Then came the explosion.
and Standish felt the brid
struck by the greatest wave in creation. As he reeled
against some unyielding object he was partially
blinded by a torrent of falling spray, his lungs
burning as the air was squeezed out of them. All about
him men were slipping and falling, yelling to each
other, while the ship staggered and
then rolled upright again.

Also in Arrow by Douglas Reeman

A Prayer for the Ship
Send a Gunboat
Dive in the Sun
The Hostile Shore
The Last Raider
With Blood and Iron
HMS Saracen
Path of the Storm
The Deep Silence
The Pride and the Anguish
To Risks Unknown
Rendezvous – South Atlantic
Go in and Sink
The Destroyers
Winged Escort
Surface with Daring
Strike from the Sea

DOUGLAS REEMAN

The Greatest Enemy

ARROW BOOKS

Arrow Books Limited
3 Fitzroy Square, London W I P 6JD

An imprint of the Hutchinson Publishing Group

London Melbourne Sydney Auckland
Wellington Johannesburg and agencies
throughout the world

First published by Hutchinson 1970
Arrow edition 1971
Reprinted 1973, 1974, 1976, 1977, 1980
© Douglas Reeman 1970

Made and printed in Great Britain
by The Anchor Press Ltd, Tiptree, Essex

ISBN 0 09 910170 X

To Gerald Austin
a good and valued friend

Contents

	Author's Note	9
1	Change of Command	11
2	Room to Bustle in	26
3	Exercise Action!	44
4	The Boarding Party	61
5	Ships in the Night	79
6	One for the Queen . . .	96
7	'The Navy's Here!'	112
8	A Matter of Security	129
9	Only Human	145
10	Morning Departure	162
11	Storm Warning	180
12	At the Captain's Discretion	195
13	Aftermath	213
14	Between Friends	230
15	The Only Place	244
16	A Full Cargo	261
17	The *Bombay Queen*	277
18	Sixty-five Days	294
	Epilogue	316

Author's Note

Over recent years there have been several cases where individual captains have been criticized, even reprimanded for using what they considered to be their right of initiative and personal judgment. Yet in time of war where would a nation's security lie? If a captain cannot demand unquestioning loyalty from his subordinates and the respect for his integrity from his superiors, it might be argued that future strategy will be decided by a computerised bureaucracy which will allow for little beyond the talent and skill of a limited few.

A case which came to my attention when I was researching for this book was that of an American officer, Lieutenant-Commander Marcus Arnheiter, who after being in command of the radar picket destroyer *Vance* off Viet Nam was relieved of his appointment without trial or warning. The *Vance* was a notoriously slack ship and Arnheiter, within the short span of ninety-nine days, set to work to put her to rights, to restore discipline and efficiency where it was most needed. On the face of the available evidence it would seem that his main crime was his eagerness to serve his country, to take his ship where she would be of the most use and purpose. His zeal it appears was not shared by some of his officers, and the way in in which the captain was destroyed would not seem out of place in Wouk's *Caine Mutiny*.

The Arnheiter Affair, as it came to be known, was one of the the worst naval disputes of the decade, and until some sort of ruling is made to prevent its happening again, there will be many captains who might be tempted to hold back when they are most needed.

The command structures of the American and British Navies

are different, but basically the ideals and traditions which have guided and moulded them over the years are very similar.

My story is and must be fiction, but the questions are still there. Was the captain of the *Terrapin* a fool or one whose real strength lay in his pride of country and his own beliefs?

If pride is indeed an enemy, then surely so too must be complacency.

1 Change of Command

THE towering sides of the fleet supply ship shone in the blazing sunlight like polished granite, and while her derricks swung busily above two frigates moored alongside the seamen employed on deck moved with equal vigour, if only to end the work and escape to the shade of their messes.

It was halfway through the forenoon watch, and already the searing heat across Singapore's wide naval anchorage had rendered movement, even thought, an unbearable effort. There was not any sort of breeze, and scattered at their buoys the moored warships seemed to crouch beneath their taut awnings, etched clearly above their motionless reflections like part of a vivid seascape. But it was Sunday, and only aboard the supply ship and the two frigates taking on stores was there any sign of activity. A few gaunt junks idled on the sluggish current, but without wind in their strange, batlike sails it was hard to tell if they were anchored or making a feeble attempt to quit the harbour.

In his cabin below the bridge of the outboard frigate, Lieutenant-Commander Rex Standish lay naked on his bunk staring up at the deckhead fan. It was quite motionless, and already he could feel the air thickening in the small compartment, bringing with it the usual irritation and frustration. He raised one hand towards the bulkhead telephone, the small movement fetching a rush of sweat to his chest and armpits, and then changed his mind. What was the point? The fans, like just about everything else, broke down too often for comment.

He wedged his hands beneath his dark, unruly hair and

closed his eyes, trying to clear his mind from the fog of heavy
drinking left over from the previous night's party.

It should have been a double celebration. Bob Mitford, the
captain, was flying home to England, and he, Rex Standish,
executive officer and first lieutenant of the frigate *Terrapin*, had
reached his thirtieth birthday.

Some heavy tackle clattered across the deck overhead and he
swore silently. The party had been more like a wake than a
celebration, with drinks getting larger every minute, and speech
becoming almost incoherent. And early this morning when he
had seen Mitford over the side for the last time, without fuss or
ceremony and with most of the ship's company still in their
hammocks, he had tried to find the words, both to thank him
and to ease his lonely flight back to England.

Instead, they had just shaken hands, and the work of getting
alongside the supply ship had pushed the other nagging thoughts
to the back of his mind Until now.

It was strange to realize he had been aboard the *Terrapin* for
only six weeks, and most of that time the ship had been in the
Hong Kong dockyard suffering repairs to one of her shafts. Six
weeks of vague routine, with most of the ship's company on
local leave and the rest merely intent on avoiding the dockyard
workers who came and went with the whistle in a jabbering
human flood.

Then the day the frigate had emerged from the dock everything seemed to happen at once. Mitford had been ashore at the
hospital when the signal had been received. To take on fuel and
sail without delay for Singapore. Perhaps they should have
expected it. In the Navy it was foolish ever to depend on
normality.

When Mitford had returned from the hospital he had received
the news almost indifferently. He had merely given the necessary orders to Standish and had retired to his cabin.

Standish turned his head and looked through the open door
to the cabin on the opposite side of the narrow passageway.
The other door was closed, the word *Captain* gleaming on the
varnished wood like an epitaph.

Without effort he could picture Mitford, as if he was still
standing there. His round, glowing red face, the loud laugh,
and his never-ending string of rugby stories. Now he was gone.

Flown back to his wife and family to tell them what he must have suspected himself for months. That he had an incurable liver disease. That he would be dead within six months.

Yet he had never spoken of it. All the while during those six weeks, while he had tried, and often succeeded, in lifting Standish from his own despair, he must have been thinking of it. Waiting for that final examination, phrasing his own reaction, and the way he would explain it to his family at home.

The fan squeaked and then whirred busily into life once more, and Standish levered himself to the deck to stand directly beneath it, letting the cool air play across his tanned shoulders and chest.

But the sudden movement brought the hammers back to the top of his skull, and he took several deep breaths to control the nausea, the bitter taste of gin at the back of his throat.

He caught sight of himself in the bulkhead mirror and grimaced. He had had a cold bath that morning but already he looked tousled and vaguely dispirited. There was only one scuttle in the cabin and the swaying grey side of the frigate alongside held back most of the light, so that he leaned his hands on the bulkhead to study his own reflection more critically.

Beneath the dark hair his level grey eyes seemed calm enough, but the shadows below them, and the deep lines at the corners of his mouth, told their own story. He tried to grin, the effort bringing back the youthfulness to his face but leaving his eyes as before. Guarded, and just that little bit too steady.

There was a tap at the door and he turned to see Lieutenant Pigott, the supply officer, watching him gravely, his forehead shining with sweat and his white shirt blotchy and crumpled, as if he had been in a tropical downpour.

'What is it, Bill?' Standish sat down on the bunk and reached for his pipe and pouch. Pigott was also O.O.D., which was just as well. It was not unknown for even fleet supply ships to give short measure, and nothing would escape his careful check of the incoming stores.

Pigott eyed him doubtfully. 'Just had a telephone signal via the supply ship, Number One.' He stepped into the cabin and closed the door behind him. 'The new commanding officer will be aboard forthwith.'

Standish stared at him. '*What*?' He dropped his pipe. 'Here, give me that bloody signal!'

It wasn't possible. Mitford barely off the ship and another here already as if poised waiting in the wings.

He re-read the sweat-stained flimsy. Commander Hector Dalziel. His eyes moved back again. A full *commander* for the poor old *Terrapin*? He looked up and saw Pigott nodding behind his horn-rimmed glasses.

'I made 'em repeat it. Dalziel's a three-ringer right enough. He's been out here for about a week, although no-one seems to know much more than that.' He fell back as Standish lurched to his feet and began to pull on his shorts. 'What d'you reckon?'

Standish paused and looked at him. 'I *reckon* we're in one hell of a mess if he arrives before we've got the ship cleaned up. You'd better call away the motor boat and instruct the cox'n immediately.'

Pigott did not move. 'Dalziel's no slouch, Number One.' He gestured vaguely overhead. 'He's *flying* in by way of the supply ship's own chopper.' He seemed amused.

'Damn!' Standish half opened a drawer to find a clean shirt, but Pigott's laconic announcement ruled out any such luxury. The suddenness of the new captain's arrival, his own hangover and all the other mounting irritations made him tug on the shirt he had been wearing when he had seen Mitford ashore, the one in which he conned *Terrapin* alongside the supply ship in the ice-clear morning light. He fumbled with the buttons and glared at himself again in the mirror. There was an oil smear on one sleeve and altogether he looked a mess.

He seized his cap and pushed past the other officer. 'Have you nearly finished loading stores?'

He winced as he reached the upper deck, the top part of the steel ladder burning his palms like a furnace bar.

Pigott grunted, 'N'other hour yet.' He sounded defensive. 'I'm very shorthanded y'know.' He was a Yorkshireman, and when riled his accent became more noticeable.

Standish hardly heard him. As he strode quickly beneath the narrow strips of awning he was conscious only of the confusion all around him. Crates and vegetable sacks, nameless boxes of tinned fruits, and all the litter of wires and blocks needed to stow it below before the sun welded it to the steel decks.

He saw Petty Officer O'Leary, the cook, gesturing fiercely towards a pile of broken bottles. It could have been jam or pickles, but in the fierce glare it looked like part of a bad road accident.

'Clear them things up!'

The seaman addressed looked at him sullenly. 'Not my fault, Chef! Can't do it all on me bleedin' own!'

Standish said quietly, 'Then get someone to help you.' He saw a small spark of defiance in the man's eyes and hardened his tone. '*Now!*'

He could sympathize in some ways with the men working around him. They *were* shorthanded. The *Terrapin* had been built to carry fourteen officers and one hundred and forty-four ratings. He paused by the ship's bell, its engraving almost polished away by the years and a thousand unknown hands.

H.M.S. *Terrapin*. Clydebank 1944.

Standish felt a small shiver across his neck in spite of the heat. She was twenty-six years old. Older than most of her ship's company, and worn out by almost constant service. He tried to picture her as she must have once looked, like her framed photograph in the wardroom, bright with dazzle-paint, with the great Atlantic rollers creaming her over as she maintained station with the rest of her killer-group. For *Terrapin* had been designed, built and created for hunting U-boats, and no doubt many of her recent engine defects were the results of the battering her hull had received so many years back, when she had blasted the Atlantic apart with her depth-charges. He stopped the train of thought. That was too far in the past. There had been so many roles since then, even other wars. Korea, Malaya and the brave fiasco of Suez, and with each passing year the ship had been by-passed by her newer consorts, and her roles had diminished accordingly.

And always she seemed to be getting further and further from the land where her keel had first tasted salt water. The blistering heat of patrols in the Persian Gulf, where her air-conditioning had originally been fitted, and which now, as then, hardly ever seemed to work for any length of time. To the trouble spots of the Far East, checking junks and doubtful freighters which sailed beneath 'Flags of Convenience', searching for unlawful refugees going one way or the other; traitors, terrorists and patriots.

The latter seemed to change as often as Britain's own policy in the Far East, and as the Navy remained aloof from the greater events in Viet Nam, so too the ageing *Terrapin* stayed more and more on the fringe of things about her.

When Standish had joined the ship at Hong Kong he had been told of her more recent jobs. Strange, vague assignments, which varied from humping stores for some Red Cross missions to carrying out an oceanographic survey along the Malacca Strait, her wardroom crammed with civilian scientists and other nameless experts who had apparently viewed the ship's voyage more as a yachting trip than one of any value.

It had been rumoured that the ship was to be paid off at Singapore and the hands sent home by air. She was to be handed over to the Royal Malaysian Navy, to end her days under a new name and an alien flag.

Now, even that seemed unlikely. Whitehall was not renowned for saving manpower, but nevertheless it was pointless to see why a new commanding officer should be appointed if the ship was to be taken off the Navy List.

A new sound intruded on his thoughts, and as he squinted up he saw the black silhouette of the supply ship's helicopter already hovering above the tiny flight deck abaft one of the busy derricks.

He said, 'Muster the side-party. I'm going aboard to meet him.'

It was strange how little he knew of Pigott or any of the others. This was the first time the whole of the ship's company had been aboard in one body since he had joined the ship.

There were five other officers apart from Pigott, and the whole company, wardroom included, totalled only one hundred. Not much of a command for a man of Dalziel's rank, he thought grimly.

By the time he had reached the circular flight deck the helicopter had already disgorged its passengers and was preparing to take off again.

Standish stood breathing hard in the glare, conscious of his own crumpled state when compared to the supply ship's officers who enjoyed more spacious quarters and every modern comfort.

He watched the handful of passengers, dismissing all but two of them. The tall, distinguished man in slacks and shirt turned suddenly and climbed with easy familiarity up one of the bridge ladders. So that left just the other one.

It was the way he was dressed which really attracted Standish's attention. A beautifully cut suit of lightweight dove-grey material, a crisp shirt and Goat Club tie; he looked exactly like one of those men in the television ads who can allegedly travel ten times round the world in the same suit which never needs pressing.

He was carrying a hat, and beneath his arm jutted an old-fashioned black walking-stick.

'You must be Standish?'

The clothes seemed to fade as the newcomer's features swam into focus.

'Yes, sir.'

'Good.' Dalziel held out his hand. It was dry and surprisingly hard. 'Good,' he said again.

As he glanced casually around the busy upper deck Standish studied him carefully. Dalziel was slim, even wiry, and would have been tall but for a slight stoop which gave him a strangely eager, thrusting appearance. But his face really interested him. It was, like the walking-stick, old-fashioned. There was no other description for it. His hair was brushed straight back from his forehead, neat and apparently impervious to the slowly revolving helicopter blades, and his deepset brown eyes were separated by a hawkish, finely cut nose, which again added to the general impression of alertness. His hair was quite dark, but the longish sideburns, which looked as if they were trimmed daily with a cut-throat razor, were grey, the colour of gunmetal.

He realized with a start that Dalziel had turned slightly and the eyes had swivelled to watch him with the same interested perusal he had used on the supply ship.

Standish said quickly, 'I'll take you aboard, sir. I'm sorry about the mess. We were ordered to take on stores, and . . .'

Dalziel lifted his hat slightly. 'Think nothing of it, Number One. I didn't expect a guard of honour or an iced cake at such short notice, eh?' He laughed lightly, his mouth opening just a little as he added, 'I know what it's like. Oh yes, I know!'

At the guardrail he paused and stared down at the slow-moving activity beneath one of the derricks.

'Smart ship, Standish.' His sleek head nodded vigorously. 'No doubt about *that*!'

Standish glanced at him quickly. '*Terrapin* is the *outboard* ship, sir.'

Dalziel ran lightly down the ladder and brushed between the other frigate's O.O.D. and some sweating seamen. At the opposite side he paused again, and Standish saw a small muscle moving busily at one corner of his tight mouth.

Surely Dalziel must have known what *Terrapin* was really like?

He followed his stare and saw his ship for what seemed like the first time. In dock you never saw any vessel at her best, but now, viewed from the upper deck of her larger consort the *Terrapin* looked even worse.

Seen from a distance it would still be possible to admire and appreciate the grace and simplicity of her lines. But close-to the reverse was equally apparent. From her raked stem to her narrow, delicate stern there was hardly an inch of her three hundred odd feet which had not gathered some scar or blemish to mark the passing of her years of service. Her outline was neat, even austere when compared with the newer frigates and all their attendant clutter of radar and sophisticated detecting gear, and with her square, tiered bridge and single funnel she had over the years retained a kind of jaunty defiance, like a tried veteran in a world of overtrained, overweight recruits.

Standish waited for Dalziel to move. He could see Pigott fidgeting nervously under the captain's cold scrutiny, the hastily assembled side-party looking strangely alien in their white shorts against the background of crates and half-naked seamen, the latter seemingly still unaware of Dalziel's arrival.

Dalziel walked instead towards the bows. The flared fore-castles of the two frigates curved away to display more of the *Terrapin's* ravages, the streaks of rust beneath her hawsepipes, the deep dents by her stem where she had nudged jetties, or her officers had once or twice misjudged a buoy or another ship.

Standish said, 'Of course she's pretty old, sir.'

Dalziel twisted slightly and looked at him. '*So*?'

'I just meant, sir, that it's hard to see what could be done to keep her in line with newer ships.'

Surprisingly Dalziel grinned. He did not merely smile, the

grin spread right across his face until his mouth seemed to join with the two neat sideburns.

He said, 'Well, we'll just have to change things a bit, eh?' He pointed with his stick, the motion jabbing like a swordthrust. 'Look at the state of those signal halliards, for instance. *They* don't need painting, do they? They just need to be *taut*, like the ship, eh?' The grin vanished. 'Can't abide slackness, you know. To me, a slack ship is about as much use as a long-tailed cat in a room full of rocking chairs.'

He strode briskly towards the break in the guardrails and clambered down the short brow to the *Terrapin's* deck.

Pigott saluted and the pipes shrilled in recognition.

Dalziel waited for the din to cease and then said, 'Your name?'

'Pigott, sir. Supply and victualling officer.'

'Good.' Dalziel glanced around him. 'You are also officer of the day, right?'

'Sir.' Pigott glanced anxiously at Standish.

'*So*.' Dalziel smiled gently. 'Next time I come aboard I want the hands at attention, right? *All* the hands on deck at that particular moment in time.' He looked at Standish. 'Just another small point, Number One.' But he was still smiling.

Then he saw the ship's bell and walked slowly towards it. No-one moved or spoke as he examined it with infinite care.

Standish found that his hands were tightly clenched in the presence of this extraordinary man. What was wrong now? Was the brass smudged or unpolished? The bellrope frayed or the whipping gone?

Dalziel turned and looked at him, his deepset eyes distant and strangely sad.

Then he said slowly, 'It really makes you *think*, doesn't it, Number One? To see this bell. All those years. All those sea-miles under her keel. The officers and men she's made or broken.' He shook his head. 'It makes you feel almost humble.'

Across Dalziel's shoulder Standish saw Pigott's earlier anxiety giving way to something like astonishment.

He replied quickly, 'As I remarked earlier, sir, she's an old ship.'

'Quite. And if she needs extra care it is because she has

earned it, eh?' He looked round briskly, the moment of humility
past. 'Cabin?'

'Follow me, sir.' To Pigott he added, 'You can carry on with
the loading now.'

Pigott watched them go and then said, 'Humble?' He looked
at the quartermaster. '*This* ship?'

Then with a sigh he walked forward to watch the men at the
slings.

*   *   *

Rex Standish paused outside the captain's day cabin and
found time to wonder at the speed with which the day had
passed. It was evening, and a small welcome breeze made the
moored ship nudge gently at her fenders and felt its way
between decks to clear away the oppressive heat of the day.

He tucked the clean shirt more firmly into his shorts, his mind
going back over the day, and more precisely the afternoon of
Dalziel's first few hours of command.

The captain had remained in his own quarters, but had sent
out a stream of instructions, not least of which had been concerned with his personal luggage. The latter had arrived offshore by way of the supply ship's helicopter, and Standish had
stood with Pigott as the small duty part of the watch had
struggled back and forth along the brow with cases and metal
trunks of every size and weight. Whatever anyone else imagined
about the future, Dalziel obviously expected a long stay in his
new command.

Now, at long last, the *Terrapin* was quiet again. Apart from
the duty hands the rest of her company were either ashore or
comfortably settled aboard the supply ship with other off-duty
personnel to watch a Western in the big vessel's cinema, or to
squander some of their pay at tombola.

He tapped at the door and almost jumped as Dalziel's voice
replied instantly, 'Come!'

When he stepped over the coaming it was difficult to realize
that it was the same place as before. Only the armchairs and
carpets appeared familiar, and the rest of the captain's day
cabin seemed to be covered with open boxes, parcels of books
and uniforms which hung from every available projection like
wares in a Cairo bazaar.

Dalziel was seated behind the table, all of which was equally well covered by papers, signal files, publications and a portable typewriter. He had changed into uniform, and his crisp white shirt and gleaming shoulder straps seemed to contrast violently with the litter and confusion around him.

He gestured towards a chair. 'Clear that gear off there and sit while I finish this report.' He skimmed down the next sheet of paper as Standish seated himself opposite the table, and then added, 'That was a good lunch you sent down, Number One, but too much of it. Can't abide fatty foods. Makes you sluggish!'

He scribbled some notes on an open pad which Standish had not noticed before and then leaned back in his chair.

'Well, Number One, that's about it for the first day.' He pulled a slim gold case from his pocket and lit a cigarette. 'I'm not offering you one. You're a pipe man, right?' He gestured with his gold case. 'Light up and puff away. This place is like a sty as it is. A bit more smoke won't hurt any.'

Standish looked round guardedly. The long talks he had had in here with Mitford. The confidences and the regained hopes. Now under Dalziel's brief dismissal it did indeed look both shabby and in need of a new paint job.

Dalziel said abruptly, 'I would normally speak to all my officers immediately upon joining ship. However, as the duty board tells me that everyone but the ship's cat is ashore, there isn't much point in it.'

'I'm sorry about that, sir. But we had orders to lie alongside the supply ship until tomorrow. We did not know about your appointment, and I thought it fair to let the hands ashore.' He paused. 'And the officers.'

'Quite.' Dalziel regarded him calmly. 'Not blaming you at all. Anyway, it has given me time to go more fully into the ship's state before I meet them, eh? To assess the *situation*, so to speak.'

'Sir?'

Dalziel puffed out a thin stream of smoke and watched as it was whipped upwards into the fan. 'A captain and his first lieutenant are a team. Must be. Usually one starts in a ship before the other, unless of course that ship is just being commissioned, in which case it's all hands to the pumps.' Again that slow smile, as if he was remembering another time and another place. 'Now take *this* ship, the frigate *Terrapin*. Rather a different set of circumstances all round, wouldn't you say?'

Standish tried to relax, but Dalziel's cool, unruffled tones seemed to be hiding something.

He replied, 'I agree, sir.'

'Good. I know, for instance, that although you are the ship's executive officer you have been aboard only six weeks, mostly in dock, and for the same period in a state of flux.' He grinned. 'Otherwise I'd not be sitting here yarning like the proverbial Dutch uncle.' He stubbed out the cigarette and studied him evenly. 'For, as you well know, this ship is a *disgrace*.' There was no anger in his voice, merely the patient disapproval of a schoolmaster. 'It is dirty and badly maintained. The hands, what I have seen of them, are nothing to be proud of. Their appearance alone is enough to make you weep. If they look like that, they must have torn and slovenly minds also, right?'

Standish stared at him. 'I . . . that is, we all thought the ship was being paid off, sir. Bob often said . . .'

'*Bob*?' One syllable, but as sharp as a knife.

'I mean Lieutenant-Commander Mitford. I'm sorry, sir.' He felt suddenly angry under Dalziel's impassive gaze. 'We were both the same rank, I suppose it made a difference at the time.'

Dalziel nodded absently and turned over two sheets of paper.

'Mitford. Yes.' He nodded again. 'Liver complaint. Drink, probably.'

Standish half rose to his feet. 'I must say that he was very good to me, sir. I always found him . . .'

Dalziel said, 'Let me finish.' He smiled gently. 'I did not know him, so I can only judge from present facts. This ship, *any* ship under the White Ensign, has to be ready for anything, even if she is going to be paid off in one hour's time. And the more thinly spread our resources become, the more important it is to keep each and every unit at first-line readiness.' His voice lifted slightly. 'Anything less than that grade is *sub*-standard in my book, and I do not intend to let it happen in this ship, even if the previous captain was a cousin of the Pope and had the sun shining out of his backside, right?'

Standish sat back dazedly. '*Right*, sir.'

'Good.' Dalziel relaxed and turned over some more papers.

'We are going to see a lot of each other in the future, and we will be working hand in glove to make this ship come alive again.' He paused and then added, 'So we had better get off on the right course, eh?'

He stood up and walked to one of the open scuttles. Standish could see the fading sunlight reflecting on his face like gold, could almost feel the man's energy like a living force.

Dalziel said suddenly, 'You know, I love the Navy. Always have. Strange really, as I come of an army family. My father, bless him, was a general, and I spent most of my boyhood being shunted from one damn garrison town to another. But I *knew* what I wanted, and once in the Service I have never found occasion to doubt my calling.' He sighed. 'As you know, you meet all sorts. The ambitious and the failures. The loved and the hated. A real potmess of a mixture.' He swung round and stared at Standish, his eyes alight with sudden excitement. 'But they all go to make the team, Number One. The Service is the thing, and not the mere individuals who come and go with the years.'

Overhead a tannoy speaker intoned dully, 'Duty part of the watch fall in. Able Seaman Dolan muster at the quartermaster's lobby.'

Dalziel smiled slightly. 'You see? It goes on forever.' He crossed to the table again and continued in a crisper tone, 'I was in America a few years ago on a NATO course. While I was there I saw a whole herd of cattle on the move. All over the plains and the hills, there seemed to be millions of them, and only a practised eye and a firm hand could control them and keep them on course.' He tapped the table sharply. 'And when the drive was over, all that effort, all that spectacle was nicely compressed and labelled into uniform tins of beef! And *that* is how I want my ship. Tight and snug inside this hull, so that the whole thing has both purpose and function, right?'

Standish put down his pipe. He had made two attempts to fill it, but this last appraisal of the *Terrapin's* role made further efforts pointless.

He said quietly, 'I don't know much about the ship's company yet, sir. But I am sure they will do their best...'

Dalziel nodded. 'I said earlier that we must get off on the right course. So let us drop the pretence. You know this ship is

a mess, so do I. What you may not realize is that it will be asked
to play an essential part in Far East strategy, and at any
moment now.' He smiled. 'I thought that'd shake you!'

Standish looked at the littered table. 'It does, sir.'

'Of course, nothing is completely settled yet, but I'm getting
my orders tomorrow. While I'm ashore with the admiral you
can get the hands to work.' He pulled a typewritten sheet from
the paperweight and handed it across. 'This will give you something to go on with. When the leading writer comes aboard I'll
want him to type out my new standing orders, too. And I'll
need every officer to read and known them by heart.' He shot
him a quick glance. 'How well do you know *them*?'

Standish looked away, feeling the rising helplessness again,
yet unable to control it.

'Not too well yet, sir.' It sounded like an admission. And it
was.

Dalziel smiled. 'Not to worry. We'll soon change that.' He
perched himself on the edge of the table and added evenly, 'So
let's begin with *you*, eh?' He did not wait for Standish to speak
but said, 'You had a command of your own it seems. The
submarine *Electra*. You were transferred to general service last
year following a fire aboard your boat in which several men lost
their lives.'

Standish stared at him but saw nothing but a swirling mist.
Like smoke. Like that day, which should have been like all the
others. A simple dive within three miles of Portland Bill, to act
as 'target' for some frigates which were undergoing anti-submarine training. The exercise should have lasted an hour, but
within a few minutes of its completion the fire had broken out
in the fore-ends. A new type of signal flare was to have been
discharged from a torpedo tube to signify the finish and to mark
their position at the end of the run.

How it had started was not clear, but within seconds the
torpedo space had turned into a raging inferno.

At the court of enquiry he had not only been praised for his
efforts, but had in due course received the George Cross for his
personal bravery.

He still did not know why he had gone to try and get those
men out. It had been pointless and might even have prolonged
their agony as well as adding further risk to the boat's safety.

Was it guilt? If he had not been worrying about Alison he might have checked further before the dive. If it had not been her brother trapped with his men in the blazing torpedo space, might he have acted differently?

And in the end he had ordered the space to be flooded, so it was all in vain. Perhaps his own severe burns and terrible pain had saved him from disgrace and awarded him instead both honour and admiration.

He heard himself say thickly, 'When I came out of hospital I was found unfit for submarines, sir.' He added with sudden bitterness, 'It happens!'

Dalziel walked to his cupboard and took out a bottle of whisky and two glasses.

'No water, I'm afraid.' He sounded almost matter of fact. 'But drink it down anyway.' He watch Standish over the rim of his glass and then said calmly, 'I'm sorry about that, Number One. But I thought it best to get it out and done with. Commander Mitford tried to help by reassuring you, eh?' He held his glass to the scuttle and examined it critically. 'I will not. For to reassure you means that I think you *need* it. You are my first lieutenant, and for me that is enough. It has to be.'

Standish felt the raw whisky exploring his stomach and realized he had not eaten for twenty-four hours, or maybe longer.

He said, 'Thank you, sir.'

'Save the thanks!' Dalziel was grinning as he had done aboard the supply ship. 'You may come to loathe my guts! But together we will make this ship live again. And for me, that is all that matters.'

He placed his glass carefully on the table and added, 'Now, if you are ready, I want to discuss tomorrow's programme.'

Outside, the sky and the water grew darker, and the moored ships merged together to lose their identity for the coming night.

The *Terrapin*, being the outboard ship, was more restless than her consorts, as if she too realized she had another, and perhaps her last captain.

2 Room to Bustle in . . .

THE *Terrapin's* wardroom ran the whole breadth of the hull
and compared even with more modern vessels was quite
spacious. The fact that her proper complement of fourteen
officers had been reduced to seven, excluding the captain, made
it all the more so.

Standish hung his cap in the lobby and walked wearily to
the letter rack, and after the usual perusal seated himself by an
open scuttle and signalled to Wills, the leading steward, for his
first drink of the day.

It was half an hour before noon, but already the dining
table on the starboard side of the wardroom was laid with a
clean cloth, and beyond the pantry hatch he could hear the
subdued chatter from the messmen as they waited to serve the
officers' lunch.

The other half of the wardroom was typical enough. Battered
armchairs, racks of tattered magazines and paperbacks, and a
much-used bulkhead sideboard, above which hung the ship's
crest, flanked on either side by framed portraits of the Queen
and the Duke of Edinburgh. In one corner, deeply immersed
in a ledger, Pigott was still at work checking the last of the
supplies which had finally vanished from the upper deck to be
stored and jammed throughout the hull until needed.

In another chair, bent forward over a NAAFI catalogue of
sports gear, Lieutenant Thomas Hornby, the electrical officer,
was equally busy making out a new list for some additional
equipment, breaking off occasionally to sip at a tall glass of

tomato juice. For Hornby was also the sports and entertainments officer, dual roles which seemed to keep him more involved and interested than anything to do with the ship's well-worn wiring and electrical circuits.

Standish regarded him thoughtfully above his glass. It was odd how hard Hornby tried to keep fit. It was almost as if the whole business of arranging sports and amusements for the ship's company were for his own benefit. Yet with little success, for the more he swam and refereed, the greater his efforts to stay in trim, the fatter he seemed to grow, and although only in his late twenties he was already well overweight, and his round pink face which defied every attempt to gain a healthy tan was shining with sweat and blotched with heat, like that of a seedy child's.

He looked up suddenly as if feeling Standish's eye on him.

'When is the captain coming off, Number One?'

Standish shrugged. 'Any minute now.' He did not feel like talking but added, 'He'll want to speak to all the officers before lunch.'

Pigott said without taking his eyes from the ledger, 'Well, my department's buttoned up.' He removed his glasses and polished them vigorously on his shirt. 'What d'you make of him?'

Standish took the first sip of gin very slowly to give himself time. If Sunday had been bad, this first Monday forenoon had been far worse.

In the breathless morning air as he had watched Chief Petty Officer Corbin, the coxswain, mustering the seamen for the day's work he had been conscious of the change which had spread throughout the ship. Few of the men had laid eyes on Dalziel as yet, but his presence had already made itself felt.

Standish took another drink and sighed. That list. Even Corbin, normally unruffled and taciturn, had been moved to say, 'Gawd knows if we can get this lot sorted out, sir!'

The list which Dalziel's had left for the day's work was impressive. It started with a complete check on bosun's stores and all the complicated tangle of mooring wires and shackles, ropes and spare canvas, and the thousand and one pieces of gear which were intended to keep one of H.M. ships free of want and unnecessary disaster. Gunnery stores and fire fighting equipment, collision mats and spare oars for the whaler, it went on and on, and as the sun grew fiercer the working parties had become more harassed and resentful as they heaved on tackles or stumbled through the bowels of the ship and into some flats and spaces which to Corbin's knowledge had remained sealed for as long as he could remember.

He said slowly, 'Commander Dalziel is making a clean sweep.'

Pigott regarded him bleakly. 'About time if you ask me. Too many captains have handed this ship over in the past with a signature and little else.'

Standish waited. He was not disappointed.

Pigott added, 'It's always dropped in the supply officer's lap. Every bloody time!'

Even Hornby smiled. 'Poor sod!' he said unfeelingly.

The stewards were getting busier with their bottles and glasses.

Sub-Lieutenant Caley, the torpedo and anti-submarine officer, entered the wardroom, jammed his thickset body in a chair and snapped, 'Glasserbeer!' Then he snatched up an old newspaper and scrutinized it until the tankard was placed beside him.

Standish noticed that Caley's eyes did not move when he studied the newspaper. It was merely his defence. His shield. Although from what, other than his own sense of inferiority, it was hard to tell.

Standish had gathered little information about his brother officers, but he knew it was Caley's first ship with a commission. He had worked his way through the lower deck, a professional at his job, until at long last he had gained the first coveted stripe of gold lace. At least that was how it should have been. But Caley was different. Standish had rarely heard him speak, unless it was to complain to the stewards about food or service, or to throw some caustic comment whenever Brian Wishart, the ship's sub-lieutenant and junior officer, chose to voice an opinion. But he drank a good deal, and usually from his own glass tankard. Never 'please' or 'thank you' to the stewards, but just his usual surly 'Glasserbeer!'

Standish had seen this in his early service when lower deck promotions had been a small and awkward minority in every wardroom. In *Terrapin*, however, but for himself, young Wishart and Irvine, the navigating officer, all the others were from the lower deck. In fact, the only man aboard he had seen getting on with Caley had been Petty Officer Squires, the head of his own T.A.S. department. Perhaps Caley regretted leaving the firm companionship of the P.O.'s mess, or maybe . . . he broke his train of thought as Lieutenant Irvine stepped over the coaming and stood for several seconds gazing around the wardroom.

Irvine was very fair, with the finely cut good looks which always made him stand out in a crowd, as if in his own personal spotlight. He was twenty-seven, a competent navigator, and very self-assured. Standish disliked him, without knowing why.

He made himself ask, 'Everything all right, Pilot?' Irvine was O.O.D.

'Fair enough, thanks.' Irvine had a gentle drawl and a lazy way of looking slightly away from the person he was addressing. He added, 'The Old Man's still ashore.' He snapped his fingers. 'Large pink Plymouth, Wills!'

Wills nodded. 'Yessir, right away, sir.'

It was strange how the men seemed to jump at Irvine's smallest demand. The lieutenant came of a naval family and had a good pedigree. He was an Etonian and used his background like a riding crop, with just enough force to get his own way.

He perched on a stool and studied his glass thoughtfully.

'Bit late to get this hulk into shape, I'd have thought?' He smiled. 'Still, I suppose the old *Terrapin's* going to be blessed with one more has-been to end her unnotable career.'

Standish said, 'You must admit that things have got a bit run down.'

'Really?' Irvine looked away. 'Just the ship for some of the wrecks we seem to gather aboard, I'd imagine.'

The door banged back and Lieutenant Quarrie, the engineering officer and the oldest member of the ship's company, walked stiffly to the letter rack and then said, 'Horse's neck, Wills.' He looked coldly at Irvine and stalked to a chair at the opposite end of the wardroom.

Quarrie was another odd one, Standish reflected. He was in his forties and could have been out of the Navy before this. He was sturdy and firm jawed, with the sallow skin and scarred hands of his trade to mark him apart from his companions and make him strangely alien. But the strangest thing of all about Quarrie was that he had apparently joined the ship when she had first commissioned as a brand new frigate and he had been a young, barely trained stoker. What had gone since and between that first meeting nobody knew, but somehow Quarrie had kept contact with his first ship. As she had grown older he had climbed up the slow ladder of promotion from boiler room to his own footplate, until at last he had come back to her. Perhaps this final meeting was to be the end for both of them.

Standish signalled for another gin, suddenly cold as Irvine's casual remarks came back to him.

Suppose this worn frigate was indeed a dumping ground for useless or unwanted men? He found himself gripping the arms of his chair, running over the other officers, probing at their roles and backgrounds. It was just possible, he thought despairingly. All except Irvine, who had too much influence, and Wishart, who was too junior, each of the rest could have been sent to the *Terrapin* as the last springboard into oblivion.

He swallowed the gin and relaxed slightly as the others became involved in some new topic of conversation.

Unfit for submarine service. It *could* have meant just that. He found himself going over it all again, as he had after leaving Dalziel's cabin the night before.

He had of course heard of it happening to others in submarines. No outward flaw, just something, *something* which made it impossible to act and think as before once the hatch was slammed shut and the depth gauges started to creep round.

The months in hospital, the pain and the anxiety of waiting had done nothing to help. The surgeons had been proud of their work. New skin on his hands, and their showpiece, two completely new eyelids. Even now when he looked in a mirror he imagined they were paler, less real than the rest of his face. They had done a good job in him, but his inner hurt was something else again.

So maybe the *Terrapin* was the end of the line for him also. And all the soothing words would come to nothing. To have commanded a submarine was to have been alive. To rate first lieutenant of this clapped-out frigate might easily be the thin edge.

It had been unnerving the way Dalziel had hit upon his

weakness with little to go on but his bare record. He had even been right about Mitford. Deep down Standish had known Mitford to be killing himself with drink, but he seemed unable to stop it. He too had been due for the axe, and it was almost as if he had been unable to face life outside the only world he knew. Another failure. And now there was Dalziel, a different being entirely, and perhaps, in spite of everything, the one man who could give them all a new chance.

The quartermaster thrust his head around the screen door.

'First Lieutenant, sir? Captain's comin' offshore now.'

Standish nodded and got to his feet. To Irvine he said, 'Get your people to man the side.'

Irvine shrugged. 'If you insist, Number One.' He grinned. 'We get a little chat now, do we?'

Standish regarded him calmly, trying not to dislike him. 'He will tell you want he wants you to know.'

On deck it was hotter than ever, and as Standish stood with the side-party he could feel the sweat running down his spine and gathering above the waistband of his shorts. He watched the motor boat curving fussily towards the gangway, the bow-man ready with boathook poised, and for once, properly dressed.

Dalziel ran lightly up the short ladder, his fingers on the oak-leaved peak of his cap as he returned their salutes, his deepset eyes already exploring the upper deck before the pipes had ceased their shrill greeting.

He said warmly, 'Much better, Number One! Capital!' Then he glanced at Irvine. 'Forrard awning's a bit slack. Get the duty part of the watch to cope, eh?'

Irvine saluted limply. 'Now, sir?'

Dalziel eyed him coolly. 'I do mean now. Whenever I give an order it means *now*, right?'

As Irvine walked away, his handsome features set in a tight frown, Dalziel said lightly, 'He seems capable enough.' He looked at some wet paint and touched it with one finger. 'Still, early days yet.'

There was a scrape of feet on the ladder and Sub-Lieutenant Wishart climbed up from the motor boat. He handed a brief-case to the captain and then stood waiting in silence. Normally he was a cheerful, if naive youngster, but now he looked positively crestfallen.

Dalziel opened the briefcase and ruffled the contents vaguely. 'Found this young chap, ashore, Number One.' He nodded towards the duty board. 'Says *there* he's still aboard. Odd, eh?'

Wishart said uncomfortably, 'I was sent with a message to the Officer's Club, sir.'

'I see.' Dalziel seemed to dismiss the matter. Then he said abruptly, 'If a rating had been looking for you aboard, *depending* on your knowledge or lack of it, you would not have been found. A man might have dropped dead searching for you, could have lost faith in his officers and his country, and all the while you'd have been in the Club!' He regarded the luckless Wishart sadly. 'Bad show. Damn bad show. I shall be watching you, Sub, watching and praying for some improvement.'

He touched Standish's elbow. 'Now let's meet the others, eh?' He tapped the briefcase. 'Tell them all the good news.'

Then he turned. 'That will include you, Sub, so take your damn chin off the deck and *jump about, will you!*'

The young officer almost ran the last few paces to the hatch, and Dalziel said cheerfully, 'These new Dartmouth types. What a shower of children they really are.'

Once below he said suddenly, 'We will slip from the supply ship in six hours, Number One.' He smiled, the eagerness bright in his eyes as he added, 'Get to sea, find a bit of room to bustle in, as someone once said, eh?'

Standish opened the wardroom door and stood aside, baffled. He saw Dalziel's smile vanish as if switched off to suit the importance of the occasion, and as the other officers shuffled to their feet he followed the captain inside.

It took only a few minutes to introduce the officers by name and in order of seniority, but Standish was conscious the whole time of Dalziel's crisp formality, the brevity of his comments which accompanied each handshake.

In theory Dalziel, like any other captain, was a guest in the wardroom, but as the introductions were completed he showed no sign of following this tradition. At least not yet.

He tossed his cap on a chair and said, 'You may be seated. I'll not keep you long, and afterwards, with Number One's permission, I'd like to stand you all a drink while we have a more informal gossip, eh?'

Every pair of eyes followed his hands as he opened the briefcase and took out a stiff manilla folder and laid it carefully on a table beside his chair.

He said, 'We will proceed to sea in six hours. Our first destination is Kuala Papan on the east coast of the Malaysian Peninsular.' He turned sharply and looked at Irvine. 'Know it?'

'Yes, sir. About two hundred and sixty miles.' Irvine's mouth moved slightly in a smile. 'It's an inlet...'

Dalziel interrupted, 'Yes, that is what Kuala means in Malay, Pilot, I'd have thought you'd know that.' He smiled calmly. 'It is actually two hundred and sixty-*five* miles from here.' The grin widened. 'Still, you weren't to know I was going to ask, eh?'

Irvine dropped his eyes, two small spots of colour showing on his cheeks. He said, 'Thank you for telling me, sir.'

Dalziel ignored him. 'I'll not bore you with a long appraisal of the Far East situation, gentlemen. My orders are to proceed to Kuala Papan and report to Rear-Admiral Curtis.' He saw their mystified expressions and continued, 'He happens to be an American. As you all know, there have been increasing incidents lately involving acts of terrorism and sabotage throughout the Peninsular, spreading as far north as Thailand, and south to Indonesia. We are, after all, only five hundred miles from Viet Nam, and as expected the communists have no intention of stopping short in *that* unhappy country.' He opened a much-thumbed chart and held it across his body. 'We have watched it happening over the years. Viet Nam, Laos, it goes on like some creeping, rotten disease, and now there are reports of communist infiltrators actually crossing the Gulf of Thailand to enter Malaysia *and* founding secret camps in Thailand as well.' He refolded the chart deftly. 'Their end purpose is only too clear, as you will no doubt agree.'

No-one spoke, and when Standish glanced around the other faces his immediate impression was one of cautious confusion. Except for Irvine, who was still smouldering, the rest were obviously unable to picture their ship set against the wider background of power politics and the tougher events of the cold war. Like Standish, such things were usually seen in newspapers, the figments of journalists' fears or imagination.

Dalziel said at length, 'The Americans have carried the can for the lot of us out here far too long. You cannot expect the U.S. taxpayer to go on footing the bill for the containing of communist aggression while the rest of us sit on our backsides and criticize, right?'

Pigott cleared his throat uncomfortably.

'Yes?' Dalziel eyed him impassively. 'You have a question?'

Pigott shifted under the combined stares. 'I'm sorry, sir, I just don't see where *we* come in. The Reds have been pushing for years. And it looks me as if they are bound to take over the whole area if the Americans lose interest and our government keeps to its policy of withdrawal.'

'Quite right!' Dalziel smiled. 'Hit it right on the button! But it does seem as if a little daylight has at last penetrated the dusty minds of Whitehall. The job of checking and policing this vast area is to be *shared*, not dominated by one solitary power. The Malaysian government is fully aware of what will happen if it is allowed to go on like this. Already there has been plenty of real trouble stirred up by these agitators. Killings and riots, their main weapon being to fan up hatred between the local Chinese and Malays themselves. Much in fact as the Japs did when they invaded here twenty-eight years ago. Divide and conquer, their basic principle. If it's not political then it's religion, but they'll use something to force the issue into open war as in Viet Nam.'

He flicked open the folder and stared at it for several seconds.

'Our role, or part of it, is to join forces with the Americans and local Malaysian patrols and keep an eye on any communist activity. Gun-running, smuggling saboteurs or even trained troops into the area; just as soon as our particular sector has been allotted to us and clearly defined.'

His finger moved slowly down a typewritten sheet within the folder.

'But first things first. I've had a good look round the ship, and also made it my business to study her state of readiness.' He seemed to be ticking off items in his mind. 'Engine room is fine. Even in a new ship I never found better.'

Standish saw Quarrie's shoulder move slightly, but his expression remained guarded, like that of a man about to rush to the defence of the thing he most loved.

'Communications, well, they appear adequate for our purposes.' Dalziel looked at Standish. 'Who is the gunnery officer? No mention here at all.'

'Well, sir, the main armament of twin four-inch guns is mothballed, and apart from humidity checks and so forth they don't warrant much attention. Petty Officer Motts, the G.I., keeps an eye on them and the four Bofors guns.'

Dalziel regarded him thoughtfully. 'Interesting.' Then he swung round on his chair and jabbed a finger at Wishart. 'And what exactly do *you* do, Sub, apart that is from carrying messages to the Officers' Club?'

Wishart flushed. 'Well, sir, that is, I deal with ship's correspondence and, and . . .'

Hornby said, 'He assists me with sport and entertainment, sir.'

'Ah, I see.' Dalziel leaned back and eyed the young officer calmly. 'It all begins to drop into place. Now, Sub, if you can be released from the duties just described, *you* will become the gunnery officer.'

Wishart stared at him. 'Yes, sir.'

'I want those four-inch weapons stripped and brought to state one readiness. As soon as we get to sea I'll expect to see a practice shoot, and it had better be good!' He frowned. 'Well, what's the matter now?'

'I have only done basic gunnery, when I was at Dartmouth, sir.'

'So?'

'I just meant that a more experienced officer might be better . . .'

His voice trailed away as Dalziel said smoothly, 'Well, this will be experience, eh?' His tone sharpened. 'More than you'll get by kicking a football or making yourself beautiful on a pair of damn water-skis!'

He shifted his gaze to Caley. 'T.A.S. department appears in good shape. But some of the seamen I questioned seem a bit vague about what the Squid mortars are *for*?' He fixed Caley with a grim stare. 'I'll want you to train two extra crews. I don't just want those mortars to look good, I want 'em ready to use if necessary, see?'

Caley half rose. 'I'll speak to my P.O. about it, sir.'

'You'll do it yourself, unless you want to change places with him!'

Then Dalziel smiled and relaxed slightly.

'That's about it for now, gentlemen. I just wanted you to know my standards, which are quite high. We may be going to one more boring bit of patrol work. But if not, and there's work to be done, work which we have all joined and trained for, then I need to be ready. And if there's any fighting to be done, then I want this ship where that fighting is!'

Irvine said quietly, 'I'd not think they'd use this ship, sir.' He appeared to have regained his composure. 'Her last commission was bad enough, but these past months have been just about pointless.'

Dalziel nodded. '*Wasted* is a better description, Pilot. Wasted and thrown away, with the result we now have a slack, dis-organized ship.' He smiled at Irvine. 'But that's all in the past. As I used to tell the lads in my last ship. Treat me squarely and I'll be nice as pie. But call me pig and I can be pig right the way through, believe me.'

Irvine asked, 'Which ship was that, sir?'

Dalziel rose to his feet. 'I'll not have time for that drink now, Number One. But I'd like to stand treat just the same.' He picked up his cap and looked at each of them in turn. 'Stations for leaving harbour at 1800, right?'

As the door closed behind him Irvine said savagely, 'Then I'll have a treble brandy if he's paying for it.'

Pigott walked slowly to the bulkhead calendar and stared at it gloomily. Then he pulled a pencil from his shirt and drew a ring around the day's date.

'Dalziel plus one,' he said dryly. 'What a way to start August in *this* ship!'

Standish returned to his chair and picked up his glass. The interview had not gone well, but it had certainly made a deep impression. As the stewards returned to pour the drinks he could hear a buzz of questions and complaints all around him, as if twice the number of officers were present.

The chair beside him creaked and he turned to see Quarrie sipping meditatively at a large horse's neck.

'Well, Chief, how do you feel about *things*?'

Quarrie replied without hesitation. '*Terrapin's* been waiting for a Dalziel for nearly twenty years. He'll do me all right.'

Wishart was saying plaintively, 'But I've never *done* a shoot with four-inch guns!'

Irvine snapped, 'Shouldn't have joined, Sub. At least you don't have to share the bridge with him.'

All Caley said was, 'Glasserbeer!'

Standish leaned back and let the gin explore the back of his tongue. Maybe Quarrie was right. Either way it looked as if they were all going to be very busy indeed.

*   *   *

Standish stood high on the gratings at the forepart of the upper bridge and watched the seamen moving about the forecastle in readiness for getting under way.

With all awnings removed and stowed there was little shelter from the sun, which in spite of the hour felt as hot as ever. He saw Wishart right forward in the eyes of the ship and wondered if he was attending to his men or still thinking about the twin guns which pointed straight towards him as a constant reminder of Dalziel's expectations. Around the bridge voicepipes muttered and squeaked, and the usual business of preparing for sea continued unhurriedly and with little outward emotion.

Some seamen were already at the guardrails of the frigate alongside ready to release mooring wires, and beyond her on an even higher plane Standish could see a few·idlers watching from the depot ship where only yesterday he had gone to greet his new captain.

A bosun's mate said, 'Cap'n's comin' up, sir.'

Dalziel looked impeccable in what appeared to be another new shirt, and had his cap tilted over his eyes against the fierce glare.

Standish saluted formally. 'Ready to proceed, sir.' He hesitated. 'There's a transport dropping anchor in the fairway, sir.' He gestured astern. 'We could wait a bit longer if you like.'

Dalziel glanced round the bridge, his dark eyes moving over the messengers and signalmen, the bosun's mate with his ear to a telephone, and lastly to Irvine who was leaning on his elbows across the chart table.

'Time, Pilot?' His tone was quite calm.

'1755, sir.' Irvine did not look up.

'Very well. Ring down stand by.' Dalziel climbed on to the gratings and touched the glass screen with his fingers.

It was hard to tell what he was thinking. That this was the first time he had moved the ship himself, and already there was the added complication of the big transport astern. The *Terrapin*, like the supply ship, was pointing towards the causeway which linked Singapore Island to the mainland, and to get clear of the other vessels it was first necessary to move astern before making a slow turn into the centre of the channel. But his face was like a mask, and he could just have easily been making a mental note of the salt stains left on the screen from the last trip.

'Take in breast ropes!' Dalziel adjusted his glasses about his neck.

Beneath the scrubbed gratings the deck began to vibrate slightly as Quarrie released the power in readiness for the next command from the bridge.

A diamond-bright light winked from the shore's hazy outline and Petty Officer Burch, the yeoman, snapped, 'Signal, sir. Proceed when ready.'

Standish glanced quickly at the masthead pendant. Moments before it had been hanging limply in the heat, now, as if gathering strength from an unknown source it lifted slightly and then flapped towards the other frigate.

The man at the telephone reported, 'Breast ropes inboard, sir.'

Standish said suddenly, 'The wind's holding us against the other ship, sir.'

Dalziel glanced at him. 'So I see.' In a louder tone he added, 'Let go aft!'

Standish crossed to the bridge wing and watched as the seamen on the narrow quarterdeck threw off lashings and tugged at the great greasy coils of wire which piled around them like so many eager snakes.

'All gone aft, sir.'

Two officers had appeared on the other frigate's bridge and Standish could see them peering down as the *Terrapin* sidled more heavily against the fenders.

Even without the telephone it was possible to hear Caley's harsh voice from the quarterdeck. 'All clear aft, sir!'

Held only by the spring and headrope the little frigate was yawing badly, and more seamen were being urged and pushed to manhandle the fenders along the flared forecastle where already there was some danger of the two vessels grinding together in close embrace.

Dalziel said in the same flat voice, 'Slow ahead port engine!'

Corbin's voice repeated the order from the wheelhouse. 'Slow ahead port engine, sir.' A pause. 'Port engine slow ahead, wheel amidships, sir!'

Standish found himself gripping his hands together behind him as very slowly at first and then with added thrust the *Terrapin* began to nudge forward. The spring took the strain, tighter and tighter until it was stretched bar-taut, and more than one man was staring at it with obvious alarm.

'Stop engine!' Dalziel moved to the starboard wing and stared down at the gap between the two ships. It was already narrowing as once more the wind playfully eased the *Terrapin* back alongside the other vessel.

Standish looked away. Dalziel's attempted manoeuvre was normal enough. To go slow ahead on the one wire which ran from the bows back to a point on the other frigate's quarterdeck. It should have acted as a spring to swing the *Terrapin's* stern clear so that Dalziel could reverse his engines and back clear. But the wind was too strong, as he should have realized.

Some of the seamen on the other ship were grinning broadly and an officer on her bridge raised a megaphone to enquire, 'Forgotten something, old chap?'

Dalziel tossed him a casual wave, his mouth set in a wide grin, but standing by his side Standish could see the muscle jumping quickly in his throat, a small droplet of sweat below the peak of his cap.

He said quietly, 'Sir, I think it would be better if...'

Dalziel looked at him. 'Not to worry, Number One.' Then he leaned over the screen and yelled, 'Get ready to jump about, Sub!' Over his shoulder he snapped, 'Slow ahead port engine!'

Again the surge of white froth beneath the frigate's counter and the responding thrust against the wire spring.

A man said thickly, 'Gawd, it'll snap and cut some bleeder's 'ead off!'

Standish willed himself to stay quite still, feeling the ship snubbing harder and harder against the captive wire. The two officers were no longer grinning from the other bridge, and he could hear the shrill of a bosun's pipe, the stampede of feet as the duty watch dashed on deck to assist.

At that very instant the wind dropped again, and with something like a prayer Standish saw the gap starting to open into an arrowhead of bright choppy water.

'Stop engine. Let go spring.' Dalziel had both hands in his pockets. 'Tell those men to *get a move on*!'

'All gone the spring!' The voice was cracked with relief.

'Good. Now let go forrard!' Dalziel hardly paused to hear the shouted response before adding tersely, 'Slow astern both engines!'

All at once they were gliding clear, the faces along the other ship's side losing their individuality, the pale hull merging with that of the supply vessel.

The yeoman said, 'That transport's swinging badly, sir.'

Dalziel turned abruptly. 'What? Where?'

Standish stared past him and saw the anchored ship, her tall sides rusted and streaked with red lead, angling from her anchor cable like a solid steel wall.

Dalziel snapped, 'And why the *hell* did nobody report that?' He gestured at a lookout. 'What have you been doing all this time, eh?'

The luckless seaman muttered, 'I was watchin' the wire, sir. I thought it were goin' to break.'

Dalziel shouted, 'I don't give a damn what you think! On lookout you keep your eyes on your sector and nothing more, *do you understand*?'

Irvine stood up from the chart table and said sharply, 'My God, we'll hit her!'

Dalziel seemed to realize that the ship was still churning remorselessly astern, her flapping ensign almost in direct line with the transport's tall funnel.

'Stop both engines!' He grasped the voice pipe as if for support. 'Slow ahead port, half astern starboard!'

Down in his gleaming world of machinery Quarrie must be

staring at his dials and wondering just what the hell was happening on deck, Standish thought. The ship was still going astern, but the starboard screw fighting in opposition to the other one was dragging her round in a tighter arc. At best she might slide alongside the other ship, and at worst she could still smash her stern right through the transport's plates.

Dalziel's face was expressionless. 'Half ahead port, *full astern* starboard!'

The ship was shuddering and vibrating like a mad thing, with every rivet and plate creaking as if to tear itself out of the bridge.

Standish said at length, 'Pass the word for fenders along the starboard quarter!'

Dalziel snapped, 'Belay that!' In a calmer tone he added, 'No need, Number One.'

The *Terrapin's* shadow glided down the transport's towering forecastle with less than twenty feet to clear.

Dalziel said sharply, 'Stop both engines!' He reached out for the voicepipe again. 'Half ahead together. Starboard fifteen.'

As she moved ahead once more, her hull leaning to the rudder, Standish saw her bow wave rippling away on either beam, watched fascinated as the disturbed water broke across the transport's anchor cable like a miniature millrace.

'Midships.' Dalziel crossed to the opposite side, turning his back on the transport. 'Slow ahead both engines.'

The other ships moored nearby had so far remained silent, either too spellbound or too horrified to speak as the little *Terrapin* had surged astern towards the anchored transport, only to turn at the very last minute before swinging ahead to circle her bows like a terrier around an elephant.

But now the silence was broken and as lights flashed from every direction Burch, the yeoman, and his signalmen wrote busily and acknowledged the lights with hardly a pause for breath.

Dalziel said, 'Take over, Number One. Fall the hands in for leaving harbour.' As he glanced at the scribbled signals, most of which were either caustic or downright rude, he added absently, 'She handles well, Number One, in spite of her years.'

Then he grinned, his teeth white in the shadow of his cap. 'I'll bet that shook some of those idle buggers, eh?'

And me too, Standish thought. 'Yes, sir.'

While the frigate wended her way slowly past the rest of the anchored warships, the pipes shrilling their respects to their seniors and the hands standing in swaying lines on the quarter-deck and forecastle alike, Standish found himself wondering even more about Commander Hector Dalziel.

Had it really been a demonstration of reckless self-confidence, or just a man desperate to succeed no matter what the consequences? And those consequences were bad indeed. A collision would have meant court martial and the instant removal of Dalziel from command.

He turned from the voicepipe to watch the captain as he raised his glasses above the screen. He was studying the out-thrust finger of Changi Point as it glided slowly past the star-board beam, its white houses still shimmering in the fading heat haze. He looked quite composed and relaxed, and when he lowered the glasses Standish could see the excitement in his eyes like a living thing.

He said, 'I have a feeling that this is going to be a profitable experience, Number One.'

He did not explain what he meant for at that moment Irvine said, 'Time to alter course, sir.'

Dalziel nodded and walked to the voicepipe. 'Starboard ten. Midships.' He lowered his eyes to the gyro repeater. 'Steady. Steer one-one-zero.'

A shabby junk glided past the port beam rocking uneasily in the frigate's wash, and the gulls which had followed the *Terrapin* clear of the harbour idled further and further astern, to wait perhaps for another source of food.

'Fall out harbour stations.' Dalziel glanced up at the mast-head pendant, gold now in the last of the dying rays. 'And tell Wishart well done. He moved quite quickly back there when the moment arrived.'

He paused with one foot still on the gratings. 'Nothing like a little challenge to get the blood pumping, eh?'

When Dalziel had gone to his sea cabin Irvine said slowly, 'Did you ever see anything quite like that?'

Standish looked past him, watching the pale smoke from a hill fire high above the nearest headland.

'It's your watch, isn't it?' He walked to the bridge wing and wiped his face with his handkerchief. 'Just see that you do *your* part, fair enough?'

Irvine watched him calmly. 'Aye, *aye*, sir!'

Darkness found the *Terrapin* steaming at ten knots north east up the Singapore Strait, her navigation lights burning like two bright, unmatched eyes and her slim hull lifting easily to the mounting swell from the South China Sea.

In her cabins and messdecks there was plenty of talk and rumour, and the story of Dalziel's spectacular departure from the harbour would gain much in the telling.

But the *Terrapin* at least seemed content to wait and see, and, as with all ships, that had to be enough.

3 Exercise Action!

STANDISH climbed on to the upper bridge and lightly touched the peak of his cap as Irvine saluted and said, 'Good morning, Number One. It's going to be another sizzler.'

'Looks like it.' Standish glanced down at the vibrating chart table with its much used instruments and tried to assemble his thoughts for the coming day.

It was a few minutes to eight o'clock, and, as Irvine had just remarked, it had the promise of a hot day, in more ways than one. Standish had in fact been up for several hours, going round the ship as the hands cleaned up decks before breakfast, checking and watching while the normal sea-routine got under way. He had found it hard to sleep, and the activity on the deck had helped to steady him, to clear his mind from its usual nagging despair.

Irvine who was waiting to hand over the watch said abruptly, 'Still ten knots. Course three-four-eight.'

A bosun's mate looked up from his handset. 'Red Watch closed up at cruising stations, sir. Able Seaman Macnair on the wheel.'

'Very good.' Standish walked up on to the gratings adding, 'You'd better get some breakfast, Pilot. You may be required shortly.'

Irvine grimaced. 'First day at sea and we're doing drills. What does the Old Man have in mind?'

Standish shrugged, feeling the heat across his shoulders in a humid embrace. 'No idea.'

Irvine grunted and clattered down the bridge ladder.

It was quite new for a whole watch to turn up for duty before time, Standish thought vaguely. There was a strange expectancy over the whole ship. He had even noticed it during a brief breakfast, where the officers had sat munching in silence, each no doubt contemplating the efficiency or otherwise of his own department. He conceded that it was not a bad way to start off a new command. He had done it himself in the past. Run through the usual drills just to keep the ship's company awake to their responsibilities. It never did any harm.

The tannoy squeaked and the the bosun's mate's voice echoed above and below deck with weary indifference.

'Out pipes. Both watches for exercise in five minutes.'

There was a step on the coaming and Standish turned to see Dalziel crossing from the small chartroom abaft the bridge.

He saluted. 'Good morning, sir.'

Dalziel nodded amiably. He looked bright and eager, his skin glowing as if from a cold shower.

'Belay that last pipe, Number One. You can clear lower deck and have the hands lay aft. I intend to address them.'

The bosun's mate saw Standish nod and picked up the microphone.

'Clear lower deck! All hands lay aft to the quarterdeck!'

There was a long pause, and then in a growing flood the seamen and off duty watchkeepers began to make their way along either side deck towards the stern.

Dalziel peered down and said, 'Two or three odd ones there. Thought we had some Wrens aboard for a moment.' He frowned. 'Can't abide long hair. Makes them look scruffy.'

Standish kept his face immobile. 'I'll tell the coxswain, sir.'

'Good.' Dalziel fidgeted with his shirt buttons. 'And you might tell Irvine to indent for new charts. The ones I've just examined are covered with more tea and coffee stains than useful information.'

Corbin appeared at the top of the ladder and saluted.

'Lower deck cleared, sir.'

He was a giant of a man, a true product of a navy which was now little seen. He had been born and raised in a London slum, and been encouraged into the Service at the age of fifteen by a mother who changed her admirers almost as often as her clothes. The hard life and early upbringing had made Corbin

shed everything which might remind him of his past. He had
become Navy through and through, but had somehow managed
to retain a strong sense of humanity which the more foolish of
his subordinates had sometimes mistaken for weakness.

Dalziel smiled. 'Thank you, Swain.' To Standish he added,
'I'll be a few minutes and then we can go to drills.'

Standish walked back to the forepart of the bridge and relaxed
slightly.

Across the gently spiralling bows the sea was stretched taut
like a sheet of glittering blue silk, above which the sky seemed
washed out by comparison and gave a sure hint of the heat to
come. A layman might have imagined the ship to be alone on
a vast ocean, for there was neither land nor another vessel to
be seen in any direction. But the chart, like the steadily revolving
radar, showed the *Terrapin* to be steaming up the Malaysian
coastline, which now lay some twenty-five miles across the port
beam. It was even possible to imagine a smudge of land there,
but Standish knew it to be a haze, a strange, pale mist which
broke down the edge of both horizons and merged sea and sky
in an unmatched, glaring void.

He said suddenly, 'Switch on the quarterdeck microphone,
Spinks.'

The bosun's mate threw a switch and Dalziel's crisp voice
flooded into the bridge, making both the signalman and one of
the lookouts jump with alarm.

Dalziel was saying, 'I have not yet had much time to speak
with you as a company. Just a few individuals to get a general
picture, eh? But time will tell me more, and until then I want
to put you in the picture, to tell you exactly what I require from
my people as a whole.'

Standish had a sudden vision of the cans of beef which
Dalziel had so eagerly described to him when he had come
aboard, and wondered what some of the listening men would
say if they saw themselves in the same category.

'I had you brought aft at this particular time for a good
reason.' There was a small pause and Dalziel's voice became
muffled as he turned away from the microphone. 'Over there,
some twenty miles on the starboard beam is the resting place of
two great ships. It is almost thirty years since *Repulse* and *Prince of
Wales* went to the bottom, carrying with them many hundreds

of brave and resolute men.' His voice became clearer again. 'In less than an hour, in the twinkling of an eye, two great ships, and with them the whole balance of naval power in these waters, were lost.'

Standish darted a glance at the young signalman. He was about nineteen, with a round open face unmarked by memory or much serious thought. But as Dalziel spoke he was staring across the screen, as if expecting to see some sign, some mark of the disaster he had just heard described.

'But this was no great deed in the making. These ships were not destroyed on some vital mission. They were thrown away by men whose minds had become addled and cramped by peace, by a system which believed that everything would be all right on the day, that nothing mattered but financial profit, self-advancement and personal comfort.'

Standish walked to the port side and found himself waiting for Dalziel to continue.

'For the want of a nail, someone once said, eh? Well, for the want of some simple common sense we lost two great ships, and consequently our foothold in the Far East.' The voice faded again. 'Over the other beam is Malaya. When most of you were either babies or just an evil gleam in your father's eye, there was a tragedy going on out there. Men were fighting and dying, some cursing their own flag and country, because at the moment of truth they knew, they *knew* they had been betrayed by the very fools they had trusted!'

Irvine walked from the chartroom, some breadcrumbs on the front of his shirt.

'God, did you hear him?'

Standish held up his hand. 'Listen. He's still speaking.'

'Well, today there are no great ships and few emblems of country. The world, our world is divided in two pieces, and we fight to preserve all that we hold dear as best we can. But we have enemies other than those across the Iron Curtain. Enemies within, of the same ilk as those who threw away those two proud ships.'

There was another pause and Standish could imagine Dalziel standing on a liferaft, hands behind him, head thrust forward as he looked around at his command.

'My requirements are simple. Loyalty, obedience and constant vigilance. This ship has been allowed to get stale. That
state of affairs ceased to exist at midday on Sunday last!'

There was a murmur of voices and then Corbin's carrying
tones as he brought the assembled men to attention.

'Switch off.' Standish looked down at his hands. He had
almost expected to see them shaking.

Irvine muttered, 'God knows what our layabouts'll make of
that. Most of them were expecting to be shipped home to
mother, or to see what the naughty neighbour has been up to
with the little woman.' He ran his fingers through his sun-
bleached hair. 'Now they'll be seeing a communist under every
bunk.'

'Not a bad thing either.'

They both turned to see Dalziel already at the head of the
ladder.

Irvine said, 'Sorry, sir, but I was just trying to see it from their
point of view.'

'Well, don't bother, Pilot. See it from mine!' Dalziel's chest
was heaving as if he had run from the quarterdeck. 'Now,
Number One, let us get started. Tell Wishart to put his people
to work stripping and preparing 'A' gun. We will have a shoot
this afternoon. This forenoon we will have boat lowering and
fire drill, a bit of damage control.' He paused and looked at
Irvine. 'If you must come on the bridge with half your breakfast
on your shirt then you might at least wear your cap!'

He turned back to Standish, his voice brisk and controlled.
'Send for Pigott and Hornby, and then tell Caley to exercise
the T.A.S. team.' He rubbed his hands, a dry, rasping sound.
'Well, Number One?'

Standish found himself smiling. 'Right away, sir.'

Minutes later the whole business was under way, with petty
officers and seamen, mechanics and even stewards struggling
with unaccustomed drills, while Dalziel peered down at the
milling confusion with obvious satisfaction. And he made sure
they all knew he was watching them, Standish thought.

Hornby and Pigott reached the bridge together, mystified no
doubt by their unexpected summons.

Dalziel nodded. 'Ah, Pigott. I want you to get your supply

chaps busy. Get all the spare crates on deck as quickly as you can. The bigger the better.'

Pigott regarded him suspiciously. 'I have to sign for those, sir.' When Dalziel said nothing he added firmly, 'I'm answerable for all my empty crates.'

'You are answerable to *me*, Pigott.' Dalziel eyed him cheerfully. 'When you have gathered all the crates on the main deck you will give my compliments to the Chief and tell him I require some empty oil drums, the five-gallon type will do very well.'

Pigott opened his mouth and then shut it again as Dalziel added, 'I know. He's answerable for all his drums! Well, just see that they're on deck in thirty minutes, right?'

Pigott had reached the head of the ladder when Dalziel called, 'When you've finished you can come back here and take over the watch from Number One.'

Pigott turned and stared at him, his pale eyes blinking rapidly behind his glasses.

'But I'm not a watchkeeping officer, sir.'

'Suppose all of 'em were suddenly to get killed, or drop dead from some of that food you so jealously guard in your stores, eh?' He grinned. 'What would you do? Just sit on your arse and wait for a bloody miracle?' He slapped his palms together. 'Now come on, Pigott, *jump about!*'

As the supply officer ran down the ladder Standish said quietly, 'He means well sir.'

'Quite. So did Eichmann, I believe!'

Dalziel turned his eyes on Hornby who was staring at him like a fat, mesmerized rabbit.

'Take twenty men and transform Pigott's boxes and drums into a raft.'

If he had asked for some blood Hornby could not have been more startled.

'Raft, sir?'

Dalziel shot Standish a grin. 'Why does everyone repeat every damn thing I say?' To Hornby he roared, 'Yes, a *bloody raft!*'

'Yes, sir.' Hornby licked his lips. 'I'll try, sir.'

Dalziel said gently, 'Of course you will. I never doubted it. In any case it will take some of that blubber off you, eh?' He pulled out a stop-watch from his pocket adding half to himself, 'Can't abide fat officers. Obesity and complacency go hand in hand in my experience.'

He thrust the watch into his pocket. 'Number three fire party has taken all of five minutes so far, and not a damn hose in view.' He beckoned to the bosun's mate. 'Get down there and tell the senior rating I'll light a fire under his rump if he doesn't shift himself.'

He rubbed his hands. 'Well, Number One, things are moving.' He snatched up the red handset almost before it had stopped buzzing.

'Captain speaking. Oh yes, Chief, those drums.' He looked at Standish and winked. 'Ah yes, I see. Quite so. I agree with you in principle, Chief, but I do require drums.' He paused. 'And of course their removal would make room for some extra spares which I might be able to get for you when we touch port again, eh?'

He replaced the handset very gently. 'Thought that would do the trick.' Then he peered at Hornby. 'Still here?' And as the electrical officer hurried for the ladder he added quietly, 'A big body, but I suspect there is a tiny man lurking within.'

Thirty minutes later Pigott returned to report that the required articles had been assembled.

'Capital.' Dalziel gestured towards the chart table. 'Course is three-four-eight. Carry on here while we go and watch young Wishart.'

Standish followed him to the ladder. When he looked back he saw Pigott still staring at the chart, his expression one of complete bewilderment.

Beside the twin four-inch mounting they found Wishart amidst his men, his shirt smeared with gun grease, his face set in a frown of concentration.

Petty Officer Motts, the G.I., saw Dalziel and saluted.

'Good as new, sir. Just another hour or two an' we'll 'ave 'em as clean as whistles.'

Dalziel nodded. 'That's what I like. Enthusiasm.' He looked at Wishart. 'This afternoon we will put Hornby's raft in the water and you can shoot at it.'

Wishart glanced at Standish and replied grimly, 'Aye, aye, sir.'

'We might find time for the four Bofors, Number One.' Dalziel peered at his watch. 'But they may have to wait.'

Standish followed him along the port side, having to step out to keep pace with him. As he passed amongst the busy seamen he watched their faces, expecting open resentment or even scorn.

But they seemed dazed, shocked perhaps by what they could do once they were set into motion. If Dalziel could make it last, it might just work, he thought.

Dalziel halted below the whaler's davits and looked at him calmly. After a moment he said, 'I understand that your wife ran off with some other chap, is that right?'

*   *   *

It was late evening when the *Terrapin* crossed the ten fathom line and headed towards the twin headlands which guarded the entrance of Kuala Papan. The sun had all but disappeared beyond the deeply shadowed hills, so that the thick jungle which ran inland as far as the eye could see was made to merge in a carpet of burnished copper.

By the time the frigate had groped her way into the sheltered water below one of the towering headlands it was practically dark, and as the anchor had splashed into a welter of dancing phosphorescence Standish had found himself wondering what might have happened if Dalziel had left his entrance any later.

For now, while the ship swung gently at her cable it was quite apparent that there were neither buoys nor beacons of any sort to mark the deep water channel, and there seemed to be no sort of pilot to help the unfortunate stranger into safety. Perhaps out here strangers had no right to protection, he thought vaguely. It was a desolate place, hemmed in by jungle and steep hills with only a small fishing village to show any sort of human life. Kuala Papan's main claim to fame seemed to be its stone pier and a road which ran inland to serve several plantations and one mine. Both pier and road had been built by the Japanese, and as Standish stood smoking his pipe at the quarterdeck guardrail he found it easy to visualise the misery and pain which had gone to their construction. On nights like this, with the stars so large they seemed to link the headlands on either side of the estuary, thousands of starved and brutally treated prisoners-of-war must have lain at the mercy of mosquitos and countless other insects, too wretched to find comfort from a brief respite, too fearful of the odds against their survival to think about any future.

On the opposite side of the inlet he could see the massive shape of the U.S.S. *Sibuyan*, aboard which Dalziel was now in conference with the American admiral. Her upper deck and twin derricks were well lit with arc lamps, and a small guard-boat spluttered slowly around her hull at regular intervals. Of about 10,000 tons, the *Sibuyan* was one of the strange, multi-purpose vessels which the Americans seemed to use more and more frequently in their efforts to contain the undeclared war around them. Rated as an amphibious force flagship she carried helicopters as well as guns, and contained all the resources to sustain a small fleet of lesser craft, as well as provide the necessary communications and headquarters facilities for her commanding admiral.

Standish tapped his pipe on the rail and saw the ash glowing above the uneasy water before being extinguished on the current. Around and below him the *Terrapin* was quiet again after the excitement and confusion of the day. From speakers on the forward messdeck he could hear the muffled pulsating beat of a pop group, and from an open scuttle in the petty officers' mess the sudden ripple of laughter and clink of glasses.

When at last, weary and gasping for breath, the ship's company had stood down from exercises, Standish had expected Dalziel to show some sort of disappointment. The drills had been, for the most part, a disaster, but as the ship had altered course westward towards the land Dalziel had squatted on his bridge chair making notes in his little book at a furious speed, pausing every so often to peer down at the forecastle or to take a few rapid paces back and forth as if to settle something in his mind.

Wishart had done better than he had dared to hope. Using local control the four-inch crews had got at least two shots within fifty feet of Hornby's raft before the right gun had jammed and brought the practice to a halt.

Undeterred, Dalziel had hurled a lifebuoy over the port rail and had yelled at the bridge, 'Exercise man overboard drill!'

The effect had been startling. Pigott had rung down for full speed and had flung the ship into a hard turn, the deck tilting as she slewed wildly and throwing many unprepared seamen from their feet. In the boiler room a mechanic fell down a ladder, and in the main galley some fifty pieces of crockery skidded to oblivion.

Dalziel had clambered to the bridge where Pigott's last reserve of calm had given way to near panic. He had forgotten to take a bearing on the bobbing lifebuoy, and seeing Dalziel watching him he had run to the voicepipe yelling, 'Hard a-starboard!'

With opposite helm put on just as violently, the *Terrapin's* wake was twisting across the blue water in a zigzagging maelstrom of white foam, while from below decks came more crashes and curses as yet more men were caught unprepared.

Standish had seen the makeshift target appear suddenly across the swaying bows, but as he had opened his mouth to warn Pigott, Dalziel had put a finger to his lips and had shot him a grin of complete satisfaction.

The frigate hit the raft at full speed, sending the crates flying in splinters and the released oil drums bobbing down either side to the derisive cheers of the guns crews.

'Take over the con, Number One.' Dalziel had scribbled a few more notes before adding to Pigott, 'Awful.' He had grinned wider. '*Bloody awful!*'

The supply officer had left the bridge pale-faced and staring straight in front of him, and Dalziel had added evenly, 'He'll remember that next time. Think before you act. Can't abide people who panic.'

As the ship had turned for her final approach towards the sunset Dalziel had remarked, 'Not a bad effort all round. They need a lot of polishing of course, but the material is there. A few leading hands will have to be disrated, and I'm not too happy about certain of my officers.' He had given a small, eloquent shrug. 'You can teach a man his job. But you cannot supply him with officer-like qualities if he is already without them. Any more than you can win the Derby with a pit pony, eh?'

Standish had heard Dalziel yelling at the ratings too on more than one occasion. And that was the odd thing about him, they took his insults, and even appeared to enjoy them. Perhaps his sudden flashes of excited rudeness were more acceptable to the ratings than the formality they would normally expect from a captain.

Dalziel seemed to have this outspoken manner for all occasions. Like that moment by the whaler's davits when he had asked about Alison.

Before, had he considered it, Standish would have expected himself to react quite differently. To tell Dalziel or anyone else to mind his own business in no uncertain manner.

And yet, even now, looking back over the day he could still find no sort of resentment at Dalziel's cool question.

He had always stored the bitter memory in his mind, padded it with phrases like 'incompatible' or 'a marriage doomed from the start.' But boiling it all down, Dalziel was right. She had in fact 'run off with some other chap.'

There had been so many uncertainties connected with Alison. Naturally enough they had met when he had commissioned his own command, the submarine *Electra*, in which her brother was appointed sonar officer. Alison was fair and beautiful, she was tantalizing and also totally unpredictable, and Standish had been stunned when she had agreed to marry him. It was still hard to work out the actual moment of disaster, or even the threat of it. At sea things were usually clearer and more precast. If two ships followed certain courses for a set distance you knew a collision was unavoidable. If the ship's buoyancy went beyond a slide-rule calculation she would certainly founder.

But Alison's change of heart towards him was vague, like most of his other memories of her. Only the beginning was clear cut, with the shining faces and uniforms outside the dockyard church, the avenue of raised swords, the jokes and the mad rush to the airport, and that first overwhelming moment of passion. And of course the end was clear enough, too.

The packed suitcases outside their flat. The taxi-driver watching with obvious interest as Standish pleaded and then finally watched her drive away and out of his life.

Even then he had still imagined it might be temporary, and had gone to see her father, a rich construction engineer on the outskirts of London. He had been unsympathetic, and looking back, perhaps even pleased.

'Never wanted her to marry into the Navy. Bad enough having my son running about dressed in fancy uniform. He should be working in the business which I built with my own two hands, without her being so stupid, too.' He had regarded Standish's angry features coolly. 'But I'll drag young Roger out of the bloody Navy if I have to bribe a minister to do it!'

But he left it too late. Roger had died that morning off Portland Bill with his men in a sealed and blazing inferno.

Being her brother Roger might have known Alison's intentions but had been too loyal to both of them to speak out. Perhaps it had been too much on his mind as he had supervised his men with the new type of flare.

The marriage, like his command, had lasted just nine months. It was not much of an achievement, he told himself bitterly.

There was a scrape of feet on the steel deck and a bosun's mate peered at him through the gloom.

'First Lieutenant, sir, signal from the Yankee ship. The captain's returnin' now.'

'Thank you, Roper. You'd better fetch the O.O.D.'

Standish walked slowly towards the illuminated gangway where the quartermaster was staring in contemplative silence at the black water alongside.

How many captains had climbed on to that brass plate with the ship's name to greet them and remind them instantly of their responsibilities?

Well, it was to be hoped that Dalziel had been given more time to get his new command into shape before he was employed on more demanding service.

Wishart appeared in the lamplight, adjusting his cap and squinting beyond the glare towards the other anchored ship.

Standish asked, 'All right now, Sub?'

He grinned ruefully. 'Still sweating a bit when I think about the gunnery today.' He shrugged. 'Still, it could have been worse, I suppose.'

But not much, Standish thought. He said, 'Well, keep at it. We might be able to organize a contest with some other ship when we get moving again.'

An engine spluttered in the darkness and the quartermaster yelled, 'Boat ahoy?'

Back came the reply. '*Terrapin!*'

It was the big motor boat from the *Sibuyan* which had whisked Dalziel away almost before the anchor had been secured.

Dalziel's head and shoulders came into the harsh lights above the gangway, his eyes gleaming as he nodded curtly to Wishart and his side-party before saying, 'Come to my cabin, Number One.'

He made to walk forward and then snapped, 'Why is the gangway sentry not armed?' To the deck at large he added sharply, 'In future, and until I order otherwise, I want an armed sentry here.' He jabbed a finger at Wishart. 'And the officer of the day will also carry a sidearm. Draw one now and write it in the log for your relief.'

In the captain's day cabin there was a strong smell of fresh paint, and Standish noticed that the one bulkhead which still awaited a new coating looked yellow by comparison.

Dalziel threw his briefcase on a chair and said absently, 'They'll start on my sleeping quarters tomorrow. At least this place looks a bit more like it, eh?' But there was little enthusiasm in his tone.

He opened his cupboard and took out a decanter and some finely cut glasses which had not been there before. He said, 'Must have a drink. American ships are more than hospitable, but their mania for abstinence makes me somewhat dehydrated.'

Standish took the proferred glass which was more than half filled with whisky. Dalziel had given him no choice of drink, and was already sipping his own glass with obvious impatience.

'How did it go, sir?' Standish tried to see beyond Dalziel's detached expression. 'Was the admiral aboard?'

Dalziel nodded and stared at his glass. 'Rear-Admiral John P. Curtis. Yes, he was there. Damn nice chap too as far as I can make out.' He moved the glass idly. 'He is in overall command —*with* the Malaysian consent, of course—of all inshore patrols until these acts of aggression cease or change direction in some way.' He smiled wryly. 'The Americans quite rightly do not want another Viet Nam, or any situation where they become so totally involved they can't withdraw or win an outright victory. They want the rest of the club to do their bit for a change.' He slammed the glass on his table. 'There was also one of our people aboard the *Sibuyan*. One Captain Philip Jerram, lately appointed as our supervisory overlord of Malaysian East Coast Patrols. In his care—God help them—he has twenty patrol boats and converted minesweepers to protect and watch over some two hundred miles of creeks, inlets and bloody islands, the names of which are probably not even marked on a chart!'

Standish watched him thoughtfully. By the sound of it Dalziel's visit to the flagship had not been a success.

Dalziel jumped to his feet and seized the decanter. 'God, they say there's no justice in this world and now I'm half inclined to believe it.' He refilled the glasses, some of the whisky spilling unheeded on the deck. 'Jerram and I are old colleagues. Oh yes, I can see that he and I are going to get on like a house on fire, I don't think!'

'Well, sir, were you told of our next assignment?' It was obviously necessary to draw Dalziel from his thoughts if he was to learn anything of what had happened.

Dalziel frowned. 'Along the coast we have all these half-trained, gibbering Malays. To the south and east we have the heavy units of the Seventh Fleet, just in case.' He fixed Standish with a flat stare. 'And on offshore patrols from here to the Thailand border we will have *Terrapin*!' He looked down at the littered table. 'It's so bloody unfair, and I told him so!'

Standish studied Dalziel from another, more personal viewpoint. Without effort he could imagine him bouncing into the American admiral's quarters, full of schemes and ideas, and having his enthusiasm knocked from under him, maybe by this Captain Jerram.

He asked quietly, 'What did the admiral say?'

Dalziel looked up and gave a wry smile. 'He told me not to *"Split my stack!"* A most descriptive phrase for the way I was feeling just then.'

'It boils down to our being given another picket job, sir.' Standish put down his glass and looked round for some water. 'Like the others she has had in the past. I'm sorry about this, and I can guess how you feel . . .'

Dalziel stared at him. '*Guess*? How can you possibly begin to understand what it means to me?' He paced twice across the worn carpet. 'They're not going to push my ship into some damn backwater just to keep me quiet, not again!' He calmed himself with obvious effort. 'The trouble with Jerram is that he's like so many in the Navy today. No imagination. No get-up-and-go! The Service seems to be driving out all the characters nowadays. Just leaving us with computers and a few white-faced pansies who squat on their arses in Whitehall!' He paused and stared down at Standish. 'Well, they're not going to push *me* around, d'you hear?'

Standish said, 'Yes, sir.' He had never seen anyone else work himself into a rage in such short time. Unless it had always been there, behind the grin and the unruffled self-confidence.

Dalziel was saying bitterly, 'The same old attitudes all over again. Be nice to the Reds and look the other way. Everything will be all right and they'll leave us in peace. God in heaven, the communist world is honest enough. They've told us plainly what they want to do, and still we seem to wait for a miracle. Believe me, if you want to win friends and influence people you don't do it by showing them you're as weak as gnat's water, do you?'

He lowered himself into his chair and sighed. 'Still, we're not beaten yet. Not by a damn long chalk.' He picked up the decanter. 'This was given to me by the Shah of Persia as a gift to remember him by. Strange chap, but quite decent in his own way.'

Standish watched the level in the decanter drop another two inches.

'Have we got our sailing orders yet, sir?'

'No. The *Sibuyan* is weighing at dawn tomorrow, and then Jerram is coming aboard to look over my ship.' He could not disguise the contempt in his voice. 'Probably not been in one for months.'

Standish stood up and felt the cabin swaying. 'I think I'd better turn in, sir. It's been a long day.'

'It has indeed.' Dalziel regarded him emptily. 'But when I've done with this ship she'll make everyone sit up and take notice.'

Standish stared at a framed picture which had appeared on one of the newly painted bulkheads. It showed a destroyer at full speed, her guns lifted skywards as if on manoeuvres. Underneath is stated, '*H.M.S. Harrier. Mediterranean 1968.*'

The whisky, which he rarely drank, was making his stomach

contract, and he knew that if he did not get away from the enclosed cabin and its stench of paint he would be violently sick. But the picture, the name *Harrier*, seemed to hold him, to open up some lost memory which he could not place.

Dalziel said, 'My last ship. But I expect you knew that, eh?'

Standish turned and looked at him. There was an edge to Dalziel's voice, like the tone he had used when speaking about Captain Jerram.

'I'm sorry, sir. I was in hospital for a long time. It must have been something else.'

Dalziel smiled thinly. 'I was very attached to *Harrier*. Unfortunately she was cut in half by the carrier *Implacable* in the Med. Sixty-five men were lost.' His voice sounded slurred. 'Not my fault of course, I but still miss her just the same. A *good* ship. Damn fine command.'

Standish picked up his cap. It was strange how important events seemed to be held at bay by some mental barrier. All those months in hospital, the comings and goings of staff officers gathering information for the court of enquiry in hushed voices, the pain and the empty void of waiting for news of Alison. And all the while, in another place, Dalziel had had his battles, too. There had been combined fleet manoeuvres in the Eastern Mediterranean, more to impress the Russians than anything else it was said, and the destroyer had been rammed by the carrier while both ships had been turning to take up stations for the night. The rights and wrongs had been lost in the same mist which made it hard to remember Alison's brother and the events which had led to that morning off Portland.

But one thing was clear. Only too clear. Dalziel was one more unwanted officer. Like himself. Filling a space until the time came to discard them along with the tired old ship which held them.

He heard Dalziel say, 'Tomorrow we will try another exercise or two. I'm not too happy about Caley's T.A.S. party. Not happy at all.'

Standish closed the door and staggered the last few paces to his own cabin and fell spread-eagled across the bunk.

In the next cabin he could hear an occasional click, followed by a metallic rattle, and knew that Hornby was doing his nightly practice. Driving golf balls into a tin cup across four feet of carpet.

Around him a discordant vibration also told him that someone in the officers' bathroom was trying to run a shower. The water system always sounded like a freight train shunting in a badly maintained siding, and normally it was considered something of a joke. Like the air-conditioning. Like the ship.

Standish buried his face in the pillow and closed his eyes fiercely.

And like all of us, he thought desperately.

4 The Boarding Party

W<small>HEN</small> the *Terrapin's* company were roused from their bunks and hammocks the following morning they found that the American vessel had already weighed anchor and was standing well out to sea. By the time work of washing down decks had commenced the *Sibuyan* had left the headlands far astern and her hull was almost lost in a curling bank of morning haze.

Standish had heard her anchor cable clanking through the hawsepipe as he had shaved himself for the coming day, and had wondered what the visit by Captain Jerram would bring for the ship, and for him personally.

As the first rays of yellow sunlight penetrated the deep inlet he saw through the open scuttle that it was not quite as deserted as he had imagined. Apart from a few gnat-like native fishing boats he could also see two low-lying M.L.s, each painted in the pale grey of the Malaysia Navy. So Jerram was presumably aboard one of them, waiting his moment to make a suitable appearance.

Breakfast and morning colours passed without event, and then as the hands mustered once again beneath the awnings a small motor dory shoved off from one of the M.L.s and headed purposefully towards the frigate.

Dalziel must have been watching from his day cabin, for within seconds of the side-party mustering at the gangway he too was there, his face set in a tight, expressionless mask.

Standish was not sure what sort of man he had expected in Captain Philip Jerram, but the one who climbed up the ship's side and returned the salutes with grave formality was not a bit like anything he had imagined.

He was small and square, with a tendency to plumpness beneath his well cut white uniform, and his face, tanned and criss-crossed with tiny compressed wrinkles, was more that of a sober business man than a naval officer. His voice was surprisingly deep and resonant, and he had a slow, ponderous manner of speaking which made Standish alter his comparison again to that of a high churchman or influential vicar.

Jerram made a cursory inspection of the upper deck, pausing only to watch the hands being detailed off for the forenoon's work before saying, 'There seems quite a good deal to be done and ample hands to do it. They could learn a lot from my Malays. They may not have much education, but they do understand that a clean ship is an efficient one. And an efficient ship is a happy one.'

Standish glanced quickly at Dalziel. His face was like stone. But he replied calmly enough, 'Early days yet, sir.'

Jerram pouted doubtfully. 'Let us hope it is not too *late*.'

The two of them disappeared to Dalziel's quarters, and Irvine who was O.O.D. said, 'Not much love lost there, I should imagine.'

The forenoon dragged on very slowly, with the sun rising more steeply above the inlet and the airless anchorage changing accordingly to something like oven heat.

'Up spirits' was piped and the decks became heady with the smell of rum as Pigott and his supply ratings made ready to serve the daily tots, although to Standish the thought of drinking the rich, watered mixture in this heat was beyond consideration.

Then Caley appeared, and seeing Irvine said testily, 'The captain wants you in his cabin. I'm to take over.' He waited grim and unsmiling as Irvine unbuckled the unaccustomed pistol and handed it to him before adding, 'And he wants the charts you were preparing yesterday.'

Irvine drawled, 'Ah, the light dawns. We are to discuss the new patrol area.'

Standish walked from beneath a Bofors mounting and Caley called, 'The captain said to tell you to go too, Number One.'

Irvine's lips curved slightly. 'Really, you must learn the

proper naval phraseology, old chap. Did the captain not send his *compliments* to number one?'

Caley flushed darkly. 'Well, er, yes he did as a matter of fact.' He looked at the pistol and muttered, 'Sorry. I got a bit mixed up.'

As Standish walked to the screen door he said quietly, 'Must you be so bloody sarcastic, Pilot? Caley finds it a bit difficult to settle in. You don't make it easier for him.'

Irvine seemed amused. 'Sometimes I think I've been out here too long. I shall return to U.K. one fine day and find the Navy, maybe the whole country, run by Caleys. Dumb, ignorant morons who'd be better off between the shafts of farm carts.'

Standish kept his voice level. 'Perhaps if he had had your advantages he would show a bit more self-confidence.'

Irvine did not appear to have heard. 'He told me once that he and his wife like to have a run ashore in London sometimes, for *special occasions*.' He chuckled. 'I can imagine. Lyons Corner-house and a visit to the Imperial War Museum.'

The quartermaster's lobby was momentarily deserted and Standish said, 'Tell me, what is it that makes *you* so bloody special?'

Irvine regarded him calmly. 'Do you know, Number One, I really cannot answer that. I just know that I am.'

'Well, for the record let me tell you something. If you speak to Caley again as you did just now, I will ask for an apology, and what is more, *old chap*, you will make one!'

Irvine stared at him. 'No offence, Number One, and I hope none taken.'

They reached the companionway and Standish added, 'Now get those charts and meet me there.'

Irvine smiled gently. 'At once.' And as Standish ran down the ladder he added, 'Old chap.'

Jerram was sitting behind the cabin table, arms folded, with a short stubby pipe jutting from his mouth. Dalziel stood by an open scuttle, hands thrust into his pockets, back turned to his superior as he said, 'Sit down, Number One. This is to put you in the picture.' He sounded tense and on edge.

Standish seated himself and waited as Jerram removed his pipe and tapped the ash carefully into a brass bowl. As he refilled it with methodical slowness from an old, much-used tin he said, 'You will have a large patrol area. Two hundred miles north to south, staying for the most part thirty miles offshore.' He tamped the tobacco home and then leaned over his chair to pick three small shreds of it from the carpet. These he replaced carefully in the tin. 'Don't believe in waste. Never have.' He held a match above the pipe and sucked for several seconds, his eyes watching Standish through the spiralling smoke. 'For that reason I do not intend to waste this ship. The patrol will be for the express purpose of watching for any unidentified craft which try to approach the Malaysian coast without permission. Your ship will shadow such vessels and contact my patrols by radio. My people can do what is necessary to investigate, and if required, detain any such unauthorized excursions. That is about all there is to it.'

There was a long silence, broken only by the lap of water below the open scuttle and the gentle sucking noise from Jerram's pipe.

Standish asked, 'Will we be having any support, sir? Another ship perhaps?'

The pipe smoke was getting thicker. 'No.' Puff, puff. 'None to spare.' Puff, puff. 'In any case I am not anticipating anything drastic, if that is what's worrying you.'

Dalziel swung round, his eyes almost desperate. 'I have read all the Intelligence reports, sir. It is obvious to me that the communists intend to force our hand in Malaysia and Thailand.

'Obviously to *you*, possibly.' Jerram's voice was cold and uncompromising. 'But others, perhaps better informed, say differently. Malaysia, and for that matter Thailand, is not Viet Nam. It is not going to be one either.'

Dalziel was breathing quickly. 'Why? Because you say so?'

Jerram eyed him for several seconds. 'I will disregard that.' He looked round irritably as Irvine knocked and stepped into the cabin. Then he relaxed slightly and said, 'Put the charts down here where I can check them properly.'

But Dalziel strode to the table, blocking Irvine's way.

'I'm not satisfied, sir! This ship is good as any in the command! In my view it's nothing short of lunacy to put her right out at sea, away from possible landing places and rendezvous areas.' He was almost shouting now. 'You have only to look at a map, the daily newspaper if you like, surely it must be obvious what's happening right here and now!'

Jerram said, 'Nothing is that obvious.' To Irvine he added, 'Would you kindly do as I asked?'

Irvine shuffled the charts. 'I was about to, sir.'

'Just stay where you are until I have finished!' Dalziel turned so suddenly that he knocked one of the charts to the deck. 'I want to make a formal complaint! I'll not have this ship denigrated to some half-baked, useless operation without proper explanation!'

Standish found that he had risen to his feet, and was conscious of the tension around him, the agony and disappointment in Dalziel's voice. He saw Irvine's face alight with interest as he looked from one to the other, and could imagine the damage Dalziel's outburst might do if it was not stopped, and at once.

He said, 'Perhaps the Americans have some scheme of their own, sir. They may not have considered our role in this.'

Jerram looked down at the table. 'Rear-Admiral Curtis does not wish to interfere with our internal matters, Number One. Quite the reverse.'

Dalziel leaned on the table, his eyes blazing. 'You *see*? I knew this would happen! Someone has got it in for this ship, and for me!'

Irvine had managed to reach the table and placed the charts casually on top of the other papers.

Standish gave him a quick nod and said, 'If Lieutenant Irvine can be spared now, sir, he can go to the wardroom and gather the other officers. I'm sure they'd like to show a bit of hospitality before you leave.'

Jerram studied him thoughtfully and then replied, 'Good idea.' As Irvine backed, still watching, from the cabin he added, 'I was forgetting, you have already had a command, Number One. Your display of tact is commendable.' He stood up and spread his arms. They were very short. 'I think I'll toddle along to your wardroom now, if I may. I've not long, and there's a lot to do.' He looked at each of them. 'Just check those orders and apply your signatures. I'll collect my copies before I leave.' He stepped out of the door and closed it quietly behind him.

Dalziel pushed himself away from the table and said tonelessly, 'I did a very stupid thing just then.'

'I'll tell Irvine to keep his mouth shut, sir.'

'Damn *him!*' Dalziel turned and studied him gravely. 'It's Jerram I'm worried about.' Then he smiled, a slow sadness spreading across his mouth. 'Thank you for what you just did. You're an odd chap in some ways. But I'll not forget.'

They both looked at the neatly worded orders. Short and to the point. No room for manoeuvre or misunderstanding there.

Then Dalziel remarked offhandedly, 'I do fly off the handle sometimes you know. When I was in hospital I had a lot of time to think . . .'

'I didn't know you were in hospital too, sir?'

Dalziel turned away frowning. 'Oh, I thought I'd mentioned it.' He rubbed his chin. 'All history now of course. But last year was a bad one all round really. For me that is.'

Standish looked at him. To think that while he was lying with his skin-grafts and his nightmares, Dalziel was probably in the next room, or the next bed even.

'Was that Haslar hospital, sir?'

Dalziel signed the papers, his signature large and sprawling. 'No.' He shook his head sharply. 'No, it was another one. Duncan House.'

Standish had never heard of it.

'Best to forget all those things, Number One.' Dalziel rubbed his hands together. 'Let's get to sea, and to hell with Jerram and his bloody piousness.' Then he gave a great grin. 'See the way he picked up the tobacco? Always was a mean bastard.' He seemed to be recovering and growing in stature with every second.

Standish smiled, strangely relieved that the man he had come to know was somehow returning to his proper image.

'Better not let him hear that.'

Dalziel looked round the cabin and then let his eyes rest on the photograph of the destroyer.

'He'll not take *this* ship away from me, no matter what he does!'

He picked up his cap adding lightly, 'Come. We've given 'em long enough to gossip behind our backs, eh? In any case, if my officers are waiting for Jerram to push the boat out we'll *never* get to sea.'

And four hours later, with rather too much smoke frothing

from her funnel, the *Terrapin* steamed from the anchorage and turned her dented bows towards the north.

*   *   *

One week and a day after leaving Kuala Papan found the *Terrapin* steaming at eight knots, her narrow hull rising and corkscrewing uncomfortably in a slow, undulating swell. During the forenoon she had turned to head south-east on another leg of her patrol area, and with the sun almost directly overhead the upper bridge was blistering in the relentless heat. Even with a strip of awning above their heads the watchkeepers drooped in the glare, their eyes squinting at a million reflections thrown back from the sea around them, a sea which was both empty and seemingly endless.

Standish stood on the sun-dried gratings, his feet well apart to take the uncomfortable motion, his body poised to avoid touching the steel plates or the instruments, all of which felt as if they had just been lifted from a glowing fire.

In his chair on the port side of the bridge Dalziel sat hunched forward, his cap tilted over his eyes, glasses hanging loosely around his neck. He could be asleep or brooding, and Standish felt it was better to leave him to his own thoughts for the moment.

For today was like those which had gone before. Hot, oppressive, and with nothing to break the painful monotony of that empty, mocking expanse of sea.

On the first few days they had sighted several ships, and Dalziel had rung down for full speed and had altered course to investigate. But each time Burch, the yeoman, had checked his lists of authorized traffic, and had reported all was well. Standish had found himself wishing that some suspicious craft would appear, if only to snap the torpor which held the whole ship and made the daily drills both uncomfortable and pointless. But the drills went on just the same, with Dalziel springing fresh ideas and new tests to drive his officers and men to the point of exasperation and defeat.

He had refrained from using the guns for target practice again, and Standish suspected that Jerram had voiced his disapproval of Dalziel's action in stripping them from their mothballed retirement when there was no prospect of replacing the covering until the next overhaul.

There had been just one episode, and for a while Standish had imagined that Dalziel's outward calm would disintegrate.

On the fourth day they had sighted a tall-funnelled freighter, and upon closer inspection found her to be Russian, her course set for the north of the Gulf, probably to Bankok.

As the *Terrapin*'s plates had quivered and vibrated to the sudden increase of speed Dalziel had said, 'This is more like it. The bloody Russians have probably got this whole Gulf sewn up into supply areas for their local guerrillas and arms dumps.'

But Burch had come up with the same weary shake of the head.

'She's the *Umba*, sir. Nothing against *her*.'

Dalziel had remained unperturbed. 'Bits of paper! What the hell do people ten thousand miles away know about her movements, eh?'

The *Terrapin* had closed to within two cables and turned to steer parallel with the other ship, above which a tattered red flag had appeared.

'Signal her to heave to!' Dalziel had fidgeted with impatience as Burch had goaded his men into action. 'We'll soon know if she's behaving lawfully.'

Several heads had appeared on the freighter's high bridge, and for a long time nothing happened. Then at length a lamp had stammered out a slow reply, the flashes almost lost in the reflected sunshine.

Dalziel had snapped, 'Well?'

Burch, like most of his trade, was a careful man. Being a yeoman he was privileged to hear and see his officers at close quarters. To know of their uncertainties and to accept or disregard their varying ways without spreading his knowledge around the ship. But this time he could find no way of translating the misspelt signal into more diplomatic language.

He had replied unhappily, 'He says, go to bloody hell.' He had swallowed hard. 'Sir.'

Standish had seen the muscle jump in Dalziel's throat, the sudden clenching of his fists. Then the captain had climbed back on to his chair and said cheerfully, 'Make another signal. Tell him it's the Tsar's birthday and . . .' but the mood seemed to elude him. He had added curtly, 'Belay that! Alter course and return to three-zero-five.' To Standish he had added, 'We'll leave him to the big boys, eh? Don't want to start an *incident*, do we?'

Irvine, who had been crouching over the gyro repeater had said quietly, 'And so another gallant episode in naval annals draws to a triumphant close.'

Two seamen nearby had heard him and had exchanged delighted grins. Standish had seen and heard all of it, but had said nothing.

Now, on the upper bridge for another watch he wondered why Dalziel had been so reckless as to expect the Russians to allow a search. Even if they had been weighed down to the scuppers with plastic explosives and armed terrorists it was unthinkable that they would permit such a thing.

The story had of course gone over the ship, growing and becoming more outrageous by the hour. When the hands went to their drills it was common enough for a rating to cry out, 'Please, sir, I think there's a Russian on the messdeck!' And once, scrawled below a gun mounting Wishart had reported finding the words, 'Dalziel go home!'

It was as stupid as it was trivial, but under these conditions even small things could only make their lonely vigil worse.

And there was not even much prospect of locating another ship today, for as was too common an occurrence, the radar was switched off for running repairs, reducing their effectiveness as a picket to the length of a man's eyesight.

Behind his back he heard the clatter of teacups and the sudden stir of feet as the watchkeepers pulled themselves from their torpor, and seconds later a bosun's mate switched on the tannoy and called, 'Stand easy!'

Standish glanced at his watch. God, how the afternoon was dragging. He turned as a voice came from somewhere overhead. 'Bridge there!'

He crossed to the wing, feeling the sun searing his neck as he moved from beneath the small awning. High above the bridge, their half-naked bodies shining like brown chestnuts against the sky, two mechanics had been working unenthusiastically to service the radar scanner. At the sound of the call to stand easy and find a few moments respite below decks they had been about to climb down when one, the man who now stood with his arm outstretched and the other hooked around a steel ladder, had turned to stare seaward.

Now, as Standish squinted up at him, he yelled, 'There's a ship of some sort, sir! On the port quarter. But I can't make her out yet.'

Standish raised his glasses and trained them across the side of the bridge wing. He had to blink to clear the sweat from his eyes, but after a slow search he could still see nothing. Nothing but a low bank of sea mist which hung above the glittering water like a fallen cloud.

He felt Dalziel at his side and bit his lip. Another second and they might have missed the other vessel. Or if the radar mechanic had not paused to look round . . . he checked his thoughts and asked, 'What do you think, sir?'

Dalziel was peering through his glasses, his mouth turned hard down at the corners in a tight grimace.

'Bit of luck that lad kept his eyes open. He can see above this damn mist.' He lowered the glasses and looked at Standish. 'What do I *think*?' He frowned. 'I'm surprised at you!'

He crossed to the compass and then snapped, 'Port twenty!'

The quartermaster sounded startled. 'Port twenty, sir!'

Dalziel kept his eyes level with the compass. 'Midships.' He smiled as if at some inner memory. 'Steady. Steer zero-one-zero.'

He straightened his back and looked at Standish. 'We'll take a look at him, eh?' He seemed to read Standish's thoughts and he added more quietly, 'We'll play it cool this time. Make it an exercise, right?'

Standish relaxed. 'Aye, aye, sir.'

Dalziel climbed back on to his chair. 'Mustn't *split our stacks*, or anything obvious like that!' He sounded almost cheerful again.

In a crisper tone he snapped, 'Send another man aloft to help that mechanic. This mist seems to be thicker than ever now.'

'Ship, sir!' A bridge lookout was peering through the mounted binoculars on the port wing. 'At red four-five!'

Dalziel hurried to the gratings, groping for his glasses as the other vessel materialized from the milky haze. It was still well hidden, its gaunt shape distorted in the reflected glare, but as

Standish peered above the screen he saw it was a native junk, larger than most he had seen around the coast, but a junk nevertheless.

He said wearily, 'Better luck next time.'

Dalziel did not lower his glasses. 'She must have been about to cross our stern when the radar mechanic spotted her.' He sounded excited. 'What do you make of her?'

Standish stepped down from the gratings and removed a teacup from the quivering chart table. What the hell did it matter? It would just mean more effort and sweat, and do nothing for Dalziel's reputation between decks.

'She's steering north-west as far as I can make out, sir. But her final landfall could be either side of the Thai/Malay border.'

Burch appeared at the rear of the bridge, blinking in the sunlight, an enamel mug in one fist.

Dalziel said, 'She's no sails up, so she must have a good engine to push her along like that. Nor'-west, you say?' He lowered the glasses. 'Just the sort of move you might expect.' He turned and saw Burch for the first time. 'What the hell are *you* supposed to be doing, Yeoman?'

Standish said quickly, 'Stand easy was piped just now, sir.'

Dalziel stared at him, his eyes grappling with this information. 'What?'

Then he brushed past him and leaned over the bridge wing to stare down at several groups of seamen who were gathered on the shadowed side of the superstructure, drinking tea and smoking while they watched the other vessel as she began to fade into another bank of haze.

Dalziel snapped, 'God in heaven, Number One, you must *think*!' He swung back to the gratings, his jaw set in a grim line. 'Well, there's no time to bugger about now.' He reached out and stabbed his finger on the red button beneath the screen, and as the alarm bells echoed throughout the hull he added, '*Stand easy* indeed!'

Cups clattered in all directions as the figures on deck started to run to their action stations, some peering up at the bridge as they dashed past, as if expecting to see it was a mistake, or that the alarm circuit had melted in the heat.

'Port fifteen.' Dalziel raised his glasses again. 'Midships.'

There were mumbled responses from handsets and voicepipes

as the men arrived gasping at their stations, and when Irvine clattered up the bridge ladder he asked, 'What is it for Christ's sake?' No-one replied, and with another curse he wedged himself behind the chart table and looked up at Dalziel as the captain barked, 'Steer, three-one-five.'

'Course three-one-five, sir.' This time it was Corbin's voice up the brass pipe. 'Both engines slow ahead, coxswain on the wheel, sir.'

The deck shook slightly as screen doors and hatches were slammed shut, and Standish found time to pity the people jammed below decks behind sealed ports and scuttles. Worse still, they would not even know what was happening.

Standish took the last report and said, 'Ship at action stations, sir.'

Dalziel grunted. 'About time. Far too long.'

Irvine whispered fiercely, 'What is happening, Number One? For God's sake, *tell* me.'

'That junk.'

Irvine stepped cautiously on to a grating and then said wryly, 'I see, *that* junk.'

The yeoman coughed. 'She's no registration mark on her hull, sir.'

'You see?' Dalziel turned and looked at all of them. 'This may be one of the bastards.'

Irvine waited until he had turned back to the screen and whispered, 'What bastards?'

Standish glared at him. 'Forget it. Anyway, it might do some of our people a bit of good to move beyond a crawl.'

Irvine shrugged and tapped a pencil on his teeth.

'Make a signal for her to heave to.' Dalziel paced to the opposite side and back again. 'Call away the motor boat's crew and muster an armed boarding party.' His eye fell on Irvine. 'You take charge. I want that junk searched from top to bottom, right?'

Irvine saluted. 'Right.'

Pipes shrilled and more men dashed for the boat davits, and as Irvine clambered over the bridge coaming Dalziel added curtly, 'And arm yourself, too.'

The junk was now about half a mile from the starboard bow on a slightly converging course. She wore no flag, and on her tall poop Standish could see several heads turned towards the frigate, and other figures on the main deck beside what appeared to be several large crates.

The signal broke from *Terrapin*'s yard, while for good measure Burch triggered busily with his hand lamp, his jaws still champing on the remains of a biscuit.

'No reply, sir.'

'And not stopping either, by God!' Dalziel rubbed his hands. 'Well, we shall see.' He glanced at Standish. 'Is that boat ready?'

'I'll take a look, sir.'

Dalziel sounded angry. 'Yes do so, please. I'm not a bloody mind-reader.'

The motor boat was already lowered to deck level, her small cockpit crammed with armed men, while her bowman and coxswain struggled to make sure the falls were indeed ready for final release. Irvine stood with one hand resting negligently on the cockpit cover, his tanned features split into a grin as he said something to the petty officer in charge of the lowerers.

'Ready, sir.' Standish bit his lip. This was no exercise. Dalziel was getting more excited with every phase of the operation. Why in God's name didn't the junk reply, or show some flag, anything to forestall the ridicule which would come Dalziel's way if this proved another false alarm?

'Stop engines.' Dalziel walked to the wing. 'Slip the boat.'

As soon as the motor boat had been lowered to within two feet of the slowing bow wave it was slipped and dropped heavily into the wash, the armed seamen cursing and clutching their Stirlings as it wallowed round until controlled by the boat rope which still held it to its mother-ship.

'Slow ahead.' Dalziel looked towards the junk as the increased way tugging at the boat rope made the small craft yaw away from the ship's side, its engine spluttering into life until with a jaunty wave from the coxswain it slipped the rope and swung round towards the other vessel.

He remarked slowly, 'Those crates might contain some interesting gear, eh?'

Standish did not reply. He was still watching the motor boat, which seemed to have stopped, a plume of petrol smoke hanging above it like a shellburst.

Burch raised his big telescope as the boat's coxswain, swaying precariously above the crowded boarding party, started to make a semaphored signal with his arms.

Burch sucked his teeth. 'Engine's broke, sir.'

Dalziel stared at him. '*What?*' He turned on Standish. 'It's even worse than I thought...' he broke off as a seaman said hoarsely, 'Junk's increased speed, sir.'

The captain ran to the wing again, his glasses banging unheeded against the metal.

'He's getting away!' He gripped the screen until his knuckles were white. 'Like bloody hell he is!'

He appeared to control himself with a great effort, and almost casually crossed to the voice pipe and said, 'Starboard ten.' He waited, tapping the gyro repeater with his fingers. 'Midships. *Steady.*'

The junk appeared to have swung inwards, although this was of course an illusion. But the *Terrapin's* shallow turn had edged round the bows so that from the bridge it looked for all the world as if the junk was pinioned on the frigate's jackstaff.

Dalziel sounded very calm. 'Tell Wishart to prepare his gun crews for boarding. He's got about five minutes.'

Standish heard the order being barked over the bridge speaker, and could imagine Wishart's sudden apprehension. From being a spectator to one of the prime actors in this little drama.

He shifted his glasses over the screen and studied the other craft more carefully. Her sides were blotched with a dozen colours, her hull patched so many times it was hard to imagine her as ever being new.

He said slowly, 'If you get too near you might stove her in, sir.'

Dalziel shrugged. 'He still has the option of stopping.'

There were more heads on the junk's carved poop now, and several figures were struggling from an open hatch just below her foremast. The *Terrapin* was a small frigate, but viewed almost bows on from the junk's deck she must look the size of a cruiser.

Far astern, the motor boat was bobbing up and down on the swell, a black sliver against the harsh expanse of blue. Whoever was responsible for the engine failure would know all about it when Dalziel got hold of him, Standish thought grimly.

Dalziel said sharply, 'Signal him to heave to again.' He drummed his fingers below the screen in time with the morse lamp and then added, 'Well, so be it!'

Wishart was below the bridge, a revolver strapped round his waist, his face turned upwards as Dalziel yelled, 'Prepare to board!'

But just at the very last moment, as the frigate's raked stem slid comfortably towards the junk's port quarter, the other vessel's master cut his engine. The effect was disastrous. As the way was lost to her ancient rudder she started to swing drunkenly to starboard, the high poop following round to present itself across the *Terrapin's* final approach in a solid barrier of carved wood.

'Full astern both engines!' Dalziel gripped the screen as the bells jangled in the wheelhouse below his feet. 'The fool! The stupid, bloody idiot!'

The bridge shook violently as Quarrie threw the engines to full speed astern, the sudden change of thrust making the whole hull quiver as if being bounced through some rapids.

When it came, the actual impact was barely felt. It was more of a tremor which died almost as soon as it was begun. But the sound was appalling. The steel bows ploughed into the junk's swinging stern like a giant axe, and the waiting boarding party scattered beneath an onslaught of splintered wood, torn rigging and one whole section of handrail which slewed across the four-inch guns like a painted foot-bridge.

'Stop engines.' Dalziel stood looking down at the chaos without moving. 'Slow ahead. Starboard ten.' He waited until the frigate started to nudge forward again before saying, 'Second time lucky.'

Standish stared at him. There was neither anger nor remorse on Dalziel's face. He seemed conscious only of the job in hand. Of getting alongside the junk, no matter what.

He shouted suddenly, 'Over you go, Wishart! *Jump to it!*'

As heaving lines and steel grapnels thudded into the junk's splintered bulwark the seamen, reluctantly at first and then with desperate enthusiasm hurled themselves aboard, their arms and legs flying as they piled after Wishart in a wild, disordered tangle.

Dalziel said, 'Stop engines.' He seemed oblivious to the fresh sounds of breaking wood as the frigate surged slowly forward, the sagging vessel lurching and bumping alongside like so much salvage.

Burch said thickly, 'There's women an' kids there, too!'

Dalziel ignored him. 'What's that fool doing?' He pointed down at one of the seamen who was struggling frantically with a tall, smock-coated Chinese. The latter was an old man with a pale grey beard, but even from the upper bridge his strength was obvious.

The rest of the seamen had become momentarily separated from the other man by a surging crowd of people. They had swarmed up from below, of all ages and sizes, and as Burch had observed, with a large proportion of women and children. Screams and yells almost drowned the harsher shouts of the seamen and Wishart's shrilling whistle.

The sudden ripping burst of automatic fire silenced the din, and every sound, while with grotesque dignity the bearded Chinese staggered to the bulwark, his fingers interlaced across his belly, his eyes glazing as he stared with disbelief at the blood which poured over his hands and across the smoking muzzle of the seaman's Stirling.

Burch said quietly, 'Gawd.'

It was pitiful to watch the way the crowd of packed figures seemed to shrink in density, to fall back across the listing deck until Wishart and his men were left quite alone in a small, tight group.

Dalziel picked up a megaphone. 'Get on with the search, Wishart! Ship's papers, the hold, you know what to do!'

The man with the smoking gun looked up at the sound of Dalziel's voice and cried, 'Worn't my fault! The silly old sod kept pullin' an' yellin' at me!' He stared at Wishart. 'Worn't my bleedin' fault.' Then he dropped his head and started to sob.

Dalziel said, 'What a sickening spectacle. Get that man aboard *at once*!'

Standish looked down at the junk. The crates were easy to see now. Most were quite empty, but two of them contained a handful of scrawny chickens. He felt sick, unnerved by the suddenness with which things had happened, and a man had died.

It seemed an age before Wishart reported to the bridge. He was pale and tight-lipped, and his shirt was filthy from the search below decks.

He said, 'Refugees from Viet Nam, sir. This is their third attempt to cross the Gulf.' He swallowed hard. 'They're carrying nothing but a few personal belongings. Nothing else.'

Dalziel had reseated himself in his chair. 'Why did the fool run away?'

'I don't know, sir. I think they've been frightened for so long that to meet us out here after getting within sight of hope...'

Dalziel held up his hand. 'I can manage without the drama, Sub. And who was the man by the bulwark?'

'An old fisherman, sir...'

Wishart recoiled as Dalziel shouted, '*Not him, I meant that stupid rating with the Stirling?*' He swung on Standish. 'Call themselves seamen! I'll give them bloody seamen before I've done!'

Wishart said, 'His name is Thomas, sir.'

'Good. I'll deal with him later. Now withdraw the boarding party and cast off.' He looked at Burch. 'Tell the W/T office to make a sighting report to Jerram's patrols. He can clean this mess up.' He scowled. 'Refugees, eh? The thin edge of the wedge if you ask me!'

There was a small spluttering sound and a seaman said nervously, 'Motor boat's comin' alongside, sir.'

Dalziel's mouth tightened.

'It seems the engine restarted. A small miracle.' He banged his hands on the screen. 'Or something else!'

Standish said, 'Will we stand by the junk until an M.L. arrives, sir?'

'No point in that. Mass interrogation is Jerram's job. I'll make out a report and let him have it later. Mark the position on the chart and then make up the log.' He shrugged vaguely. 'Usual thing. Stopped and searched unidentified vessel. Refugees alleged from Viet Nam. One suspected terrorist killed resisting arrest. That should cover it.'

Standish looked away. 'The man in question would probably disagree, sir.' He could feel his limbs shaking. As if from fever.

'He was probably afraid. Saw the man with the gun, and panic did the rest.'

Dalziel eyed him impassively. 'Supposition, Number One.' He turned to watch the motor boat being run up to its davits. 'And that is something I have little use for.' His eyes narrowed as Irvine appeared at the top of the ladder. 'Any more than I have for disloyalty.' He walked to his chair. 'Now bear off and bring the ship back on course.'

Irvine opened his mouth to report his presence but saw Standish's expression and closed it again.

Instead he said, 'Well, here's a fine thing.'

Standish looked at him bitterly. 'You were well out of it, it seems? I have never seen the motor boat break down before.'

Irvine smiled gently. 'To think anything else would be supposition too, surely?'

The bosun's mate switched on his speaker. 'Fall out action stations.' Then after a pause and while the listing junk dropped slowly astern in the frigate's rising wash he added, 'Continue stand easy . . .'

5 Ships in the Night

STANDISH waited until Leading Steward Wills had removed the last of the empty coffee cups and then said, 'That will be all for now.' He saw Wills glance curiously around the other officers and added, 'And close the pantry hatch as you leave.'

Dinner, such as it was, had been consumed in almost total silence, and now as the others slumped in the battered armchairs or squatted on the bench seats below the scuttles Standish picked a folder from the deck and opened it across his lap. All through the meal he had been thinking about this moment, the weary necessity of telling the others of Dalziel's latest requirements. On the opposite side of the wardroom he saw the straight purple edge of the horizon mounting slowly along each open scuttle, hanging for a moment and then falling with equal slowness and monotonous regularity.

It would soon be dark again. Another night on this senseless patrol. He glanced around the wardroom, his eyes taking in the familiar scruffiness, the disordered little world where they came and went with the passing hours, dragging out each day to the prescribed times of duty and routine. On the bulkhead the calendar was no longer a joke. But Pigott still encircled each passing date with his pencil. *Dalziel plus nineteen*, and a whole week since the swift and unexpected encounter with the junk.

He said, 'The captain has asked me to tell you about the new programmes.'

They were all watching him. Irvine and Hornby, Quarrie and young Wishart. Pigott was sharing the bridge with Caley,

enduring Dalziel's close supervision while he passed the watch
away by thinking up some new test to put them on their mettle.
Every so often the hull would give a shudder, or there would be
a scramble on deck to show that the duty hands were running
to complete some further drill against Dalziel's stop-watch.

He continued, 'Starting tomorrow every officer will take
turns to produce a programme, an exercise if you like, to be
carried out during the afternoon of each working day.'

Irvine asked, 'How about poker?'

The others smiled and Standish said, 'I'll put it to the
captain.' He frowned and added shortly, 'It's his idea to keep
our people from becoming bored sick. I think that anything
other than actual sport, which might include poker, should be
considered.'

Irvine grimaced. 'If the Old Man had not been so mad keen
to put this ship on a Dunkirk footing none of the lads would
have known any difference.' He spread his hands and yawned.
'As it is, it turned out to be a great let-down, just as I
prophesied.'

Standish looked at him calmly. 'There will be no discussion
on the captain in front of me. You should know that.'

Irvine smiled. 'Just as you say, Number One. But if this is
to be an informal discussion, then I think we should put our
views in the open.'

Standish looked across at Quarrie. 'Chief?'

The engineer placed his scarred hands palms down on his
knees and studied them.

'What you do on deck is your affair. My department is
always on top line. It doesn't matter to me what you do with
your time.'

Standish smiled slightly. Quarrie was a hard man to know,
but he always spoke his mind.

He looked at Hornby. 'What about you?'

The electrical officer dabbed his forehead and eased his bulk
carefully away from the chairback.

'Yes, I think we ought to be frank about it.' He flushed as
Irvine laughed quietly. 'Although I can't really see what the
captain expects to get out of this ship.'

Wishart said quickly, 'Well, I think he's done wonders. For
me anyway. All the months I've been aboard I have been used

either as an errand boy or a filing clerk. At least under Dalziel I've *learned* something.'

The deck canted slightly and faint shouts filtered down from above.

Irvine said dryly, 'Sounds as if Bill Pigott is learning, too. The *hard* way.'

Wishart met his amused gaze and replied hotly, 'And why not? I think any officer should be able to take charge of the bridge, in a limited fashion at least.'

Standish looked at each of them in turn. 'You all know the state this ship was in.' Even saying the words made him feel uneasy. It was like betraying Mitford's memory. He added harshly, 'Petty officers almost had to plead with some men to get things done. Now they at least know they have the captain's backing, and several faults have been ironed out.'

'And there are more men at the defaulters' table!' Irvine dragged out a cigarette and lit it irritably. 'Dalziel talks as if there was a war on, for God's sake. You can't expect our people to play war games just because he's happy to have a ship again.'

Standish eyed him coldly. 'That's a bloody stupid attitude to take.'

'In your opinion.' Irvine looked at the deckhead fan. 'When Captain Jerram was aboard I did get time to ask him about Dalziel and the big collision. Jerram was there, too. He had a staff job and was temporarily aboard Dalziel's ship, the *Harrier*.'

Quarrie said dourly, 'Took you into his confidence, did he?'

Irvine glared at him. 'My father still has some influence, you know. I imagine Jerram is well aware of that fact.'

Standish said, 'Get it off your chest and then drop it for good.'

'Well.' Irvine seemed momentarily off guard. 'It seems that the wrong helm order was given and the carrier had no chance to avoid the *Harrier*.'

Quarrie gave a rare grin. He had small teeth, each spaced apart from the next, like a line of matched stones.

'Well, the court martial let him off with a reprimand. I remember the case quite well now. And that was for placing too much trust in the officer of the watch.'

'Who was killed in the collision.' Irvine's smooth interruption was perfectly timed. 'There was only our captain's word.'

'Are you disputing it?' Standish closed his folder with a snap. He had been wrong to let it go on. It was a bad mistake and he was to blame for misjudging the situation. Yet when he had decided to call this informal meeting to discuss the programmes he had thought it best to bring it all into the open. Clear the air and release each of them from his own theories and apprehensions.

He continued sharply, 'You know as well as I do that the captain, any captain, is well within his rights to use all legal means to get his ship to first-line efficiency. So far he's not had much help from his officers, or at least some of them. Like that business with the motor boat for instance. Because of it breaking down the Sub here had to do your job.'

Irvine said uneasily, 'He was just saying it was a good thing for officers to know each others' jobs.'

'Because of this failure a man died, Pilot, so just think about it.'

'I hope you're not blaming me for that?' Irvine half rose to his feet. 'When the captain tried to stop a Russian ship I thought things were going too far. But when he charged alongside that moth-eaten junk I knew he had no idea what he was doing.'

The bulkhead telephone buzzed and Wishart answered it, his eyes still on Standish's face. Then he said, 'Captain wants you on the bridge, Number One.'

Standish stood up, suddenly thankful for the summons. He paused by the door and said slowly, 'In future we'll have a bit more co-operation all round. Or I'll want to know why.'

When he had gone Hornby said in an aggrieved tone, 'I don't see why *he's* so edgy about it.'

Irvine pressed his fingertips together and replied evenly, 'Because he too is sweating on another command. Anyway, whatever he really thinks, he still has to back up the commanding officer.' He glanced coolly at Wishart. 'And next time you feel like a bit of death or glory just remember one thing, Sub. To cause a disaster in the Service is bad, but not overwhelmingly so. As we all know, a court martial can often bring an officer into the limelight, and therefore to advancement by other, less tedious means.' He frowned. 'But to *condone* a disaster is something else. The stigma can follow you everywhere, can wreck your career just as much as if you had been the principal offender. If you live long enough, you'll learn that when the chips are down it's no use saying you were only obeying orders.'

Wishart flushed and walked to the door. 'I'm going to my cabin.'

Irvine remarked, 'Wants beating with a sixth-form cane, does that one!'

He looked at the others and sighed. Quarrie had dropped into a doze and Hornby was already studying another catalogue of sports gear.

To the wardroom at large he said, 'No Dalziel is going to foul *my* yardarm. Not now and not ever.'

Quarrie opened one eye. 'You on watch soon?'

Irvine looked at him coldly. 'In about ten minutes.'

Quarrie closed his eye. 'Thank Christ for that!'

*   *   *

Standish found Dalziel in the small chartroom at the rear of the upper bridge, his white shirt gleaming in the gathering shadows as he stared through an open scuttle at the horizon.

'You sent for me, sir?'

Dalziel did not turn. 'I did. Odd thing just happened. Petty Officer Keeble's chaps picked up an S.O.S. Very strange indeed.'

Standish waited. Keeble was the radio supervisor, a competent, nuggety little man, who like Quarrie spent most of his time amidst his outworn equipment.

Dalziel continued in the same calm tone, 'Very faint, and extremely brief. Good chap that Keeble, didn't waste any time. I must see that he is encouraged to sit for promotion.'

Through the open door Standish could see Pigott's figure framed against the darkening sky as he prowled along the gratings in the forepart of the bridge. He may not have learned much more about standing a watch, but he certainly looked the part, Standish thought.

He asked, 'Did Keeble get a fix on it, sir?'

Dalziel turned and peered at him searchingly. 'Capital thinking!' He nodded. 'Due south of us somewhere.'

Standish looked down at the illuminated chart, feeling Dalziel's eyes on him as he studied the ship's plotted position. She was heading north-east by north, creeping along the furthest extremity of her patrol area.

He asked, 'Any other ships in the vicinity, sir?'

'None as far as I know.' Dalziel leaned on the table, dropping his voice suddenly. 'And nobody else attempted to reply to the signal, according to the W/T office.'

Standish straightened his back and said carefully, 'Even supposing it was genuine, it would take us well out of our area, sir. We could make a signal to ask for an air search, I suppose.' Even as he spoke he knew what Dalziel would say. The captain was itching to break away from the destructive boredom of patrol, and to him this vague and unfinished S.O.S. was an obvious chance.

Dalziel said, 'Be dark soon. If the S.O.S. was from a ship in real trouble, sinking perhaps, they'd be too late to save anyone. The sharks would see to that.'

There was some sense in what he said. But a last note of warning made Standish ask, 'Will you inform Captain Jerram too, sir?'

'No need, Number One. I'll cope with all that side of it later, eh?'

A shadow fell across the door and Irvine stepped inside the chartroom.

Dalziel said, 'Ah, Pilot. Lay off a new course. We will carry out a sweep to the north for fifty miles.' He looked at Standish and added crisply, 'Tell Pigott to bring her round to zero-one-zero and ring down for full speed.' He grinned. 'No sense in wasting time!'

Pigott listened to the new instructions and replied grimly, 'Here we go again!'

'Shall I take the con?' Standish saw the lines of strain round Pigott's mouth and found time to sympathize with him.

'No. I don't mind this part of it so much.' He leaned over the voicepipe. 'Port fifteen.' His spectacles glittered in the dying red sunlight as he turned to watch the curving wake astern. Then he glanced at the gyro and snapped, 'Midships. Steady.' To

Standish he said, 'The captain just gave me *my* programme.
I've to put topics of interest into a hat and pass them round the
wardroom.' He cocked his ear over the voicepipe and then
replied, 'Very good. Steer zero-one-zero.' He bit his lip and
added, 'Full ahead both engines.' To Standish he added, 'Once,
I'd have increased speed *before* the turn. With all that broken
crockery listed in my stores returns things are bad enough
without adding to the trouble.' He frowned. 'As I was saying,
each officer will draw a slip of paper, and whatever topic comes
his way will be the subject of a lecture to any off-watch people
who are either too slow or stupid to be somewhere else at the
time.'

The deck trembled as the revolutions mounted, and Standish
saw Quarrie, hatless and almost running as he hurried to his
engine room to find the cause for such violent treatment.

Pigott rested his hands on the screen and smiled. 'It does *feel*
good, I must say!'

Dalziel strode on to the bridge and glanced up at the masthead pendant. 'Fine weather for a search. Capital.'

From the chartroom door Irvine called, 'No moon tonight to
speak of, sir. If there is a ship out there, or survivors in the water,
we'll be hard put to find them.'

Dalziel looked at the radar scanner. It was revolving steadily,
and from the funnel came an increasing plume of smoke.

'Men on the moon, heart-transplants are as common as
corned beef, and *we* can't find a bloody ship, Pilot? Really, I
must see what can be done about you!'

Irvine looked away, and a signalman lowered his head to hide
a smile.

Dalziel climbed on to his chair and settled himself comfortably to watch the distant horizon.

Standish turned slightly and studied the captain's profile, the
hooked nose, the gunmetal sideburns on his tanned face.

What do we know about him? Really know. He could be
married or divorced. A secret drinker, or a man so driven by
some inner compulsion that even now he was carrying the ship
and everyone in her to disaster.

He thought suddenly of Irvine's words, his obvious contempt
for what Dalziel was trying to do. It was unlikely that Jerram
had discussed anything important with him, but Irvine was

nobody's fool, and what was unsaid was almost as important as evidence.

He heard Dalziel say, 'Ah, Caley, I did not see you hiding over there.' A pause, and the T.A.S. officer mumbled some sort of reply. Then Dalziel added cheerfully, 'Better go and check our budding Kildare in the sickbay. He may have work to do before he's much older.'

As Caley hurried away Dalziel murmured, 'We should have a qualified doctor aboard, not just a medical assistant. No foresight, that's half the trouble with our so-called planners.'

He turned and looked suddenly at Standish, his teeth shining in a broad smile of pleasure.

'*Feel* her, Number One? She's just loving this, you know. I'll bet many a U-boat sailor wet his pants when he heard her screws grinding overhead, eh?' The smile faded. 'I always regret that I was too young for the war. Korea was all I got, but even that was better than most of the present day Navy has had. They're getting soft, like a lot of bloody women. A nine-to-five Service, with the little wife and the television waiting every night.' His voice rose slightly. 'Semi-detached minds, that is all that sort of nonsense produces!'

Standish said, 'I take it you're not married, sir.'

'Never found the time. One day perhaps, but from what I've seen, it's not worth a candle. Once upon a time women married sailors either because they liked it or because they just wanted a man. Now, well I ask you, all they think about is status and respectability. Result? Moral oblivion!' He reached out and gripped Standish's wrist. 'I was forgetting. That was quite unthinkable, Number One, in view of your own, er, misfortune.'

'It was nothing like that. I can assure you.' Standish looked at the shadows on the heaving water beyond the bows. 'Anyway, I'm trying to forget it.'

Dalziel nodded, apparently reassured. 'That's the ticket. No sense in brooding, eh?' He swung round and yelled, 'Where the *hell* are the navigation lights? Come on, Pigott, jump about then!'

Standish walked to the port wing and stared out across the creaming bank of foam which swept from either bow in a solid, unbroken arrowhead.

No wife, and he suspected, few real friends. The more he

learned of Dalziel, the more remote and unreal he seemed to become.

At that moment the big light below the bridge wing came on, bathing his hands in deep red. He shuddered and thrust himself away from the jerking steel plates as the memory came back like part of a nightmare.

Before the drugs had carried him down into an empty, painless world he had seen his hands like that. Stripped and burned raw by the fire, shining in that mad enclosed world of screams and curses before the watertight door had been screwed shut and only his own cries had followed him into the blessed darkness.

He gritted his teeth and pressed his hands hard against the screen. He had to forget it. Shut it from his mind forever. After all, Alison had found it easy to forget him, so why was her memory still so necessary and so constant?

Dalziel said suddenly, 'Pass the word to keep a good lookout for anything unusual. Lights in the water, things like that.'

But as the first pale stars appeared above the flapping masthead pendant the *Terrapin* kept the sea to herself, with only the hard white line of her wake to show for her efforts.

*　　　　　*　　　　　*

By midnight it was pitch black on the bridge, and after the unwavering heat of the day the air touched the watchkeepers like ice. Beyond the quivering glass screen the upsurge of the ship's bow wave rolled away into the darkness, tinted eerily on either beam with the red and green of the navigation lights.

The sound of the sea breaking away from the stem was masked entirely by the many other noises which made talking almost impossible. Creaking metal, the clatter of loose gear and signal halliards, the discordant chorus was continuous and kept time with the racing screws which had maintained full power for almost four fruitless hours.

It was a strange, unnerving sensation, Standish thought, quite unlike a submarine in every way. On watch at night in the cockpit of a submarine's high fin, even more so in the open conning tower of the older conventional boats, you had the feeling of being on a partially submerged rock. But beneath your feet there was another living world, a whole synchronized and dependable mechanism waiting for the merest word, when at the slam of levers you could be carried deep to smooth safety, to wait or to ponder, and if need be escape from the dangers overhead.

But now, standing with one arm wrapped around a stanchion he could feel no such security. The ship was charging further and further to the north, as if she cared nothing for the puny creatures on her bridge, or those who lay in their hammocks and bunks cursing the racing shafts while they tried to close their minds in sleep.

Irvine stepped out of the chartroom and crossed the gratings below Dalziel s chair.

He sounded tired and resentful. 'Captain, sir?

'Hmm?' Dalziel turned and glanced down at him, his shirt etched against the dull steel and the sky beyond.

'We've logged twenty-two miles beyond your search limit.'

'I see.' Dalziel seemed to be considering it. 'Seventy-two miles all told. You know that just shows, doesn't it? The Chief must be very pleased with his department tonight. I do not suppose this ship has maintained such an excellent average speed since she was launched.'

Irvine said, 'I did not mean it as a compliment, sir.' He sounded as if he was speaking through clenched teeth. 'We should break off now and make a signal to that effect. If there is a wreck somewhere, then it certainly seems to have kept clear of *us*.' He paused before saying, 'And if the W/T office picked up some false static by mistake it leaves us *seventy-two miles off station.*''

'Thank you Pilot. I shall bear your survival ratio in mind.' Irvine turned sharply and walked back to the chartroom. Standish heard the door slam, and imagined him swearing amongst his charts and calculations.

Dalziel said quietly, 'He is unhappy about it.'

Standish stepped up beside the chair so that the others should not hear him.

'He has a point, sir.'

Dalziel looked away. 'But suppose there is a ship out there. Could be just a handful of poor devils in an open boat. They might be able to see our lights *right now*.' In a more subdued tone he asked, 'Do *you* think I should turn back?' He did not wait for an answer. 'Don't reply to that. My decision. Right or wrong. No other way.' He lapsed into silence and stared straight into the salt-stained glass screen.

Standish crossed to the opposite wing and jammed his unlit pipe between his teeth. If Dalziel failed to alter his decision soon, Pigott would have very few more dates to encircle on his calendar. Whatever had bred the dislike or mistrust between Dalziel and Jerram, it obviously needed very little to bring it to a new flashpoint.

'Bridge . . . Radar!'

The metallic voice from the microphone beside the hooded chart table made him swing round and he saw Dalziel already beside it. How he had moved from his chair to the centre of the bridge in such a short time was hard to understand, but the tone of his voice did give some hint of the strain he had been careful to hide from all of them.

'Bridge . . . Captain here!'

'Echo, sir. Green oh-two-oh.' The radar operator cleared his throat noisily as if suddenly aware of his captain at the other end of the line. 'Range oh-eight-oh.'

Dalziel snapped, 'Who is that speaking?'

'Leading Radar Operator Vine, sir.'

'Well, Vine, would you mind explaining why we are within four miles of a ship without your people spotting it earlier?'

Vine sounded defensive. 'Too much vibration, sir.'

Dalziel's head nodded sharply in the darkness. 'Good. Capital.' He snapped, 'Reduce to one-one-zero revolutions.'

He crossed to the radar repeater, his eyes glowing faintly in the twisting mass of back-echoes and strange guttering reflections as he peered fixedly into the screen.

'Ship all right. No doubt about it, Number One.'

He stepped back to allow Standish to see. It was just visible, blurred and indistinct, like an unmoving flaw in the radar's swinging probe.

Dalziel said, 'Bring her round to zero-three-zero.' As Standish leaned over the wheelhouse voicepipe he added irritably, 'The echo is firm enough. What is the fool playing at? He must be able to see our lights.'

Corbin's voice came up the brass pipe. 'Steady, sir. Course zero-three-zero.'

Standish looked up at Dalziel's shoulders above the screen. He was swinging his glasses back and forth, leaning forward in that characteristic way as if to smell out the other vessel.

He said, 'She could be abandoned, sir.'

'Maybe. But there should be some flares or something, damn it!'

Vine's voice again. 'Range now oh-seven-five. Appears to be stationary, sir.'

Dalziel said something under his breath. Then he called, 'Is the yeoman there?'

'Sir.' Burch stepped into the centre of the bridge.

'Is that big searchlight of yours still working?'

'Yes, sir.'

'Well, get some of your bunting-tossers to uncover it. We're going to need a bit of light around here shortly.' He returned to the screen. 'In more ways than one!'

Standish found time to wonder if Hornby was still awake and within easy reach. If the big searchlight blew itself when it was switched on it would need more than a set of sports gear to appease Dalziel.

Several figures had appeared below the bridge, dark and indistinct against the surging water alongside. Some of the older hands probably. It was odd the way seasoned seamen seemed to feel things before they happened. Like the coxswain, for instance. He should be below in his bunk, but there he was now, on the wheel. At his place, in case he was needed.

And it was more than likely that Quarrie was on his foot-plate, never having left it since his hurried exit from the wardroom.

Dalziel said sharply, 'Nothing happening yet.' He sat stiffly on the edge of his chair, as if willing himself to relax. 'Reduce speed to seven-zero revolutions. Don't want to run some poor chap down in the water, do we?'

The vibrations eased in response to the telegraphs, and once more the sea-noises intruded into the bridge. The sluice of water around the bows, the steady hiss of spray thrown back over the forecastle like tropical rain.

The minutes dragged by, broken only by Vine's regular

reports, while in the radar repeater the strange, unlit ship remained across their line of approach like an unmarked reef.

Burch came back breathing heavily. 'Searchlight ready, sir.'

Standish said, 'Perhaps you'd better stay with it. Just in case.'

Burch's shadowed features split into a broad grin. 'S'all right sir. The electrical officer's down there in 'is pyjamas takin' charge 'imself!'

'Stop that damn muttering!' Dalziel slid lightly from the chair. 'We'll edge round a bit to port and take a look at him.' He lifted his glasses again. 'Port ten.' He seemed to pivot in time with the ship, as if he was part of her, while he moved the glasses slowly along the screen. 'Midships. Steady.'

'Steady, sir. Course zero-zero-five.'

'That should do it. Right, switch on!'

The bosun's mate with the handset had hardly finished speaking when the great glacier-blue beam swept out from amidships, before swinging with painful brilliance towards the starboard bow.

Burch muttered, 'Thank the Lord for that!'

They all watched in fixed silence while the hard-edged beam moved purposefully above the heaving water, throwing back thousands of diamond-bright reflections where seconds before there had been only darkness.

'There she is!'

Every pair of glasses settled on the shining line of scuttles, and then as the beam lifted steadily, on the tall white bridge and slung lifeboats and the single funnel with its painted insignia.

She was barely a mile away. The searchlight's glare held her as if at the end of something solid and unyielding, and Standish was conscious of the tension around him while the *Terrapin* moved slowly towards her.

'Shall I signal her, sir?' Burch had his lamp at the ready.

'No.' Dalziel crossed the gratings in two strides. 'The searchlight must have blinded everyone aboard, I should think.' He reached a handset which was connected with the bridge loud-hailer system.

A signalman said excitedly, 'There's someone on her bridge wing, sir!'

Standish nodded and then turned to watch as Dalziel's voice

boomed across the narrowing strip of gleaming water, magnified and metallic like that of a robot's.

'This is a British warship! What ship are you?'

In his powerful glasses Standish could see several heads beyond the first one, some in the wheelhouse and a few more by what appeared to be a radio shack. The bridge ladders seemed to be gleaming in the glare, and with a start he realized they were enmeshed in layers of barbed wire and protected by stout metal gates.

Burch said helpfully, 'That's in case they get attacked by pirates, sir. Does 'appen sometimes, though not much in these waters.'

Someone had raised a megaphone and back over the water came a man's voice, very distinct and surprisingly loud.

'S.S. *Cornwallis*! Three days out of Saigon and bound for Songkhla with general cargo.'

Dalziel snapped, 'Check that, Yeoman!' Then he switched on the loud-hailer again. 'Do you require assistance?'

'No, but thank you.' A long pause. 'We had a fire in the radio room, but it is all right now.'

There were plenty of dark stains around the little radio shack, and it was possible to see the broken glass of its scuttles now that the ships had drawn closer together.

The voice added, 'Burned through a whole lot of cables, which was why we couldn't put on our lights or signal you.'

Burch muttered, 'Just like that bloody line. Only four old freighters in it, and all on a shoestring.' In a more formal tone he said, 'The *Cornwallis* is on our cleared list, sir.'

At that moment the freighter's navigation lights came on, and along her island superstructure several scuttles lit up, giving the ship both personality and life. At her high counter a solitary screw churned the water busily, the froth pale blue in the reflected glare.

Dalziel said harshly, 'Are you sure, Yeoman?'

Burch was watching the other ship with professional interest. 'Know her well, sir. I was just tellin' the first lieutenant here that she an' three other old tubs work out of Hong Kong.'

Irvine had appeared on the gratings, his face smooth in the glare. 'Well, well,' was all he said.

The freighter had gathered slight way when a voice called,

'I'll tell my owners you were offering to help. What name shall I say?'

Dalziel said, 'H.M.S. *Terrapin*.' He paused and Standish could see his knuckles bunched into a tight fist around the handset. 'Commander Dalziel.'

The voice grew fainter as the ship began to forge clear. 'Goodbye, and thanks again.'

Burch said sourly, 'Mean buggers. Afraid of gettin' a salvage claim, I expect.'

Dalziel turned sharply. 'Switch off that damned light, will you!'

When it died the darkness seemed to come sweeping inboard like a solid canopy, and as Standish peered across the screen to look for the freighter he could barely see her shaded sternlight. Even the stars seemed faded now.

A telephone buzzed like a trapped insect and the bosun's mate said nervously, 'W/T office 'as a signal, sir. Immediate.'

Dalziel was on his way back to his chair. 'Have it decoded and bring it up.' He sounded tired.

Somewhere in the darkness below the bridge a man laughed, the sound unnaturally loud above the slop of water against the hull.

Standish bit his lip. Another build-up for nothing. The man who laughed was probably spreading the yarn around his messdeck right now. S.O.S., and it had turned out to be little more than an electrical failure, and that was common enough aboard *this* ship, let alone the battered *Cornwallis*.

Pigott stepped forward from the chartroom, a signal pad in his hand. He said, 'Signal is from S.N.O. East Coast Patrols, sir.'

Standish tried not to watch Dalziel's bunched fists. It would have to be Jerram now.

'Go on.' Two words, toneless and devoid of emotion.

'It reads,' Pigott's glasses gleamed in his torchlight as he held up the pad, '*Terrapin to rendezvous with Force Tango Zulu twenty miles east of Chenering Head at 0600.*'

There was a stunned silence and then Irvine said quietly, 'Well, that really does put the fat in the fire.'

Without consulting any chart Standish knew what he meant.

At any other time the *Terrapin* could have reached the rendezvous no matter where she was on her patrol area. But Chenering Head was over one hundred and forty miles astern. It might just as well be on the moon.

Pigott asked, 'Acknowledge, sir?'

Standish could almost feel Dalziels' disappointment. He was glad it was pitch dark, if only to hide his face from the others.

Feet grated on a ladder and Quarrie's square shape moved uncertainly across the bridge.

Dalziel asked flatly, 'Yes, Chief?'

Quarrie rubbed his chin, suddenly aware of the mood around him.

'I could leave it, sir.' Then he said firmly, 'No, I'll speak my piece and go.'

Dalziel watched him, his face in shadow. 'Well?'

'I came up for a breath of air and to watch the old *Cornwallis*, sir.'

'You know her too, do you?' Again the same lifeless tone.

'That's just it. We was in Hong Kong for months at a time when I first came aboard. We was always running into the old *Cornwallis*.'

'Get to the point, please.'

'Commander Mitford was a regular visitor aboard her. Used to play golf with her master and first officer. Great buddies they was.'

Pigott stared at him. 'That's right. I remember now.'

Dalziel stood up very slowly, as if he was standing on thin glass.

'The *Cornwallis*'s master would have recognized this ship, you mean?'

Quarrie nodded decisively. 'More'n that, sir, he'd have been bound to ask after Bob Mitford when you gave *your* name as captain!'

Dalziel removed his cap and turned it over in his hands.

'Thank you, Chief.' He looked away. 'Thank you very much.'

Irvine said, 'But this signal, sir. What are we going to do?'

'Do?' Dalziel clamped his hat back on his head. 'Disregard it for the present.'

Irvine lowered his head. 'Christ Almighty.'

'Number One, bring the ship round to one-seven-zero at

once.' He seemed to be speaking his thoughts aloud to the bridge.

'In one hour we will go about again and go after the *Corn-wallis*. When we turn we will extinguish all lights and make no further transmissions on W/T, right?'

The ship swung slowly round in response to Standish's orders, and as she steadied on her new course Dalziel added half to himself, 'Two can play this bloody game. Make no mistake about it!'

He turned on his chair and Irvine whispered fiercely, 'He's really done it this time. Oh, my aching God, *has* he done it!'

6 One for the Queen...

'CHAR, sir?'

Standish took the enamel mug from an anonymous figure in the darkness and held it with both hands. 'Thanks.'

After heading away from the *Cornwallis* at maximum speed they had turned to make another dash through the night until the radar had again reported the ship some six miles distant, steaming as before towards the Thai mainland.

It felt strange without the lights, Standish thought. True to his word Dalziel had ordered a complete shut down of scuttles and screen doors, and had even sent Hornby round the ship in person to ensure his orders were being carried out. The fat electrical officer was here now, his pyjamas showing faintly above his jacket while he sipped nervously at a mug of sweetened tea.

Dalziel said, 'Check the *Cornwallis* again.'

Irvine's face glowed above the radar repeater. 'Bearing three-oh-oh degrees. And she's still maintaining a westerly course, sir.'

Standish held the mug to his lips. There was no mistaking the triumph in Irvine's voice as he added, 'Seems innocent enough.'

Dalziel replied swiftly, 'Guilt often *looks* innocent, Pilot.'

Standish wondered just how much longer Dalziel could keep this up. It was no good at all. The freighter was still heading for the Thai port of Songkhla, and it would be better if Dalziel turned back now, if only to avoid the spectacle of his ship steaming into Thai waters in broad daylight without any possible reason for doing so.

And twice so far the W/T office had reported further signals from Jerram, the last one demanding *Terrapin*'s exact position and E.T.A. at the rendezvous.

Dalziel had momentarily lost his temper when the radio supervisor had come to the bridge with the last message.

'Do I have to say everything one hundred times? No transmissions means just that, Keeble, so for God's sake stay off my back!'

But that seemed an age ago. The *Terrapin*'s reduced speed added to the impression of failure and absurdity as she steamed after the other vessel. The old freighter's progress was so slow that it had been necessary to alter course several times merely to stay at a safe distance. She was out there now, about four miles off the port bow and heading away almost at right angles from their own line of approach. It was not possible to see her lights, but the angle was probably too extreme, or perhaps her electrical circuits had failed again, Standish thought wearily.

And all the while the patrol area was fading further and still further astern. Had Dalziel turned at once after meeting with the freighter he might still have held his own with Jerram. After all, an S.O.S., no matter how doubtful, was a fair reason, if not a true excuse, for his behaviour. But now there was no such extenuating reason, and nothing would save him from the consequences.

Standish went back over what Quarrie had said but could find little comfort. It was all too vague, a straw in the wind which had gone in the *Terrapin*'s wake like every other explanation which they had *wanted* to accept.

Perhaps if he had been more insistent with Dalziel, instead of merely abiding by his snap decisions without comment, this might still have been avoided. Maybe he believed even now that the old *Terrapin* was just a stepping stone, a limbo for his own personal use while he waited for the chance to strike out to something better.

He stepped up beside Dalziel's chair and said quietly, 'I suggest you make a signal to the squadron, sir. Captain Jerram can decide how to handle this at the Thai end.' He had spoken almost without realizing what he was saying. 'If we head back to our area now we could claim W/T interference, anything but this.'

'Your part in all this is quite clear to me.' Dalziel leaned back in his chair, his voice impassive. 'No blame will rest on your shoulders.'

'I wasn't thinking of myself!' Standish stared at Dalziel's outline, suddenly angry.

'I see. I'm glad of that. But I could hardly blame you anyway. From what you have already told me, and from a whole lot more which you carry round inside yourself, I have gathered a good deal. But the Navy is not the distant future, or what happened six thousand years ago, it is the here and the now. The ship around you at any given moment of time, the situation as you see it, and as you translate it into worth and deed.' He shrugged, the movement like one of resignation. 'If you were not thinking of your own reputation, then you must have had mine in view, eh?'

'Something like that.'

'It does you credit. But beware of too much sentiment. You know what they say in the Service.' He sounded suddenly bitter. 'One hand for the Queen, but keep one for yourself.'

He tensed as the speaker came to life behind him.

'Bridge . . . Radar.' Vine's voice. His eyes must be squinting from strain by now, Standish thought.

'Radar . . . Bridge.' Irvine's slim figure was swaying easily to the slow roll of the hull.

Vine sounded less sure this time. 'I'm getting a lot of bad interference, sir. It might clear but . . .'

Irvine snapped impatiently, 'Get on with it, man!'

Dalziel slid from his chair and crossed to his side. 'Give me that! If Vine is the best operator we have, you'll get nowhere by flustering him with bloody rudeness!' When he spoke into the handset his tone was quite calm again, even soothing. 'Captain speaking. Tell me.'

'Well, sir, I thought the set was on the blink and I was going to request that you increase speed to close with the freighter.' There were muffled mutterings over the speaker from another operator and then Vine said excitedly, 'I was right, sir! The *Cornwallis* is turning!'

From the repeater Irvine said sullenly, 'Can't see anything on this yet.'

'Turning? Are you sure?' Dalziel was crouching over the handset like a sprinter awaiting the pistol.

'Quite sure, sir.' The voice was confident again. 'Ship bears three-oh-oh, range oh-eight-five. Her present course is about two-four-zero, but still turning.'

Dalziel looked round the bridge. 'Well, Number One, is there anywhere else she could be heading?'

'I can see no reason for the change of course, sir.'

'Right.' Dalziel replaced the handset and returned to the chair. 'Port fifteen.'

The speaker intoned, 'Ship has settled on new course, sir. Now steering approximately one-six-zero.'

Dalziel grunted. 'Midships. Steady.'

Corbin's reply echoed up the voicepipe. 'Steady, sir. Course three-three-zero. Revolutions seven-zero.' He sounded very intent.

'Steer three-three-five.' Dalziel raised one hand in the darkness. 'Tell Vine to shut down all radar transmissions immediately.' He waited for the order to be passed and then said calmly, 'No point in proclaiming our arrival, eh? Even *that* old freighter might have some sort of detection gear aboard.'

Irvine muttered, 'I should think it unlikely, sir.'

Dalziel turned suddenly in his chair and snapped, 'Well, *you* didn't think the *Cornwallis* was acting suspiciously in the first place, did you? I'm afraid your sense of judgment leaves a lot to be desired!'

Irvine crossed to Standish's side and whispered savagely, 'No radar, and we're almost on a collision course! What the hell did he expect me to say, for Christ's sake?'

Dalziel said, 'Pipe the hands to action stations. We'll not use alarm bells this time. I don't want to wake the whole world.'

Muffled below decks the brief pipes and hoarse bark of orders brought the off duty hands unwillingly to their stations, some still so dazed with sleep that they called to each other in the darkness, their voices confused and some openly scornful.

On the four-inch gun mounting a man yelled, 'Wot is it, sir? Another friggin' drill?'

And Wishart's voice, sharper but equally confused, 'Keep silent, that man, and do as you're told!'

Someone kicked over an empty mug, probably Hornby, Standish thought, freed at last from the anguish of waiting for some of his circuits to explode while he was on the bridge.

Dalziel said slowly, 'We'll use the searchlight on him again and see what happens. We'd have seen his lights by now if he had any on.' He slapped his palms together. 'I wonder what the hell he's up to?'

Irvine raised his head from a telephone. 'Ship closed up at action stations, sir.'

'Good. It's as well to be ready.' Dalziel seemed completely absorbed.

Standish said, 'I estimate that we'll pass port to port if he's still on the same course. It'll be close.'

'My thinking, too. Tell the Chief to be ready for instant speed when required, I don't want another bloody accident.'

There was a startled shout from one of the lookouts and then Dalziel yelled, 'That light! What was it?'

A small yellow beam flickered in the water below the raked forecastle, died and then licked out stronger than before.

A petty officer called, 'One of the messdeck scuttles, sir! The deadlight must 'ave become unclipped!'

Like a badly controlled signal lamp the loose deadlight swung open and shut across the scuttle, the light flashing at irregular intervals in time with the ship's roll.

The effect was immediate. A great red eye seemed to light up in the sky itself, so close that Standish could see Dalziel's face shining in the glare as he shouted wildly, 'The *Cornwallis* has seen us! They've switched on their lights, damn them!'

Everyone was speaking at once, and as he watched Standish saw the red light fading slightly, and then with sudden shock saw the brighter gleam of the green starboard light.

Dalziel's voice lifted above the startled voices around him. 'He's turning across our bows!' He almost fell as he ran to the voicepipe. '*Full astern both engines!*'

Irvine said tightly, 'If we'd had *our* lights on this could never have happened.'

Dalziel stared past him, his eyes green as he watched the

towering pale rectangle of the freighter's superstructure rising beyond the swinging navigation light.

'Shut your damn mouth!' The deck shook violently to the reversed thrust and he added, 'Stand by searchlight!'

'We're getting sternway, sir.' Standish felt the deck shaking madly beneath his feet and imagined how it would feel to Quarrie in his sealed world of roaring machinery.

The green light vanished but for a faint glow along the other ship's bridge wing, and Standish saw the single funnel clearly silhouetted against the stars, and realized just how close they had all been to disaster.

'Stop engines.' Dalziel reached out and grabbed his wrist. 'Did you see that? Not a bloody word of protest!'

It was odd that in the confusion and sudden threat of danger Standish's mind had failed to record the fact. Yet in spite of everything Dalziel had noted it, was even now showing his teeth in a grin of excitement or relief.

'Slow ahead both engines.' Dalziel waved his hand. 'Search-light!'

The other ship was almost end on now, her rising wake boiling beneath her high counter while she swung awkwardly away from the pursuing frigate. Because of the angle the searchlight was only able to illuminate part of the freighter's hull, leaving the rest darkened by the shadow of *Terrapin*'s own bridge.

The loud-hailer squeaked and then Dalziel's voice boomed across the water.

'Stop immediately! This is a British warship and I am going to board you!'

In the harsh glare Standish saw the freighter's wash leaping and writhing above the single screw. It showed no sign of lessening.

Dalziel said grimly, 'Like that, is it?' He snatched up a handset by his chair and snapped, 'Captain here. Give me the gunnery officer.'

Burch looked at Standish and muttered, 'Crumbs!'

'Sub? Captain.' Dalziel sounded crisp and formal as he kept his eyes on the other ship's stern. 'I am going to turn slightly to port in a moment. Once on a new course I want you to fire a star-shell across his bows.' His teeth gleamed in the reflected light. 'Close as you like without hitting the bugger. I need it to be spectacular rather than lethal, right?'

He slammed down the phone, and Standish pictured Wishart and his gun crews, the sudden responsibility which had been thrown down from the bridge.

'Port ten.' Dalziel swung round to watch the searchlight's beam as it followed the other ship in time with the turn. 'Midships. Steady.'

Below the bridge there was a metallic click and a voice yelled, 'Right gun loaded, sir!'

Burch said between his teeth, 'I 'ope they've not put a lump of H.E. up the spout by mistake.'

The communications rating wearing the headphones looked up at Dalziel's squared shoulders.

' 'A' gun ready, sir.'

'Capital.' Dalziel was almost gentle. 'Now we shall see, eh?' Then he nodded curtly. 'Fire!'

The righthand gun of the twin mounting lurched back in a savage recoil, the sound of the explosion echoing and re-echoing across the sea like a miniature bombardment.

Seconds later the star-shell burst far ahead of the other ship. the peardrop of brilliant light hanging and drifting slowly above its own reflection.

In the sudden silence someone said, 'Bloody good shot!'

Dalziel merely remarked, 'It appears to have worked.'

The freighter's wash was falling away even as they watched, and by comparison the *Terrapin* appeared to be forging ahead with increased speed towards her port quarter.

There was neither signal nor any sign of anger from the other ship's bridge, and Standish wondered if Dalziel felt as calm as he now appeared. Even at the last moment Standish had been expecting the *Cornwallis* to demand an explanation, or the W/T office to report that she was screaming to the listening world that she had just been fired on. But there was nothing.

'She's hove to, sir.'

'Good. Stop engines. But keep a weather eye on the drift. Don't want to get too close.' Dalziel crossed to the wing and raised the handset again. '*Cornwallis* ahoy! Stand by to receive boarding party *now!*'

Over his shoulder he added, 'You go, Number One. Enthusiasm is fine, but this time we want a bit of experience as well, eh?'

Standish nodded and then turned for the ladder, his mind grappling with the job ahead. In his heart he had known Dalziel would choose him, but now it was actually happening he was suddenly conscious of that same blockage, that too familiar sensation which seemed to render him momentarily confused and unable to think clearly.

As his feet groped for the top rungs of the ladder he saw Dalziel close above him, his face shadowed by the searchlight's beam at his back.

He said quietly, 'No heroics or anything like that. I'll be keeping an eye on you, so take all the time you need.'

His tone was so calm, so completely assured that Standish felt himself thinking and breathing more easily. He nodded quickly and continued on his way to the deck below.

Torches flashed here and there in the darkness and he heard Caley snapping out orders to the lowering party beside the motor boat's davits.

Petty Officer Motts, the gunner's mate, loomed between the busy seamen and Standish felt him clipping a pistol belt around his waist as he said cheerfully, 'Boardin' party mustered, sir. I've squeezed two extra bodies in this time, just in case like.'

Standish peered round as the boat began to jerk squeaking down its falls towards the heaving water alongside. A scrambling net was already lowered, and torch beams flashed on intent faces and the muzzles of Stirling guns as the small party of seamen waited to climb down to the boat.

Motts said, 'The engine'll be all right this time, sir.' He grinned. 'Since the skipper disrated the coxswain it seems to 'ave gone bloody well.'

Standish swallowed hard, his mouth suddenly dry. It took real effort to move, to stop thinking of vague possibilities and fears.

He snapped, 'Over you go, lads. Safety catches on, and no talking.'

He followed Motts across the guardrail, dimly aware of the vague faces above him as he climbed down the scrambling net, of the fact that he was leaving the ship. The latter suddenly seemed very important, and he could feel the sweat cold beneath the rim of his cap.

Perhaps his mind had been more damaged than even he had suspected? That the pain and shock he had suffered had left him mentally scarred, as vulnerable as a man who has lost a limb or a sense of balance.

'Shove off forrard!' Cully, the boat's coxswain, swung the tiller and waited as the engine roared into sudden life. ''Old tight all!'

Standish found that he was gripping the gunwale with all his strength, feeling the spray soaking over his arm, yet unable to move it.

Motts said, 'Better get down, sir. May be a bit choppy once we gets clear of the old *Shellback*'s lee.'

Standish stared at him. It was strange that he had never heard the ship's nickname before, and the realization seemed to steady him. *Shellback* was about right, too, old and somewhat comical. He lowered himself on to a thwart as the boat pushed noisily around the frigate's bows and headed for the search-light's dazzling carpet which lay between the two ships like something solid.

But then, he knew so little about anything or anyone aboard if it came to that. Pain, bitterness or just self-pity, he had failed completely to make himself a part of the ship, as if by so doing he might admit his own vulnerability.

Then he saw the freighter glittering in the beam, her hull rising like a cliff against the backcloth of stars and dark sky.

He heard two of the seamen whispering, and one of them actually laughed aloud. They were unworried, perhaps even glad something had at last happened to break the boredom and frustration they had come to take for granted.

He wiped his forehead with the back of his wrist, knowing too that they were untroubled because he was with them. An officer, one who would know what to do if things went wrong. He felt a sudden surge of apprehension. He did not even know what the *things* were. Back there on his own bridge Dalziel would be watching, hiding his impatience as he awaited the first report from the boarding party.

Standish found himself cursing Dalziel, his mind suddenly filled with unspoken, nameless words. Dalziel could have waited until daylight, or ordered the other ship to follow him into port. But no, he had to act at once, regardless of the risk. Perhaps Irvine was right after all. That the captain thought more of his own glory than any possible consequences.

Motts said, 'They've thrown a ladder down, sir.'

It looked more like a long snake in the harsh glare, and made the freighter's side appear all the more invincible.

The coxswain shouted, 'Stand by in the bows!'

Motts turned and looked at Standish, his face like a circus clown's in the searchlight's unwavering eye.

'Shall I go first, sir?'

Standish stood up and then staggered as the boat ground heavily against the ship's pitted plates. Every rivet seemed to stand out in the light, and the great patches of uncovered rust looked like dried blood.

'Follow me.' He hardly recognized his own voice. 'The boat will return to the ship and await orders.'

He seized the rough ladder, his legs soaked to the groin as the boat dropped sluggishly in a trough, and with his eyes fixed on the rail far above, began to climb.

He had almost reached the top when a slight movement to his left made him turn his head. A small figure in a white shirt had appeared on the flying bridge and seemed to be watching him. The man did not shout or wave or show any sign of emotion at all other than the casual interest of a spectator. Then another appeared slightly further forward of the first, but he moved straight to the screen, his shirt gleaming in the light as he stared down at the motor boat which was already chugging stern first away from the side.

Standish could feel the ladder jerking beneath him and knew that Motts and the seamen were pressing hard on his heels. But something made him remain motionless, his eyes fixed on the two figures on the flying bridge.

Then, even as the motor boat started to curve round away from the freighter's side, the second figure came to life. In the arctic glare Standish saw him point something down across the screen, and as he yelled a warning his words were drowned by the searing rattle of automatic fire.

He started to climb again, his knuckles and knees bleeding from a dozen cuts as he scraped against the rough plates, but his mind recording nothing but the savage burst of firing, the smash of splintering wood as the hail of bullets swept across the motor boat from end to end.

Then he was up and over the rail, his feet stumbling on a carelessly stowed rope, while his fingers plucked desperately at his holster. The firing stopped abrubtly, and in the sudden stillness he heard a man screaming, a terrible bubbling sound which went on and on like some tortured animal, until like the firing it ceased with the suddenness of death.

The searchlight went out, although whether on purpose or from some of the bullets Standish neither knew nor cared.

His men were tumbling and cursing around him, their weapons clashing against the deck while they groped like blind cripples in the unfamiliar surroundings, their voices cracked and close to panic.

One side of the freighter's boat deck lit up briefly and another burst of automatic fire whined and ricocheted across the crouching seamen, striking sparks from a winch and hammering into the planks on every side.

Standish yelled, 'Spread out to either beam!' He ducked as a solitary bullet smacked the deck by his feet. 'Motts, take charge to starboard!'

The seamen started to run and then faltered, blinking and dazed as the big clusters of cargo lights came on above their heads, illuminating every hatch and stanchion, and making their figures stand out stark and unreal like creations in a nightmare waxworks.

It was the signal for more firing, the bullets ripping down from the bridge and boat deck until it seemed that they would all be slaughtered within seconds.

Motts dropped on one knee and opened fire with his Stirling. Faintly between bursts Standish heard breaking glass and several shouts from beyond the blinding lights. He yelled, 'Put a burst into those clusters!'

A seaman gaped at him and then nodded, but before he could raise his gun he was plucked from his feet and hurled against the bulwark like a piece of torn rag. Standish felt blood spurting across his leg as he snatched the fallen Stirling and then poured a full magazine at the nearest light cluster above the mainmast.

Another seaman fell kicking and screaming, his hands on his face as he rolled from a hatch top and dropped between two of his companions below.

Standish crouched on one knee behind the winch, his eyes aching with effort as he tried to see beyond the remaining lights. Before a burst from Motts' gun shattered the cluster to fragments and the deck was plunged again into pitch darkness, he saw the two sets of ladders to the bridge, the barbed wire and the heavy gates. It was like a fortress.

Motts crawled across to his side, his forehead bleeding badly. 'What d'you think, sir?' He sounded out of breath.

'God knows. But whoever has taken over the ship has got us pinned down right enough. If we rush that barricade they'll pick us off in the wire like . . .' He ducked as a burst of gunfire ripped along the hatch top, hurling wood splinters and torn canvas in all directions.

Motts muttered savagely, 'They'll never get away with it!'

Behind them a man was whimpering piteously and another shouted, 'I'm comin', Ginger! 'Old on, mate!' But more shots from the bridge silenced the wounded man, and the one who had called to him yelled, 'You murderin' bastards! You stinkin', butcherin' sods!'

Standish said slowly, 'This is no use at all.' It was surprising how calm he felt. As if he was suspended in space, remote and cool, dangerously so.

He added, 'We'll have to do something before first light. They'll soon winkle us out when the sun comes up.'

Motts said, 'But who are *they*, sir?'

'The yeoman said something about pirates earlier on.' He steadied the Stirling against the winch and then relaxed slightly. It was only a shadow. Earlier on? Was it possible it had all happened within hours? And somewhere in the darkness Burch and the others on *Terrapin*'s bridge were watching, expecting them to be killed. What the hell could Dalziel do but stand off and await daylight?

A seaman whispered, 'There's a bloke coming down the starboard ladder, sir!' He raised his Stirling, adding harshly, 'I'll get that bastard!'

But Standish gripped his wrist. 'Hold your fire!'

The man in question was unlocking the iron gate at the foot

of the ladder, held all the time in a beam of torchlight directed from somewhere on the boat deck. He was a small bald man, and on his torn shirt wore the shoulder straps of a ship's officer.

Once through the gate he locked it and then after a brief hesitation threw the key up towards the light. Then with his arms above his head he started to walk unsteadily towards the mainmast, his shoes loud in the silence.

As he blundered level with the winch Motts reached out and dragged him into cover.

Standish said, 'Who the hell are you?'

The man slumped against the winch gasping for breath. He smelt of sweat, and fear.

'Hamlyn, chief officer.' He had a Yorkshire accent, and Standish was reminded vaguely of Pigott. He added thickly, 'I've been sent down to parley with you.'

Standish stared at him. 'Who by?'

The man let out a groan. 'I don't know, an' that's the truth. We were on passage for Songkhla when we came on two junks. One was towing t'other and they seemed in a bad way. We stopped to help of course.'

Standish looked at Motts. *Of course,* he had said. The unspoken code of the sea. He asked, 'What happened?'

'It was all so quick really. We had a deck cargo of Chinese passengers. They were supposed to be cleared, had work permits for Thailand an' all that stuff, but as soon as we got alongside the junks they rushed the bridge and took command. The junks carried about two dozen more of 'em, armed to the bloody teeth. It was all over in minutes.'

Motts gestured towards the ladders. 'What about the wire an' gates?'

The officer shrugged. 'Someone aboard had been careful to open them up at the right moment.' He added bitterly. 'It was no bloody chance affair. They knew we were coming all right!'

'The cargo?' Standish tried to control his impatience.

'General mostly. But we've fifty cases of rifles and automatic weapons for the Thai army and twelve tons of drugs and medical supplies.' He became suddenly desperate. 'I've been sent down to tell you to signal your ship to stand off. The leader of these bastards has given me ten minutes.'

Motts said grimly, 'Some 'opes 'e's got!'

'You don't understand!' The officer struggled on to his knees. 'We've got twelve other passengers aboard, eight of 'em women! He's going to kill the lot if your captain stays in company! That was why the skipper played along with him when you first stopped us.'

Motts said quietly, 'Jesus!'

'Would he do it?' Standish tried to clear his mind, to produce some solution, even though he knew it was hopeless.

'He shot the quartermaster and third officer. Our Sparks was killed when the bastards threw a grenade into the radio room. The poor bugger was trying to get off an S.O.S.'

'I know.' Standish looked at the stars. They seemed paler already. This leader, whoever he was, probably intended to rendezvous with some other ships and unload the precious cargo at sea. It would not be too difficult for someone who was so obviously well trained and informed. Jerram's M.L.s would be many miles to the south. The leader probably knew that, too.

He said slowly, 'I can't make any bargains.'

'D'you know what you're saying, man?' The officer clutched his arm. 'They'll murder the lot of them!'

Motts said sharply, 'The first lieutenant means that they'll kill the lot of us anyway. Where would be the point in lettin' *us* live?'

'Where are the passengers?'

'Under guard in two cabins, port side of the boat deck.' He sounded suddenly despairing. 'They've got several armed men in the engine room to watch the black gang, and the rest are on the bridge with the master, Cap'n Tothill. It's no use. They've thought of everything.'

Standish made up his mind. It was a crazy, impossible risk, but there was nothing else left.

'Go back and tell them I must signal my captain. They'll be expecting that, I should think. It'll give *us* a bit more time.'

'If you say so.' He stood up and would have fallen but for Motts holding his arm. 'I'm getting on a bit. I was going to retire from the sea this year.' He shuddered. 'But now . . .' He reached suddenly into his shirt, and after some fumbling produced a battered money belt. 'Only safe place to keep it in this old bucket. They steal everything that's not screwed down.'

Standish waited. Knowing the man was making time, trying to come to some decision.

He continued in the same breathless tone, 'I've been at sea for thirty years, mostly out here.' He thrust the belt into Standish's hands. 'See that my old woman gets this if you come through.' He released himself from Motts' support, adding gruffly, 'But I'll not die knowing I didn't lift a finger.' He turned to leave. 'There's a spare key to the starboard gate in there, too.'

With something like a sob he was gone, and as he approached the bridge the torch came on again, and in the pale glare Standish saw a key hanging down from the boat deck on a length of codline for the officer's re-entry.

When the torch was extinguished Standish felt the man's own key between his fingers. It was still warm from contact against his body.

Motts said quietly, 'Well now, there's a thing.'

'Get the lamp and signal the ship, Motts. As quickly as you can, but make sure you turn it away from the *Cornwallis*'s bridge as you send.'

He wondered briefly why Dalziel had made no move. Had not even attempted to make contact with the loud-hailer.

'Ready, sir.'

They froze as a piercing scream shattered the silence. Then there was another. Then nothing.

A seaman said thickly, 'Christ, that was a woman!'

Standish looked away. 'Start sending, Motts. Word for word, just as I tell you.'

Motts shuttered his small lamp, and back across the black water came an instant acknowledgement. That must be Burch, Standish thought. It was some comfort. Something familiar to hold on to.

No shots came down from the bridge, nor was there any attempt to stop the message. It was a gamble on both sides, he thought grimly. But in this game everyone could lose.

Eventually Motts lowered his lamp and looked at him. 'It's been nice knowin' you, sir.' He sounded very calm. 'If I ever get to Pompey again, I'll stay there for good.'

Standish peered past him. Trying to see the ship's outline. Imagining the scene on her bridge at this moment.

Then he replied slowly, 'Be ready to move. And if I catch it, you'll have to manage on your own. There's no margin left for failure now.'

In his mind he imagined he could hear Dalziel's voice. *Can't abide failures!* And in spite of the tension he felt his mouth twist in a smile.

Motts said, 'I'll tell the others, sir. What's left of 'em.' He showed his teeth. 'I 'ope to Christ it's the right key!'

Standish turned to watch the bridge again. It would soon be over. He wondered momentarily if Alison would ever read about it in the papers. And if she did, would she care?

He gripped the dead seaman's Stirling even tighter and shut her from his mind.

Dalziel had said *it is the here and the now*. Well, now they all knew what that meant.

7 'The Navy's here!'

PETTY Officer Motts slithered across the freighter's deck and touched Standish's elbow with his fingers.

'I've told the lads what to expect, sir.' He lifted his head above the winch and strained his eyes towards the superstructure. 'I think it's gettin' brighter already.'

Standish did not reply. He had hardly moved a muscle since the brief message had been flashed across to the frigate, and his eyes felt raw from peering at the upper bridge and the deeper shadows around the boat deck. He tried to picture Dalziel, and wondered what he would have done had he been in the captain's position.

Motts muttered, 'Jesus, what's takin' so long?'

'It's not long.' Standish stiffened as a brief glimmer of light showed itself beyond the shattered glass of the radio shack. A man lighting a cigarette. They must be confident, he thought grimly. Then he thought of Motts and the other seamen, and how much worse it must se:m to them. The *Cornwallis*'s engine had started again, and against the pale stars the darker tracery of rigging and blocks were shaking violently to the screw's renewed effort.

He said more calmly, 'The captain seems to have fooled them.' *For the present anyway* . . . 'It'll be any minute now.'

He eased back from the winch and brushed against something by his knee. It was a man's leg, outthrust and relaxed, the attitude accepted at the moment of death.

Tightly he added, 'Pass the word round, Motts. There's

going to be a hell of a lot of noise. So keep together, and think of nothing but that bloody ladder!'

He heard Motts whispering in the darkness and thought of those unknown men above him on the bridge. Did they really expect Dalziel to haul off and let them get clear? But they had no choice now, and nothing left to gamble with but their hostages. He remembered the chilling screams and tried not to imagine their cause.

Motts hissed in his ear, 'Look!' He seized his arm excitedly. 'Port quarter! The old *Shellback*'s comin'!'

Standish half rose, his eyes fixed on a hardening moustache of white water beneath the frigate's stem as she pounded out of the darkness at full speed, her bows pointing straight for the freighter's hull.

To go alongside an anchored ship in the dark was always dangerous, but to attempt to close with a moving one was courting with real disaster. Standish found that he had risen to his feet, and the seamen around him were staring at the onrushing patch of broken foam with something like awe.

Overhead a voice called out urgently and two dark shapes flitted along the bridge wing. As Standish pulled the key from his pocket the *Terrapin*'s searchlight came on, lighting up the bridge and funnel in a dazzling glare, while at the same time her siren rent the air apart with a jarring banshee wailing, the deafening sounds adding to the nightmare unreality.

Standish yelled, 'Now, lads! While they're all busy!'

Then he was running, heedless of nameless shapes in the harsh glare, of disjointed cries and the occasional sounds of shooting, his whole mind concentrated upon reaching that gate.

Men lurched against his back, and while he fumbled with the crude lock he heard one repeating fervently, 'Oh God, oh God,' as if he would never stop.

The gate clanged aside and they were dashing up the ladder, blinded momentarily as the boat deck hid the searchlight like a curtain.

And all the time the siren kept up its insane wailing, louder and nearer until Standish could also hear the roar of fans, the steady swish of screws as the frigate charged headlong towards the other ship's tall side.

There was more shooting now, and sparks flickered from

bridge and boat deck alike as bullets cracked and whistled, or whimpered impotently across the opposite beam.

A pale shape loomed across the catwalk beside the radio shack, saw Standish and made to step back into the shadows. He felt the hot wind of bullets past his face and saw the crouching shape plucked aside and fall kicking to the deck below. The seaman who fired must have missed Standish's head by inches.

But they were on the catwalk, and between the radio shack and the tall funnel Standish saw the frigate's grey outline as she surged close alongside, her bridge lit occasionally by short bursts of automatic weapons as she replied to the fire from the other ship's superstructure.

Then came the first impact. Standish felt the deck stagger beneath him, heard the terrible shriek of torn metal as the frigate's raked forecastle ripped through the freighter's rusty plates like a timber saw. In the weird reflected light he could see hammocks and fenders draped along the *Terrapin*'s hull to withstand the first shock, but they were already being ripped away as both hulls ground together again with a prolonged metallic roar.

Motts shouted, 'Up 'ere, sir!' He dashed towards the bridge, his Stirling held in front of him while the deck gave one more terrible convulsion.

Standish kicked open a wooden screen door and saw the figures around the wheel and telegraph swinging to stare at him as if he had fallen from the sky. There were about fifteen of them, anonymous in the smoke and dazzling reflections. Then one made a dash towards the opposite wing, that one small movement triggering off all the fear and hatred which the remaining seamen had endured since climbing aboard.

Stirlings hammered viciously from the door and through the shattered bridge windows at the rear, shutting out the screams and cries, concealing their brief harvest in wreathing coils of blue smoke.

Standish knocked Motts' arm down. 'Enough! Cover what's left while I go for the boat deck!' He saw Motts nod, his eyes wild in the glare.

As he ran with three seamen towards the first door in the superstructure Standish noticed that the savage jerking had stopped and the ship was wallowing heavily in what must be the frigate's wake. So *Terrapin* had done her bit. Had created a fantastic and crazy diversion while he finished the job.

He pushed open the door and stumbled to the opposite side of a darkened cabin. He found another door and almost fell into a brightly lit passageway which ran fore and aft through the boat deck superstructure.

A shadow moved by a door at the far end and a bullet ricocheted against the steel behind his shoulder. Muffled screams answered the shot and Standish yelled, 'End cabins! *Move!*'

At that moment another figure dashed into view, a grenade held above his head as he seized the handle of a door and jerked it open. Standish heard the women's terrified screams even louder and knew that this was the one where they were being held. The grenade was to ensure that they at least would not be spared.

Standish raised his Stirling and fired. The magazine was almost empty, but he saw the man spin round, heard the click of steel as the lever flew from the grenade, and shouted, 'Down, lads! *Get down!*'

Confined closely by the sides of the narrow passageway it was more of a sensation than an actual sound. Standish did not hear any explosion at all, but was conscious of tremendous pressure on his ears and lungs, of stinging smoke and chipped paintwork across his outthrust arms like imitation snow.

Then as his hearing returned he lifted his head and saw what remained of the would-be executioner. His trunk and legs were smashed into a corner of the passageway, and the rest of him spread across the punctured deckhead and doors like some hideous mural.

He turned and looked at his men. One was slumped against the side, blood pumping between his fingers as he squeezed them round his thigh, his teeth gritted against the pain. The others seemed dazed but unhurt.

Standish said, 'Dobson, you stay and look after him until help arrives. Put a dressing on it.'

The wounded man peered up at him and grinned. 'S'all right, sir. Don't feel too bad.' Then he fainted.

Standish reached the last door and seized the handle. It had swung shut as the grenade thrower had died and its surface was scarred with splinters and droplets of blood.

He drew his revolver for the first time and stared at it. Then he pushed down the handle and heard more screams, suddenly close and personal.

He shouted, 'You're safe now!' There was a sudden silence and he added, 'The Navy's here!' He half turned and saw the seaman beside him grinning broadly, the shock draining from his eyes as Standish said awkwardly, 'A bit theatrical, but it seems to have worked.' He tried to return the man's grin but his lips felt frozen.

Standish thrust open the door and stepped across the coaming, his eyes passing over the upended suitcases and torn bedding, the crouching shapes of several women, wild-eyed and staring at him like those who cannot believe in their own reason.

One, a young girl with dark hair, was sitting on a bunk, her knees drawn up under her chin. She was almost naked, and as she looked at Standish she began to weep. There was no sound and no tears, just a steady, pitiful shaking.

Standish asked, 'Is everyone here?'

A tall, grim-faced woman in a dressing gown said, 'In the next cabin.' She shuddered. 'The master's wife. They killed her when your ship came alongside.'

She sat down and put her arm round the sobbing girl's bare shoulders.

'Is she all right?' Standish felt sick and dazed after the first few moments of madness.

'Several of the Chinese raped her.' The girl made no sign that she had heard as the older woman added quietly, 'She might get over it. I was at Singapore in the last war. I did.'

Standish turned to the seaman. 'Stay here. I'll go and see...'

He did not finish but opened the other door and pushed into the cabin. The light had been smashed so he groped for the deadlight and clipped it above the wide scuttle. Astonished he saw the sea spread out beyond him, blue and green in the early light. Then he turned and looked at the large double bunk, at the elderly woman who lay spread-eagled across the bloodied sheets, her eyes watching him but devoid of understanding. He pulled a rug from the cabin floor and threw it across her.

Could men really do that to a woman? To any living thing? He doubled over a chair and vomited uncontrollably.

Then he re-entered the other cabin and locked the door behind him. They were all staring at him, their eyes white, unmoving, watching his mouth like so many deaf mutes.

He said, 'Get Petty Officer Motts.'

But it was the ship's master who returned with the seaman. He was a big, craggy man, white-haired and built like a rock.

He said thickly, 'Thank God you found us!'

Standish watched him, his mind still cringing, suddenly hating this man without knowing why.

'If you had been more careful . . .' Then he thought of the locked cabin behind him and added quietly, 'Your wife is in there, Captain.'

The other man licked his lips and then replied, 'Thank you.' He looked at the women and added, 'I have released my other hands. I will return to my bridge until . . .' His eyes moved to the locked door. Then he said harshly. 'I will await your captain's directions.'

Standish held out the money belt. 'It belongs to your chief officer.'

'He's dead, too.' The words hung in the enclosed cabin. 'They hacked him down as soon as your ship came back.'

'He was a brave man.' Standish looked away.

'Aye.' The master walked slowly to the passageway, his arms hanging at his sides like dead things. 'I never realized it before. But he was indeed.'

Motts passed the other man and looked at Standish questioningly. 'Orders, sir?' He nodded to the women. 'Mornin', ladies. Soon 'ave you right as rain again.' He became serious. 'The lads 'ave got ten of the bastards lined up on the foredeck, sir. All Chinks, an' not one over the age of twenty by the looks of 'em.'

'And their leader?'

'Gawd knows, sir. One of them clobbered on the bridge, I should think.'

From the end of the passageway a voice called excitedly, 'The ship's signalling, sir! Will you come?'

Standish looked around him. 'Yes.' It was nearly over. 'At once.'

As he followed Motts into the growing daylight he thought of the girl, of what she must have been through.

Above the boat deck, outlined against the shattered bridge windows he saw the ship's master training his glasses on the approaching frigate. How could he bear to stand there, in that bloody shambles?

Motts said quietly, 'Looks fine, don't she, sir?'

Standish followed his stare and saw the *Terrapin* steaming slowly abeam on a parallel course. Even in the poor light it was possible to see the buckled plates on her forecastle, the torn guardrails and the broken remains of the whaler hanging from its davits in two equal halves.

He nodded slowly. 'Fine. She'll do me.'

Stranger still, he found that he meant it.

*   *   *

Dalziel lowered his glasses as one of the *Cornwallis*'s big lifeboats pushed off from the side and turned slowly towards her own ship.

'Capital.' He turned and looked at Standish, his head cocked on one side like an eager bird. 'You feeling better?'

Standish swilled the strong coffee round the bottom of the mug, tasting the liberal dose of rum which someone had added for him. 'At the moment, sir.' He still did not trust himself to speak more than few words at a time. Instead he looked above the screen at the washed-out blue sky, the dark line of the early horizon. It seemed almost impossible to believe that barely two hours before he had been fighting for his life. Killing.

Dalziel was saying, 'The motor boat coxswain and mechanic were killed in that first burst. We did manage to pick up the bowman, however.' He nodded thoughtfully. 'So that's four dead and two wounded all told. Could have been worse. Much worse.'

Standish shivered. He kept seeing that girl. The look of complete destruction on her face. The rest consisted only of vague pictures and confused sounds. Of Irvine greeting him on his return to the ship aboard one of the lifeboats. Irvine of all people, wringing his hand and yelling, 'Well done, old lad! Bloody well done!' And Wishart, eyes filling his face, watching him and staring, saying nothing. And all the others, showing relief, or surprise that he had lived.

Caley clattered up the ladder and saluted.

'All the women are in the wardroom, sir. I've put the wounded in the P.O.'s mess and prisoners under guard.'

'Fine.' Dalziel moved to his chair, humming to himself.

Pigott appeared on the opposite ladder, his face unshaven and crumpled with fatigue. He saw Standish and grinned with obvious pleasure.

Then he said, 'Sir I do feel that the cook is being a bit hasty about the rations.'

Dalziel eyed him calmly, '*I* gave the order for extra food today, Pigott. God, man, a good breakfast is just what we all need. If tinned pheasant is all you have, then give 'em that too, eh?'

Pigott said stubbornly, 'It's all very well, sir, but my calculations do not allow for . . .'

They all turned to stare at Standish who had burst into a fit of uncontrollable laughter.

Pigott removed his glasses and polished them vigorously against his shirt.

'You can laugh, Number One. But a supply officer has to consider everything.' He moved towards the ladder muttering, 'No help from anybody, that's the trouble. Always the same!'

Dalziel slid from his chair and guided Standish to the chartroom. It was cool and dark after the open bridge.

'All right?' His eyes were concerned. 'Would you like to go below?'

Standish removed his cap and wiped his forehead with his fingers. The skin felt clammy and unreal, like his own voice and the laugh which he had been unable to control. It was strange that Dalziel was the only one to realize how close he had been to breaking dowm completely.

Dalziel continued, 'Poor old Pigott. Good chap at heart, but does go on a bit.' He watched as Standish leaned against the chart table. 'You did well. If your plan hadn't worked you would have been in real trouble.' He grimaced. 'A right potmess, eh?'

'What now, sir?' Maybe the rum had done it. There was a

roaring in his ears, like the moment when the grenade had exploded. He pushed his mind back on course, away from the grotesque remains splashed across the deckhead, from the mutilated corpse in the cabin. 'Or don't we know yet?'

Dalziel squared his shoulders and stared reflectively at the open scuttle.

'I have informed the squadron of our movements. Just the main details of course. We will give them a fuller account when we dock.'

'Dock?'

'Didn't I say?' Dalziel sounded very casual. 'Received a signal to proceed forthwith to Singapore.' The grin appeared, spreading from sideburn to sideburn as it if had been lurking there all the time. 'I don't think we shall have any more rude comments about our place in affairs, eh? Our worth has been proved for everyone to see.'

Standish dropped his gaze. Proved. Proved by four British sailors and God knows how many others. And that girl who had no tears left.

'A few days in dock'll put the ship to rights.' Dalziel seemed far away. 'Not much damage, not to us that is.' He walked back and forth across the chartroom. 'Plot foiled, ship rescued, and a good handful of prisoners as visible evidence. Bloody good show.'

Irvine looked into the doorway. 'Ready to proceed, sir.'

'Good. Bring her round on the new course and signal *Cornwallis* to take station astern.' He glanced at Standish. 'Her owners have apparently agreed to let her come with us.' He frowned. 'Bless my soul, they're lucky to have a ship left if they go on like this.'

Irvine watched them impassively. 'And the radar's broken down again, sir.'

Dalziel glared at him, and then very slowly allowed the grin to return.

'Well, we can't have everything, can we, Pilot?'

When Irvine had left Dalziel added warmly, 'Do you know, Number One, I feel we are on the threshold of something big this time. *Really* big.'

Standish looked down at his legs. There were patches of dried blood on his trousers. Like the rust streaks on the freighter's hull. He swallowed hard, feeling the nausea returning. Fighting it.

He said, 'We were lucky.'

'There was some luck, certainly.' Dalziel cocked his head as the telegraphs jangled in the wheelhouse and the deck began to tremble again. 'But I prefer to rely on judgment.' He nodded, apparently satisfied. 'Judgment, and something else which you don't find by sitting on your arse ashore, eh?'

He walked to the door. 'You use my sea cabin. Have a wash and a lie down. After that and the biggest breakfast this ship has ever witnessed, you'll feel all about again, right?'

Standish nodded wearily. 'Right.' The door was tightly closed and he realized he must have been staring at it for several seconds after Dalziel had gone. He realized too that Dalziel had been freshly shaved and was wearing a clean shirt.

While they had been rounding up the last of the Chinese attackers who had fled from the boiler room to escape the released stokers, and while the dead had been sorted into neat lines below the bridge, Dalziel had been acting in the only way he knew.

Standish looked at his hands and steadied them against the table. Surely no man could be as confident, as remote from personal feelings as that?

He sat down heavily on the top of a chart locker and leaned his back against the bulkhead. Through it he could feel the gentle, insistent tremors of the engines, as if, like Dalziel, the old ship was trying to revive him, to restore him to their world.

When Dalziel returned to the chartroom ten minutes later he found Standish fast asleep, sprawled across the locker like a corpse.

He smiled slightly and stepped back through the door.

*   *   *

The return to Singapore took the best part of four days. For apart from the necessity to maintain a painfully slow speed in order to remain in company with the *Cornwallis*, there were other, more unexpected delays.

During the first day the *Cornwallis* had hove to, and while the *Terrapin* idled nearby on a gentle swell flags were lowered to half-mast and the officers and crew members who had been killed in the fighting took their last passage over the side into thirty fathoms of water.

Dalziel had watched stern-faced from his own bridge while the pathetic little bundles had been slipped clear of the freighter's rusty hull, and had remarked bitterly, 'Pity we can't do the honours for our own people. Damn pity.'

The last bundle to fall had been the master's wife. Standish had known this for he had seen the elderly captain in his glasses as he had thrown a crude wreath after her, his face like stone in the powerful lenses.

Standish had also known the reason for Dalziel's annoyance at being denied his own sea burials. A curt signal had ordered him to expect the arrival of two Malaysian patrol boats. The four dead ratings would be transferred ashore and be flown by helicopter to Singapore in company with the two wounded ones.

And in due course the two boats had made contact, and after more frustrating delays while one of them had struggled to get alongside the business of transferring the dead had begun.

Both the patrol boats were loaded with military police. In fact, there were more of them than sailors. One, a dapper little major with a black moustache had produced a warrant and informed Dalziel in impeccable English that the Chinese prisoners were also to be transferred to his custody forthwith.

As the two boats had headed back towards the land Dalziel had said irritably, 'Bloody lot of red tape! It's suppose to be a Malaysian matter. Not considered prudent to allow *us* to take take the prisoners to Singapore. Damn load of rubbish, I call it. But for us they'd have had those jokers ashore right now blowing up their bloody police stations, I shouldn't wonder!'

And so, but for the battered plates along the forecastle and the loss of both boats, the *Terrapin* had little to show for her venture. Except for the women, who had remained throughout the voyage in the wardroom and in Dalziel's own quarters.

It was strange how unwilling they seemed to show themselves on deck. It was as if they were ashamed of their ordeal rather than grateful to be alive.

But the strangest thing of all as far as the ship's company was concerned was the total absence of news on the radio about their rescue of the *Cornwallis* from her attackers. Perhaps the powers, both civil and military, were awaiting Dalziel's personal account before they gave their verdict to the outside world.

Personally, Standish did not care much either way. There was plenty for him to do, for following the collision with the *Cornwallis* there seemed to be more defects and mechanical failures than ever, which under the circumstances was hardly surprising. For the whole four days he hardly left the upper deck except to sleep, and even that was little enough.

He knew inwardly that he was trying to work himself to a standstill, to drive himself so hard he would forget all which had happened, and above all his own part in it. If Dalziel noticed what he was doing to himself he said nothing about it. He on the other hand seemed to become more affable and excited the nearer they got to Singapore, and once when he had seen some seamen splashing new paint on the forecastle he had shouted, 'Leave it as it is! Let everyone see what it cost us!'

Standish wished he could join in this strange air of unreal gaiety which seemed to cover the whole ship. He guessed that the obvious pride and pleasure in their achievement was more from relief than any earlier enthusiasm. As Corbin had remarked sadly, 'Well, sir, I expect the old girl'll be paid off now. At least she's going out with a bang.'

On the morning of the last day at sea, as the *Terrapin* steadied on a westerly course through the Singapore Strait, Dalziel came to the upper bridge, and after his usual cursory inspection of chart and compass, settled himself in his chair.

He said, 'I've received our docking orders, Number One.' He looked up to watch the gulls as they twisted lazily above the motionless radar. 'But we have to pick up a buoy first. I've told Pilot to lay it on.' Then he glanced directly at Standish. 'I want a smart entrance. Get our people properly dressed and fallen in well before time.' He nodded as if to emphasize the importance of it. 'We'll show 'em, eh?'

Standish lifted his glasses and watched a small fishing boat until it was well clear of the ship's bows. 'What about the passengers, sir?'

'All taken care of.' Dalziel was still watching him, his eyes shadowed by the oak-leaved peak of his cap. 'The P.M.O. is arranging a launch and accommodation ashore. Seems to be running smoothly for once.'

Standish replied, 'I hope so.'

Dalziel leaned back and thrust his hands into his pockets, his eyes dreamy. 'I expect there'll be quite a few visits to do. Press, interviews and so forth. The U.S.S. *Sibuyan* is already in harbour here, and I'll have to see the admiral right away. You too of course. Just as well you were the boarding officer.' He grinned widely. 'I could have sent young Pigott, and just think what he might say to the admiral. Probably go rabbiting on about his precious stores, eh?'

A signalman called, 'Minesweeper on the starboard bow, sir.'

It was a small coastal minesweeper, one of the hard-used maids of all work which did just about every local duty, except minesweeping.

The signalman raised his glasses as a light started to stammer from the small ship's bridge.

'*Rokesmore* to *Terrapin*.' The signalman's lips moved in time with the lamp. 'What hit you this time?'

Dalziel stood up and stared across at the other ship which was already steaming past on an opposite course.

'What's the matter with the idiot?' He was still grinning, but as he turned Standish could see the sudden anxiety in his eyes.

Irvine, who had just climbed on to the bridge to take over the watch said flatly, 'They haven't heard. They don't know a damn thing about it!'

Burch snatched the lamp from his young signalman and rasped, 'Permission to reply, sir?'

He looked hurt, Standish thought. He could imagine the sort of retort Burch would send. Short and probably obscene.

Dalziel said, 'Tell them to read their newspapers.' He returned to his chair and lapsed into silence.

Irvine looked at Standish and shrugged. 'What d'you make of that?'

'I don't know.' Standish walked to the rear of the bridge as the forenoon watchkeepers clattered up both ladders to take their stations.

Irvine rubbed his chin and added thoughtfully, 'When I was at school we had a lower master.' As Standish said nothing he continued, 'We always knew when there was going to be trouble, or if someone was going to get a flogging, this chap never said a word. Not a single bloody word.'

Dalziel called sharply, 'Get your breakfast, Number One. I'll want you with me as soon as we reach Changi Point, right?'

Standish left the bridge and went straight to his cabin. Leading Steward Wills passed his door and then came back to peer at him.

'Breakfast, sir?'

'Bring it down to me.' Standish pulled off his stained shirt and threw it on the bunk. 'Just coffee will do.'

Wills chuckled. 'Not much else anyway. Be glad to draw some more grub when we berth, I can tell you. I'll fetch it down right away, sir.' He seemed to sense Standish's tenseness and added, 'I've just got to see to the last of the passengers.'

Standish stared at himself in the mirror and ran his fingers through his tousled hair. Poor Wills, he had been a nurse and mother to the women since they had come aboard, but he seemed to have thrived on it.

There was a step in the passageway and he saw the same severe woman in the dressing gown he had found in the freighter's cabin. She was still wearing it, and carried a towel across one arm, like a schoolmistress in a second class hotel. She paused by the open door and looked at him.

'I expect you'll be glad to see us leave?'

Standish put down his razor, suddenly feeling crumpled and dishevelled.

'More likely the other way round.' He smiled. 'I hope you all get to wherever it was you were going when . . .' He looked away. 'And that you can forget what happened.'

She smiled back at him. It made her look years younger.

'My husband's a planter. I don't suppose he'd notice if I went to America.' She held out her hand. 'Thank you. I'll never forget what you did. Neither will the others.'

She turned to go but Standish said abruptly, 'That girl. The one who was . . .' he faltered as she turned to watch him, her face suddenly severe again. 'Has she anyone here? Anybody to help her?'

'I have friends in Singapore. She will stay with me until things are settled.'

'Good.' He wished she would not stare at him. 'I'm glad. I just thought . . .'

'I know what you thought, and thank you again. Your family will be very proud of you. I know I would be.'

Standish picked up his razor. 'Thanks.'

He heard her walk away towards the wardroom and tried to shut her grave kindness from his mind.

Family. What family? He switched on the razor and then threw it savagely on to the bunk with the shirt. The power circuit had gone again.

He snatched the handset from its hook beside the bunk and snapped, 'Tell the electrical officer to send someone to fix my razor point.' He watched his own despair and growing anger in the bulkhead mirror.

Family. Father killed at sea during the war, and his mother had long since remarried and gone to Canada. And Alison . . . He barked into the handset, 'I don't give a bloody damn where he is, *find him!*' He slammed it down and sank wearily on the edge of the bunk.

Later, changed into a clean shirt and shaved with only minutes to spare, he stood beside Dalziel while the frigate moved slowly between the anchored warships, half listening to the shrilling pipes, the blare of bugles from the larger vessels, and every so often Dalziel s voice as he conned his command towards a vacant buoy.

Someone had had the thoughtfulness to provide a boat and two buoy-jumpers. The latter were already squatting on the fat buoy, and in the eyes of the ship Wishart was waiting to signal the last few yards of approach so that the mooring wires could be passed down to them. A sleek harbour launch hovered nearby, and anchored firmly in the centre of the bigger ships Standish could see the uneven bulk of the *Sibuyan*, the Stars and Stripes somehow alien amidst so many British colours.

'Steady as you go.' Dalziel moved across the gratings to watch the buoy. He was wearing dark glasses and it was even harder to tell what he was thinking at this moment. All the way up the naval anchorage, past each moored ship, he had appeared to be waiting. Hoping.

There had been several signals, but just the usual greetings you always received when returning to harbour. But not one word about the frigate's gashed hull or a message of congratulations.

'Stop both engines.' Dalziel jabbed his finger towards the stem. 'Tell that idiot to get ready with the Jack!'

Burch pouted. 'Aye, aye, sir.'

'Slow astern both engines.' Dalziel leaned out over the wing to watch as the buoy vanished beneath the stem and the waiting seamen were galvanised into sudden activity.

Wishart turned and raised his arm.

'Stop both engines.' Dalziel leaned against the screen as the shackle was secured and then straightened his back to watch the Jack break out from its staff above the stem, while simultaneously from the quarterdeck a crisp new White Ensign broke to the gentle offshore breeze.

Then he removed the sunglasses and said, 'Ring off main engines. Rig awnings as soon as the fo'c'sle party has secured.'

'Launch comin' alongside, sir.'

Dalziel frowned. 'Tell it to stand off until we've rigged the gangway, damn his eyes!'

Burch sucked his teeth noisily. 'Can't do that, sir. It's the officer of the guard.'

'More delays.' Dalziel rested one hand on the compass as the engines' vibrations cut and died.

The smart lieutenant who climbed to the bridge was polite but firm. His words, Standish thought, were carefully rehearsed.

'I have orders to take your written report to the U.S.S. *Sibuyan* immediately, sir.'

Dalziel thrust his hands into his pockets. 'I'll get it from my safe. I'll expect your signature in return.'

The officer seemed very relieved. 'Naturally, sir.'

When Dalziel had left the bridge Standish asked quietly, 'This is unusual. I would have thought the C. in C. would want to see the captain first?'

'It's all been arranged like this, sir.' The officer fidgeted with his swordbelt. 'The American admiral is in control of your operations, so to speak, and I expect feels more able to deal with this situation.'

Irvine looked up from the chart table. 'Situation? I call it sheer bloody bad manners!'

Standish shook his head. 'Easy, Pilot.' To the lieutenant he added, 'Then you don't know anything about it either?'

They heard the door of Dalziel's sea cabin slam shut and the sound of his feet in the chartroom. Then the lieutenant said quickly, 'Look out for squalls! The wires have been buzzing like mad for the last few days. I thought another war had started. So watch your step!'

Dalziel stepped into the sunlight and handed him a sealed envelope. Then he stood aside to watch the lieutenant scribble his signature on a receipt.

The officer of the guard straightened his back and saluted. 'Welcome back to Singapore, sir.'

Dalziel watched him go down to his launch. Then he left the bridge muttering under his breath.

Irvine asked, 'What did the captain just say, Yeoman?'

Burch looked at the guard boat as it sped towards the shore. 'I think it was, get stuffed, *sir*.'

8 A Matter of Security

THE quartermaster poked his head inside Standish's cabin and cleared his throat discreetly.

'Beg pardon, sir, but there's a boat alongside to take you an' the captain across to the Yankee ship.'

Standish had been lying on his bunk. He looked at his wristwatch. It was over two hours since *Terrapin* had made fast to the buoy.

'Have you informed the captain?'

'Yessir.'

Standish nodded and stood up. 'I'll be right there.'

Then he glanced slowly around the cabin, automatically patting his pockets to make sure he still had his pipe and tobacco with him. So something was happening at last. After the waiting and the complete lack of information, someone had apparently decided to break the silence.

On deck the sun was as bright as ever, and as he strode aft to the gangway he noticed how quiet the ship seemed after the excitement and speculation of their return to Singapore. There was a smell of rum still hanging over the ship, and in the messes most of the hands were getting ready for their midday meal, but, all the same, it was quieter than it should have been.

There was not much moving on the flat water of the anchorage, just a few small craft and a heavily loaded boat full of tourists which was steering as close as possible to the grey warships in order that the movie cameras could obtain the best results.

Wishart was O.O.D. and was watching the tourist boat intently as Standish walked up to him.

He said suddenly, 'Ah, I thought so.' He pointed to the sleek guard boat which had appeared as if by magic from behind an anchored supply ship. 'That's three times it's happened.'

He did not have to elaborate. Standish watched the guard boat as with the dexterity of a well-trained sheepdog it pushed close to the slow moving pleasure craft, the coxswain standing up to shout something through a megaphone. The tourists were going to be disappointed as far as *Terrapin* was concerned, Standish thought angrily. It was as if the whole ship was diseased in some way, that she was to remain isolated at her buoy forever.

Wishart said, 'Perhaps you'll get it sorted out when you see the admiral.' He looked at Standish, his eyes puzzled. 'What does it all mean?'

'Security, I expect.' Standish glanced down at the launch alongside. 'If there's a reason for doing nothing, you can bet your boots it's always *security*!'

The side-party stiffened to attention as Dalziel appeared through a screen door. He looked alert and quite composed after his show of anger on the bridge, and as he took a quick glance around the upper deck his expression gave nothing away.

'Right, let's get on with it then!'

The pipes shrilled and the American seamen saluted as Dalziel and Standish climbed down into their boat.

Dalziel said, 'I expect we'll be dining aboard the *Sibuyan*. God knows, I've never felt less like eating.'

Standish looked at him with surprise. 'Worried, sir?'

'Apprehensive.' Dalziel turned to watch a powerful destroyer as they surged past. 'Too many amateur politicians in the Navy these days. Can't abide amateurs in any profession. They're too damn dangerous.'

He fell silent and did not speak again until the launch was within yards of the *Sibuyan*'s main gangway. Then he looked at Standish and whispered fiercely, 'If anything goes wrong, you just stay out of it, see? You obeyed my orders and nothing more. I'll not have my officers badgered by outsiders for doing their duty.'

Standish followed him up what seemed like an endless gangway until they reached a broad entry port and a side-party of American enlisted men and marines. More pipes and salutes, and then a tanned officer was ushering them into the cool half-light of the *Sibuyan's* hull.

It was more like being swallowed than going aboard in the accepted sense, Standish thought. As he followed Dalziel and the American O.O.D. through one great passageway after another he was conscious of the vast complex of machinery and equipment all about him. Through open doors he saw men sitting at typewriters and teleprinters, and in what appeared to be a vast steel cavern he saw masses of plot tables and perspex monitoring screens, complicated graphs and a whole barrage of telephones, most of which appeared to be in use.

They hurried still further into the ship's interior until Standish had lost all sense of direction and position. Then they passed a wooden-faced marine and through a door marked *Reception* where a bored looking yeoman sat behind a desk reading a paperback and chewing gum.

He did not look up as the O.O.D. said politely, 'If you'll wait here, gentlemen. I'll tell the admiral you've come aboard.'

Standish looked round the big cabin. It was fully carpeted, and there was a gleaming array of coffee percolators arranged on a small sideboard, above which hung a full length picture of the President.

'Quite a place.' Standish walked to a scuttle and peered out. He could see the *Terrapin* almost end-on, and guessed he was somewhere below the *Sibuyan's* main bridge structure. The frigate looked small from this distance. Small and shabby.

Dalziel said, 'If you think this is grand, then wait until you see the admiral's quarters.' He tried to smile but then turned and asked sharply, 'How long will the admiral be?'

The yeoman looked up, his jaw open in mid-air. 'You gotta be kidding, Commander. He takes his time, an' when he says jump, we *all* jump.'

Dalziel turned away, his face like a mask. 'Thank you.'

The yeoman returned to his paperback. 'My pleasure, sir.'

Dalziel said quietly, 'Strange chap.'

Standish said, 'I expect he sees more senior officers every day than we do in a lifetime, I . . .'

He broke off as the other door swung open and the O.O.D. said formally, 'This way, gentlemen.'

They walked on to another, even thicker carpet, and as the O.O.D. closed the door and vanished Standish found himself confronted by the largest cabin he had ever seen. Yet in spite of its size it seemed somehow spartan, and the giant desk at the far side below the open scuttles appeared to be the centrepiece, the nerve centre of this whole complicated ship.

Rear-Admiral John P. Curtis was tanned and lean, almost a head taller than Dalziel, with a slight stoop which told of cramped service in earlier days aboard less spacious craft than the *Sibuyan*. He had cropped hair which was almost completely grey, but his smile was youthful, and his eyes were those of a man used to making decisions, regardless of outside opinions. Not a man to try and fool, Standish decided.

There were others present, too. Captain Jerram and a harassed looking lieutenant were seated by some well-stocked bookcases, and near the desk was a round-faced captain in the uniform of the Royal Thai Navy.

Curtis said, 'Sit down, gentlemen. I'm sorry to keep you on a limb like this.' He shrugged. 'You know how it is today. Diplomacy first, action second.'

Dalziel seated himself stiffly opposite the desk.

'I hope my report was satisfactory.' He could not keep the bitterness from his tone. 'If so, I am sure my ship's company would appreciate a word in that direction.'

Curtis leafed through some papers on the desk, the movements regular, well-timed.

Then he replied evenly, 'Yes, I've read your report. It was full, and very definite on certain points.' He swung his chair round until he was facing a great coloured chart which completely covered one bulkhead. 'When I was given this command I had my doubts that it would work out. It is so easy to get panicked by a whole series of incidents, to see a communist plot in each one, when in fact they may be just unconnected co-incidences. Too much force too early and we get accused of crepe-hanging. Too little and you've lost another battle before it's begun.' He swung back again and asked, 'What's on *your* mind, Captain Jerram?'

Standish shot a glance across the cabin. Jerram had been

sitting quite still, as if holding himself in the chair with real effort, but now he jumped to his feet, his face working with barely suppressed concern.

'I know this was to be an informal discussion, sir, but certain of Commander Dalziel's actions are in dispute. There may be occasion to proffer them as evidence at a later date.'

Curtis nodded, his eyes moving lazily between them.

'I see. Well, as I was saying, when I was appointed to this task of welding some sort of combined force together I knew one thing above all else. The Reds' strongest weapon is, and always has been, the disharmony amongst their adversaries. I would not attempt to interfere in the internal matters of the Royal Navy, Captain Jerram. *However*,' the word seemed to hang in the air above them, 'while I am in overall command I will expected to be consulted at all times.'

Jerram bit his lip. 'I will accept that, sir.'

'Great.' The admiral leaned back in the swivel chair and stared at the deckhead. 'Now let us get to the bones of Commander Dalziel's report.' Without consulting any notes he ran briefly through the parts relating to the S.O.S. and the first sighting of the *Cornwallis*. Then he asked, 'Tell me, Commander, what is your personal assessment of the facts at your disposal?'

Dalziel replied, 'When my executive officer and his boarding party came under fire I knew there must be a definite connection between the S.O.S. and the shipmaster's failure to identify *Terrapin* when we first made contact. When Lieutenant-Commander Standish signalled that he had a plan and the unpleasant alternatives proposed by the enemy, I knew I had to act, and at once.'

Standish saw Jerram frown at the word 'enemy', and he knew that Admiral Curtis had not taken his eyes from him since Dalziel had mentioned his name.

Dalziel continued, 'It has been my contention for some time that the present system of patrol and investigation is outdated and misplaced. I believe that the Chinese communists are making renewed efforts to infiltrate Thailand and Malaysia just as they have succeeded in doing elsewhere, but I do *not* believe they are using the methods described by our Intelligence.'

Jerram snapped, 'You are forgetting yourself, Dalziel! This

attitude has already brought a score of complaints from the Russians after you tried to stop one of their ships. And then you nearly sunk an unarmed junk, an action which resulted in the death of a civilian.'

The admiral held up one hand. 'It should be noted that there *were* three terrorists found aboard that junk by your inshore patrols, Captain.'

Dalziel said calmly, 'If I had not found and retaken the *Cornwallis* I believe they would have landed those arms and supplies without any trouble at all.' He looked at Jerram for the first time, his eyes gleaming in the reflected light. 'The rendezvous which you were using, and at which my ship would have been but for the courage of the *Cornwallis*'s radio officer who sent the S.O.S., was hopelessly misplaced, and made I suspect after your being given false information.'

The admiral stood up. 'Take it easy, Commander. We will just keep to the other facts, if you don't mind.'

Surprisingly Dalziel smiled. 'Certainly, sir. The other thing which bothered me came when I inspected the prisoners.'

The admiral nodded. 'In the report you say they were regular troops. How come? As far as I know, none of them has spilled a thing yet.'

Dalziel grinned. 'All young and much the same age at that. All fit and well disciplined. It was obvious to me anyway.'

Standish glanced quickly at the American, but he was smiling gently at Dalziel's curt appraisal of the matter. He realized with a start that Curtis was looking at him.

'And what do you think about it?'

Standish saw Dalziel watching him, his fingers on the arms of his chair.

'I agree with my captain, sir.' Dalziel's fingers relaxed slightly as he continued, 'They were too well organized right from the start. One of the freighter's officers said that it was timed to the minute.'

Curtis nodded. 'You did well.' He smiled lazily. 'But I hear you were a submariner. Well, so was I.'

Dalziel said, 'I think we should follow through with more patrols. Hunt them out before they can close the coast and pick their own landing places at leisure!'

'I admire your concern.' The admiral watched him curiously.

'But you must try and see the broader pattern. As I said earlier, we must have co-operation, which is why I requested you to give the prisoners to the Malay patrols. SEATO or any other set-up out here requires that each country manages its own internal defence. If other, non-committed nations think we are taking over the whole shoot they'll be terrified of being turned into another Korea or Viet Nam, a battleground for the big powers who might see fit to withdraw from the ashes without either winning or losing the final conflict.'

A telephone buzzed quietly and he lifted it from the desk. 'Yes. I see. Okay.' He replaced it and looked at his watch. 'Lunch is about ready, gentlemen.'

Dalziel stood up, his face suddenly anxious. 'But, sir, what about my ship's part in all this? My men have worked damn hard, some have even died to carry out what I think was a fine piece of work.'

Curtis looked at him, his eyes thoughtful. 'Here's the deal. Tomorrow morning the Press Bureau will issue a statement. That the S.S. *Cornwallis* was overrun by pirates, the attack being repulsed and defeated by H.M.S. *Terrapin* which was on routine patrol at the time.'

His eyes hardened slightly. 'I know how you feel, Commander, and I can guess what the ship means to you. But we are here to do one all-important job and nothing more. I do not want the whole world and ten thousand reporters clamouring over my command, not unless or until I know exactly what the Reds are up to.' He looked round their intent faces. 'And I don't give a sweet goddamn who steps out of line. If he's under my flag, I'll break him, okay?'

Then he looked at the Thai officer who had said nothing throughout the interview.

'Captain Pumhirun is the kind of officer I like. He speaks no English, so we get on just fine.'

He crossed to Standish and held out his hand. 'Sorry I can't have you to lunch too. But this is strictly for the heads of departments.' His handshake was firm but brief. 'Take care of yourself. I have a feeling you are going to be useful around here.' He turned his back on the others and dropped his voice to a mere whisper. 'Especially if you can stop your captain from blowing his cool every time we meet. I have troubles enough without an internal riot!'

Dalziel caught him as he moved to the door. 'I'm damn sorry about this, Number One. But I expect it is to be another informal get-together.' He looked at him fixedly, his eyes suddenly bitter. 'I'm not going to let them forget our part in all this. I don't care what it costs!'

Two white-gloved marines had opened a pair of doors at the far end of the cabin, and through them Standish could see the well-laid table, other senior officers and the glint of silver and perfectly matched china. He thought suddenly of the *Terrapin*'s shabby wardroom, the others who would be waiting hopefully for his news.

He said, 'I'll be going, sir. If we're docking tomorrow there'll be a lot to do.'

Dalziel stood up and then said impulsively, 'Look after her, eh? She's a good ship, you know.'

Standish nodded. 'I will.' She's all we've got, he thought.

Then he was through the doors and past the same unmoving marine, his mind still busy with what he had seen and heard.

Would it have been any different with another captain? Did Admiral Curtis propose this negative report because of Dalziel or in spite of him, or because Jerram had already spoken against him in private?

A grinning sailor touched his arm. 'Not that way, lootenant. Follow me if you wanna see daylight agin.'

Standish smiled. 'Lead on.' And suddenly he was glad to be leaving. Glad to be going back to the *Terrapin*, where for once he felt he was going to be needed.

*   *   *

Dalziel returned to the *Terrapin* in the late afternoon. There was an official from the dockyard waiting to see him, and while they discussed the matter of the ship's repairs in the captain's cabin Standish watched him closely and tried to discover his present mood.

He seemed quieter than usual but in no way subdued, and when the dockyard official had departed he said briskly, 'Soon get this bit of damaged hammered out, eh?'

Standish asked, 'How did it go, sir?'

'The lunch? Dalziel sounded vague. 'Quite well really. Chicken of course. It's always chicken aboard American ships. Odd chaps.'

He stood up and paced across the worn carpet. 'Rear-Admiral Curtis was very friendly, I thought. Plenty of get up and go in that one.' He halted suddenly in his pacing and stared at Standish. 'How did the others take the news?'

Standish thought of the brooding silence as he had outlined their reception aboard the *Sibuyan*.

'Disappointed, sir. But I thought you'd like to fill in the picture yourself.'

'Quite. Good thinking. As a matter of fact I may be able to tell them some more inspiring news after I've seen the C. in C.' He saw Standish's surprise and added, 'Made an appointment for this evening. Don't want to let the grass grow under us, eh?'

He crossed to his cupboard and took out the beautifully cut decanter and glasses.

'Bit late in the afternoon, I know, Number One. But I'm rather hoarse after all that talking and tinned chicken.'

He held the decanter to the scuttle and swilled its contents about in the sunlight.

'Good bit of glass this. Got it as a small mark of appreciation when I was escorting the Royal Yacht.'

Standish opened his mouth and closed it again. Perhaps he had misheard the first time, or maybe there was a twin decanter which Dalziel had received from the Shah of Persia.

He asked instead, 'Do you think Admiral Curtis will act on your report, sir?'

'Depends.' Dalziel swallowed the neat whisky with obvious relief. 'Jerram is the one who bothers me. Such an old woman, and absolutely no idea of the real situation we're facing out here.' He perched himself on the table and leaned towards Standish. 'As I see it, the Chinese communists are in a hurry. They're not going to mess about subverting and infiltrating right round the northern coast of the Gulf of Thailand. In Viet Nam it was quite different. They helped the North Vietnamese to by-pass the frontier and demilitarized zone by using Laos, where the Americans could not get at them. But this time they will try and take a short-cut, pop up right in the middle of their next objective, so to speak.'

Standish watched the whisky splashing into the glasses again. 'I can understand that.'

Dalziel smiled warmly. 'I know. That's why I like you. You see beyond all this nonsense about rules and so forth.' He hurried on before Standish could speak. 'The U.S. Seventh Fleet is absolutely bogged down with its commitments throughout the whole South China Sea and as far north as Korea. It is a vast organization, a naval way of life more than an individual concern. You saw Curtis's flagship, well that should give you some idea. It's all so connected, so dependent on long drawn-out lines of communication that personal initiative is almost heresy.'

Standish thought of Curtis's great desk, the radio links which connected him with every corner of the Western world, or perhaps in the end to just one man at an even larger desk in Washington.

Dalziel said, 'Whatever anyone tells you to the contrary, wars are won by pre-thinking and individual action. No other way.'

'I take it that Captain Jerram is satisfied with your explanations, sir?'

'No other choice, has he?' Dalziel grinned widely. 'Everything I said was true. His Malaysian patrols were useless when the time came, and so would we have been if we'd been at the rendezvous.'

He eyed Standish crookedly. 'You're thinking it was sheer luck, eh? I can see it written on your face.' He crossed to his bookcase and ran his fingers along the top shelf. 'Look at these names. Nelson, Collingwood, or John Paul Jones if you like. They all took risks when older, more stagnant minds were dead against them. Failure would have meant ignominy and disgrace, if not worse. But they trusted their own judgment, and were proved right.'

Standish watched him gravely. Dalziel's voice was getting louder and there were patches of colour on his tanned cheeks. It was as if his energy and enthusiasm needed a safety valve, but one over which he seemed to have little control.

'That rubbish of Jerram's, for instance. Are we supposed to cruise up and down the damned ocean with blinkers on? I say that if the communists know we are here, then we should show them we mean business. It all stems from today's politicians, hypocrites almost to a man if you ask me. No thought of honour, not them. Just *what is in it for me?* or *how much money will we lose if we go to help a nation which trusted our word!* Lot of bloody parasites living off the state!' He whirled round and snapped, 'Enter!'

Leading Steward Wills looked through the door. 'Shall I lay out your best uniform, sir?'

'Yes.' He seemed to relax. 'Sword and medals for a visit to the C. in C.'

He reached for the decanter, paused and then poured another full glass. 'Never hurt anyone,' he remarked absently. 'Still, I expect the politicians will stop that too one of these days. No drinking for the officers or rum for the ratings, so that they can spend the money themselves on some bloody party rally at Broadstairs or something.'

He looked at Standish thoughtfully. 'Might have a little party tonight, what do you think? Just our own officers and a few drinks to celebrate.'

'I'll lay it on, sir.'

'Capital. One good thing about this sort of commission is that you live together as a ship's company, not running off every night to watch television.' He frowned. 'Did the ladies get ashore all right?'

'They had gone when I returned from the *Sibuyan*, sir.' Standish recalled the strange sense of disappointment when Wishart had told him. He added shortly, 'I've heard that the lads turned out to see them go. I think they feel that the women were the only ones who really appreciated what they did.'

'Hmm, I can understand *that*. Still, we mustn't mope about it. We've shown everyone what we can do. Now it's up to us to see we go on paving the way.'

Standish stood up and moved towards the door, but Dalziel added slowly, 'I shall speak to the ship's company myself. Explain to them about all this security nonsense.'

Standish was not quite certain but he thought Dalziel winked as he added gravely, 'Of course, it's not always possible to keep Jolly Jack quiet when he's on a run ashore, is it? So give leave to all but the duty part of the watch until midnight and lay on some tenders to bring them back aboard, right?'

He saw Standish hesitate and asked, 'Something on your mind again? Well, spit it out. You know me better than to keep it bottled up.'

'I was thinking about what you said earlier, sir. Perhaps Captain Jerram was anxious to overrule you, or maybe *he* had someone breathing down his neck, too. I think it would be unwise to tempt fate so soon after the last trouble.' He looked down at his hands. 'Our people are disappointed because they feel their little victory is being overlooked. But later, if there's another let-down, they might start to ask if any of it was worthwhile. Men died aboard the *Cornwallis*, and they'll start remembering it when this excitement has worn off.' He thought of the gun in his hands, the suddenness with which he had killed. Like the swift reaction of a wild animal with thought of nothing but survival.

Dalziel reached out and punched his arm, the gesture playful. 'Then it's up to us to see that the excitement does not wear off, right?'

As he walked along the passageway Standish thought he heard Dalziel humming to himself.

*   *   *

Lieutenant Marcus Irvine leaned back in his chair and blew a stream of cigarette smoke towards a deckhead fan.

'This is the stupidest party I've *ever* attended!'

Standish crossed to a scuttle and stared at the thousands of glinting lights along the shoreline, the occasional pale wash of a power boat before it was swallowed up in the darkness of the anchorage.

All the frigate's officers were present, their mess kit strangely formal against the worn furniture and faded paintwork. A messman was stirring a giant china bowl of punch, while Wills stood by the sideboard staring gloomily at an array of delicacies which he and the cook had prepared between them. The slices of toast upon which they had arranged tempting portions of anchovies and local tinned fish were already curling like damp cardboard, and the sandwiches looked decidedly stale.

Irvine said angrily, 'A party, he says, and the principal guest is still absent.' He looked at his watch. 'I could have been at the Tang-Liun Club tonight instead of sitting here like a bloody twit.'

Hornby passed the sideboard for the twentieth time, his eyes on the untasted food. 'I suppose we *could* start without him?'

Pigott showed his teeth. 'Watch it! I can't abide fat officers!'

Standish smiled in spite of his nagging apprehension. It was strange that Dalziel was still ashore.

He said, 'All right. Serve the punch, Wills.'

Quarrie grimaced. 'Punch? Tastes like gin and diesel.'

'Got the recipe out of a book, sir.' Wills eyed him defensively.

Irvine smiled gently. 'Which book?' He looked at Caley. 'I expect *you*'d prefer a glass of beer, eh?'

But if the punch tasted unusual, it was certainly potent. Standish noticed the level dropping in the bowl, and when he glanced at the sideboard he saw that the food had equally diminished.

Hornby was munching as if his life depended on it. 'I expect the captain'll bring a few bottles off for us too, if we're lucky.'

Irvine grinned. 'I think your luck is fast running out, old son.'

'What?' Hornby's last sandwich halted halfway to his mouth.

'Do you remember when we were attached to the American squadron a year ago? How mad keen you were to compete with them on equal terms?'

Hornby frowned. 'Vaguely.'

'You'd better be more precise, my fat comrade. The captain asked me this morning about a "special sports fund" you were holding at that time.' He nodded as Hornby's face paled. 'I see that the jolly old memory is returning a little.'

Standish saw the others watching and asked, 'What was it for?'

Hornby did not seem to know what to do with his sandwich. 'We were very short of good sports gear. The Americans seemed to have everything, and as we were the only British ship in the squadron I thought...'

Irvine interrupted smoothly, 'You thought you'd gather a little nest-egg of your own!'

Hornby lurched to his feet, his eyes blazing. 'That's a bloody lie! I intended to use it for some more water-skiing and aqua gear. How was I to know we were leaving the Americans to go on that survey job?'

'Well, the captain knows about it, so you'd better prepare your defence.' Irvine glanced languidly at Standish. 'Even Hornby's court martial will be better than nothing.'

Hornby sank down in his chair and said wretchedly, 'I've not spent a penny of it.'

Quarrie eyed him bleakly. 'Why the hell didn't you pay it back to the lads?'

'Half of them had left the ship by then. It was all gift money, for the good of the ship as a whole. I didn't see anything wrong in it!' He sounded as if he would burst into tears.

Standish said quietly, 'I expect the captain will see it your way.'

It was odd Dalziel had not questioned him about it. But perhaps as Irvine had been aboard longer and was the next senior officer, he saw no point in wasting time.

Irvine asked calmly, 'How much cash is there in the old kitty?'

Hornby mopped his brow anxiously. 'Don't you remember, we had several raffles, and I made some more at tombola in Hong Kong?'

'You really are a nut.' Pigott was grinning broadly. 'But as Number One says, you should be able to explain it.' He spread his hands. 'Most of the officers I've known have *lost* the money, not added to it.'

The quartermaster appeared in the doorway. 'Officer of the day, please?'

Wishart looked round. 'Yes?'

'Boat shovin' off from the pier, sir.'

Standish said, 'That'll be him. I'll come up with you, Sub.'

They stood together by the gangway in the circle of light below the main awning. Standish saw the pinprick of green light reflected above a boat's bow wave and found that his stomach muscles had gone taut. It was not difficult to recall that other great green eye hanging above the *Terrapin*'s hull, the terrible closeness of disaster. But even that would have been better than what had followed.

Wishart asked quietly, 'Will there be trouble about that money?'

Standish breathed out slowly to relax his limbs. Although he had made light of it in the wardroom, if only to save Hornby from Irvine's calculated persecution, he was still not too sure. More officers had been broken over mishandling money than anything.

'We shall have to wait and see.'

The quartermaster cupped his hands and yelled, 'Boat ahoy?'

Back came the call, 'Aye, aye!'

Wishart said, 'It's not the captain after all.'

'Probably another officer paying us a visit.'

Standish watched as the harbour launch chugged alongside the gangway, pausing only long enough for one passenger plus two large suitcases to be dumped without ceremony on the gratings before merging once again into the darkness.

It was a lieutenant, and as he stepped cautiously into the lamplight Standish saw the gleam of scarlet between his two gold stripes.

He smiled. 'Hello, Doc, what brings you out here?'

The newcomer blinked and pulled an envelope from inside his jacket. 'Surgeon Lieutenant Peter Rideout. Come aboard to join, sir.'

Wishart grinned. 'The captain got his way, Number One. He said he would get us a doctor.'

Standish guided the doctor through the screen door and heard a thump as he struck his head against the steel frame.

'First ship, I'm afraid.' Rideout rubbed his head ruefully. 'Pity if I became my first casualty, too.'

Standish opened a cabin door. It smelt musty and humid and he explained, 'I gather this ship has been without a doctor for some time. But at least you've a cabin to yourself, and it's not too far from the sickbay.'

He waited until the quartermaster had deposited the two cases on the deck, taking the time to get a good look at the newcomer in the brighter lights of the cabin. He was slim and willowy, almost as fair as Irvine but with the pale complexion of one fresh out from England.

Rideout crossed to the handbasin and turned the tap. 'My

God!' He stepped back with alarm as the noisy juddering of the water system preceded the first spurting jet into the basin.

Standish watched as he lathered his hands very methodically, as if he was just about to perform a delicate operation.

'There's a party going on in the wardroom. I'll take you there and introduce you when you're ready.'

Rideout turned and looked at him. He had very pale blue eyes and it was hard to tell if he was really serious or merely mocking as he replied, 'Thank you. That really is most kind of you.'

Standish tried not to watch him as he busily wiped each finger with a clean towel which he had taken from a suitcase.

'Don't go too much on first appearances, Doc. She's an old ship.' Strange how defensive he sounded.

'It doesn't mean much to me.' Rideout looked at his hands and seemed satisfied. 'As I have never been afloat before.'

'Well, that's all right then. But I expect you looked the *Terrapin* up as soon as you got your orders. I always did when I got a ship.'

The pale eyes flickered very slightly. '*Did*?' Then he smiled showing a set of perfect teeth. 'Actually I flew out here to an appointment at the base.' He shrugged. 'I had no idea I was coming aboard until the P.M.O. sent for me, almost before I had put down my cases. I gather that some captain by the name of Jerram requested the arrangement. It was all rather vague really.'

Standish felt that same sense of warning. 'Been in the Service long?'

'Two years. Here and there. I suppose this will be a nice change really.' Rideout was obviously not one to part with information easily.

'Were you at Haslar?' Even the name brought back the bitter memories as strongly as before.

Again the gentle smile. 'No, Chatham mostly.' He frowned and examined the thumb of his left hand. 'And a short while at Duncan House.'

Standish turned away, wanting to leave it right there.

Instead he asked quietly, 'I've not heard of it?'

Rideout straightened his uniform and beamed. 'Now lead me to the party!' He seemed to realize that Standish had spoken. 'Duncan House? Oh, it's a Combined Services hospital.' He nodded emphatically. 'You know, for mental cases!'

9 Only Human

THE nightmare seemed to be reaching a climax. The main impression was of heat. The next that of complete helplessness. Flames were all around, but pointing inwards, like the petals of some hideous flower, the centre of which contained an obscene tableau of interlocked, writhing figures. Without seeing her face, Standish knew it was Alison, watched horrified while the bobbing, grimacing figures tore and probed at her naked body. He knew he was calling her name, could even feel the heat of the flames as he struggled to reach her side. Then, as the figures merged and swirled into a mist he saw her turning her head to look at him. Before she finally vanished he saw too that she was laughing. Laughing at him.

He rolled on to his side, fighting the sheet across his body, and only then became aware that part of the light still remained.

But it was a shaded torch beam, and behind it he heard Wishart ask anxiously, 'Number One, are you all right?'

Standish groaned and propped himself on one elbow. In the nightmare he had been burning, and he could feel his chest and thighs running with sweat. But unlike the dream, he was ice cold.

He raised his wrist to his eyes and peered at the luminous dial of his watch. It was three in the morning.

'For Christ's sake!'

Wishart crouched beside the bunk, his face pale in the torchlight. 'I'm sorry about this.' He sounded worried. 'But the quartermaster called me. The captain came aboard just now.'

Standish sat up slowly, tasting the gin in his throat, feeling the pitiless hammers around his skull.

'Oh, I see.' He switched on a small reading lamp above the bunk and tried to rub the tiredness from his eyes. 'Did he say what was wrong?'

Wishart shook his head. 'Only that the captain came in a motor boat from the base and told him not to wake the O.O.D.'

'Well, that's it then.' Standish felt unreasoning anger welling inside him, alongside the vague pictures of the wardroom party which had finally dissipated itself in the mixed attitudes of drunkenness.

'Is that all?'

'No.' Wishart sounded less certain under Standish's angry stare. 'That is, I thought you ought to know. The captain's on the bridge. He didn't turn in, and the Q.M. thought I should be told about it.'

'God.' Standish stood up and steadied himself against the bunk. 'I'd better see what's up.'

He tried to grin and then caught sight of himself in the mirror. He was naked, and he knew Wishart was staring at the patches of discoloured flesh where the grafts had been taken from his thighs and upper arms.

He said savagely, 'For Christ's sake leave me alone! If you can't cope with your duty then let me get on with it!'

As Wishart shrank back towards the door he pulled a shirt over his head and added quietly, 'Forget it, Sub. It's not your fault. Just forget I spoke.'

Wishart turned and looked him full in the face. 'I'm sorry, too. I'd heard you had a bad time.' He shrugged helplessly. 'How you managed to do what you did in the *Cornwallis* after all you'd suffered before, I can't begin to think.'

Standish ran a comb through his tousled hair. In the mirror he could see the look on Wishart's open features, the expression of complete wonder. Like that of someone privileged to share a precious secret.

He said shortly, 'It's surprising what you can do on the spur of the moment. Frightening, too.' He dragged his cap from a hook. 'Now hop back to bed. All hell will be breaking here in a few hours. The tugs are taking us into dock at eight bells, so one of us at least should be wide awake when that happens.' He placed one hand on Wishart's shoulder. 'And thanks.'

It felt very cold on the upper deck and he walked briskly towards the bridge, letting the keen air clear his head, conscious of the paling sky, of the other ships nearby sleeping at their moorings.

The upper bridge was deathly quiet, like that of a ghost ship, the instruments and the gratings empty of life. Even the cold steel felt clammy to the touch. It was hard to think of the ship as a moving, vital thing at moments like these.

He thought he heard a sound and then noticed a patch of light showing from the chartroom scuttle. He raised his hand to the door and paused. He could hear Dalziel murmuring to himself, the scrape of feet as he moved about the small compartment with hardly a pause.

He turned the clip on the door and heard Dalziel say sharply, 'Who's that? Get out whoever you are!'

Standish stepped into the chartroom and closed the door quietly behind him.

'So, it's you, is it?' Dalziel rested both hands on the table and peered at him fixedly. There was only the plot table's small light switched on, so that his features looked accusing and more angular. 'What do you want?'

Standish replied, 'The Q.M. reported you were back aboard, sir. I had already left word I was to be informed.' The lie came easily but Standish felt far from calm as he watched the other man across the table.

Dalziel had taken off his jacket and the front of his shirt was patchy with sweat. Or from the smell it could be whisky. His tie lay beside his cap on the deck, and his eyes looked bright, even wild.

'Well, in that case.' Dalziel did not finish the sentence. Instead he stared down at the table, and Standish saw that there were several charts and coloured maps spread there, one on top of the other in a disordered pile.

'Is anything the matter, sir?'

Dalziel stared at the topmost chart, his hands around the Gulf of Thailand as if holding it for himself. He muttered vaguely, 'I made it clear enough surely. Even a mental pigmy like Jerram ought to be able to understand.'

His usually immaculate hair was awry, and one piece had fallen across his eyes and shone in the light like a polished quill.

He looked up sharply and glared at Standish. 'I told them. I talked and talked until I was blue in the face. They listened of course. Nice and polite as always. Polite and bloody stupid, the lot of them!'

Standish waited. Any word from him now might really make Dalziel crack wide open.

'Only saw the C. in C. for a few seconds. I realize his appointment could not wait.' The scorn in his voice was bitter. 'Dinner with some visiting Minister is far more important than dealing with communist aggression in the Far East!' He beat one palm slowly and regularly on the edge of the table. 'He handed me over to three of his staff. They must have been told what to say. How to react.' He pushed himself away from the table and walked to the door of his sea cabin. 'I did my double-damndest to make them understand. I even took my own map along to show them. I've spent days outlining my ideas.' He vanished into the other cabin. 'Might just as well have thrown it all in the bloody drink!' He reappeared suddenly, a bottle in one hand and two cups in the other.

Standish said, 'Anyway, you tried, sir.' It sounded stupid, but he had to say something. Just to stand and watch Dalziel's anger and disbelief was more painful than he could have imagined.

Dalziel filled both cups almost to the brim and said, 'I tried to push home the lesson of experience. They weren't interested.' He stared at Standish, his eyes dazed. 'Would you believe it?' He tossed the cup to his mouth, some of the drink spilling down his shirt.

Then he said flatly, 'But my report stands. They couldn't shake me on that! They'll have to take all of it in bloody Whitehall. The recommendations I made about patrols, the full evidence of the work done by young Wishart on his first boarding job.' He paused and looked sideways at Standish, his eyes clouded. 'And of course about what *you* did.' He raised his hand to touch Standish's arm but overbalanced and cannoned against the bulkhead, the whisky splashing over the charts.

'Sod it!' Then he smiled. The effort made him look incredibly sad. 'We'll show 'em, eh? Teach the mealy-mouthed bastards a thing or two!'

He busied himself with the bottle again and then remarked, 'Sorry 'bout the party. Got tied up. All go off all right?'

Standish thought of Hornby being sick in a wastepaper basket. Of Pigott and Irvine duelling with broken chairlegs while Caley drank himself scarlet with glass after glass of beer. And on top of that punch. Even the memory made Standish feel close to vomiting.

He replied slowly. 'Quite well.' He watched the whisky going down. The way Dalziel kept turning to stare glassily at the charts. He added, 'A doctor has joined the wardroom, sir. A Surgeon Lieutenant Rideout.'

There was no sort of reaction at all. Dalziel said thickly, 'Rideout? That's a bloody stupid name if I ever heard one.' He banged his chin with the cup. 'Still, I got a doctor for the old *Terrapin*. There's some spark of hope for those lamebrains yet.'

Standish bit his lip, judging the moment. 'He seems a good chap, sir. He's only done hospital work so far and no sea-time at all. He says he spent a short time at Duncan House.'

Dalziel swallowed hard and rubbed one hand across his stomach. 'Never heard of it.' He swallowed again and swayed against the lockers. 'So long as he's a doctor, that's all I care about.'

As he turned towards the light Standish saw that his face was shining with sweat.

Dalziel said between his teeth, 'A hand, Number One! Give me a course to steer for my quarters, eh?' He closed his eyes tightly as Standish guided him towards the door. Dalziel was leaning more heavily against him every second. How in God's name would they get down three ladders without falling and rousing the watch?

A figure moved in the gloom of the signal bridge. It was Wishart in his pyjamas.

'I thought you might need me.' He seemed to expect a rebuff and hung back by the ladder.

Standish whispered fiercely, 'Take his other arm. Never more glad to see anyone in my life.' Dalziel sagged between them, his voice muffled in vague, indistinct mutterings.

'Is he ill, Number One?'

'Not *ill*, Sub.' They staggered backwards towards the top of the ladder. 'Drunk I know, and tired out from arguing too by the sound of it.'

Later, after an agonizing journey along the brightening deck and down to Dalziel's sleeping cabin, Standish said, 'Keep this to yourself. Captains are human, like the rest of us. But it sometimes pays off to forget that fact.'

Wishart followed him along the passageway, his slippered feet noiseless as he replied firmly, 'You can rely on me.'

Standish returned to his own cabin and stared at the crumpled sheets with distaste. It was hard to know who you *could* rely on, he thought.

*   *   *

Surgeon Lieutenant Rideout seated himself carefully at the small table and beamed at his companions. 'So this is the Planters' Bar? Really fascinating!'

Standish wedged his legs under the table and tried to catch the eye of a passing waiter. The bar was attached to a modern, air-conditioned hotel, and to give some weight to its name had been extravagantly adorned with masses of imitation palm fronds and mock bamboo screens, as well as large areas of bright plastic leather.

But for Irvine's insistence it was unlikely they would have got a table at all, for the place seemed crammed to overflowing and the noise almost deafening. The people around the tiny, circular tables were mostly tourists, British and American, with a sprinkling of French and German engineers and businessmen for good measure.

Irvine said dryly, 'When you do a tour, Doc, you really do it.'

Standish seized a waiter by the sleeve and shouted, 'Four iced beers!' Then the man had gone, his eyes glassy from work and the din around him.

Standish was still not sure why he had agreed to accompany the others on a tour of the city's highspots. Perhaps he was still afraid there could be some link between Dalziel and Rideout, a connection from the past which might be exploited if the doctor was left alone with Irvine.

It had been a difficult day, starting with the moment when the tugs had warped *Terrapin* into dry dock and all the business of inspection and estimating the damage had got under way.

If Dalziel recalled anything of the previous night he gave no sign of it. When Standish had finally found time to introduce him to the new doctor Dalziel had been pleasant, if a trifle distant, but there had been no sign of recognition on either side.

With the ship in the hands of the dockyard workers and most of her company ashore there seemed little way of avoiding Rideout's suggestion of an evening 'seeing the sights.'

Standish had visited Singapore several times throughout his service but never like this before. Rideout had not only acted like a tourist, he *was* a tourist. Between their feet beneath the the table was a great bag of souvenirs which he had bought regardless of advice or warning, ranging from brass ashtrays to crudely painted figurines, most of which had originated in Birmingham.

They had followed him down side alleys, sampled a dozen mixtures of food from pavement stalls and had dropped in at several bars which were normally frequented by the more doubtful of Singapore's citizens.

Now, jammed between Irvine and Wishart the doctor appeared to be finally content.

The waiter reappeared with the beer and Irvine said firmly, 'Bring some champagne!'

The man said, 'It's German, sir.'

Irvine groaned, 'Bring it anyway.'

Rideout smiled. 'What a scene! Wait until I tell my mother about it. The meeting place of the seven seas.'

Standish sipped the iced beer and eyed him thoughtfully. Rideout seemed simple enough. Not very forthcoming perhaps, but there was little sign of any guile either.

Above the bobbing heads of the people around him he saw a tall sweating half-caste in a white dinner jacket and pink cummerbund jerking his head in time with a small orchestra as he crooned breathlessly into a microphone. It sounded like, 'Ahdunnawah ahluvyah lakkadu!' As his ear adjusted itself above the din Standish realized he was in fact singing, 'I don't know why I love you like I do'. He thought of Rideout's description and smiled. The meeting place of the seven seas.

Irvine said, 'It sounds as if we'll be out of dock before the paint dries.'

Standish nodded. Either Dalziel had some influence with the dockyard manager or someone higher up was even keener to get rid of the *Terrapin* again. It had been agreed that the work would go on for most of the night, which was, to say the least, unusual.

'I'll not be sorry to leave.'

Wishart turned to watch a striking looking blonde on the arm of a plump escort as they pushed past on their way to the hotel lobby.

Irvine said softly, 'He'll be all right with that one, I should think.'

Wishart flushed. 'It might be his daughter. She looked a nice girl to me.'

Irvine glanced at Standish and winked. 'Ah, the innocence of youth!'

Rideout leaned forward to watch the waiter pouring the first of the champagne. Then he raised his glass and said cheerfully, 'I think I'm really going to enjoy my stay on the *Terrapin*.'

Irvine grimaced. '*In* the *Terrapin*.'

Rideout looked at him curiously. 'Pardon?'

'Forget it.' Irvine sipped the glass and then licked his lips. 'Not bad.' He glanced at the doctor again. 'Well, tell us about yourself. What great store of experiences have you brought to brighten our little monastic world?'

'Oh, I've just done all the usual things. But after a few months barrack duty, inspecting sailors' private parts for V.D., I had a go at the old head-shrinking bit.'

Wishart swallowed hard. 'Steady on, Doc. I'm still having a job to hold down that raw fish you got us eating.'

Irvine grinned. 'Where was that?'

'A place called Duncan House in Hampshire.'

Standish tried to think of some quick remark, anything to break this line of conversation without making it obvious. None came.

Irvine folded his arms. 'I'll bet the whole place was full of nutty sub-lieutenants.'

Rideout frowned. 'Actually I was only *attached* there on general medical duty.' He seemed momentarily caught in his own thoughts. 'No, as a matter of fact many of the patients were quite senior. I remember there was a brigadier who insisted on searching his bed every night for mice. Extremely promising.' He sighed. 'Turned out to be advanced D.T.'s. Bit of a disappointment really.'

Standish placed his hands on his knees below the table and tried to relax. It was stupid to let it affect him like this. It was obvious that neither Dalziel nor Rideout had ever made contact. And yet . . .

Wishart said, 'I wonder what job we'll get after this.'

'Just so long as we stay clear of trouble.' Irvine shook the bottle and muttered, 'Empty!' He signalled to a waiter and added, 'One more stroke like the last one and we'll *all* be writing reports for the rest of our lives.'

Rideout watched him, his pale eyes contemplative. 'Now that *is* interesting. Your, I mean *our* captain strikes me as a real man of action. Not one to be trifled with.'

Irvine eyed him calmly. 'You mean he's a *type*?'

'Not exactly.' Rideout took another glass and beamed at it. 'It's only that one does not often make contact with officers of his kind nowadays.'

Standish said, 'I suppose that means you'll be watching all of us and making notes for some future use?'

The others grinned and he let himself relax a little more.

Irvine yawned hugely. 'You wait until he gives you a programme, Doc! I'll bet a day's gin he'll find a nice subject for you to lecture on. Something to make the lower deck really sit up and take notice.'

Rideout looked at him gravely. 'A lecture? Is that what happens?'

Wishart smiled. 'I'm to give one on the place of the computer in today's society. God knows what it'll come out like.'

'It's not as bad as it sounds, Doc.' Standish knew Irvine was watching him but added abruptly, 'On these long stretches of isolated patrol it often pays to keep everyone on the jump.' He forced a smile. 'Otherwise we might all end up under your care!'

Rideout nodded. 'I see. Well, of course you'd know a great deal more about that than I do.' He was frowning again. 'All the same . . .'

'I'll go across to the Club for a bit.' Irvine stood up. 'What about you?'

Rideout shook his head. 'Thank you, but no. I've had enough excitement for one day. I think I'll return to the ship and turn in.'

'I'll come with you.' Wishart helped him to gather up the great bag of souvenirs. 'I promised I'd give Bill Pigott a break as O.O.D. while he slips ashore for an hour.'

They all looked at Standish who had remained seated. He said, 'I'll stay here awhile. I've left word at the desk in case I'm wanted.'

Irvine shrugged. 'Unlikely. Unless of course the ship is ordered to sea with half her plates lying on the pier.'

Standish leaned back more comfortably and allowed the noise to wash over him while he considered that last conversation. Why should he worry about it? It was useless to make barriers before trouble came in sight.

He turned and saw the waiter hovering above him.

'Sorry to bother you, sir. But there is a hotel guest who would like to speak with you. A lady.'

Standish stood up quickly. 'Lady?' He felt suddenly anxious and confused. 'Where?'

The man stood aside. 'If you will follow, sir.'

As Standish pushed after him he noticed that the table was occupied almost as soon as he had stepped clear.

After the mingled roar of voices and music in the Planters' Bar the hotel lounge was like a tomb. A few of the more elderly guests were sitting around enjoying a late night coffee or examining their newest batch of photographs, and through the darkened windows he saw the distant lights of the harbour shining and blinking on the hidden water.

'Lieutenant-Commander Standish, ma'am.' The waiter bowed himself through the doors and vanished.

'Good of you to leave your table like this.'

Standish stared at her for several seconds without speaking. He was aware of a sense of disappointment even as he told himself he had been ridiculous to hope for anything else. What had he expected as he had hurried after the waiter? That it might be Alison who had tracked him down to throw herself in his arms? To offer him back some sort of future again? Or had he been anticipating something else?

The woman who was watching him was slim and fair, and he supposed, in her early thirties. Her eyes were calm and very steady, and seemed vaguely at odds with her mouth which was both wide and sensuous. All these thoughts rushed through his mind as he heard himself ask, 'How can I help? Will you let me order you a drink?'

She sat down in a cane chair, the movement both easy and elegant. She said, 'I will order.' She raised her arm and a hotel steward appeared as if by magic. 'I am having brandy and soda. And you?'

She had a quiet but very direct manner of speaking. The sort of woman who would be used to her own way, Standish thought.

'Pink gin will do me.'

As she turned to speak with the steward he ran his eyes quickly over her clothes. Alison's extravagance had taught him one thing, and that was how to recognize expensive tastes. And this woman, whoever she was, would have gone through a month's pay just to cover herself for one evening.

She turned and looked at him calmly. 'I flew in a few days ago. I had intended to go up country if necessary.' She shrugged. 'But now it seems I am saved that prospect.'

She took her glass from the tray and stared at it.

'I saw your ship come in and made a few enquiries. When I heard you had left your name at the desk I decided to meet you.'

Standish cradled the drink in his hands. 'I see.'

'You don't, of course.' Then she smiled. It altered her completely, lighting up her face and making it almost beautiful. 'I should introduce myself. I am Sarah Dalziel.'

Standish placed his glass on the table. Giving himself a few more seconds to think.

'Why did you want to see me, Mrs. Dalziel?'

The smile had gone. 'My place is with my husband. Isn't that what they say?' She touched the glass with the tip of her tongue. 'He made no arrangements for me out here. Fortunately I am not totally reliant on Service pay, so I came anyway.' She seemed to come to a decision. 'I had to meet you. To know what sort of man you are.'

'And now you know?'

'I know what you are *not*. That is probably more to the point. You could have been one those watery-eyed subordinates, or you might as easily have been a fool. You are neither.'

'Thanks.'

'There is no need to be sarcastic.' Her eyes flashed angrily. 'I know I had the advantage over you. I read of your exploits in the *Straits Times* today, about your battle with Chinese pirates. They gave you quite a write-up. Even mentioned your past career, or some of it. Hector seems to have been lucky with his second in command this time.'

Standish rose to his feet. 'Look, I don't see how I can help you, Mrs. Dalziel. Even if I knew what you wanted, I would still be unable to interfere.'

'Please sit down.' She uncrossed her legs and leaned towards him. 'You didn't even know he was married, did you? So please hear me out before you start judging and condemning my actions!'

Standish sat. He said slowly, 'Have you tried to contact him?'

'I thought I'd wait a bit longer. I have a few friends here, and I have heard some rumours about him, and the ship.'

Standish waited. Here we go. No secret was ever safe for long in a naval base.

'People are saying that my husband nearly got himself court martialled.'

'What people?'

She met his eyes frankly. 'Just people. But they are high enough to know what they're talking about.'

'I don't think I can listen to any more...'

She reached out and seized his hand. 'Don't start talking like a round-eyed midshipman! You know the Navy and how it all works. Well then, so do I. I was born into it, christened into it and married into it. When my father was born, his choice of career was already mapped out for him, too.' She dropped her voice as two other hotel guests turned to glance curiously in her direction. 'My husband's rank is the lowest ever carried by a single member of my family, so even if I was stupid I could not fail to have learned *something* about your precious Service!'

She seemed to realize her hand was still resting on his and

added quietly, 'Excuse the drama. I'm a bit overwrought.' She took it away, but he could still feel its smoothness.

'As a matter of fact I only flew out here because I'm worried about him. He's had a bad time lately. I wouldn't want anything else to go wrong.'

'The collision?'

She nodded. 'And other things. In a way it's partly my fault. I knew he was eating his heart out to get a ship again. So I asked a friend of my father to pull strings.' She smiled sadly. 'So he got the *Terrapin*.'

Standish watched her. He wanted to get out, but something about her candour, her complete lack of evasiveness seemed to hold him in the chair.

'You want me to tell him you've arrived in Singapore?'

Surprisingly she shook her head. 'No. At least, not yet. I just want you to know I'm here. In case anything happens.'

Standish leaned towards her, aware of her perfume, the closeness of her hand.

'You must tell me. What *could* happen?'

She stood up, gracefully, like a cat.

'I don't know.'

He followed her to the door, conscious of the watching eyes from the other chairs, the silence about him.

Outside she turned and looked at him steadily. 'You'll say nothing of our meeting, will you?' Then she held out her hand to him. 'You know where to find me.'

He smiled. 'It was just luck. I've never been here before.'

As she turned towards the stairway she said quietly, 'I'd have found you anyway.' Then she was gone.

Standish walked out into the street and looked round for a taxi. It was getting worse, not better, and the more he thought about it the more he felt he was being made to take sides. To play some part in a conspiracy which he still did not fully understand.

There were no available taxis, so with his hands deep in his pockets he started to walk through the crush of carefree people, none of whom knew anything of his predicament, and probably would have cared even less if they had.

*   *   *

Dalziel strode briskly along the edge of the dock and then stood by the brow until Standish caught up with him. He pointed with his black walking stick towards some Chinese workers who were mixing paint on the frigate's deck below the four-inch gun mounting.

'Better tell the O.O.D. to keep his eye on those jokers until they're all ashore and finished, eh?'

He ran his eyes over the ship from bow to stern and then added, 'Looks *much* better.'

Standish watched him and replied, 'Out of dock tomorrow then?'

'Yes.' Dalziel started to walk along the wall until he had reached the great dock gates and peered down at the oily water beyond them where two boats were being warped against the piles by some of the *Terrapin's* seamen.

'Are *they* our new boats?' He sounded incredulous.

Standish nodded. 'The whaler's not too bad, sir. But the motor boat is more patches than planks, and its engine was certainly not new even when this boat got it.'

Dalziel rubbed his chin. 'So that's all we get for replacements, eh? Bloody lot of misers!'

Standish glanced at him, expecting more. But Dalziel was still looking at the two replacement boats, his eyes glinting thoughtfully. Standish wondered if in fact the dockyard could have given them some better boats. Or whether someone was getting his own back for all the urgency which Dalziel had thrust his way.

And the work had certainly moved, he thought. It was less than two weeks since the ship had returned to that discreet silence. Two weeks of work and frayed tempers, while Dalziel had harried his officers and dockyard officials alike to get what he wanted and in double-quick time.

Dalziel faced him and asked calmly, 'Have you seen Hornby this morning?'

'He's working in the T.S., sir.'

'Good.' Dalziel started back towards the brow, swinging his stick like a sword above the worn stones. 'I'll have him in my day cabin right away. Get things squared up before we sail, eh?'

'Sir.' Standish saw Dalziel turn to watch him again. 'If it's the matter of that sports fund, I did speak with him about it. I am sure it was an oversight.'

'Of course, Number One.' Dalziel was smiling crookedly. 'I'm sure you're right.' He frowned. 'But still, we can't have the ship's name impaired by that sort of carelessness, now can we?'

They passed the saluting gangway sentry and Dalziel added, 'Trot Hornby down then, will you? Make it as smooth as you can for him, eh?'

Standish found the electrical officer squatting amidst a litter of wiring and various switches, his face creased with concentration.

He looked up and said wearily, 'All old stuff, but I thought I might be able to salvage something useful.' He paled. 'What is it?'

Standish said gently, 'The captain wants to see you.'

'The money?' Hornby looked sick.

'Yes.' He helped him to his feet. 'Get a grip on yourself, man!'

Hornby fumbled with his boiler suit. 'I'm just putting my kid into a decent school. If anything happened over this I don't know what I'd do.'

They did not speak again until they were in Dalziel's cabin.

The captain was examining a long-barrelled sporting rifle, darting occasional glances at what appeared to be a maker's handbook.

He looked up and smiled. 'Ah, Number One. Capital.' He placed the rifle on top of a locker beside several boxes of ammunition. When he turned again he was not smiling.

Standish said formally, 'Lieutenant Thomas Hornby, sir.' He could almost feel the man's terror beside him.

'Well, Hornby, I've read the executive officer's report and I have examined your own, ahem, ledgers. For the want of a more suitable word, I would say that you have been a complete bloody *fool*.'

Hornby moved his heavy shoulders wretchedly. 'I'm sorry, sir. I'm really terribly sorry, I . . .'

Dalziel's eyebrows came together. '*Shut up!*' Then he walked round the table and eyed the other man coldly. 'Do you know how many men have said they were sorry before they were hanged?' His head came forward with a jerk. '*Well, do you?*'

Hornby whispered, 'No, sir.'

'Then that is a bloody pity!' He leaned back against the table and crossed one leg over the other. 'How you ever became qualified as an electrical officer I shall never know. I personally would not allow you at large with a number eight torch battery, do you know that?'

'Yes, sir.' It was pitiful to hear him, Standish thought.

Dalziel shook his head. 'I do not know, Hornby. I really do not know about you.'

Hornby's hands were screwed into tight fists as he said desperately, 'If I could have another chance, sir?'

Dalziel frowned severely. 'Don't grovel, Hornby. On some it looks fine. But on fat men it merely looks obscene.' He held up his hand and grinned. 'I know what we'll do, Hornby.' He pointed at the two crumpled ledgers on his table. 'We can't give back the funds to people who've vanished to the other ends of the earth. People who probably still fondly imagine that their old sports officer was as intelligent as he was gross. So we'll spend it. How does that strike you, eh?'

Hornby stared at him, his eyes glazed as if from shock. '*Sir?*'

'That's what we'll do then.' He nodded firmly. 'Lieutenant-Commander Standish will witness your signing over the money to my care, and *I* will spend it before you do something even more cretinous, from which even I cannot save your disgusting body.'

Standish watched Hornby's relief with something like amazement. Another few minutes of Dalziel's onslaught and he would have broken, he was quite sure of that.

Dalziel folded his arms and nodded. 'Just remember this in future, Hornby. Remember it every time you start hatching up schemes you can't control, right?'

'Yes, sir.'

'Now get out of my sight!' As the lieutenant lumbered to the door he added, 'I'll make an officer of you yet, Hornby! If it *bloody well kills you!*'

The door slammed shut and he said cheerfully, 'I said it was nothing we couldn't handle.' He consulted his watch. 'I've to go to the C. in C.'s office in an hour.' He could hardly restrain his grin. 'Orders at last, Number One.'

Standish followed him to the upper deck, his mind still in a whirl. 'What about the money, sir?'

'We'll spend all of it.' Dalziel paused and looked suspiciously at two Chinese workers. 'Came to me just now. Know just the very thing to buy with it.' He chuckled. 'Sports Fund indeed. I hope to God Hornby never gets as close to a court martial again. Still, I expect he lost a few pounds in weight back there, one way or the other.'

Standish saluted as Dalziel marched purposefully up the brow swinging his stick. Hornby might live to resent what Dalziel had said to him, but he had certainly been lucky.

He turned as the quartermaster said, 'Shore telephone call, sir.'

He took the telephone, his eyes still on Dalziel's silhouette as he strode along the top of the basin. 'Standish here. Who's that?'

'Sarah Dalziel.' Her voice seemed right alongside him. 'I'd like to see you if you can manage it.'

Standish stood very still. He could hear her breathing. 'Is it urgent?'

'Very.' The telephone went dead.

He looked at the quartermaster. 'Tell the O.O.D. I'm ashore for an hour.'

The seaman watched him leave and then winked at the sentry. 'Jimmy the one's got hisself a bird! Lucky bastard!' He straightened his face as Irvine appeared at his side. 'Pardon, sir, but the executive officer's ashore.'

Irvine eyed him bleakly. 'Where was the call from?'

The man paled. 'Th' Bates 'Otel, sir.'

Irvine walked away, his mind busy. 'Very interesting.'

The quartermaster muttered fiercely, 'Big-eared sod! 'E was listenin' all the bleedin' time!'

The sentry grinned unsympathetically. 'Shame, annit? One of 'em'll probably catch a dose an' give the new sawbones a job.'

Irvine was out of earshot now and stood looking after Standish as he hurried towards the gates. So that was why Standish had stayed behind in the bar. It would bear looking into if nothing better turned up.

10 Morning Departure

SARAH Dalziel's suite was on the tenth floor and had an uninterrupted view of the sea and the busy harbour roadstead below the city.

She said, 'I'll mix you a drink. Perhaps you will stay for lunch?'

Standish glanced round the big room, the comfort and elegance. 'I'm afraid I can only spare a few minutes.' He thought of the taxi waiting at the entrance and wondered if the driver would keep his word and stay there until he returned. 'It's over ten miles to the dockyard. That's more like fifty out here.' He watched her as she moved unhurriedly to a drinks table. She wore another expensive dress.

'Then I will try to be brief.' She brought him the drink and seated herself in a chair, her figure in silhouette against the harsh glare beyond the balcony. 'You look different in uniform. It suits you.'

He felt vaguely cheated without knowing why. 'You sounded on the phone as if there was no time to change.' It had meant to be sarcastic. Instead it sounded childish, he thought angrily.

'My husband is collecting his orders today.' It was impossible to see her face against the bright light. 'A friend told me this morning.'

'Your friend would do well to remember there's such a thing as security.'

'Some place their trust where it has value.' She turned slightly and he saw the quick movement of her small breasts. She was not so composed as she sounded.

She said abruptly, 'I really am worried. Your ship is returning to duty as before. It will be the last thing she does before . . .' she paused, 'before she is paid off for good.'

'I think everyone was expecting that.'

'But don't you see?' She got to her feet and moved restlessly to the table. 'It is Hector's last chance. If he tries to make more of it than it is, he'll never be allowed to continue in the Service.'

Standish looked at her steadily. 'Mrs. Dalziel, I don't know what you're really worried about. Your husband's reputation, or your own. How can I be expected to take anything seriously just because of some rumour handed to you by an *old friend*?'

She swung round, her mouth moist in the sunlight. 'Is Captain Jerram good enough to be considered reliable? Do you imagine I like talking with you like this?' She was shaking with either anger or emotion.

Jerram's name seemed to be everywhere. 'Perhaps he has his own axe to grind, too?'

'Captain Jerram is an old friend of the family. I have known him for years. Some think him conservative, even dull, but I have never known him to be dishonest. And he is genuinely worried Hector might do something rash. The situation out here is reaching a difficult phase. If anything were to go wrong it would rest hard on my husband.'

Standish stood up. 'Jerram was with your husband when he lost his ship. From what I've gathered recently it seems he didn't do much to speak up for him at the court martial.' He could not keep the coldness from his voice. 'Not for an old family friend, that is!'

She replied, 'Perhaps he took a greater risk by keeping silent.'

As Standish made towards the door she said quickly, 'Please wait. Perhaps I've not been completely frank. It's difficult.' She tried to relax as Standish sat down again. 'After the court martial and Hector's illness I tried, I really tried to help him. But he wanted another ship, and the more I attempted to dissuade him, the more he shut me off. He's like that, you know. Anything he dislikes or mistrusts he blocks off from his mind. Completely. As if it wasn't there. You'll find that out soon enough.'

She seemed to expect Standish to contest her words but then added, 'So as I told you, I asked someone to pull strings and he got his ship.' She plucked the front of her dress. 'I really did think he was better, a lot better by that time. So it's my fault in a way. I've made it worse for him. And for me.'

Standish eyed her calmly. 'I have to ask you. Are you going to leave your husband?'

For a moment he thought she was going to shout at him. Or cry.

Instead she replied very quietly, 'Yes. He doesn't want me. He doesn't even allow me to exist in his own mind.'

'I see. He got his ship and you were to get a divorce.' Standish looked away. 'Now you're worried because you're afraid he'll spoil his record at the last minute, be thrown out of the Service and become an embarrassment for you.'

When he looked at her again he saw that she had gone very pale.

'Don't set yourself up as a judge.'

'I've had some experience, Mrs. Dalziel.'

She did not seem to hear. 'I'm still young.' She faced him challengingly. 'And attractive. I have my own life to consider.' She tried to smile. 'I even thought of seducing you when we first met. Just to make you agree with me. But you were not quite what I expected.'

Standish stood up again. He wanted to go, and quickly.

'Your husband must decide his own future, as you must yours. But I can't stay here and listen to a one-sided attack on my own commanding officer. I've heard too much already.'

She said, 'He's not changed one bit. He thinks only of himself. You talk of his standards, but even they belong to other people. From books, from past leaders. Even his own background is what he believes it should have been.'

'If what you say is true, then why does he refuse help?'

She shook her head bitterly. 'His pride. His damned, bloody pride!'

'Then leave him that.' He reached the door. 'My loyalty is to him. It must be.'

She replied, 'Hector is lucky to have you. But it may prove otherwise in your favour.'

With something of her earlier composure she added, 'I will be flying to Rangoon shortly. And then to England.'

'I suppose there's someone waiting to hear your news?

Wanting to know if there will be another marriage, without scandal?'

She studied him coolly. 'You put it crudely. But I don't want to end my life married to the Navy. Or to a man who doesn't even begin to accept his own failings. I've made one mistake. I'll not do it again. This time I know what I'm doing.'

'Then I wish you luck.' He stood outside the door, his cap in his hands. 'You loved him once surely?'

She smiled. 'It was a long time ago. I've grown up since then.' She called after him, 'Take care.' Then she slammed the door.

All the way back to the ship he kept going over her words, sifting and examining, but with little to show for it. Viewed at a distance Sarah Dalziel's explanation and plan of action seemed cold-blooded to a point of callousness. Dalziel had been ill, but had been discharged as fit. All men, wounded, injured or merely shocked came back with some of the scars remaining. He knew that better than most.

He still could not see Jerram's part in it. Some old enmity perhaps which had come to a head after the collision. Or maybe his friendship for Sarah Dalziel's influential family had caught him somewhere in the middle.

But by the time he had reached the basin he had decided he would say nothing to Dalziel of the meeting. If he was still under some lingering strain then this last pressure might put the whole ship in jeopardy. It was unnerving how much he seemed to have in common with Dalziel. Both injured in their different ways, and each with his own marriage in ruins. He looked at the ship and recalled how she had been when he had first joined her. Whatever else had happened, Dalziel had certainly changed her, and for the better.

Irvine was waiting for him at the brow, his face a study of curiosity. 'Thank God you're back, Number One.'

'Trouble?'

Irvine shrugged. 'You could put it like that. The Old Man was aboard and informed us that the ship is being refloated this afternoon instead of tomorrow. It will be a real scramble, I shouldn't wonder.'

'Did he want to see me?'

Irvine looked at some point above Standish's left shoulder, his eyes half hidden by his fair lashes. 'He did bellow something to that effect. However, he's gone dashing off ashore again now and told me to pass the word that you're to take charge of operations if he's delayed.'

'I see. Is that all?'

'He seemed normal enough, if that's what you mean.' Irvine smiled gently. 'I did telephone you at Bates Hotel to tip you the wink. But you'd just left.'

Standish regarded him calmly. But it was impossible to find anything beyond Irvine's casual remark.

'In that case I'll have my lunch.'

Irvine nodded. 'My thought entirely.' He stiffened. 'My God, what is *that*?'

Standish turned and stared towards the top of the wall.

That was a long, semi-articulated truck upon which was cradled a gleaming fibre-glass launch. It was dark blue with a white gunwale, and painted on the bow was the name *Whizz-Kid*. It was about twenty-five feet long, and lashed just behind it on the rear of the truck were two giant outboard motors and a brightly-painted board which stated, 'Tang Fu Boating Enterprises for Happy Sailing.'

Irvine breathed out hard. 'The captain will just love that when he sees it cluttering up the jetty. I'll bet some local merchant has bribed a dockyard matey to allow him a berth for it.'

The truck halted with a jerk and the passenger door opened smartly.

Standish said quietly, 'It's the captain.'

Dalziel was already clambering over the truck, feeling the boat's hull as if searching for possible damage, and followed discreetly by the Chinese driver. Then he looked towards the ship and waved his stick in the air.

'Capital, eh?' He climbed down and hurried towards the brow.

Standish saluted. '*Our* boat, sir?'

'Naturally. Just the thing. Worth every penny.'

'Hornby's fund?' Standish looked at the boat, aware that several seamen had also crowded at the guardrails to watch.

'That's right.' Dalziel dabbed his forehead with a handkerchief. 'The only one any good in the whole place. Took a bit of bargaining, but I beat the fellow down to our price.'

Irvine asked, 'Is it for water-skiing?'

Dalziel looked at him coolly. 'Can be used for that. Yes, of course it can. I'll bet Hornby's mouth will water when he sees it.' He became serious again. 'They're opening the dock gates this afternoon. After lunch you can tell the Chief to send some mechanics to check over those outboards. The buffer can arrange a working party to sway the boat inboard.' He ran his eye critically along the upper deck. 'We'll shift the R.N.S.A. dinghy and put some more chocks there. Get some new tackles rigged so that we can drop her in the water at short notice.' He glanced at his watched and nodded abruptly. 'Right. Lunch.' Then he was gone.

Irvine said softly, 'Now I've seen everything.'

Standish crossed to the screen door, leaving him staring at the new boat.

Dalziel had said nothing about orders. No word of further disappointment or impatience. So perhaps Sarah Dalziel's fears had been empty after all. The boat seemed to point to the fact that the captain intended to keep his men happy by less dangerous methods from now on. That too seemed to prove she had misjudged him in several ways.

He hung up his cap and then saw Wills watching him by the wardroom door. Wills beamed, showing a line of uneven teeth.

'There's a letter for you, sir.' He bobbed his head as if to share Standish's pleasant surprise. 'Though you'd like to know right away like.'

Standish took it from him and then turned away. He did not recognize the handwriting at all.

He walked in the wardroom and slumped in a chair as Wills placed a large pink gin beside him on a table.

Another chair creaked and Quarrie asked, 'Letter from home, Number One? That makes a bloody change in this ship.'

Standish folded the letter blindly and thrust it inside his jacket.

'My wife was killed in a road accident. This is from her father.'

He was only dimly aware that the buzz of conversation around him had stopped as if to a signal. He knew Quarrie was staring at him, his rough features working with surprise and pity. He picked up the glass and swallowed the gin, almost choking as he tried to get it down.

Quarrie said thickly, 'Hell, I'm sorry. I really am.'

'Six weeks back. Nobody thought fit to tell me. Until now.' He gritted his teeth, trying to keep his voice level. 'The driver of the car was drunk. Went off the Kingston By-pass into a tree.'

Pigott crossed to the chair and placed his hand on Standish's shoulder. 'The dirty bastard! God, what a rotten thing to happen!'

Standish stood up very slowly, conscious of little but the fact that Pigott's voice had lapsed once again into broad Yorkshire. He said quietly, 'Mustn't think too badly of him. He'd apparently been living with her for months.' Then he pushed past them and strode out of the wardroom.

Pigott was the first to break the silence. 'He's been waiting for a letter since he came aboard. The poor bastard.'

Wishart bent down and picked up the discarded envelope. 'It's not even a private one. It's written on company note-paper.' He sounded shocked.

Rideout murmured, 'This won't do him any good at all.'

At that moment Irvine entered the wardroom and strode to the sideboard. 'Well, well, well! All brooding again?'

Quarrie turned savagely. 'Just for once, Pilot, keep your stupid blatherings to yourself, eh? I've just about had your supercilious, snotty-nosed wit up to here!' He drew one hand across his throat. 'So stow it!'

Irvine faltered and then shrugged. 'Point taken.' He signalled to Wills. 'Horse's neck. Large one.'

In his cabin Standish stood staring at himself in the mirror, his mind completely numb. She had had no intention of coming back to him. He would not have taken her if she had. But now she had gone, and like this. He was equally aware of a complete sense of finality.

He thought suddenly of the letter and withdrew it from his pocket. Her father must have scribbled it at his desk between business appointments. *Just to let you know.* Standish crumpled it into a ball and hurled it through the open scuttle. Her father seemed to be more accusing than sympathetic. As if it was his fault. He recalled the nightmare and wondered if Alison had been laughing at the moment of impact.

He sat on the edge of the bunk and lowered his head into his hands. *Just to let you know.* It was like an epitaph.

*   *   *

By the time the *Terrapin* had been refloated and warped clear of her dock to the loading jetty it was early evening and most of her weary company were ready to drop. On the jetty were piles of stores waiting to be restowed aboard, and there was something like a combined sigh of relief when the pipe came to clear up decks and secure until the following morning.

Dalziel walked slowly around the upper deck, examining and commenting as he went, pausing occasionally to single out a petty officer or rating and fire a brief question about his duty or how long he intended to remain in the Service.

Right forward in the eyes of the ship he paused at last and leaned against the guardrail, his eyes relaxed as he looked aft along the length of his command.

'Still a few lower deck lawyers and skates amongst them,' he remarked absently, 'but the rest are beginning to settle down as a ship's company. A single force instead of that damned shambles I inherited.' He paused until two seamen with hoses and scrubbers had moved away and then looked quickly at Standish who had followed him on his inspection. 'Heard about your news, Number One. Don't have to say how sorry I am about it. Bad show all round, but it may still turn out for the best.'

Standish watched Wishart on the jetty walking with Petty Officer Harris, the chief bosun's mate, as they checked the mooring wires and fenders along the port side.

He said flatly, 'You think so, sir?'

'Impossible to go through life without trouble.' Dalziel was watching him gravely. 'Your main disadvantage was to have so much all at once. I gather there was a delay before you were informed? Well, that is on the credit side in my opinion.' When Standish said nothing he added, 'Otherwise I'd have had to fly you back to U.K. to deal with all of it yourself. Nothing would have changed the situation for you, and the ship would have been denied a good officer when she most needed it.'

'It was a six weeks delay, sir. You were not even aboard at that time.' He shrugged. 'But you're probably right. It was too late for anything by then.'

'Good.' Dalziel nodded. 'I'm glad you see it like that. No sense in brooding.' He shook his head firmly. 'I shall not mention it again, unless you wish to speak about it.' He looked at his watch. 'They seem to have finished clearing up decks so have the hands piped aft. I wish to address them before we give shore leave for the night.'

Standish beckoned to a bosun's mate and then said, 'I'll not be sorry to get to sea again. Wherever it is.'

It was strange, he had spoken almost the same words that night in the bar with Irvine and the others, when he had been worrying more about Dalziel than himself. Now they had changed roles yet again. He was back to when he had first stepped aboard the *Terrapin*.

The tannoy boomed around the upper deck, halting the tired and grubby seamen even as they prepared to go below to their messes.

'Clear lower deck! All hands lay aft!'

Dalziel said, 'Just put 'em in the picture about our new orders.' He chuckled. 'Not that I know much myself yet. But it might buck them up a bit.'

Chief Petty Officer Corbin stepped heavily over an anchor cable and saluted. 'Lower deck cleared, sir.'

'Very well, Cox'n. I'll come now.' He frowned with sudden irritation as a car nosed its way between the piles of crates on the jetty and stopped in the shadow of a giant gantry. 'Blast him!'

Standish saw that it was Captain Jerram, pausing beside a smart marine driver to peer up at the frigate and at the assembled ratings on her quarterdeck.

Dalziel snapped, 'Well, he will have to wait. You see to him, Number One. If he must come popping up at inconvenient times then he'll have to *be* inconvenienced.'

Standish walked to the gangway and saluted as Jerram climbed slowly on to the deck. He looked tired and much older than his years.

'The commanding officer sends his respects, sir, but he had already arranged to address the ship's company.'

Jerram glanced aft and then said bleakly, 'So I see. I might as well take a look at the repairs while it's going on.'

Standish followed him up on to the forecastle and waited until Jerram had examined the newly painted plates.

Then Jerram said slowly, 'You're off to sea again tomorrow.' He seemed ill at ease and Standish guessed that he had heard of his meeting with Sarah Dalziel.

He replied, 'So I understand, sir.' Well, he would not give the first opening.

Jerram took out his blackened little pipe and peered at it without recognition. Then he said, 'Try and keep the ship out of trouble, eh? Otherwise the disposal people won't be able to. *give* her away, let alone sell her when the time comes.' He appeared to reach a decision. 'When a ship pays off, finally and completely, she leaves many memories behind. The same ship in a lifetime can break one man and bring distinction to another. But she leaves more than memories. Her people who are serving at the time when her commissioning pendant is hauled down are suddenly without purpose. They are scattered and must begin again elsewhere. You'll be affected like that.' He forced a smile, the effort adding to the criss-cross of tiny wrinkles across his face. 'Take young Irvine for instance. He'll be due for his half-stripe in a few months, and probably a command of his own. Of course he'll never stick it. His sort never do. Become a captain maybe, and then plunge off into politics or some family business.'

Standish waited. It was coming soon.

Jerram continued in the same tired voice, 'Then there's you of course. Quite a different matter altogether. You had some bad luck, but that's nothing new. This short appointment to the *Terrapin* could be the new start for you, too. And who knows, if all goes well there might be a command waiting again.'

Standish looked away, suddenly tired and sickened by the fencing.

'And what about the captain, sir? Are we discussing him, too? Or wouldn't that be quite the thing?'

Jerram looked surprised and then smiled. 'A bit touchy today, eh?'

Standish shook his head. 'Not that, sir. I'm just sick to death of hypocracy. I've had my share lately.' Now that he had started he could not stop. Even if he had wanted to. 'If you're dissatisfied with Commander Dalziel, why did you accept his appointment? And if you're confident in his ability to command this ship, then why doesn't everyone get off his back? When I held a command and I disliked what a subordinate was doing, I told him to his face.' He added harshly, 'I didn't try to make trouble through my admiral, nor did I get at him under his wife's apron strings!'

Jerram said coldly, 'I think we've both said enough.'

'And so do I, sir. In spite of what the captain may say, I know that I was partly to blame for the state this ship was in when he took command. And believe me, it was a pretty mess. Commander Dalziel's methods seemed a bit strange at first and there was plenty of resentment, not only on the lower deck either. Whatever else he has done, he has made this ship come alive again.'

Jerram walked to the gun mounting and switched on the speaker system. Dalziel's voice flooded around them, and Standish was suddenly reminded of that first time when he had spoken to his new command.

'...and so we are returning to Kuala Papan for further duty. I will not ask you to expect any miracles. After all, we can't hope to keep on snatching ships full of armed terrorists away from those who *should* have caught 'em, eh?'

Standish heard some of the assembled company laughing in the background, and when he looked at Jerram he saw him running his hand across his face as he muttered, 'Oh, the damned idiot!'

Dalziel was saying, 'We've shown them what we can do. You joined a fine service to serve your country, and if necessary die for it, although I think some had let that fact slip their minds until I came aboard.' There was more laughter, louder this time. 'When you go ashore tonight I want you to do something for me. Don't just think of yourselves as naval men, or even British naval men.' There was a pause and Standish could hear Jerram breathing heavily behind him. 'I want you to remember, each and every one of you, that *you are of the Terrapin*. When you go down into the town, I want you to swagger, for if the rest of the world is in ignorance, I want you to know that I personally am proud of you.'

Jerram switched off the speaker and looked at Standish.

'Would you ask the commanding officer to see me as soon as possible?'

There was a light step on the forecastle ladder and Dalziel said curtly, 'I'm here, sir.' He was breathing hard and the front and armpits of his shirt were dark with sweat.

Jerram seemed to have forgotten about Standish.

He said coldly, 'You are sailing to Kuala Papan to rejoin the squadron. This time there will be no independent actions, no further hit-and-miss operations without first obtaining permission.'

Dalziel eyed him calmly. 'I know that, sir. I was just telling our people about it.'

'I heard some of that.' Jerram walked to the guardrail and gripped it with both hands. 'You knew when you were speaking that your next duty is pure routine, an attached picket if you like. Yet you stood up there as if you were just going into the biggest battle ever visualized.' He swung round angrily. 'In God's name, man, what do you think you're doing?'

'My job, sir.' Dalziel was smiling, but his eyes were like flints. 'As I see it, and as I was taught, to keep the peace you must be prepared for war.' His tone hardened. 'Once already my ship has been edged into the sidelines. I accepted it. I even tried to see some sense in it.'

Jerram seemed to be speaking to himself. 'Your new assignment will involve little more than local patrol and survey. You may even be required for carrying stores for the squadron.'

Dalziel thrust his hands into his pockets. 'Carrying stores, sir?' He nodded. 'Then we'll carry stores better than any other damned ship in the command, never mind that collection of iron they call a squadron!'

Jerram straightened his back and looked round as several seamen appeared on the opposite ladder. Some of them were laughing and chattering.

Jerram said quietly, 'I hope they'll still be laughing in a month or two, that's all.'

He made for the ladder and Dalziel said, 'Thank you for coming, sir. Was there any specific reason?'

Jerram faced him. 'There was. I was going to warn you. But when I heard your speech I knew I was too late.'

Dalziel followed him to the gangway and saluted.

The car moved unsteadily across the jetty and vanished from view.

Standish said quietly, 'We'll be seeing him in Kuala Papan, I suppose?'

When Dalziel failed to reply he turned and saw that he had walked inboard and was touching the ship's bell with one hand, feeling it almost gently.

Standish followed him, and as Dalziel turned slightly felt something like shock.

Gone was the cool insolence Dalziel had used when defending his ship against Jerram. Or even the rabble-rousing attitude he had presented on the quarterdeck. Beneath the tan his face was pale, and his eyes were bright, even moist as he said between his teeth, 'The *bastard*. To use my ship to get at *me!* The *bastard!*'

Standish said, 'It was true what he said, I suppose. The new duty is just another job on the fringe.' He looked away as Dalziel wiped his eyes with the back of his hand, and added, 'All your visits to the C. in C.'s office were no good?'

Dalziel replied, 'I couldn't stand there on the quarterdeck and tell them that! My God, we've not been left much in this world, but pride is something they'll not take away. Not from me or my ship.'

When he spoke again his voice was almost normal. 'Gave you you a bad time, did he? Sorry to leave you with him, but I had to speak to our chaps before he could get his oar in.'

Standish followed him towards the screen door. 'I don't think he likes me very much.'

Dalziel paused with one foot poised above the coaming. 'Really? Then you must come and have a gin with me, Number One.'

Standish thought of the decanter and two beautiful glasses. He found too that he was able to smile again as he replied, 'I think I need it rather badly.'

Dalziel's voice was muffled as he ran lightly down the next ladder. 'Capital. Can't abide . . .'

The rest was lost as the tannoy boomed, 'Attention on the upper deck! Face aft and salute!'

It was sunset. The end of a very long day.

*   *   *

Standish paused on his way to the upper bridge and looked up at the sky. Even though it was still early morning the change in the weather was apparent, and the long banks of streaky cloud which moved purposefully overhead seemed vaguely menacing, their underbellies tinged with dull copper from the low sunlight.

Through the open door of the wheelhouse Corbin remarked, 'Looks as if the weather might break sir,' He was neither curious nor worried. It was just a statement of fact.

Standish nodded. 'Could be.'

It even felt different. Normally the morning was about the only time you could hope for any sort of freshness. Now the air was sultry and clammy, and his shirt already felt as if he had slept in it. From the frigate's single funnel came a steady trail of greasy smoke, streaming abeam towards the other ships, and through it Standish saw the masthead pendant standing out stiffly like a small lance. Yet the wind was without vitality, and only succeeded in making the air more humid.

Corbin grinned. 'Quite a string of defaulters for you, sir. Seems they had a good run ashore last night.'

Standish glanced down at the forecastle. The seamen were already taking the lashing from the mooring wires, and he guessed that some of them might soon have their hands gashed by stray barbs, their minds still too blurred from the night's drinking to take proper precautions.

He had seen and heard some of them staggering back aboard himself. Drunkenness amongst shore-going sailors was as common as the ships they served. But as they had reeled, or had been carried bodily up the brow by their companions, he had sensed something different. A kind of defiance. Or maybe resentment.

More than one had been in fights with sailors from other ships, and several had been escorted on board by shore patrols and the local police. Now, with the hot wind and the threatening sky it seemed as if the whole ship was suffering from one giant hangover.

'I'll weigh 'em off later, Swain.' Standish half listened to the subdued voices of the sea dutymen, the discreet stammer of morse from the radio room, while around and beneath him the bridge superstructure trembled like a nervous animal to the controlled beat of engines far below.

He saw Dalziel's head and shoulders framed against the sky and continued his climb to the upper bridge. There it seemed normal enough. Bosun's mates and the duty signalmen. The lookouts, and a rating mopping up spilled coffee from one of the gratings.

Irvine was leaning on the chart table, his chin propped on one hand while he compared his calculations against a small notebook.

Standish saluted. 'Ready to proceed, sir.'

Dalziel faced him, his eyes hidden by dark glasses. 'Well, we can't leave yet.' He sounded sharper than usual.

Perhaps he had good reason, Standish thought. Like the dark glasses, the captain's edginess was probably a leftover from his own private drinking.

Dalziel added, 'I've had a signal to take on some medical stores for Kuala Papan. And two passengers.'

At that moment a lorry ground on to the jetty and Dalziel snapped, 'Bosun's mate! Tell Petty Officer Harris to get those medical stores inboard at once!' He glared at the dull-eyed seaman. 'Well, go on, man, *chop bloody chop!*'

A car had followed the other vehicle, and Standish saw two figures emerge from it, accompanied by a Malay with several cases.

'Women passengers?' Standish looked at Dalziel. 'For us?'

'My God, Number One, that is a crashing glimpse of the obvious!' He relented slightly. 'As a matter of fact, I was asked to take them as far as Kuala Papan. They'll go on overland after that. I suppose that as we took 'em off the *Cornwallis* in the first place it's fair enough.' He cupped his hands and yelled, 'Tell that fool to get a move on, for heaven's sake! We're sailing this morning, not bloody Christmas!'

He removed the dark glasses and rubbed his eyes. 'They can

have my quarters. I'll be using the sea cabin anyway. We may be in for a blow.' He looked at the sky and blinked rapidly. 'But there's worse to come, a whole lot worse.'

Irvine said, 'No storm warnings yet, sir. I've checked.'

Dalziel turned and eyed him calmly. 'The day I rely on weather reports will *be the day*.'

He added irritably, 'Go and hurry those idlers, Number One. I'm not anxious to hang about here forever.'

Standish pushed between the hastily summoned working party and the mounting pile of wooden boxes by the brow. Rideout was there, peering and checking each one against a list, and seemed more hindrance than help.

The two passengers were standing hemmed in by busy seamen and their own luggage. Sub-Lieutenant Caley saw Standish approaching and showed his relief with a deep sigh.

'These here are the passengers, sir.'

'Are you going to sign for us?'

Standish turned and saw that the grey haired woman wearing a tweed costume so completely unsuitable for the climate was the one he thought of as 'the lady in the dressing gown.'

He smiled. 'Welcome back, Mrs. Penrath.' He faltered as he glanced at her companion. The girl was dressed in a plain khaki bush jacket and slacks, and stood quite still, as if waiting to be told where to go next.

She had jet black hair which he thought was probably very long, but as it was pulled tightly to the nape of her neck he could not be sure. She was, he imagined, in her early twenties, and had a grave sort of beauty which he had never seen before.

He realized he was staring and said quickly, 'I'm sorry. But the captain told me you were both from the *Cornwallis*'s passenger list.'

The girl dropped her eyes and said, 'Can't we be shown our cabin?' She had a low, almost husky voice, and was speaking to her companion and not to him.

Standish saw Mills and beckoned him over. 'Lead the way to the captain's quarters.'

Two seamen picked up the cases, and as the girl followed the steward through the screen door Standish felt the other woman's hand resting on his arm.

'You really didn't recognise her, did you?'

Something in her voice, pity or sadness, made him turn and look at her. It was then that it came back to him with the suddenness of an inner pain.

Perhaps when he had been looking at her his mind had recorded someone familiar, or something about her which had remained in his memory. Now, as the woman's words returned to him he wondered how he had been so stupid.

Without effort he could see the half-naked girl on the bunk, the absolute despair in her eyes as he had crashed into the cabin, the gun in his hand.

He asked quietly, 'Where is she going?'

She did not reply directly. 'Her name is Suzane Gail. She was working as a teacher at a mission school in Saigon and was en route for Thailand with the rest of us when we were attacked.' She looked away. 'She is going to get married there. The man is an engineer. Someone she met when he was working in Viet Nam.'

'He's a lucky chap.'

She squeezed his arm. 'I can tell you meant that. But you don't know much about women, do you?' She added heavily, 'She resigned her job, sold up everything for her new life. Now she won't look at any of the things she bought to wear. She seemed so happy, so full of hope. But perhaps it'll be all right once she's living an entirely different sort of life again.'

Standish saw Caley's men letting go the brow. 'You must excuse me now, Mrs. Penrath. We're about to get under way.'

Dalziel was waiting for him, his features working with obvious impatience. 'I thought you'd decided to go ashore.' Then he shot him a sideways glance. 'Put your foot in it again, did you?'

Standish watched the wind pushing the ship away from the jetty, the mooring wires tautening and sagging to the uncomfortable motion.

'Something like that.'

Dalziel grunted and then walked out on to the port wing.

'Ring down stand by on both engines.' To Burch he called, 'Request permission to get under way, Yeoman.'

Back came the reply. 'Affirmative, sir.'

Dalziel paused and then said slowly, 'The next time we come

here there will be no holding back.' He could have been speaking to himself. Or the ship. 'Security indeed. They know as much about security as my aunt does about strip-poker!'

In the very next breath he was himself again. 'Right, let go aft, and tell Caley that if he lets his people wrap a wire round the screws I *personally* will hang his entrails on the galley funnel!'

Half an hour later, with her seamen fallen in forward and aft, the *Terrapin* passed the last of the anchored warships and turned towards the widening channel. As her stem bit into the first uneasy roller she lifted above it with the contempt of a veteran, and like many of those who served her, she seemed glad to be leaving.

11 Storm Warning

LEADING Steward Wills touched Standish's outflung arm and then stepped back as he groaned and propped himself on one elbow.

'Mornin', sir. I brought yer tea.'

Standish rubbed his eyes and then stared while Wills' body appeared to tilt over at an impossible angle. Also, as sleep reluctantly cleared from his brain he noted a new sound, that of steady, torrential rain sluicing against the ship's side and the sealed scuttle above his bunk.

Wills grinned. 'Comin' on to blow a bit, sir. You'd better get yer breakfast soon, while you're in the mood like.' He chuckled unfeelingly. 'I just took tea to poor Mr. Hornby. 'E's spewing 'is guts out next door.'

Standish took the cup and swung his legs over the side of the bunk as Wills departed whistling cheerfully. All the previous afternoon the weather had become more threatening, the air growing more and more sultry and oppressive with each slow mile up the Malaysian shoreline.

Now, as he spread his feet on the carpet, he could feel the ship reeling heavily from beam to beam, her hull shaking at irregular intervals as one or other of her screws lifted free of the water. He had to switch on his light to shave himself, for through the salt-stained scuttle the sky seemed almost as dark as night. It was going to be a bad ending to the trip, he thought wearily.

A quarter of an hour later he entered the wardroom and noticed that the battered furniture had already been lashed firmly together by the messmen, and fiddles were rigged on sideboard and table.

Surprisingly the wardroom was empty, so pausing between rolls he crossed to his chair at the head of the table and poured himself a cup of black coffee. He saw Wills peering through the pantry hatch while behind him a messman struggled to arrange strips of bacon on a plate before they wriggled independently to the deck.

'Oh, good morning.'

Standish turned in his chair and saw the two passengers by the door, gauging the moment for the last open stretch of carpet.

'You must have a strong stomach, Mrs. Penrath.' Standish stood to help them the last few feet, his eyes moving quickly to the girl as she gripped the edge of the table. She was dressed in the same plain khaki jacket and slacks, and there were shadows beneath her eyes. As if she had not slept for days.

The older woman watched Wills as he glided skilfully round the table, the plates and cups balanced like a professional juggler.

'My stomach has never given me trouble. My legs are less reliable, however.'

Caley ambled through the door and slumped down in a chair, reaching for toast and coffee automatically as he muttered, 'Blowin' like bloody hell up top.' The toast hovered in mid-air as he said awkwardly, 'Sorry. Forgot meself.'

Mrs. Penrath smiled. 'My husband never apologizes for his language, so why should you?'

Standish leaned towards the girl and asked quietly, 'Have you ever been to Thailand before, Miss Gail?'

She did not lift her eyes from the plate but replied in the same low voice, 'Never. I expect I will get used to it.'

Caley said through a mouthful of buttered toast, 'Wouldn't do for me, Miss. Full of jabberin' wogs for the most part.'

Standish saw her fingers move below the table, watched as they locked into the material of her slacks so that her hand looked like a small frightened creature trying to escape.

He said, 'With better roads and communications coming along it'll be very different in a year or two.'

She lifted her head and looked at him for the first time. Her eyes were very large and unnaturally steady. 'Is there going to be a storm?'

'Later. But we should be safe and snug in a sheltered anchorage before it breaks.' He smiled. 'I'm only sorry your journey couldn't have been more pleasant.'

'Journey?' She dropped her glance again. 'Yes. I hadn't thought of it like that.' Her mouth quivered slightly. 'I...I've been trying to sleep.'

'Perhaps our doctor could help.' Standish saw Mrs. Penrath give him a quick glance, an almost imperceptible shake of the head. He added quickly, 'But once you get ashore you'll feel differently.'

Pigott appeared at the table and sighed gloomily. 'Waste of good food. Most of it'll go down the gash chute today.' He looked at Standish and raised his eyebrows. 'Never known you to be adrift for a watch before, Number One.' He shook his head. 'Must be the pleasant company, eh?'

Standish stared at him and then at the bulkhead clock. It was two minutes past eight. He lurched to his feet, aware of the others watching him. Pigott's amusement, the woman's concern, Caley's indifference. But in the girl's eyes he saw something else. It might have been a returning fear, or it could be a desperate unwillingness to break their small contact. The first she had shared with anyone since the *Cornwallis*.

He said, 'When you've had some food why not come up to the bridge?'

He watched her, saw the conflicting emotions of doubt and despair. Only her eyes gave anything away. It was like seeing someone trapped within a controlled and dangerously calm exterior. A face behind a sad and beautiful mask.

Then she said, 'Perhaps I will. I have never seen the sea like this. So restless.' She paused. 'So cruel.'

On deck the wind and rain met him with savage glee and almost knocked the breath from his body. As he struggled up the bridge ladders he felt the rain hammering on his hastily donned oilskin, heard it gurgling and cascading down the superstructure in a dozen eager waterfalls.

Irvine greeted him with a mock salute, his wind-reddened features set in a sarcastic smile.

'Good morning, *sir*. The forenoon watch is closed up, and

only I am left unrelieved and apparently abandoned.' He lurched against the gyro repeater as the hull lifted, paused and then slid heavily into a deep trough, the spray leaping above the screen in a solid sheet before hissing into the bridge with the rain.

· Standish thrust his head and shoulders beneath the hood above the chart table and peered at Irvine's neatly pencilled calculations.

He could almost feel Irvine's impatience as he said, 'Our E.T.A. at Kuala Papan is 1400 then.'

He stood up and tightened the collar around his neck. The oilskin was shining with the rain and blown spray, but inside it his body was already wet with sweat so that he felt clammy and unclean.

Irvine moved to the ladder. 'The Old Man has been up twice during my watch.' He scowled. 'Doesn't trust me maybe.'

'Well, you were wrong about the weather, Pilot.' Standish grinned. 'You should be more careful.'

Irvine was already on his way down. 'Wrong? Yes, me and three million others!'

Standish climbed on to the port gratings and peered abeam. The *Terrapin*'s course was five miles offshore, but it could have been a thousand. He watched the great sullen rollers, unbroken but nevertheless impressively large as they pushed slowly towards the ship's starboard quarter, lifting her, holding her for several long seconds before thrusting on towards the hidden shore while the hull slid down into the eager trough to await the next long roller, and the next. He remembered the girl's quiet words. *So restless. So cruel.* And for her it had been just that, he thought grimly. He tried not to allow his mind to dwell on it, to recall that first scream he had heard while he had crouched on the freighter's deck with Petty Officer Motts and the others.

He wondered if her husband-to-be knew what had happened. If he would be able to take her mind clear away from it. He felt suddenly uneasy. Perhaps he would not even try?

Dalziel coughed behind him and then said testily, 'Are you asleep or something?'

Standish saluted. 'Good morning, sir. I was watching the

rain.' Dalziel followed his glance as he added, 'It's shut off both sky and land. Like a steel fence.'

Dalziel grunted and took a pad from beneath his dripping coat. 'Not damn well surprised.' He held out the pad. 'From Hong Kong Radio. Typhoon of unknown intensity situated within fifty miles of latitude six north and longitude one hundred and nine east.'

Standish pursed his lips and peered at the signal pad which was already sodden with rain. 'Moving west to nor'-west. We should be clear of it.'

Dalziel looked at him distantly. 'Glass is falling a bit. But as you say, we should be at our *base* when it breaks.' He clutched the screen as the deck staggered and plunged beneath him. 'I told Wishart to make sure the new boat is securely lashed. I've made it his responsibility.'

Standish shrugged. 'The buffer could have done it, sir.'

'Ah, but the chief bosun's mate is not the gunnery officer, is he?' Dalziel nodded firmly. 'Wishart's department.'

Standish looked away, aware of that same uneasiness returning. 'I'm afraid I'm not with you, sir.'

Dalziel sighed. 'Came to me quite suddenly. We needed a fast, manoeuvrable boat, right? Our own was no good, and the replacement is a damn sight worse. So I decided to get one which would suit our requirements.' His eyes gleamed in the dull light. 'When we get more stable conditions I want the Chief's department to construct a machine gun mounting in the bows of the boat so that we can do something more useful next time.'

Standish closed his mouth tightly. In spite of the warnings and the barely concealed threats Dalziel was off again. He thought of the gossip on the lower deck, of water-skiing and scuba parties. Dalziel had never had any intention of using the boat for anything but an extension to his own arm. He must have thought of it from the start, even from the time he had discovered about Hornby's sports fund.

He shot him a quick glance, trying to picture him as his wife had described him. A bad time, she had said. But how badly had it really affected him?

Dalziel said, 'A good Browning in the bows and a couple of Stirlings for the crew and we'll have a real little terror, eh?'

The rain seemed to be getting heavier, the drumming roar of it across the bridge making it difficult to speak or hear.

Dalziel shouted, 'We'll shift the con down to the wheelhouse if it gets much worse.' He grinned, his face shining. 'It's when the rain stops altogether you've got to jump about.'

He touched the screen and added, 'Breakfast. Call me before you alter course.'

Standish returned to his thoughts, his body jammed against Dalziel's chair while he watched the rain's steady onslaught.

He recalled the quick headshake Mrs. Penrath had shown him, just as if she had been reading his mind, had known he was about to suggest some of Rideout's sleeping pills. Could it really be as bad as that?

A bosun's mate called, 'Visitor, sir.'

She was enveloped from chin to toe in a seaman's oilskin, and as she pulled herself round the side of the bridge towards him he felt the sudden urge to take hold of her. To reassure her in a way that he had found lacking for his own despair in the past.

She said, 'It looks wild.' Her face was already running with spray, but when he offered her a sou'wester she shook her head, shouting above the din, 'I'll be fine like this.'

It was true that the wind had brought back some colour to her face, and as she turned once more to stare at the oncoming rollers some of her hair whipped out from the coat's collar and floated defiantly against Standish's arm like a banner. As he watched her he thought she looked more child than girl, so that her inner suffering was made all the more unbearable.

He said, 'Get into the chair. The captain'll not be back for some while.'

She brushed some hair from her eyes. It was like soft black weed on a drowned face, he thought vaguely. The thought made him add, 'You look fine. You really do.'

She studied him gravely, her face suddenly relaxed and defenceless. 'Do I?'

Then she lifted herself on to the steel chair. At that moment the deck plunged dizzily to one side, and as she began to fall Standish jumped towards her and wrapped his arms around her shoulders. 'Easy! We'll soon have you seated more firmly.'

In those brief seconds they seemed isolated in an unreal world of rain and noise, with the swaying panorama of grey water beyond the screen like some crudely painted backdrop. Through the dripping oilskin he felt the softness of her body, and then as her hands darted out to push at his shoulders, the sudden tensing resistance, while in her eyes he saw both terror and revulsion.

She said, 'Please, don't touch me!' And as the ship's tilt continued she added wildly, 'Leave me alone, oh God, *leave me!*'

The ship returned reluctantly to an upright position, the water swilling beneath the gratings like a culvert.

Standish said slowly, 'I'm sorry. Believe me.'

She did not look at him, but against the salt-stained glass he saw her profile etched like that of a perfect statue. Perfect but lifeless. Her eyes were half closed, and the rain across her skin made it appear as if she had at last found the tears which would not come.

He heard himself say, 'It would be better if you went below. The rain is getting worse, and we shall clear the upper bridge shortly.'

She turned and looked at him. 'Yes. I . . . I'm sorry about just now.' Her hands moved vaguely across the front of her coat. 'It was not your fault.'

He stood back as she slid from the chair, wanting to steady her yet afraid of what might happen. 'Mrs. Penrath told me I don't know much about women.' He felt his mouth trying to smile. 'She was right. More than she realised.'

The girl moved slowly towards the ladder, her hair plastered against the oilskin. She said, 'I just need to be . . .' But the rest was lost in the rising chorus of wind and rain.

He waited until she had reached the signal deck and then said, 'Go with her, Spinks. Just in case.'

The bosun's mate eyed him curiously. 'She sick, sir?'

He turned back to the screen. 'Not sick.' He waited until the man's feet clattered on the ladder and then added to himself, 'That girl is terrified. But where is the cure?'

Then he picked up a telephone handset and waited for Dalziel to speak.

'Ready to alter course, sir.' He replaced it and crossed to the opposite side. Alter course towards the shore. To Kuala Papan and the end of more than a journey.

The thought of her leaving, walking from the ship and his life moved him more than he would have believed credible. Maybe she was just another escape, a momentary distraction from his own uncertainty. He sighed and returned to the radar repeater and its small enclosed world of dancing reflections.

He found himself wondering what the girl's proposed husband was like, and discovered at the same time that he was filled with envy.

Dalziel sloshed across the bridge and squinted at the compass. Then he said, 'Bring her round. But pass the word first. Don't want the rest of our crockery broken up, do we?' He watched Standish thoughtfully and added, 'I'd leave it alone if I were you. There's enough trouble in the world without begging for it.'

Standish looked at him in silence. Two men separated by a patch of rainsoaked steel. What did they know of each other?

He replied flatly, 'New course is two-nine-zero, sir.'

Dalziel shrugged. 'Carry on then.'

Resentfully the *Terrapin* turned her stern into the following sea, her twin screws churning to retain a grip, a hold over her constant enemy.

Below in the wardroom Mrs. Penarth still sat at the deserted table, an untouched cup of coffee vibrating in the fiddles, her eyes on the door as the girl came inside.

'Are you all right, Suzane?'

The girl had discarded the oilskin and her hair hung around her shoulders, damp and unmoving.

She replied, 'Cold.' Then she asked quietly, 'Do you think he'll still want me?'

The older woman left the table and reached her as she began to shake uncontrollably, her body pressed against hers as the sobs were muffled in the thick tweed coat.

Mrs. Penarth did not reply, for she knew the girl was no longer listening. And she was thinking of her own youth and the way her husband had looked at her all those years ago when she had been released from the Japanese prison camp. It had taken a long while, but for them it had perhaps been that much easier. They had known the same suffering, the same torment of separation. She squeezed the girl's shoulders more tightly. Something must have happened up on the bridge, she thought.

A careless word or a curious glance. Eyes which asked, what was it like? Or, how did you feel?

Then she remembered Standish and knew the answer. In other circumstances he might have been good for Suzane, she decided. He was quiet and understanding, with that touch of outward recklessness which was always appealing.

Wills entered the wardroom and began to gather up the empty plates as the two women stepped into the passageway, their bodies angled to the deck as the ship continued to turn towards the shore. He had only three more years to do in the Service. After that he would get himself a little pub in Hampshire. Somewhere between Pompey and Southampton. His eyes were distant as he clattered between the table and his pantry hatch. A pub with a nice snack counter for holidaymakers and matelots on a run ashore. No more officers, no more clapped out ships like this one where you never knew if you were on your arse or your elbow. Just a nice, friendly pub.

Lieutenant Hornby lurched through the door, a handkerchief clapped over his mouth. His face was the colour of porridge.

He managed to gasp, 'Does someone want me, Wills?'

'Yessir. Call from the bridge. The chartroom lights have blown and the captain's yellin' blue murder.' Wills grinned. 'Bit rough up top, sir.' He watched Hornby reel wretchedly through the door. Bloody officers, he thought. Always in trouble of one sort or another.

*   *   *

Dalziel prowled restlessly from one side of the wheelhouse to the other as under reduced speed the *Terrapin* crept slowly beneath the blurred outline of the nearest headland. The atmosphere in the sealed wheelhouse was like a Turkish bath, with the sides running in condensation, the air damp and heavy, and made worse by the press of figures and wet clothing.

Standish raised his glasses and held them against a clearview screen to look at the headland. How different from the other visit, he thought. Now it was just a dull hump which changed size and shape in each fast moving eddy of rain. But the rain seemed less heavy, and almost before they had reached the first outflung spur of land the motion had been reduced to a steep offshore swell.

Dalziel muttered, 'Better tell Wishart to prepare a second anchor in case it gets any worse. These storms usually dissipate themselves once they reach land, but you can never be certain.' He turned his head. 'Port ten.' Then he crossed to the other side again. 'Midships. Steady.'

Corbin was on the wheel, his heavy face glowing in the lighted compass repeater. On either side of him the telegraphs-men and bosun's mates stood like statues, their eyes shining faintly in the reflected glare from the scuttles. Through an open door at the rear came the almost continuous murmur of morse and static, accompanied by a monotonous bleep from the echo sounder, as like a blind man with a stick the ship felt her way towards the deepest part of the inlet.

Standish could see the anchor party already on the forecastle, their oilskins shining in the grey light, their bodies hunched against the pounding rain. The rest of the inlet was hidden in the downpour, the water seething under the onslaught as if boiling from some submarine furnace.

'Down two turns.' Dalziel wiped his forehead with his sleeve. 'Keep her steady now, Cox'n.'

The revolution counter tinkled noisily, and Standish imagined Quarrie on his footplate, watching the dials, feeling the power all around his private domain.

Further and further along the wedge of headland and the vague slope of the first hill beyond, with Dalziel passing his orders and the acknowledgments coming back regularly to mark every part of the final approach.

Dalziel said, 'From the sound of the signals it seems as if every damn ship has run for shelter. God help the native craft caught out at times like these.'

Irvine said, 'Half a cable, sir.'

'Very well.' Dalziel looked at Standish. 'Go down and see Wishart, will you. He's probably bothered by all this.'

Standish pulled on a dripping oilskin and groped through the door and down the ladder to the deck. As he squinted up against the rain he noticed that the bridge and funnel were shining like grey glass, while the dark clouds seemed to be skimming just a few inches above the masthead. The illusion added to the sensation of being enclosed, pressed down by the weight of the weather.

He found Wishart gripping the guardrail, his eyes slitted as he peered aft at the bridge. The men in his anchor party stood around like strangers, their faces sore and wet while they waited in miserable silence.

'Not long now, Sub.' He had to shout. 'Get the second hook ready to drop in case we start dragging.'

Wishart nodded and turned as his leading seaman looked up at him, the telephone handset cradled beneath his oilskin.

'Stand by, sir.'

The deck trembled as the engines churned briefly astern.

'Let go!'

Standish watched the cable jerking and banging through the hawsepipe, the chipped paint and rust clinging to ship and men as if from a spray.

The leading seaman looked at his telephone and wrinkled his nose.

Wishart saw him, in spite of watching the outgoing cable. 'What's wrong, Neal?'

The man grinned. 'Thought the wire was burnin', sir. But it's all right.' He sniffed again and added uncertainly, 'But I'm sure I smelt somethin'.'

Half hidden by the rain the nearest land appeared to swing slightly towards them, as with her screws halted the ship took her first pull on the cable.

Wishart hung over the stemhead and peered down at the heavy links and the small tiderace of water which surged around them.

'Inform the bridge, Neal.' Then he stiffened and shouted, 'My God, I saw flames!'

Standish looked across his pointing arm and watched in silence as a freak gap in the rain laid bare part of the inlet for just a few moments. At the far end he could see great shooting tongues of flame, falling and rising in spite of the rain, while all around them the land seemed to be steaming like a cauldron, so that the inland hills were completely hidden.

He snapped, 'Stay here and keep watch, Sub. I'm going to the bridge.'

When he reached the ladder he saw Dalziel already climbing

back to the upper bridge, his shirt and legs soaked through, his glasses banging against the ladder as he hauled himself to the top.

As Standish arrived on the gratings he said, 'Saw it too, did you? The whole of that bloody village must be ablaze.' He lowered his glasses and added, 'The rain's blotted it out again.' He stood looking at the deserted bridge and then said, 'There don't seem to be any of Jerram's M.L.'s here, or any other damn ship for that matter.'

Standish waited. He could see the emotions crossing Dalziel's face like the pages in a book. He just needed to get his appraisal sorted out and things would start happening.

Dalziel nodded. 'Chance to test the new boat. Have the buffer sway her out now. Take an armed party and the doctor with you and find out just what in hell's name is going on.' He walked ahead of Standish to the chartroom, his shoes squeaking on the wet plates. 'Pity we haven't had time to fit up the machine gun, still, it can't be helped.'

They found Irvine shaking drips from a chart, and Dalziel snapped, 'Tell the W/T office to find out if any other vessels of the squadron are in the vicinity. No panic, just a routine check.' He rubbed his chin impatiently as Standish telephoned his orders to the lowering party. Then he continued, 'No fire would spread like that by accident. Not in this downpour.' He looked at Standish and said slowly, 'Trouble. That's what it means.'

Petty Officer Motts waited beside the break in the guardrail as Standish hurried down the side deck towards him. The sight of him brought back several stark pictures all at once. The towering side of the freighter's hull, the patches of rust, and the outflung leg of a dead seaman. And the girl. She was always there to remind him.

He said, 'Boat in the water?'

'Aye, aye, sir.' Motts handed him a pistol belt. 'The engine room have provided a good mechanic to keep an eye on those flamin' outboards. Don't fancy swimmin' back to the ship in this lot.'

Standish looked down at the pitching hull alongside. He had almost forgotten about it, and now seeing the bright paintwork and daintily varnished thwarts he was conscious of the grim unreality of the whole situation.

He said, 'Better than the other motor boat, Motts.' He jerked his thumb to the tired looking hull hanging dejectedly in its davits. 'With that you'd probably have to swim both ways.'

He swung his leg over the side, his mind fighting the clogging battering of rain across his head and shoulders.

In the boat his small party were waiting for him. There were no smiles this time, no jokes either. They gripped their Stirlings and peered towards the land, their faces set and grim.

He called, 'Be ready, lads. No shooting unless I pass the word. It may be nothing at all . . .' He swung round as Rideout fell down beside him, his medical satchel dangling from one shoulder.

'And about time!' He thrust the doctor into the crowded cockpit. 'Start up!' He saw the mechanic was Petty Officer Barrett, one of Quarrie's most valued and experienced men. The realisation that Quarrie cared that much steaded him and he said, 'We'll see what this fancy *Whizz-Kid* can do!'

Even the mechanic was surprised at the startling speed with which they thrust away from the frigate's side. There was more vibration than noise, and several of the seamen almost fell into the bottom of the boat as the bows lifted steeply to the twin motors.

Rideout shouted, 'What do you expect to find?'

Standish straddled his legs and tried to see beyond the rain. 'Not the Planters' Bar, that's for sure, Doc!'

Rideout clutched his satchel against his chest and gasped. 'God, I wish I felt as calm as you look.'

Standish grinned down at him, tasting the salt and rain in his teeth. You don't know the half of it, my friend. Aloud he shouted, 'Well, you must admit it's better than a V.D. clinic!'

Motts, who was crouching in the bows like a shining gargoyle, turned his head and yelled, 'Hard astarboard! Quick, for Christ's sake!'

Barrett threw his weight on the tiller and the hull slewed round with the violent ease of a skimming dish.

As the spray lifted and dashed against the crouching men Standish saw what looked like a tall beacon swaying down the port side, a great arrowhead of shining, blackened wood.

Barrett yelled hoarsely, 'It's the forepart of a boat, sir!'

Standish nodded. 'Go round it again, slower this time.'

As they circled the swaying shape once more Standish had no doubt where he had seen it before. There was even half of a number still showing on the scorched and charred planking.

Rideout seized his arm, his face white as he watched the drifting wreck. 'What is it?'

Standish gestured to the mechanic to continue towards the shore before replying.

'One of Captain Jerram's patrol boats, or part of it.'

He saw the young signalman who had been detailed for the landing party staring up at him. The walkie-talkie on his back beneath his oilskin made him grotesque and bowed, but he tried to smile as Standish said, 'Call up the ship, Bunts. Tell them what we've just seen.'

The boy hesitated and Standish added, 'In your own words. You might be making a bit of history today, so don't stammer, eh?'

Motts looked at him above the signalman's back and nodded. 'Get 'is name in the Sunday papers!'

As they pounded nearer to the village they could see the darting flames more clearly and almost without a break. Fanned by the wind and occasionally controlled by rain they leapt and reeled in several directions at once. There was a stench of burned wood and smoke, and mingled with the downpour's noise they could hear the hissing roar of the fire itself.

The signalman looked up suddenly. 'Message, sir. The captain is lowering the whaler and sending some more hands to help.'

Standish unbuttoned the top of his pistol holster and touched the metal inside. It felt warm. As if it had already been fired.

'It'll be some time before they can pull a boat across here.' He watched the paler outline of the jetty sweeping towards him through the rain. 'So watch out and be ready to take cover.'

Then he clambered along the boat and stood beside Motts, his eyes on the jetty.

A seaman cursed. 'Hell, there's no bleedin' boathook, sir!'

Motts swung on him. 'Then use yer teeth!'

He sounded unusually edgy, Standish thought. But then, like

himself, Motts was probably wondering what was waiting for them, or what they were all doing here anyway.

The boat lurched against the rough jetty and Standish jumped bodily on to a sagging beam of timber below the top edge.

Somewhere in the village a building must have collapsed, for as he pulled himself over the wet stonework he saw a great cloud of orange sparks being whirled up into the rain.

Beside him Motts said harshly, 'Gawd, it's like Belfast on a Saturday night!'

Then for the first time Standish heard firing, vague and indistinct above the other sounds, but there was no mistaking the sharp rattle of small arms.

He said, 'Let's get it over with.' Then as the others stared up at him he got to his feet and began to walk along the deserted jetty.

12 At the Captain's Discretion

At the end of the jetty Standish paused to get his bearings while the rest of his party took cover against the remaining wall of what had once been a storeshed. Most of the building had been burned to the ground, the charred beams shining in the dull light like great black teeth. Beyond the one stone wall the nearby huts were still steaming under the rain, and he guessed that this part of the village had been attacked first. Some had been so thoroughly burned that they were little more than dark rectangles of wet ashes spaced out along the roadway.

Motts said, 'The fishin' boats 'ave been gutted too, sir.' He raised his Stirling sharply and peered towards the far end of the village where the flames still showed as strongly as before. 'More shootin'. Who the blazes is doing it?'

Standish looked round at his men. Apart from Motts it seemed unlikely that any had had experience of land fighting. To take them blindly into an unknown place where they might at any minute be attacked by guerillas or bandits would be sheer murder. And yet the very sound of gunfire told him he must do something, and quickly.

He beckoned to the signalman. 'Call up the ship again. Tell them we're going to move along the waterfront. Explain that we have heard shooting.' He saw the boy nod and then added quietly to Motts, 'I imagine the villagers have hidden in the jungle.'

He waited until the signalman had finished his message and then walked slowly down the slope and on to the road, which by now was little better than a yellow bog. He found time to wonder why the Japs had not brought their fine inland road right down here to the jetty. Perhaps the war had ended too soon.

Motts hissed, 'In that 'ut, sir! Look!'

But Standish had already seen it. A quick flash and nothing more. Like that moment on the *Cornwallis*'s bridge when he had seen someone calmly lighting a cigarette. He could feel the hair rising on his neck as he said, 'Spread the lads down the other side of the road.' He wanted to shout to make himself heard above the drumming rain. 'I'll take a closer look.'

Motts looked at him calmly, his face streaked with mud from the track. 'I'll do it, sir. I've 'ad some of this before, when I was in Korea.' He grinned. 'You can do the explainin' if I gets me 'ead shot off.' He did not wait for an argument but cocked his Stirling and walked almost casually towards the hut.

The roof had gone, and the door was hanging from its hinges, charred and pitted with holes. Another store hut, Standish thought. It had been a well planned raid right enough.

Outside the hut Motts stooped to pick up a large piece of stone which had fallen from the wall, and after a second's hesitation lobbed it over the roof to fall into the burned-out shell on the opposite side. Even as Standish heard a gasp of surprise he saw Motts leap forward, smashing down the door with his boot while he hurled himself bodily through the opening, the Stirling level with his stomach.

But there was no firing, nor did Motts fall back into the mud.

After a moment he called, 'It's okay, sir.'

Standish pushed two seamen towards the opposite end of the hut. 'Cover the road.' Then he ran through the blackened doorway and saw Motts kneeling beside a massive figure who was propped against the opposite wall, his clothes filthy from wet ashes and mud, his eyes fixed on Motts as if he could no longer trust his senses.

He was fat and quite bald, and when he spoke Standish guessed him to be Australian.

'Jesus! I nearly died just then, mates!'

Motts said, "E's been shot in the leg.'

'Get the doctor.' Standish knelt beside the big man and asked quietly, 'We're off a ship anchored below the headland. What happened here?' He saw the strain and stubborn resistance starting to give way to shock and added, 'Everything you know. There's not much time.'

'Happened this morning. I'm an engineer from the Salik mining village, 'bout twenty miles inland from here.' He swallowed hard as Rideout entered the hut and began to open his bag. 'We were expecting a storeship to come, so I brought a convoy of trucks good an' early because of the bloody rain. You can get bogged down in seconds, mate, if you're caught out in it.' He gritted his teeth as Rideout started to slit open his torn trousers. He continued heavily, 'The bastards ambushed us from behind. Blew the one good bridge, an' when we high-tailed it for this village they were waiting for us in strength.'

Standish asked, 'Didn't you have any escorts?'

'Sure. A troop of Malay police. But nobody was bothered. There's an ambush every day out here. Anyway, we all knew there was a patrol boat anchored off the village. It was to keep an eye on the unloading when our supplies arrived.'

He gasped, and Rideout murmured, 'Sorry, old chap, but it's necessary.'

Standish saw the sweat pouring through the grime on the man's face and added quickly, 'And then?'

'Then?' He lay back against the wall and closed his eyes. 'There was one bloody great bang. For a moment I thought the boat's magazine had gone up, or maybe some joker had landed a mortar bomb on her. But I was in the army in the last lot. I've heard more mortars than most blokes have had hot dinners. It was sharper and louder, and the boat just blew apart.' He sighed. 'I dunno what happened much after that. My truck was on fire and so was the village. Two Malay troopers got me in here and they went off somewhere. I've just been sitting and waiting. Had my last cigarette, or was about to when that rock nearly smashed my brains in.'

Rideout said, 'I've given him a shot to make him sleep. I can't remove the bullet amongst all this filth.'

The Australian eyed him dully and grinned. 'Gawd help you if you'd been in the infantry, mate!'

Standish stood up and looked at Motts. 'Any suggestions?'

The petty officer kicked at the slush around his boots. 'Well planned again, sir. But I think the ambush was an accident.'

Standish frowned. 'Go on.'

Motts walked to the doorway and waved his Stirling towards the jetty. 'These guerillas, terrorists, or whatever they call their bleedin' selves, must 'ave known the road convoy was empty if they always come 'ere early to dodge the rain, an' my guess is that these other jokers were caught on the 'op.'

Standish rubbed his chin. 'It makes sense. Once they saw the convoy coming they had to hold it until they had done what they wanted.' He was thinking aloud. 'The patrol boat was blasted apart.' He looked at Motts again. 'A rocket?'

''S'my guess too, sir. The main force of attackers didn't come down the road at all. They come right 'ere direct. From the sea!'

Standish watched Rideout fixing a dressing over the Australian's wound. The man was breathing heavily and completely unconscious.

He said, 'Get P.O. Barrett from the boat, Doc. He'll give you a hand to make a stretcher and carry this chap along the jetty.'

Rideout crouched on the floor, seemingly oblivious to the mud on his legs and buttocks. In the grey light his face looked deathly pale.

'What are you going to do?'

'Must try and find out if there's anyone else alive. You tell the party in the whaler, when it gets here.'

He turned to leave but Rideout called hesitantly, 'God, but I was bloody scared.' He said it so calmly that Standish smiled.

'As Pilot would say. You and three million others!'

Then he followed Motts on to the road. 'If only this rain would stop.' But Motts did not hear him, and as they struggled through the mud and fallen huts he knew the others were following. They had all read of it. Even seen it on television. But this was happening right here and now, and they were in it.

'Sir!' A seaman halted and pointed into a ditch. It was almost overflowing with yellow water, but not enough to hide a man's feet which had caught in an outflung branch. They were tied together. And further along the bank was another corpse, a woman this time, with half of her face shot away. A cooking pot lay nearby, mute witness to the actual moment of murder.

Standish heard someone being sick, but could feel nothing

himself but a cold, unreasoning rage. He thought of the butchered woman in the master's cabin aboard the *Cornwallis*, the deliberate, senseless savagery.

He said harshly, 'Keep going. And watch the trees!'

All the trucks were burned out, too. Some still in line where they had stopped. Others upended, as if their drivers had died behind their wheels under crossfire. The seamen plodded past them, their eyes averted from the charred, unrecognizable things which crouched obscenely in the burned out cabs, or lay in the rain and the mud.

A Malay policeman was crumpled against an empty cask, his uniform soaked but without a trace of blood on it. He stared at them as they passed, his eyes bulging from a contorted face, his tongue swollen to twice its size. He had been garrotted with a piece of wire. It had been done very slowly, Standish thought.

Feet splattered in the roadway and two more Malay troopers almost ran headlong into the sailors before they saw them. They collapsed, gasping and retching while Motts tried to reassure them.

He said, 'This one speaks English, sir.' 'E says that the guerillas 'ave gone. These two 'ave bin tryin' to pick off some stragglers.'

Standish saw Motts' expression and knew he shared his own thoughts. Neither of the troopers had any weapons, and both were terrified out of their wits. They had been running, not fighting.

But the gunfire had stopped, and apart from the rain and the ripple of water in the gully beside the road they seemed to have the place to themselves.

Motts said, 'I suppose the villagers'll come back soon. Maybe they're used to this sort of thing.' He shook his head. 'Poor bastards.'

A man shouted, 'More of our lads comin', sir!' He sounded cracked with relief.

Standish turned and saw them sloshing along the track and said, 'So he's come himself.' It was the captain.

Dalziel hurried through the mud, his head swinging from side to side as he studied the burned out village and the charred corpses around him. Standish saw that he was carrying his black stick, and across his shoulder was slung the sporting rifle he had seen in his cabin.

Dalziel said tersely, 'No point in going on. Never catch up with 'em in this rain.' He sniffed the air like a terrier. 'I've been on to the authorites of course. No sense from them. It appears there have been raids and ambushes in all directions. One ambush was only thirty-seven miles from the Kedah state capital, Alor Star.' He waved his stick. 'But it's going on all over the northern territories, just as I predicted. The communist guerillas will do what they can to keep the defence forces spread out over wider and wider areas.' He stopped to peer at one of the Malays. 'This one seems to understand what I am saying.'

Motts nodded, 'That's right, sir.'

Dalziel glared at him. 'I see. Useless, was he?'

Standish said quietly, 'Frightened.'

Dalziel looked at him curiously. 'This isn't doing much good, is it?' Then he unslung the rifle and removed the waterproof cover from its muzzle. Almost casually he asked, 'Tell me what you saw?' He lowered the rifle and prodded the trooper's foot with it. 'You must have seen something, eh?'

'We shoot. We lose officer.' The man watched the gun barrel with staring concentration.

'You *bloody liar!*' Dalziel pointed the rifle at the nearest huts. 'All these men killed, and the village burned! You've no weapons, and I suspect you've been hiding right here since the fight started.' He worked the bolt deliberately. 'I'll give you five seconds to remember.'

Standish stepped forward. 'Did you see a ship?' He was sickened by the man's fear. 'Any sort of ship?'

The rifle moved very slightly towards the man's stomach and Dalziel said coldly, 'He'll say he saw anything now. I'll not waste any more time on *him*.'

'Please!' The man rolled over in the mud, his eyes round with terror. 'I am corporal. I not coward.' He sobbed and then added, 'There was a boat, I think.' He closed his eyes, the effort of remembering making him wrinkle his face like an old man. 'There was the explosion. It was after that I saw it.'

Dalziel nodded. 'Better. Much better.'

Standish asked, 'What size?'

'I not know.' The man opened his eyes and looked at the rifle. 'But not big. I am sure of that.'

Dalziel pulled the trigger and the rifle clicked harmlessly. He said, 'Get everyone back to the ship. We'll tow the whaler with the launch.' He glanced quickly at the dripping trees above the village. 'No sense in wasting time. We'll take these two and the Australian with us. Might get something out of them later, eh?'

Standish looked at him as the men started to move back along the track towards the jetty. 'What are you going to do, sir?'

'I've been calling up damn near everyone.' Dalziel strode after the seamen. 'The coastal patrols are scattered and in shelter from the storm. The army and police have all their work cut out as it is.' He smiled grimly. 'No one knows where the hell Jerram is. Probably cut off on some waterlogged airfield, blast him.'

'Did you reach the admiral, sir?'

'Briefly. He has given me the job of sorting this out.' He chuckled. 'The usual rider of course. *Use your own discretion.* In other words, if I make a hash of it I carry the can. If not, someone else will have a great and passionate yearning for all the credit.' It seemed to amuse him. 'I remember being told that they don't want another Viet Nam on their hands. Well, they're getting it, whether they damn well like it or not.'

Standish said, 'You intend to go after that boat?'

'Correct.'

They had reached the jetty and stopped to watch the seamen helping the two Malays into the whaler. Compared with the sailors they looked almost untouched. Motts and the others were covered from head to foot in mud, their eyes showing white through the layers of filth.

Dalziel added, 'We can still get ahead of that damn storm. If we wait at anchor we could be penned in for days.' He looked at Standish and smiled gently. 'Well?'

Standish shrugged. 'If there *was* a boat it must have gone north along the coast. South or east and we'd have seen it on our radar. We wouldn't have known what it was, but we'd have seen it all right.'

'Now you're getting the picture. So let's get weaving, shall we?'

By the time they had churned clear of the jetty all the fires were out, and Standish wondered if even now some of the villagers were peering down at the ruins from the protective jungle. Also, how many others lay dead, and whether the woman with the cooking pot had understood the need of her own murder before she had been shot down.

He noticed that the motion was heavier again, but the *Whizz-Kid* seemed well able to tow the pulling boat as they bounced through the drenching rain.

When he looked inboard again he saw that the seamen were very quiet, their eyes dull and unseeing, as if they were reliving those moments in the village. He found he was suddenly grateful. They were all here. They had survived. It was strange to look back and realize that when he had first climbed from the boat it had been with a kind of fatalistic bravado. A sort of madness. As he had walked along the open jetty he had expected to feel the crashing agony of a bullet, just as he had known that if he had waited any longer he would probably have turned back.

The ship loomed over them, and he followed Dalziel up the dangling ladder, his mind recording the shouts of welcome and concern, the helping hands, and an immediate bark of orders for the boats to be hoisted.

Dalziel looked up at the sky and nodded. 'Stations for getting under way immediately.'

Standish watched him gravely. 'Would you have shot that Malay?'

Dalziel paused in his stride and smiled. 'Would you have stopped me?' He hurried away without waiting for an answer. Irvine shot past on his way to the bridge. He saw Standish and grimaced. 'Another storm warning. It's backed a bit more.' He smiled. 'What with one thing and another I forgot to welcome you aboard.' Then he too dashed towards the bridge ladder.

Motts took Standish's pistol belt and muttered, 'I'll get it cleaned up a bit, sir.' He looked at the rain. 'Personally I'd rather be at sea than stuck in 'ere. You've room to run then.'

Standish watch him walk aft, his body swaying easily to the uneven motion. A good petty officer. A man who had not even hesitated when the time had come to go for the hut and whatever lay inside.

He saw Wills lurking by a screen door and said, 'Fetch my pipe and pouch from my cabin, will you.' Strange he had forgotten to take them with him. Had he really expected to die?

Wills said, 'The ladies'll be stayin' for a bit longer then?'

'Looks like it.' He added quickly, 'No need to tell them too much about the village. They'll find out soon enough.'

He climbed the ladder to the forecastle and walked stiffly towards the bows.

The men of the anchor party watched him in silence, and even Wishart seemed unnaturally subdued. He said awkwardly, 'You look all in.'

Standish watched the mechanic by the capstan and then looked up at Dalziel's outline on the open bridge. 'Thanks.'

The capstan gave a metallic grunt, and link by link the cable began to jerk back through the hawsepipe. Standish frowned. How long had the anchor been down? An hour, or was it three? His mind refused to remember.

Several men coughed as a down-draught of wind brought a cloud of greasy funnel smoke swirling forward over the bows. It was going to be rough beyond the headland, he thought.

Wishart yelled, 'Up and down!'

When the anchor finally tore itself free from the bottom the ship seemed to stagger sideways before rudder and screws brought her back under command. Even so, it took Dalziel another fifteen minutes to turn her towards the open sea, the hull shaking wildly as the engines were put ahead and astern with hardly a pause while the stem edged round. Finally the broken water was spread before them in a criss-cross of leaping whitecaps, and Standish knew that whatever else happened, they would not be able to return until after the storm had spent itself along the shore.

He said, 'Make sure you've secured the anchor, Sub. Don't want it to stove the plates in, do we?'

He made his way aft towards the bridge, his body reeling like some Liverpool drunk as he looked astern towards the village. But the rain was still too heavy to see anything. It was, he decided, just as well.

* * *

'Steady on zero-four-five, sir.' Corbin's big hands eased the polished spokes very carefully while his eyes remained fixed on the gyro repeater.

Dalziel nodded. 'Good.' Then he looked sharply at the coxswain. 'Hand over the wheel to the chief quartermaster.' He seemed to sense Corbin's unwillingness and added, 'You'll need all your skill later on, and so will I.'

Standish stood by one of the clearview screens and watched the endless terrain of broken rollers. With the ship's head pointing away from the land they were cruising almost directly towards the starboard bow. And the colours were different. The angry, serried crests were dull yellow, like the muddy water on the village road, and the sides of the rising waves were very steep and dark, like black glass. The wind had mounted too, and he could hear it wailing around the wheelhouse and smashing the blown spray against the screens like slivers of ice.

The whole ship was trembling, and he could guess the effort which Quarrie's men had produced to give Dalziel the speed he had demanded. The *Terrapin* was making fourteen knots, in spite of the sea and wind, and he wondered if ships could remember, and if so did she recall seas like these in those far off Atlantic days and months?

Dalziel snapped, 'I'm going to the chartroom, Number One. Take the con. We'll alter course in ten minutes.'

Rideout stepped aside to let Dalziel pass and then groped his way clumsily to the forepart of the wheelhouse. He murmured, 'What a sight.'

Standish looked away. It was bad now, but when *Terrapin* turned on her next course towards the north she would be at the mercy of those rollers.

He replied, 'Visibility's down to three miles and the glass is still falling.' He saw the uncertainty on his face and added, 'We'll be all right, Doc. The path of the storm will be clear of us.' He smiled at Rideout's confused expression. 'We're on the fringe, so to speak.'

'I see. But what exactly are we doing?'

'The boat we're looking for is apparently small. She'll have to make good speed to keep out of trouble, but she'll not want to keep too close inshore. In these seas it might be dangerous. Also, we have informed the shore patrols. We're trying to get a bit of sea-room before following the coastline and making a full radar sweep.' It sounded easy. Too damned easy.

Leading Seaman Porter, the chief quartermaster, had taken over the wheel and said between his teeth, 'The old *Shellback*'s takin' it well, sir.'

'Yes.' Standish did not feel like talking. 'Watch your helm. She's yawing a bit.'

The red telephone buzzed faintly above the sounds of sea and wind. It was Quarrie, his voice blurred and indistinct from the bowels of the engine room.

'Yes, Chief?'

Quarrie sounded angry. 'Will you tell the Old Man to cut down the revs? She can't take much more of this, y'know.'

'I know.' It was hard to picture the engineer as the same man who had been so moved at the news of Alison's death. He added, 'Do your best. I'll tell the captain.'

'Tell me what?' Dalziel stood in the doorway at the rear of the wheelhouse, his body reeling with the ship.

'The Chief's worried about the revolutions, sir.'

Dalziel grimaced. 'Have you ever known a bloody plumber who was *not* worried about his precious pistons?' He walked to the screens. 'We will make the turn now and begin the sweep. I've informed the radar people and sent Wishart up to keep an eye on them.' He rubbed his hands. 'There's not a decent anchorage or niche of shelter for miles. We'll run that murdering lot of bastards aground or sink them before we're much older!'

Irvine was in the doorway, his face composed but grim. 'Ready, sir.'

Dalziel wrapped one arm around a stanchion. 'Very well.' He looked at the helmsman. 'Port fifteen.'

Porter licked his lips. 'Port fifteen, sir.' He swung the wheel deftly, his eyes glued on the ticking gyro. 'Fifteen of port wheel on, sir.'

The effect was instantaneous. As the ship began to swing she heeled steeply taking a great wave full across the starboard side of the forecastle, so that the deck was completely hidden as far aft as the bridge. The four-inch gun mounting shivered as the tons of incoming water cascaded around it, leaving it isolated like some metal reef. Then as the sea boiled back along the main deck and sluiced angrily through the scuppers the bows rose heavily once more towards the low clouds.

'Midships.' Dalziel did not even blink. 'Steady. Meet her, you fool!'

There was sweat on the quartermaster's intent face and he sounded almost breathless. 'Steady, sir. Course three-five-zero.' He gulped. 'I can't hold her, sir. She's still going! Three-four-five!'

'Put the starboard engine to slow astern!' Dalziel turned to watch as another great wave thundered against the side and threw a wall of spray high above the bridge so that the squeaking clearview screens were momentarily blinded.

Porter said hoarsely, 'Steady, sir. Three-five-zero.'

'Full ahead starboard.' Dalziel looked at Standish, his eyes like stones. 'Steady as you go.' He waited until the next big roller had boomed against the hull and added, 'Not too hard now, was it?'

Porter swung the spokes and forced a shaky grin. 'Sorry, sir.'

'I should damn well think so.' But Dalziel was grinning, too.

Standish watched him and wondered. He seemed to be enjoying it. As if he was fighting the sea and the ship single-handed.

Dalziel said suddenly, 'Rain's eased a bit, but it's too late to be much use. With this low visibility it will be quite dark before long.' He frowned. 'Call Hornby and tell him to check the radar unit again.'

Standish passed his order and crossed to the opposite side to watch the yellow-toothed banks of breakers as they surged towards the ship's quarter. Driven hundreds of miles, he thought, with nothing between them and the great expanse of the Gulf but *Terrapin*'s fragile hull.

Perhaps the vessel for which they were now searching had already reached safety, or had even been driven ashore as a total wreck. He found that he was hoping it was still there somewhere ahead of the labouring frigate. Just so they could catch them. So he could see the faces of the sort of men who could butcher without mercy in the name of brotherhood.

Minutes dragged into another hour, with the motion making their minds and bodies bruised as the ship heeled and plunged, corkscrewed and staggered, like a thing gone mad.

Wills reached the wheelhouse gasping. 'Coffee, sir.' He was soaked and his hair was plastered across his eyes. He said, 'I put somethin' good in it.'

Standish took a mug and tasted it. There was more rum than coffee, he thought. But it was what they needed at this moment.

Irvine had spent most of the time by the radar repeater, his face lined with strain. He reported for the hundredth time, 'Nothing yet, sir.'

Dalziel said, 'Better go round the ship, Number One. Make sure everything's secure.' He smiled, 'Cheer them up, eh?'

Standish dragged on his oilskin. He was glad to leave, if only to be doing something.

Little groups of men were huddled everywhere. Burch and his signalmen, their coats making them look like wet seals on a rock. Lower down, Harris, the chief bosun's mate, a heavy knife hanging from his waist on a lanyard as he watched the whaler jerking in its davits as one sea after another swept along the deck from end to end. Motts was about too, clinging to a lifeline while he guided his working party along the treacherous deck, gauging the time between moves, watching the sea and cursing with the rest of them.

Caley was right aft, his thickset body bent almost double as he crawled around the depth-charge mortars accompanied by two of his ratings. He saw Standish and yelled, 'One of the Carley floats has gone! God knows when or where, but it's bloody missing now!'

Standish hooked his arm around a wire stay and felt the receding water dragging greedily at his legs and feet. 'If we can keep ahead of this front we should be all right.' He saw Caley nod doubtfully. 'After we've found that boat we can keep on going until it blows itself out. We've the rest of the Gulf if need be.'

Caley wiped his streaming face. 'We gotta *find* the bloody boat first!'

Down below decks it was quieter but no less menacing. The cabin flat seemed unnatural and deserted, with some of the doors sliding and squeaking as if being moved by invisible fingers. And all the time the sea thundered along the hull and drove hissing overhead in a never-ending onslaught.

It was not quite deserted. In one cabin he saw Pigott jammed in a corner of his bunk while he pencilled notes in a long ledger, his glasses slipping to the end of his nose as he tried to keep upright.

In the sickbay the Australian engineer was still doped or asleep, his body held in the swaying cot by two traps, while Mackie, the leading medical assistant, slept almost as deeply in Rideout's swivel chair, his mouth wide open while he snored obliviously in his dreams.

Standish found the two women in the wardroom. They were sitting in two chairs which someone had lashed against a steam-pipe.

He said, 'I just came to tell you we're still making good speed.' Now that he was here he did not know what to say. They were both looking at him, and when he glanced down he saw that his legs and shoes were still caked with filth from the burned village.

The girl said quietly, 'It was good of you to come. Down here you feel cut off. Helpless.' She gripped the chair as the deck canted steeply, the hull quivering to another great wave. 'But it must be worse for you.'

Standish removed his cap and shook it on the carpet. 'Like the ship. Battered but unbowed.' He smiled. 'She has seen worse. They built ships to last in those days.'

Mrs. Penrath asked, 'Will you find this boat?' She was watching him gravely. 'And if so, what then?'

Standish listened to the shafts, the shuddering jerk of screws as the stern lifted above the quarter sea.

'Keep it in sight until the weather eases, I expect.' It was odd, he had hardly thought about it up to now. 'We can always radio the Malaysian patrols, or the Thai army too for that matter.'

She nodded. 'We are going as far north as that then?'

'Maybe.' He thought suddenly of the *Cornwallis*. Strange they should be driving towards the same area where she had been. He glanced quickly at the girl and wondered if she was thinking that, too.

He said, 'You'll be safe enough.'

He looked around the shabby wardroom and recalled the smart elegance of Sarah Dalziel's hotel suite. It seemed like a million years ago. The stark contrast filled him with pity for the girl who was watching him so intently. It was terrible enough for her with what had happened and the uncertainty which lay ahead, without all this.

'I must go now.' He thought of the sea and the strained atmosphere in the wheelhouse. 'Wills will be here if you want anything.' He looked at the girl. 'Anything at all.'

He left the wardroom and lurched back along the swaying passageway between the cabins. Something made him turn and he saw the girl standing behind him, her slim figure outlined against the open door.

'Yes?'

She came towards him, feeling her way along the safety rail, but with her eyes on his face.

'I wanted to see you. To explain...' She faltered and dropped her eyes.

'I understand.' He reached out and took her wrist. It was very slender and quite cool. 'Try to shut it out. It'll take time, but...'

She shook her head, the black hair falling forward across her face. 'Not that. I didn't want to let you go on thinking I was ungrateful. I'll never forget what you did for us. For me.' She lifted her head and he saw the desperation in her eyes. 'I heard some of the others speaking of your trouble. What you've been through. I didn't know. Didn't stop to think.' She stared down at her hand in his. 'I'm so sorry.'

He replied, 'It's over. Forget that, too.' He waited as the ship dipped heavily into a trough. It seemed an age before the water stopped cascading across the deck above their heads. And all the while he was conscious only of her. Of her nearness. Of his need for her. He said, 'When this is over...' He paused. 'If you ever find you can't cope, I'd like you to write to me. Will you do it?'

She reached out and touched his coat, watching the salt water dripping across her wrist. 'I promise.'

Wills burst from the wardroom and shouted, 'Sir!' He seemed to sense what was happening and added more quietly, 'Captain wants you up top double quick, sir. The radar has made a contact.'

Standish looked at the girl. 'Damn.' Then he added, 'Tell them I'm coming up.' As Wills dashed away he said, 'It's hard to be alone in a ship.'

As he ran towards the companionway he retained a clear picture of her face. He had seen her smile for the first time.

Dalziel turned to the wheelhouse door as he pulled himself inside. 'Well, what did I tell you, eh?' His eyes were blazing with excitement. 'A firm contact at red four-five. Range ten miles or thereabouts.' He followed Standish to the radar repeater. 'Not much of an echo, but I'm grateful they found it at all in this weather.'

On the small screen it was certainly difficult to make out anything but a mad mixture of flickering lights.

Dalziel said, 'I've been up to the radar cabinet. Better picture there, I can tell you.' He frowned, 'Smaller than I expected. Probably a launch.'

He looked at Irvine. 'Tell the engine room I want maximum revolutions. Emergency full speed.'

Corbin appeared in the wheelhouse and Dalziel said dryly, 'A fine entrance, Cox'n. Right, take the wheel now, please.'

The speaker crackled above the door. It was Wishart's voice which followed. 'The other vessel has altered course, sir. Now steering approximately zero-five-zero.'

Dalziel muttered, 'Impossible. That's *away* from the land, for God's sake. They'll run smack across the path of the storm if they maintain that course.' More sharply he added, 'Keep checking.' But he was unable to stay still. 'Go up, Number One. Have a look yourself.'

The radar cabinet was streaming with condensation, and the faces of the operators gleamed in the big scopes like wax masks. Wishart was there, Hornby too, and they turned to watch as Standish peered over the shoulders of Vine, the senior radar operator.

'What do you make of it?'

Vine fiddled with his knobs and switches and said bluntly, 'This set should have been scrapped years ago, sir. With the new model you can find a fly on a whale's back.' He shrugged. 'I thought I knew, but now I'm not sure.' He stiffened, and Standish saw a small blip momentarily clear and bright on the flickering scope. 'Launch, I thought, or something small like that. Quite fast.' He sighed as the screen faded in a blur of back echoes. 'Lost it again.'

Dalziel's voice crackled over the intercom. 'Well, say something!'

Standish replied, 'Appears to be heading zero-five-zero, sir.' He waited, seeing the others watching his face. 'It's the only living thing as far as I can see.'

'Come down here, Number One.'

Dalziel greeted him in the wheelhouse with, 'Must be that bloody radar again. And I thought...' He saw Standish's expression and asked quickly, 'What is it?'

'No small boat would head out to sea in this. Not even a maniac would do it.' He saw the disappointment returning to Dalziel's dark eyes. 'But I was thinking, sir . . .'

'For God's sake spit it out!'

'What if it's not a launch at all?' Standish turned his back on the others. 'Just suppose it's a submarine's conning tower.'

Dalziel stared at him for several seconds. Then he said softly, 'Mother of God. You've hit it. The size and the speed.' He waved towards the salt-dashed screens. 'The waters round here are too shallow to dive in comfort.'

Standish nodded gravely. 'She's making for deep water right now.' He thought suddenly of the Malay trooper's indecision. A partly submerged submarine would baffle a native policeman under such circumstances. And Kuala Papan was one of those rare and deep inlets. Deep enough for a ship like the *Sibuyan*. Or a submarine.

The red telephone buzzed and Irvine said, 'The Chief wants to reduce speed at once, sir.' He looked from one to the other, his body pitching back and forth as the ship rolled under him. 'The starboard shaft is bothering him, sir. He wants to do an inspection.'

Dalziel crossed to the telephone and snatched it from his hand. 'Chief? This is the captain.' His eyes were fixed and unblinking as he listened briefly before snapping, 'Then you don't know anything's *really* wrong, do you?' Another pause and then he shouted, 'I don't give a bloody damn about your instincts, do you hear? There's an enemy submarine on the surface and I intend to get it.' Another pause, with only Corbin too intent on wheel and compass to listen. Then Dalziel said very calmly, 'If you had seen that village, Chief, you might think differently. However, you will remain at full revolutions until I say otherwise.' He dropped the telephone and looked hard at Standish. 'No war on indeed. Just where the hell has he been all these years?'

He turned towards Irvine. 'Give me a course to intercept, Pilot, and move yourself.' To the wheelhouse at large he added, 'No angler is considered anything but a liar until he produces the fish. Well, I'll give them a catch that even the blindest politician can get his teeth into!'

Standish waited until Dalziel had returned to the forepart of the wheelhouse and then said, 'I could have been wrong, sir.'

'We'll worry about that later.' Dalziel eyed him evenly. 'But I think not. You may know damn-all about women, but by God you do understand submarines.'

Irvine called, 'New course is zero-two-zero, sir.'

Dalziel nodded. 'Warn the ship before we turn. It may get a bit unsteady from now on.' He smiled. 'Picket duty, eh? Carry stores, will we? By God, we'll see about that.'

Irvine said, 'Ready, sir.' He sounded hoarse.

Dalziel linked his arm through a stanchion. 'So be it then.'

13 Aftermath

OUTSIDE the wheelhouse the sky was almost completely dark, with only the careering wave crests to mark any sort of division between sea and cloud. Standish clung to his position by the starboard clearview screen and watched as once more the forecastle disappeared under a thundering cascade of water, and felt the deck sliding away beneath him, the screen misting over in a distorted mirage of grey and white. He could also feel the bruise on his hip where the pressure of unyielding steel had grated against him as time after time the ship had slid almost beam on into a steep trough, only to emerge shaking and corkscrewing for the next onslaught.

He had lost all sense of time, and the whole meaning of existence seemed to have shrunk to within the wheelhouse and the efforts of Dalziel and Corbin to keep the ship under control.

The men around him were mostly just shadows, with an occasional face picked out by the compass light or the gleam of the radar repeater.

At irregular intervals Vine's voice came over the intercom. The other vessel was still there. Mocking their efforts to outpace and overhaul it.

Dalziel snapped, 'How is it now?'

Vine again, tired and hoarse from strain. 'Echo bears red oh-oh-five. Range oh-eight-oh.' A pause and somebody coughed in the background. 'Course appears to have shifted slightly. Now zero-six-zero degrees.'

Dalziel turned and stared at Standish. 'He'll cross our bows. He must be doing sixteen knots at least!'

Standish watched the forecastle lifting again, the steel shining dully against the cascading seas beyond as the old ship struggled upright towards another roller.

'Must be a submarine, sir. No small surface craft could keep such a steady course under these conditions.' He added slowly, 'She'll dive soon if I'm any judge. According to the chart the bottom starts to fall away to thirty-five fathoms directly across his present course. He'll be in a comfortable position in half an hour.'

Dalziel struggled up the sloping deck and gripped his arm. 'We can still head him off.' He swung round and shouted, 'Alter course five degrees to starboard!' He paused and waited until the last wave had crashed against the bridge superstructure. 'More speed. Tell the engine room I must have *more speed.*'

Standish picked up the handset, his eyes on Corbin as the coxswain's tall figure rose and then leaned over at almost thirty degrees.

But it was not Quarrie's voice this time. It was Petty Officer Barrett, the man who had handled the outboard motors so expertly.

'The Chief's right aft, sir!'

Above his voice and the roar of spray and rain Standish heard the pulsating beat of machinery, the whir of fans as the *Terrapin*'s engines turned the ship's afterpart into one vibrating mass of metal.

Standish said, 'The captain wants everything you can give him.'

'We've been doing that for hours, sir.'

'I know. But do what you can.' He replaced the handset and almost fell as the deck swooped and then staggered from under him.

He heard Corbin shouting, 'She's paying off, sir! Zero-two-zero; zero-one-five; zero-one-zero!' He was clinging to the spokes, his face shining with sweat in the compass light.

Dalziel had one arm around a telegraph, his head craned towards the gyro. 'Half astern starboard engine!' He used both arms to hold on as the deck leaned over still further and men fell headlong across the wheelhouse in a confused, shouting tangle.

'Starboard engine half astern, sir.'

It seemed suddenly quiet beyond the steel sides of the wheel-house, and Standish realized with sick horror that the ship was lying in the confines of a steep trough, being pushed along and over by the force of one great, towering roller. Fascinated he watched the roller's crest start to crumple, heard Irvine gasp behind him as with the force of an avalanche the great mass of water crashed down on the ship's exposed side.

Corbin yelled, 'I can't hold her, sir! She won't answer!'

'Put the starboard engine to full astern! Emergency!' Dalziel's voice seemed unnaturally loud in the imprisoned stillness of the trough.

The hull shook savagely as the screws fought against sea and rudder to bring the stem round.

A seaman sobbed, 'She's goin'! Oh Jesus, she's goin' right under!'

No one answered, but as one more great wave battered against the listing hull Corbin croaked, 'She's coming, sir!' The gyro ticked round. 'Zero-one-five. zero-two-zero.'

'Get ready.' Dalziel laid his hand on that of the mesmerized seaman at the telegraph. 'Now. Full ahead starboard!'

As the bows slewed sluggishly above the creaming wall of water the noise and violence came back as savagely as ever.

Dalziel said, 'Steer zero-three-zero.' He waited as Corbin brought her round. 'That'll give better steerage way for a bit.'

Irvine called thickly, 'The rain's stopped!'

Nobody seemed to care. But Standish saw Dalziel's quick jerk of the head before he turned his attention back to the compass. He remembered what Dalziel had said in the past. It is when the rain stops you have to watch out. *In the path of the storm.* The words drummed into his mind like a voice in a nightmare.

Irvine clawed his way round the wheelhouse and whispered into his ear, 'The bottom has dropped out of the glass. We're heading almost straight to the storm centre, for God's sake!'

Vine called, 'Echo bears red oh-oh-five. Range oh-seven-oh.'

Dalziel peered at Standish and Irvine, his teeth making a white crescent in his shadowed face. 'We're holding him! The last turn made some difference after all. If we can get another knot out of her we'll have that bastard cold!'

Standish seized the rack of telephones as the bows climbed

steeply up another unbroken roller. Up, up, until the stem seemed to be pointing at the skudding clouds like a shining black arrowhead. Then, as the roller broke and roared down either beam he felt the forepart of the ship drop sickeningly into the waiting trough, and pitied the men crammed in the dripping messdecks as they were plummeted some forty feet before smashing into the solid force of water below.

He thought too of the nameless submarine and her commander. He was leaving it as late as possible before diving, was even driving towards the approaching storm before making his dive to that other level of peace and stability. It pointed to the boat being an ordinary one and not nuclear, he thought. Her commander was probably charging batteries after his recent exploits around the Malaysian coast and elsewhere.

It was unnerving to realize that if *Terrapin* failed to make contact the submarine's crew would be able to glide away in comfort, listening to the frigate's screws as she fought her way back from the approaching typhoon.

The engine room telegraph buzzed again and the bosun's mate called, 'Mr. Quarrie wants to speak to you, sir.' He handed it to Dalziel and used both hands to hold himself to a fire extinguisher as the ship lifted her stem towards the next leaping wave crest.

'Captain.' Dalziel crouched forward to peer towards the nearest clearview screen. 'So?'

Irvine muttered, 'The ship will fall apart in a minute!'

Standish ignored him and tried to guess what Quarrie was saying. Dalziel said very little, and his voice was devoid of expression.

'Impossible, Chief. Out of the question.' He lowered the telephone slightly and barked at Corbin, 'Bring her round a bit, Cox'n. Steer zero-three-five.'

Rideout reached Irvine's side and said excitedly, 'It's wild, but the motion is better.' He peered from one to the other. 'Isn't it?'

Irvine said bitterly, 'It's always better when you face oncoming seas like these. But soon now we have to turn.' He swung away, adding, 'Work it out for yourself.'

Dalziel slammed down the telephone and said, 'I think the wind's veered a point or so.' He seemed quite calm.

Rideout swallowed hard as the ship plunged forward and down, his eyes fixed on the incoming sea as it rushed aft along the forecastle and leapt high over the gun mounting. Standish saw his lips moving, as if he was counting seconds, willing the bows to reappear. It seemed to take a long while, as though the ship was already starting to plunge to the bottom.

Rideout breathed out noisily as the deck emerged shining faintly against the tossing waves and said, 'Some of the guard-rail's gone.'

Standish turned away. You've not seen anything yet. He looked at Dalziel as Vine's voice echoed above the din.

'I'm sorry, sir. I've lost it. I think it has dived.'

Dalziel glared up at the intercom speaker and rasped, 'Keep watching!' Then he dragged himself to the screen and pressed his face against it as if seeking his quarry for himself.

Irvine said flatly, 'We must turn now, sir. While there's still time.'

Dalziel swung on him. 'Hold your advice to yourself!' He seemed to see Rideout for the first time. 'And you, what the hell are you whispering about, eh?' He staggered and reached out to grasp a voicepipe. 'Get off my bridge and attend to your own department at once!'

As Rideout hurried for the door he was thrust aside by a thickset, dripping figure. It was Quarrie. He had come straight from the engine room along the treacherous upper deck wearing neither oilskin nor lifejacket.

Standish could see the black oilstains on his chest and legs, could almost feel the man's fury as he reeled towards Dalziel and shouted, 'Are you all mad up here?' He saw Standish and added, 'There's a bearing running hot in the starboard shaft, in the after gland space!'

Dalziel replied, 'Kindly control your emotions.'

'Emotions?' Quarrie looked as if he might strike Dalziel. 'It's the after bearing, don't you understand?' He faced the others, suddenly desperate and appealing. 'It might be a blocked oil-pipe, and if I can't fix it the whole shaft will seize up solid as a bloody rock!'

Irvine said quietly, 'Hell.'

'Damn fine time to tell me that.' Dalziel was still by the voicepipes, his face in shadow.

'I've told you already!' Quarrie waved his hand wildly. 'I warned you, I explained exactly what would happen if you kept this crazy speed going.'

Standish said, 'Easy, Chief. There's been a lot going on here, too.'

Dalziel remarked, 'We will keep closing on the last fix and continue with a sonar sweep. There's still a chance of locating that submarine. A very good chance, in my opinion.'

Quarrie seemed dazed. 'In *my* opinion this ship will be lying deeper than any bloody submarine in about thirty minutes!'

Irvine looked at Standish and asked quickly, 'What do you think, Number One? You know about subs.'

'I can see your little game, Pilot.' Dalziel sounded dangerously calm. 'Well, forget it. I am not interested in opinions, only facts. And the one true fact around here is that submarine!'

He turned and peered through the screen as a dull boom echoed dismally above the hiss of bursting spray. The hull lifted, staggered and then plunged headlong through another breaking roller and the same sound repeated itself. It was like a giant oildrum being beaten with a bar of iron.

The bosun's mate snatched up a handset and reported shakily, 'The buffer says the port anchor is comin' adrift, sir.' In the compass light his eyes were like marbles.

Dalziel plucked at the neck of his crumpled shirt. 'Anchor?' Then in a sharper voice he snapped, 'Get Wishart down here at once!' Almost to himself he added, 'Is there not one single man I can rely on?'

Wishart entered the wheelhouse and almost fell back under Dalziel's sudden anger.

'Don't you ever do anything right? What sort of bloody officer do you imagine you will be, eh?' He raised his fist as the dull boom came again. 'Did the executive officer warn you about doubly securing the anchors, or did he not?'

Wishart glanced at Standish and muttered wretchedly, 'Yes, sir.'

'Yes, sir, *what*?' Dalziel leaned towards him. 'Answer me!'

'He did warn me, sir. I thought I'd taken all precautions . . .'

He faltered as Quarrie interrupted roughly, 'Never mind that. What about my shaft? I must *insist* that you slow down at once!'

Dalziel did not appear to notice him. 'Well, Sub, you can damn well take your men forrard and see to it, *right now* ...'

He broke off as another speaker intoned, 'Wheelhouse ... Sonar. No contact.'

Standish said, 'Nobody can stay alive up forrard, sir. Not under these conditions.'

'Quite so.' Dalziel was tugging at his collar again. 'Well, due to this officer's carelessness I seem to have no alternative but throw away the one real chance we've had of proving our worth.' He looked at Wishart. 'Get your men together and await orders.' To Quarrie he said, 'And you can return to your engine room, Chief. I will begin to turn the ship in ten minutes.'

Quarrie said stubbornly, 'And the shaft, sir?'

'I will reduce speed when we have altered course.' As Quarrie reached the door he added coldly, 'Unless of course you'd like to stop engines altogether and have us take to the boats!'

Quarrie went out, slamming the door behind him.

Dalziel continued in a more level tone, 'We'll let the sea do the work for us. I shall turn to port. Be ready to go half astern on the port engine.'

Boom. The sound jarred the strained minds of everyone in the wheelhouse.

Standish said, 'I think Wishart did all that he could, sir. Maybe that big breaker snapped something. Most of the cable and anchor gear has been aboard ever since the ship came out East.'

'It's not the gear.' Dalziel was squinting into the radar repeater as if still hoping for a returning contact. 'Nor the ship either.' Then he glanced across at Irvine. 'But if that's the way they want to play it, then heaven help them as far as I'm concerned.'

The bosun's mate said, 'Call from the engine room, sir. Standing by.'

Dalziel grunted. 'Port fifteen. Port engine half speed astern.'

Corbin had hardly completed a full turn of the wheel when the ship reeled wildly across an advancing wall of water and began to topple drunkenly on to her beam. Pieces of gear tore loose and clattered through the bridge, and somewhere below a man cried out in sudden terror.

Dalziel seemed to be speaking through clenched teeth. 'Increase to twenty. Port engine *full astern*.'

The next careering wave hit the exposed bow and thrust the ship hard over, the deck angling so steeply that from his position jammed against the port scuttles Standish found he was staring straight down into the frothing water alongside. Another few degrees and the hull would capsize completely. He found that he could accept it. Was even able to breathe. Then through the leaping spray he saw a piece of buckled guardrail and knew that the ship was coming upright again.

He felt the fierce pressure against his chest and thighs easing, and turned stiffly as Dalziel barked, 'Half ahead both engines. Wheel amidships!' He rubbed the screen with his sleeve. 'Steady now! *Steady!*'

Corbin said, 'Steady, sir. Course three-four-zero.' He cursed softly and swung the spokes to meet a sudden challenge, and added grimly, 'She's holding it, sir.'

Standish looked around him, at the weary, clinging watch-keepers. At Corbin standing straddle-legged and stubborn, as if nothing would break him. And at Dalziel by the gyro again, his face like a mask as he peered at the luminous figures inches from his eyes.

He said, 'I'll go and watch Wishart, sir.' There was no response. 'Is that all right?'

Dalziel still did not answer so he pushed into the small passageway abaft the wheelhouse and stumbled across Rideout who was trying to blow up a lifejacket. But the doctor was not alone. There seemed to be dozens of dark shapes jammed everywhere, their orange lifejackets giving them a strange anonymity. He thrust his way between them, saying nothing. It was useless to tell sailors it was pointless to climb to the highest point in a ship when they were terrified beyond reason. It had been bad enough on the bridge, but to men off watch and imprisoned with a reeling, creaking hull it must have been a living torment.

He found Wishart with his men huddled together below the bridge, their faces showing occasionally as a torch flashed amongst them. Beyond the watertight door he could hear the sea sluicing along the deck, the boom of the anchor like a curfew bell.

Wishart looked at him and said, 'Thanks for coming down.' He sounded as if he was shivering.

Another voice spoke beside him. 'I've got a new slip fixed up an' ready, sir.' It was Petty Officer Harris, the chief bosun's mate. He seemed unperturbed. 'An' I've sent two good leadin' 'ands below to break the cable.'

Standish nodded. Harris, like Motts, needed no telling. It was useless to try and secure the anchor. That great weight of water must have moved something just enough to allow the anchor to slip clear of the hawsepipe. Now, suspended on its shackle it was swinging against the frail plating each time the ship plunged. If it stove the bows in the sea would do the rest, bulkheads or no bulkheads.

Wishart said, 'It'll have to be fast.' He cleared his throat. 'I . . . I'll go first.'

Harris chuckled. 'We'll *both* go, sir.' He jabbed the two seamen behind him. 'White an' Bundy, take the wire strops. Dobson, cop 'old of the lifeline. When I raps on the deck with me 'ammer the lads below will break the joinin' shackle and we'll do the rest, right?'

They nodded. One of the seamen asked thickly, 'What if we gets caught by one of them big waves, Buffer?'

Harris grinned. 'Don't you worry yer 'ead, Knocker. Your old woman'll get 'er pension a bit earlier, that's all!' Then sharply he added, 'Right, lads. Let's get that bloody door open!'

Now that the ship had turned her stern towards the great following sea it was surprisingly sheltered below the bridge. Cautiously, feeling their way along a lifeline the men groped towards the gun mounting and around it where they paused beneath the twin muzzles.

Standish pulled himself to the front of the crouching figures and peered towards the stem. The ship seemed to be making hardly any headway at all, but that was merely because her speed was almost matched by that of the pursuing waves. The deck was still vibrating fiercely, and he knew Corbin would be watching and feeling his wheel, ready to warn Dalziel the instant he was losing steerage way. If that happened the ship would broach to, or be pooped and driven under before Dalziel could get more speed.

The bows dipped slowly and he saw the spray feathering

back through the bullring and spurting up over the crumpled guardrail.

He said, '*Now!*'

While the bows lifted wearily again they dashed forward along the slippery deck, clinging to the single wire stay which spelt life or death for all of them.

Harris threw himself astride the port cable shouting, 'This one never was much bleedin' good!' He laughed into the spray and held up a piece of metal. 'Sheered off like a carrot!'

The deck canted again and more water swept over them, choking their cries and curses, blinding them until the bows fought back once more.

And all the time Harris was busy with his slip and his strops, while the seaman named Dobson controlled his movements with the rest of the lifeline.

Harris rapped his hammer on the deck and shouted, 'Now we'll see!'

The cable groaned and stiffened as the steel slip took the strain. He banged twice on the deck, and from below they all heard the sudden rasp of metal and then an answering signal.

Harris yelled, 'Thank the livin' Jesus that wasn't rusty, too!'

Standish jerked the wire stay. 'Get back, the rest of you! The buffer will knock off the slip!' He saw Wishart's face close by his arm, pale and staring. 'Got to judge the right moment!'

He made himself wait, knowing that Harris was having real difficulty in holding on. But knock the slip off too soon and the anchor would smash through the hull long before it could drop clear.

The bows started to dip and he yelled, 'Slip!'

Harris leapt clear and swung his hammer, ducking into Standish's arms as with a growling roar the short length of cable trundled along the deck and then vanished through the hawse-pipe.

Harris clung to the two officers, his face split into a huge grin. 'That'll give some fish a 'eadache!'

They struggled aft along the wire towards the gun mounting, half blinded, and almost deafened by the wind in their faces.

Wishart yelled, 'Never thought it had taken so long.' He was half laughing, half sobbing. 'Be daylight soon!'

Standish peered past him and then froze. The pale line

etched against the cloud was not the dawn. It was the thin crest of the greatest wave he had ever seen. It stretched away on either quarter until it was lost from view and seemed higher than the masthead.

He shouted, 'Run for the guns! Quick!'

The wave came on, lifting the stern higher and higher until it was tearing forward and down like a surfboard. Had it broken it would have smashed the ship apart, but as it reached the bridge it seemed to stagger and break into several gigantic waves of equal size and ferocity.

Standish saw the nearest one lifting above the port rail, so tall that it was like something solid. He watched it curve inboard and felt the ship slew heavily to one side as the full force of it exploded against the foot of the bridge before thundering forward towards the bows.

His breath was being pushed from his lungs. It was like being buried alive, and in the blind maelstrom of sea and noise he could hear himself shouting, his words choked by salt water as it swept over him, dragging at his sodden body, tearing at his fingers as he fought to hold on.

Then it was past, and as he struggled painfully against the gun mounting he realized that he was alone.

He reeled round the streaming steel and saw a crumpled figure poised right on the edge of the deck, draped around a buckled stanchion like a discarded puppet. He reached it and dragged desperately at the man's coat. It was Wishart, and as he hauled him back over the side he heard him gasp, 'Buffer! He's here!'

Standish saw two seamen dashing from below the bridge to seize Wishart's body, and as he lowered himself to the side again he found Harris directly beneath him, his hands locked into a drooping piece of guardrail like two pale claws. Standish felt someone holding his legs, and reached down to seize the petty officer's wrists with all his strength.

Harris croaked, 'Bloody fine thing! Me leg's busted!'

Standish adjusted his grip and called back to the men behind him, 'Pull us inboard, lads!' It was then that he saw the next wave coming down the side of the hull towards him.

This time he heard nothing at all, but was conscious of the overwhelming, choking water, and the fact that Harris's wrists were slipping through his fingers. He knew he was trying to shout to him even though his lungs seemed full of water. Knew too that Harris was staring up at him, watching him, knowing he was going to die.

He thought he too was dying, for even as the two cold hands slipped away so also did his senses. Then there was nothing.

When he opened his eyes it took him several minutes to grasp what had happened. There was a light burning on the opposite bulkhead, and everything was white. Clean, clinical and pure white. He moved his cracked lips and tried to laugh. Like a soap advertisement.

He saw Rideout looking down at him, smiling and sad at the same moment.

'Take it easy, Number One. You had a rough time of it.'

It was coming back now. Fast and terrible.

He asked quietly, 'Harris?'

The doctor looked at his hands under the light. 'You did your best. Couldn't be helped.'

Standish closed his eyes. They seemed to be pricking him. He noticed that the motion around him was easier, and through the hull he could hear the sea pounding more evenly. He gripped the sheet tightly. It sounded pleased with itself.

He asked, 'How long have I been out?'

'Five hours. I had to do it. You were trying to get back on deck.'

Standish looked at him emptily. 'I don't remember anything about it.'

'Just shock, old chap.' Rideout studied him curiously. 'Quite normal.'

'Not for Harris it wasn't.' He wanted Rideout to go. To leave him to readjust his mind.

'I know. However, but for you young Wishart would be gone, too.'

Standish turned his face away. He could feel the sleep returning, and when he closed his eyes he could picture it quite clearly. Like smoke advancing across the sea's face.

Rideout watched him until he was asleep and then walked unsteadily to the sickbay door. Outside he found Irvine, leaning against the side and smoking a cigarette.

'I'm afraid you can't see him yet. He's still doped.'

Irvine looked at his cigarette and said tersely, 'It's you I want.'

'Oh?' Rideout's eyebrows lifted very slightly. 'How can I help you?'

Irvine looked over his shoulder. 'Come to my cabin. I want your advice about something very serious.' He eyed him coldly. 'For all of us.'

*   *   *

It took another thirty-six hours for the storm to blow itself out, with the *Terrapin* keeping just clear of its fringe, like someone dodging the wheel of a monstrous juggernaut. During that time the wind altered direction to the north and the rain returned as heavy and as drenching as before, but as the W/T office listened and prayed, the reports became calmer, and they knew that the real danger was at least passing them by.

Sleep for off-watch officers and ratings was almost impossible. Messdecks swilled with trapped water, and as the ship rolled her hull through every conceivable position and angle the sea spurted past sealed scuttles and doors, pursued the dazed and weary seamen with relentless zeal.

On the bridge it was no better, for most of the watchkeepers were too tired to take proper care and to avoid the sudden leaps and plunges. Rideout stayed in his sickbay dealing with a growing list of injuries. Bruises and cuts, and a few fractures, evidence of the sea's constant attacks.

In spite of Rideout's warnings Standish returned to his duties, and was shocked to find the deep change which had come about. Even when the cloud began to break up and the first rays of watery sunlight brought back life and colour to the sea around them he was immediately aware of the depression, the air of despair which seemed to pervade the whole ship.

The sky cleared, and as the first real warmth raised a steamy haze from the dripping decks and superstructure watchkeeping returned to the upper bridge, and with it a first real awareness of what the ship had endured.

Gratings were scattered and chipped, and the ready-use chart table was smashed to fragments. The paintwork looked as if it had been carefully scoured from the steel by several giant razors.

Dalziel had remained without sleep for most of the time, but apart from the shadows under his deepset eyes and a stubble of beard he seemed little the worse for it. Not physically anyway. But in the time Standish had been in the sickbay he had nevertheless changed and was remote to the point of coldness.

He said, 'I have had a signal. We are to proceed to Songkhla forthwith and anchor. We will carry out internal repairs and await instructions.' He looked at Standish and added, 'I'm going to my sea cabin. E.T.A. at Songkhla is 0900 tomorrow.' That was all.

When dawn came up the following day it was hard to appreciate there had been any storm at all. Standish stood on the fore gratings and watched the long stretch of coastline emerging in the early sunlight until it reached out on either bow, lush and green, as if to embrace them. There were only a few clouds, and they were soft pink, without threat or malice as they glided slowly with the growing dawn light.

And when he moved his feet he felt dust beneath his shoes. Dust carried by a lazy offshore breeze which defied the memories of towering whitecaps and great sluicing seas, of men falling and slipping waist deep in water, and of one man in particular being dragged to his death.

Petty Officer Harris had been a popular member of the ship's company. He had been Motts' best friend. But the sense of heavy depression seemed to go far deeper than that, although few had expressed their feelings openly to give some clue of the course it might take. It was like a storm, he thought. The signs were there, but no one knew the cause, or how each would react when it finally broke over them.

He heard a step behind him and saw Wishart climbing on to the gratings, one arm in a sling.

'How is it, Sub?'

Wishart looked past him towards the brightening strip of land. 'Thailand,' he said vaguely. Then, 'It's only a sprain. Nothing at all really.' His mouth trembled. 'I keep thinking about Harris. He was trying to save *me* when he slipped. Every time I try to sleep I see his face.'

Standish replied, 'It could have been any of us. Or all of us.'

What use were words? He had thought about Harris, too. He had even wondered what it had been like in those last terrible seconds. Harris might have lived just long enough to see his ship fading away. Might even have survived until he was plucked into the whirling screws.

He added harshly, 'It wasn't your fault. That's all you can remember now.'

Irvine appeared on the bridge and asked quietly, 'Can I have a word, Number One?'

'What about?'

Irvine glanced at Wishart. 'Alone.'

'Can't it wait?' Standish could not face another discussion. One more list of recriminations.

Wishart said, 'I'll leave.'

As he climbed down Irvine said, 'I suppose we'll have to anchor offshore until some of the brass come and see us again?'

'Did you send Wishart away merely to tell me that?' The tiredness brought an edge to his voice. 'If so, you can take over the watch now and I'll have some breakfast.'

Irvine eyed him flatly. 'I can manage without that young hero. When I want to hear from him, I'll yawn.' He looked above Standish's shoulder. 'The fact is I feel we should get together and discuss this last fiasco before we all get involved.'

Standish glanced through the salt-encrusted glass screen and saw a few seamen moving gingerly around the bows. They were looking at the empty hawsepipe, the scars where the broken cable had made its last journey.

'Involved in what?'

'Look, I know all about your position, and I will respect it. But it's also your responsibility to listen to the rest of us.' He cleared his throat. 'The officers, that is.'

Standish turned and studied him, feeling neither anger nor surprise.

'Have you been voicing your opinions again?'

Irvine's mouth tightened. 'Don't worry, I've not been rallying a mutiny! But it must be said. The captain nearly had us in the middle of that typhoon, and you damn well know it.' When Standish said nothing he added, 'Maybe there was a submarine, and maybe not. We'll never know now. In any case, what could we do? There's no proof it was responsible for the patrol boat's destruction, and apart from depth-charging it, do you imagine it would allow us to arrest it? It's sheer, bloody stupidity!'

'You seem to have reached some conclusion. Get it off your chest if it helps.'

'There's a lot we don't know about the captain. He got off with a reprimand after that collision with the carrier, but how do we know it wasn't really his fault?' He watched Standish narrowly. 'Another thing, he says he's not married. We both know that's a lie, don't we?'

Standish looked at him impassively. 'You should have been a private detective. But is it any of your business?'

Irvine frowned. 'Not directly, but added to the other symptoms I'd say the captain is not all he tries to appear.'

'Symptoms?' Standish let it hang in the air. 'Have you been discussing this with the doctor?'

Irvine seemed less sure of himself. 'I just mentioned a few things.'

'Did you? Well let me give *you* some advice. Put this in writing and I'll give it to the commanding officer myself. You can request a transfer, or you may make an official complaint to the C. in C.'s office. I will see that it gets officially noted.'

Irvine bit his lip. 'That would put me in a bad spot.' His eyes flashed angrily. 'You know what it would do to my chances of promotion!'

Standish turned and stared at the land again. He could see strips of white against the green. Low-lying houses by the water's edge. People would be there. Room to breathe and think. He said quietly, 'You make me sick, do you know that? You want others to do your work for you, to carry the can if it goes wrong. I can admire a genuine coward, but you disgust me.' There was no reply, and when he turned his head he saw that Irvine was already going down the bridge ladder.

He gripped the vibrating screen and breathed out very slowly. Like Dalziel's wife, Irvine wanted him to take sides, to join their own conspiracy.

A signalman called, 'Launch approaching port bow, sir. Royal Thai Navy colours.'

'Very good. I'll inform the captain.' He crossed to the telephone, his mind still dwelling on Irvine's words.

Suppose he was right? He paused with his hand on the

telephone. If he had not pressed on into the storm it would
have been less hazardous to turn the ship, and Harris would
still be alive. And the anchor. If it had not come adrift would
Dalziel really have carried on regardless of consequences? He
thought of Quarrie's angry defiance and of his own uncertainty
about the submarine's reality. After all, it might have been a
small vessel. The radio had already reported several fishing
craft sunk in the storm and one freighter completely vanished
in its path.

He realized he had the telephone to his ear. He said, 'The
anchorage is four miles distant, sir. There is a Thai launch
approaching, possibly with a pilot aboard.' He heard Dalziel
breathing heavily.

'Very well. I'll come up.'

Standish walked to the rear of the bridge and looked down
at the side deck where some seamen were replacing the lashings
on the whaler. It was a wonder the boats had survived at all.
Then he craned over the rail to watch as the two women
appeared below a Bofors mounting.

The girl had a green headscarf but was still wearing her
khaki jacket. Beside Mrs. Penrath's tweedy figure she looked
slight and defenceless.

The storm must have kept her mind occupied, he thought.
But now the ship was moving towards the shore again. To the
very destination intended for the *Cornwallis*. He thought too of
their brief contact, the moment of hope and trust. With the
passing of the storm it seemed to have been broken, and there
was no longer any more time left.

A light blinked from the fast moving launch, and as the
signalman triggered the recognition back to her Standish saw
the girl raise her eyes to the bridge and look directly at him.
He raised his hand and saw her return the wave. Across the
heads of the seamen, the flaked paintwork and buckled rails
they retained that contact for just a few more moments.

'Well, where's this launch, Number One?' Dalziel strode to
the gratings and lifted his glasses.

Standish dropped his arm and turned towards him. The
contact was broken.

14 Between Friends

Lieutenant Pigott entered Standish's cabin and placed a typed list on the small bulkhead desk. 'Petty Officer Harris's personal effects.' He wiped the back of his neck with a grubby handkerchief. 'Not much to show for twenty odd years service.'

Standish leaned his spine against the chair and studied him thoughtfully. 'All quiet on deck?'

Pigott shrugged. 'The work's going ahead in a sort of fashion.'

Through an open scuttle the afternoon sunlight blazed down across the anchored ship, and Standish could tell from the lack of noise above his cabin that there was very little work being done at all. The captain had gone ashore in the Thai navy launch during the forenoon to see the local authorities about the possibility of unloading the medical stores which had been intended for the Malaysian side of the border. He had taken the two women with him and had not so far returned.

He said, 'Well, they'd better get cracking all the same. The longer the repairs take, the longer we'll be bogged down here.'

In his heart he knew he should go himself and chase them up, jerk them out of their new torpor. He recalled Jerram's words. *I hope they'll still be laughing in a month or two.* And that had been less than a week back.

He said, 'I'm going on deck.'

Together they climbed up to the quarterdeck and paused beneath one of the well-worn awnings. Over the rail the sea looked very clear and inviting, and it was possible to see small

regiments of brightly coloured fish darting towards the motionless screws, pausing stockstill and then flashing away in another
direction. Here and there about the upper deck parties of seamen were working without enthusiasm, their skins brown against
the sky and the haze-shrouded beaches below the town. Few
craft had come near the ship, and although the distant town
looked quiet enough, Standish guessed that even there the
storm's edge had left its mark, and they too were tidying up
before another visit.

The boats had been lowered alongside, and in the battered
motor boat he saw two seamen pumping it dry, their naked
backs shining with sweat in the glare.

In the *Whizz-Kid* two mechanics were putting finishing
touches to a gun mounting above the stemhead. Whatever else
was on Dalziel's mind when he had gone ashore, he had made
quite sure that this job was to be given priority.

Petty Officer Motts, who had been watching the work, came
aft and saluted wearily.

Standish asked, 'All right? Any complaints?'

Motts shrugged. 'I was just lookin' at the new toy, sir.' He
paused before adding bitterly, 'An' wonderin' who the next
poor bugger is who's goin' to get hisself killed.'

Pigott glanced at Standish and then said quietly, 'Can't
really blame you.'

Standish rested his hand on a newly-spliced guardrail and
looked up at the bridge. He thought he saw Irvine moving
about in the chartroom. Somehow they had avoided each other
except for the brief necessity of duty. But it was there right
enough. A latent hostility which they both now accepted.

He thought of the girl and wondered if she had met the man
she would marry. She was probably still in the town. Waiting
and fretting.

Motts said suddenly, 'Some of us 'ave been a bit bothered,
sir.' He dropped his eyes as Standish looked at him. 'Will there
be an inquiry after what's 'appened? I know I shouldn't be
askin' like this, but, well, it don't seem right the way things
are going.'

Pigott said mildly, 'You've been aboard longer than most. I
think you've a right.'

Standish thrust his hands into his pockets. 'You've been

aboard long enough to know that you've no right at all, Motts.'
He saw the changing emotions on Motts' face and guessed what
it had cost him to speak out. He stifled the sudden pity and
added, 'What are you, a leader of some deputation or something?'

'I'm no lower deck lawyer, sir.' Motts looked suddenly
defiant. 'But everyone in our mess knows that the old *Shellback*'s
days are numbered. She's nearly worn 'er guts out, an' there
don't seem any point in gettin' killed, 'specially when there's no
war on.'

Standish eyed him calmly. 'I know Harris was your friend.
But in a storm, a man, anyone at all, can lose his life. It's got
nothing to do with war, and you know it.'

Pigott said, 'There were the others of course.'

Standish replied, 'There may be more. Either way it's not for
you to question your orders, Motts, so carry on with what you
were doing.'

As he walked away Standish turned to Pigott. 'That was a
bloody stupid attitude to take in front of him. Have you been
talking to Irvine?'

Pigott coloured slightly. 'What's the use of beating around
the bush? Everyone's blabbing about it. They won't speak in
front of you because either they respect you too much or they're
afraid you'll take them in front of the captain.' He forced a grin.
'I want to stay in the Service too, y'know. I wouldn't stick my
neck out unless I was damned worried. Which I am.'

Standish tried to shut out the nagging apprehension which
had dogged him since Harris's death. And before that. There
was nothing to be gained by listening to Pigott's interpretation
but he had to do something. But what?

The quartermaster called, 'Boat approaching again, sir.' He
shaded his eyes and added, 'Not the captain.'

It was the same Thai launch, but it contained two different
passengers this time. Both were dressed in neat, lightweight
suits, but from the easy way they climbed up the accommodation ladder Standish guessed them to be naval men.

The first, a sleek-haired man with quick, restless eyes,
introduced himself as Standish stepped forward to meet him.

'Lieutenant-Commander Lamb. British Operations Liaison

Officer to Rear-Admiral Curtis.' He smiled briefly. 'My companion is Lieutenant Rhodes, United States Navy, also from the *Sibuyan*.'

The latter was tall and rather studious looking, with very sparse hair for so junior an officer.

He said, 'Communications are my interest.' He had a lazy drawl, and appeared very relaxed.

Standish ushered them towards a screen door. 'The captain's still ashore I'm afraid, but if I can help you in any way?'

'Yes, maybe you can.' Lamb seemed untroubled at Dalziel's absence, and Standish suspected he knew already.

In the deserted wardroom Lamb said, 'I have just a few instructions which you can pass on to the commanding officer, if you would be so good. Pure routine for the most part.'

The American was wandering around the wardroom, glancing at the ship's crest, the letter rack, and anything which took his fancy.

Lamb continued evenly, 'For the purpose of security your stay here is being described as a courtesy visit. The Thai authorities have expressed the hope you have all you need, as local facilities are somewhat primitive.'

Standish thought of Quarrie and his men who were struggling to put their machinery to rights again.

He said, 'I suppose you could fly any spares to us if need be?'

Lamb glanced round and frowned severely as the American laughed and said, 'Jeez.'

'You'll know soon enough, so I'll get to the point.' Lamb glanced at his watch. 'The *Terrapin* will be returning to Singapore in three months to be paid off. Both the C. in C. and the integrated command to which you are now attached will be grateful if all spares demands are minimal, if not completely nil.'

'I see.' Standish made himself relax and consider the verdict. Paid off. Finished. He had been anticipating it ever since he had stepped aboard, but something about Lamb's dismissal, his offhand words about this old ship filled him with sudden resentment.

The American asked, 'Okay if I go and hunt out the communications department?'

Lamb nodded. 'Not more than fifteen minutes.'

'Sure.' The lieutenant glanced idly around the wardroom. 'Which way do I go?'

Standish said abruptly, 'The quartermaster will take you.'

As the American left the wardroom he said, 'I'd have thought he would have known where to go.'

Lamb shifted in his chair but made no comment. Then he said, 'I wanted to chat to you alone. Off the record, so to speak.' He seemed ill at ease. 'I expect you know what a lot of dust has been stirred up recently. Well, now there's this submarine you allegedly sighted.'

'It was there.' Standish watched the other man's discomfort. It was happening all over again. But this time he was prepared, even eager to see how Lamb would handle it.

'Perhaps. We had no reports of any submarines in the area, but I suppose the Chinese, or the Russians for that matter, might have slipped one through the net. It is a remote possibility.'

'Is that the admiral's opinion?'

Lamb flushed. 'He was interested in the report, naturally. It will be looked into, have no doubt on that score.'

'I take it that Captain Jerram is not so enchanted with the idea?' Standish saw the shot go home, watched the mounting confusion on Lamb's face.

He stood up and walked to an open scuttle before replying, 'You could put it like that.'

Standish watched him coldly. 'In three months time this ship will be dropped from the Navy List, right? So if you wish it, why not just sit back and wait until then, or have your lords and masters already got their axes sharpened?'

Lamb faced him, his face grim. 'Look, I didn't want to come here. But I'm a staff officer, and I do what I'm told just as much as you. There has been a lot of talk. Rumours if you like. I'm not asking you to make a statement, I merely want you to speak to me as you would across the bar in Fort Blockhouse.' He took a deep breath. 'If, and I'm only saying *if*, you were asked, would you accept command of this ship on a temporary basis, until she is paid off?'

Standish stared at him. 'And what about Commander Dalziel?'

'Ah, well, that is a little delicate.'

'Why should that be?' Standish leaned back in his chair and watched him calmly. 'Couldn't he be kidnapped or run over by a truck? Surely a staff officer is well versed in these *delicate* matters?'

Lamb look away. 'I guessed you'd take this attitude. In your shoes I hope I'd have done the same. But I doubt it. However, whatever I believe, you must hear me out. Officially, Dalziel is completely fit and well after his other trouble. Nevertheless, it seems unlikely he'd have got this command but for an oversight somewhere. Maybe some pressure was brought to bear, I don't know or care. What I do know is that Her Majesty's Government is not prepared to get involved in some great Far East commitment merely because of a tactless or ill-devised incident, do I make myself clear?'

'The Americans are equally disinterested in that surely? After Viet Nam they will want to remain on the sidelines for a while.' Standish added bitterly, 'But nobody but a fool would ignore a real threat from the communists again.'

'Quite. Yes, I'm sure you're right.' Lamb consulted his watch. 'I take it then you'd not be interested?'

'No.' Standish was surprised that he had not even hesitated. 'How would you have done it anyway?'

Lamb shrugged. 'Had you been willing to accept command without comment there would have been little fuss. Commander Dalziel might have been prematurely retired. It has happened before, I believe.'

Standish rose from the chair. 'But of course you wouldn't be sure, would you?' He added dryly, 'No fuss. Just a man dropped from circulation because his views don't happen to coincide with someone else's. No inquiry, nothing loud or vulgar like that. Just bang, and oblivion, is that it?'

Lamb faced him. 'We were just *talking*, remember that.' He moved to the door adding, 'I hope for your sake you're right about the next three months. If not, there will be something other than an inquiry to finish this commission, I can assure you!'

On deck they found the American lieutenant leaning on the guardrail watching the work being done to the *Whizz-Kid.*

He looked up and smiled easily. 'Smart boat. Should be a real asset, I'd say.'

Lamb said bleakly, 'We'll leave now. There's a lot to get done before we fly out.' He glanced at Standish. 'Local leave is all right for your people. But they must abide by the military patrols and stay in the town limits. There's been a bit of trouble recently. Ambushes on the roads, you know.'

'I do know.' Standish recalled the burned out village. The charred corpses. 'But nothing you can't handle, eh?'

The American was watching him with quiet interest. As Lamb made for the ladder he reached out and touched Standish's arm. 'See you around. Very interesting visit.' His eyes gleamed in the sunlight. 'That storm must have been quite something.' Then he followed Lamb down the ladder.

As the launch glided away Standish saw the radio supervisor walking aft from the bridge.

'Did you show the American around, Keeble?'

The petty officer shrugged. 'No, sir. 'E didn't want nothing to do with me. 'E was more interested in the radar department an' the chartroom.'

Standish nodded. 'Did Lieutenant Irvine look after him?'

Keeble replied, 'I think so, sir. Funny sort of officer, if you ask me. All questions. Like 'e'd just stepped out of college.'

Standish walked back to the quarterdeck, his mind busy with Keeble's words. Lieutenant Rhodes certainly showed little knowledge of communications, but in Standish's view was no sort of fool. Rear-Admiral Curtis was not the kind of man to have dead-weight on his staff, so where did he fit in?

He was still pacing back and forth beneath the awning when the quartermaster reported that the launch was returning with the captain aboard.

Dalziel listened to the report on the first day's work, and when Standish mentioned the visitors he merely asked, 'What about Rhodes, the American?'

'Communications.' Standish paused. 'So he said.'

'You don't agree?'

'I think he is an Intelligence man, sir.'

Dalziel seemed distant. 'Could well be.' He shot him a quick glance, his deepset eyes suddenly tired. 'We're being paid off in three months, but I suppose they told you?'

'Yes, sir.'

Dalziel looked moodily along the upper deck, his head jutting forward like the day he had come aboard. Standish pictured him in the months and years ahead, with two framed photographs to remind him of his life's work. The destroyer which had been cut in half by a carrier, and this one, the elderly *Terrapin*, which would be taken from him by means more subtle, but no less brutal for him.

Dalziel seemed to feel him watching and said tersely, 'I'm going to shower. I'll be staying aboard if you wish to visit the town.'

'Thank you. I might do that.'

Dalziel turned towards the hatch. 'The Hotel Europa should suit you.' He hesitated, as if struggling with his emotions. 'Miss Gail might still be there, but I could be mistaken.'

Standish watched him as he vanished through the hatch. All at once he was glad he had said nothing about Lamb's cautious questioning and hints.

If Dalziel deserved nothing else he deserved loyalty. No, he thought bitterly, he *needed* it, even if he would never admit it. Perhaps one day in the future he would be able to look back and see all this as an episode. The action aboard the *Cornwallis*, the submarine's blip on the radar, even Dalziel himself would become blurred against the other things which might happen. He would eventually let them all slide into memory, even as his own suffering was now doing.

But as he looked slowly along the littered deck and at the storm-scarred paintwork he found himself doubting, knowing that he did not want to lose the *Terrapin*, any more than Dalziel did.

There was no reason or sense in it. Any fool could see that. Just as there was no point in going ashore in the hopes of seeing that girl. But he would go nevertheless, just as he knew he would back Dalziel in spite of his own doubts. Or perhaps because of them.

*   *   *

The Hotel Europa stood on the corner of a wide street facing the sea. By the time Standish had got ashore the sun had already disappeared beyond the inland hills, and the lengthening purple shadows of evening were broken here and there by lighted

windows and open doors. It was not too dark to see that the
hotel hardly lived up to its name. It was three stories high, with
the upper rooms opening on to well-weathered verandas, and
the paintwork was scarred and blistered by many suns. Only the
nameboard was freshly painted, and he guessed that in its lifetime the hotel had changed its title to suit the times. Many
conquerors had been and gone, and it was likely that the name
would one day change again as a matter of expediency or tact.

The town, or what he had seen of it on his way from the jetty,
was as varied as he could have imagined. Across the street from
the hotel was a small cinema surmounted by a giant and garish
hoarding depicting an American western with Thai lettering.
Immediately outside the cinema was an ornate and delicately
carved shrine, below which sat three Buddhist monks, their faces
quite expressionless and unmoved by the people who thronged
around them in a slow, colourful tide.

The military were much in evidence. Jeeps were parked in
several side streets, their uniformed occupants idly watching the
passing crowds, their hands never far from their weapons.

Yet in spite of them the atmosphere was peaceful, even gentle,
and as he walked quickly towards the hotel he was conscious of
the different dialects, the mixed aromas of incense and fish, the
dusty American cars vying for position with handcarts and
rickshaws.

Inside the hotel entrance he saw some servants extinguishing
oil lamps as the overhead fans started to revolve in squeaking
unison.

The round-faced clerk at the desk beamed at him and rolled
his eyes to the roof. 'The electricity has only just returned.' He
made an eloquent shrug. 'Storms or bandits, who can tell?'

Standish glanced towards the main lounge and bar. There
were several Europeans there, some in crisp slacks and coloured
shirts, their cropped hair and youthful exuberance suggesting
them to be some of the many American airmen who were
serving at Thai bases up country.

He asked, 'Is there a Miss Gail here?'

The man regarded him with new interest. 'Perhaps.'

'Could I see her?' Standish felt uneasy under his inscrutable
stare.

'It might be arranged.' He coughed and then smiled as Standish placed some money on his desk. 'At once, sir.'

He snapped his fingers and a small boy scampered from a stool beside the entrance. He spoke to the boy quickly and then looked at Standish. 'If you will follow, he will take you to the English lady, sir.'

As Standish started after the minute Thai youth he noticed that the clerk was busy counting his easily gained bribe.

On the next floor were several smaller lounges, obviously for the convenience of hotel residents. They looked shabby and much used, and Standish imagined they were usually occupied by visiting engineers and servicemen on leave who would care little for the lack of comfort.

The boy opened a door and nodded emphatically towards the opposite side of the room. There was a double door which opened on to one of the verandas, and outlined against the darkening sky he saw someone looking towards the sea.

When she turned into the lamplight he hardly recognized her. She was wearing a plain yellow dress, her tanned arms and legs bare, while the long black hair hung across her shoulders, loose and shining in the light.

Standish said uncertainly, 'Thought I'd come and see that everything's all right.' He had made a fool of himself again. Gone was the drill jacket and despair. She was lovely and quite unreachable in her new guise, and he saw a kind of defiance in her eyes as she replied, 'That was nice of you. Please sit down.'

Before he could reach a chair she had turned again and walked on to the veranda.

'I have been watching your ship. She looks so small from here.'

Standish followed her and leaned his hands on the blistered rail, very aware of her nearness, her warmth, and the scent of her hair.

He made himself look towards the dark blue water in which some early stars were already mirrored like tiny lanterns. The *Terrapin* was little more than a black shadow, but even a mile offshore he could see her bright anchor light, the faint glow of scuttles beneath her awnings.

He asked quietly, 'Has anything happened yet?'

She shook her head. 'There was a message. A car was being

sent to the hotel for me. Perhaps it was delayed in some way.'
It sounded like a question.

Standish said, 'Perhaps. There has been some trouble on the
roads. The army might have stopped all traffic for a bit.' He
hesitated. 'Has Mrs. Penrath gone?'

'Yes. Her husband came for her. She did not want to leave
me on my own, but it was unfair to keep her. Her husband had
to get back to his work. He was a nice, jolly little man. I liked
him.'

Standish said gently, 'You shouldn't be up here like this. You
could go outside, have a look round. You might enjoy it.'

'I tried earlier.' She turned away. 'I suppose it was my fault.
There were several young men. They kept looking at me.
Following me.'

Standish cursed himself. 'Probably Americans on leave. You
can hardly blame them for looking at you. When I came in just
now I thought . . .'

She swung round suddenly, her hair half hiding her face.
'What did you think? That she looks like a girl who would be
easy, is that what you thought?'

She let her arms fall to her sides as Standish placed his hands
on her shoulders and gripped them tightly.

'You know I didn't think that.' He felt her resist and then
give in as he pulled her against his chest. 'I just want you to be
happy, to try and forget everything else.' He touched her hair
very gently and felt her spine stiffen again. 'I had no right to
come, but I'm glad I did all the same.'

'What shall I do?' The defiance had gone. She sounded
confused and uncertain.

'I need not return to the ship until tomorrow morning.' He
was speaking very carefully, afraid that he might break the
fragile link. 'I will send word to them where I am and book a
room in the hotel.' She made as if to release herself but he
continued, 'It will be all right. I promise you. Your future
husband would not like to think of you alone, be sure of that.'

'Why are you doing all this?'

He replied, 'If you were my sister I'd not like to think of you
here on your own either.'

She leaned back and looked directly into his face. Her eyes
were searching and very grave. 'But you are not my brother.'

'No.' He tried to smile but it would not come. 'I'm not anything.'

Then she stepped away from him and touched his arm with her fingers.

'I would like you to be here. Thank you.' She tossed the hair from her face and smiled. 'I always seem to be thanking you, don't I?'

Angry voices and the sound of breaking glass echoed up from the street, and when Standish glanced down he saw some pale, hurrying shapes before they vanished into a side alley. Some of *Terrapin*'s libertymen. There would be more bleary-eyed defaulters to face tomorrow after a night on the town. When he looked round again he saw that she was watching him, her face serious and troubled.

'When I was looking at the ship I was wondering what would happen to you also. I hope, no I *want* you to be happy, too.'

She brushed a strand of hair from her eyes as a cool breeze fanned across the veranda. Even that movement was painful for him to see, and the thought of not seeing her after this night was even more unbearable.

'It will be another ship sometime. New faces.' He shrugged. 'I'll have to get used to the idea.' It was strange how distant and unreal the other problems seemed now that he was here. With her. Dalziel, Irvine, even the ship were another part of him, out there, waiting to reclaim his loyalties or his enmity.

The door opened slightly and a white-coated servant said hesitantly, 'There has been a message. Mr. Winter has been delayed. He will arrive some time tonight.'

Standish watched her, realizing it was the first time he had heard the man's name. Perhaps he had tried to shut out even that piece of reality.

She said quietly, 'It's Roger. He's coming.'

'I see.' He watched her hands clenching into tight fists, saw the quick painful thrust of her breasts through the yellow dress, as if she was on the verge of panic. 'Would you like a drink? It might help to steady you.' He made the smile come. 'I'll bet he's a lot more nervous than you are!'

She stared at him as if she had not heard. Then she replied quickly, 'No, thank you.' She walked vaguely to the centre of the room and stood by the light, her hair shining like black silk beneath it.

'I think I'd better go. To my room.' She waited for him to reach her. 'I might have to leave tonight. I . . . I don't know.'

'I'm staying anyway.' He gripped her hand firmly. 'Just in case.' He did not know how to go on, nor did he want to stop. 'The ship will be anchored offshore for several days yet. We might see each other again if . . .'

She held up her hand and touched his lips. Her fingers were very cool.

'Don't say any more. Please. It won't do any good. For either of us, will it?'

He gripped the hand and held it against his mouth. 'No. I'm sorry.'

'Don't be.' She took her hands away and moved back towards the door. 'You've done so much for me. More than you'll ever know.' Her eyes widened as if from shock. 'I don't even know your name!'

He stood quite still. 'Rex.' It sounded flat and final.

'Goodbye, Rex. I'll remember the promise. I will write if . . .' She turned and almost ran from the room.

He looked at the open door for several seconds, his mind empty of feeling. Knowing it would soon return, like an old pain.

'Goodbye, Suzane.' The empty room seemed to echo his words, and he walked slowly down the stairway to the desk to make his arrangements.

The clerk listened attentively and then watched as Standish took out his wallet.

'I will send a message in my brother-in-law's boat, sir. It shall be done.'

'Thanks.' He hesitated, only half aware of the noise and laughter from the bar. 'Do you have any gin?'

'So sorry, sir. No. Mostly Americans come here.' He shrugged. 'They seem to prefer whisky or vodka.' He gestured towards a shelf behind him. 'The whisky is, er, Japanese. The vodka I cannot vouch for.'

Standish said, 'Get me a bottle of vodka and send it to my room.'

Later, as he sat in a battered cane chair beside the bed he

wondered what he was going to do. Before, things had been planned, even predictable. After the submarine *Electra* he had intended to transfer to nuclear boats, the new way of life. But the fire and Alison had changed all that.

When he looked at the bottle he saw it was half empty, yet he felt ice cold sober.

What was there left for him? And to what purpose?

He thought of the girl along the corridor, and what might have been. Another delusion, one more hopeless dream.

Below his window a police klaxon brought an answering chorus of shouts and the shrill cries of some seabirds which had been dozing on the hotel's corrugated iron roof.

Slowly, almost without thinking, Standish started to fill his pipe, his eyes distant as he watched the stars beyond the veranda. The pipe was still unlit when his head lolled against the back of the chair and he fell into a deep, mindless sleep.

At five in the morning a barefooted servant padded into the room with a pot of black coffee. After shaking Standish's shoulder until he was awake he stood back to stare at the untouched bed with something like disapproval.

Standish stood up and examined his crumpled clothes and felt the stubble on his chin. He had brought nothing ashore from the ship, and he was conscious of the hammers beating against the lining of his skull.

He asked, 'The young English lady. Is she awake?'

The man shook his head and gave a toothy grin. 'She leave in the night. Her man come in great hurry.' He nodded cheerfully. 'Great hurry.'

'And I was asleep.' Standish turned towards the window and the shimmering expanse of sea below the horizon.

'Any message for me?'

The servant frowned. 'From the British ship, sir?' He saw the look on Standish's face and added hastily, 'No messages, sir.'

What could she have said anyway? He walked on to the veranda and stared down at the cool, deserted street.

It was over.

15 The Only Place

IN three days, to the casual observer at least, the ship's storm
damage had been put to rights, and Quarrie announced that
the starboard propeller shaft was as good as could be
expected under the circumstances.

The *Terrapin*'s brief visit had not altogether been a happy
one. There had been more trouble ashore, including fights with
the police and several incidents of brawls with the town's
shopkeepers for no reason at all. One able seaman had been
sent overland to Singapore after receiving a severe head wound,
the cause of which was as obscure to him as to the patrol which
had found him bleeding in a back alley with half his uniform
torn from his body.

Dalziel had received several complaints from the local
authorities but had remarked on each occasion, 'Just high
spirits. It'll pass.'

But on board his attitude had been somewhat different. In
spite of growing resentment he had driven officers and ratings
alike with no less determination than he had shown when he
had first taken command.

On the last evening as the officers gathered in the wardroom
the place stank of fresh paint, while from the bathrooms came
an unending rattle of pipes as the libertymen prepared for one
final run ashore to mark the end of the 'courtesy visit.'

Apart from the regular inspections of work progress about the
ship Standish had had little contact with the captain. When he
was not goading and threatening, Dalziel had spent most of his
spare time ashore. Pigott had told Standish that he had seen the

captain on one occasion in company with Lieutenant Rhodes, the studious looking American, who had apparently flown in unheralded on some mission or other. Mostly, Standish suspected, to keep an eye on the *Terrapin*'s progress and report back to Admiral Curtis.

Standish sat in his usual chair, an untouched glass by his elbow as he watched the others grouped around the open scuttles.

Somehow or other a bag of mail had at last caught up with the ship, and for once the talk was not of the *Terrapin*'s inner problems, but of that other, remote world which Standish had almost forgotten.

Caley was unusually talkative, and even this early was well flushed with beer. It seemed that his daughter, the apple of his eye, was to be married. She was only seventeen, and the lucky man was apparently a marine corporal on the Admiral's staff at Portsmouth.

He was saying thickly, 'A good lad to all accounts. He's got a cushy little number an' should be able to make sergeant if he keeps his nose clean.' He frowned. 'Still, I don't see why there's such a bloody hurry to get spliced. I might not be home in time to see it.'

Pigott glanced at Rideout and raised one eyebrow. The doctor turned away hurriedly to hide his expression from a baffled Caley.

On the other side of the wardroom Quarrie was listening with obvious resignation to Hornby's news from home. His son had been made captain of the school's cricket team.

'Did I say, he's only ten, you know!' Hornby's flabby face was shining with pride.

Quarrie nodded gloomily. 'Yes. You did mention it a few dozen times.'

Rideout had received a whole bundle of letters, but had opened the most official one first. After a quick examination he had taken it to his cabin to read in privacy. Looking at him now, Standish was unable to imagine what had caused so much interest.

He glanced at the full glass beside him and swallowed hard. He would wait a bit longer. In the last few days he had been drinking a lot, so there never seemed to be any time when he was completely clear-headed. The work, the sun, the constant stream of problems and complaints had been made almost bearable in this way, but as he looked at the glass he felt something like disgust. The others were friendly enough, but seemed embarrassed by him. They probably imagined he was still brooding about his wife. He picked up the glass and let the gin burn the back of his throat. But for a few moments they had forgotten about him, and were unconscious of the hurt they might be offering as he listened to their talk of home, of wives and of security.

Wishart crossed to his chair and sat down beside him.

Standish said, 'No letters for you Sub?'

'Only one.' Wishart relaxed slightly. 'Just a bill from Gieves though.' He dropped his voice. 'We're off tomorrow then?'

Standish thought of Dalziel's face an hour earlier when he had told him of the new orders. An independent patrol again, but this time higher up into the great Gulf of Thailand. Until the patrol was cancelled, or the ship was relieved, they would never get closer to land than one hundred miles.

He replied, 'Yes. There have been reports of fishing boats in our allotted area.' It sounded vague, and it was. 'Intelligence apparently think there might be a possibility of smuggling. Exchanging arms and illicit goods at sea.' He took another drink. 'It's another stop and search job.'

Wishart nodded. 'A bit lonely.'

'You could put it like that.' Standish ignored the curious look on Wishart's face. He had said almost the same thing to Dalziel, half expecting him to agree. But he had said firmly, 'In a way, Number One. But I cannot agree altogether. It does give us elasticity, a fluidity of movement, eh?'

Standish could not be sure if Dalziel meant it, or whether he was just making the best of what must now be evident as the ship's last active task.

Dalziel must have had a letter from someone, too. As Standish had turned to leave the cabin he had remarked, 'It seems that young Irvine will be going on his commanding officer's course after this commission ends. He'll get his half-stripe, and then . . .' He had stopped there and had looked slowly round the small, outdated cabin. 'All this will have been excellent training for him.'

Even now, just thinking about it, made Standish feel uneasy. Dalziel had seemed so pathetic, so unusually lost in his own thoughts that for a few brief moments his guard had dropped.

Wishart asked, 'What will become of the ship?'

Standish signalled for another drink. 'They'll probably try and sell her to some up and coming power. You know the sort of thing surely. A country that takes all our aid and spends the cash on building its armed forces. It's a great incentive for the newly freed colonial people. Join the army, or bloody well starve!' He looked at Wishart and smiled. 'Sorry. Not my day.'

God. I'm beginning to sound like Dalziel now. Why should Wishart's question affect him like this, or at all? It was just a ship. One more for the breakers. But it did matter, and he could not help himself.

Feet clattered on the deck outside the door and a massive figure staggered over the coaming, supported on two sticks. It was the giant Australian engineer they had found in the burning village. He was scarlet in the face and had a bottle protruding from each jacket pocket.

He grinned broadly as they pounded his shoulders and boomed, 'Had to come out and see you before you goes off again. I heard you was leaving, so I decided to cadge a lift with my two friends here an' make it a party.'

His friends were a pair of Thai customs officers who had been regular visitors to the ship during her stay at anchor. They spoke little English but were beaming from ear to ear with pleasure at their unexpected treatment.

The Australian tapped his nose and added, 'Course, I'll be sure of a lift back this way, eh, lads?'

He saw Standish and hobbled over to greet him. As he flopped into a chair he said wheezily, 'Jeez, I'm glad I caught you. Wanted to shake yer paw once more to thank you for all the trouble an' that.' He raised his leg gingerly. 'It was a near thing that time.'

Standish signalled to Wills. 'We were all lucky. Anyway, I've already been ashore once.'

The man eyed him strangely.'All the same.' He waited until Wills had brought the drinks. 'With a lovely little sheila like that I'd have thought you'd have been dancing a bloody jig by now.'

Standish smiled to hide his sudden despair. 'I didn't think anyone had noticed. But she's gone. Left the ship three days ago.'

'Well, there's a thing.' He swallowed deeply and smacked his lips. 'I'd have liked to speak to her too before I shove off back to the bloody job. A real nice little sheila.' He sighed. 'But what with the traffic and my gammy leg, I wasn't fast enough. When I got across the street she was gone.'

Standish stared at him. 'When was this?'

'What's the matter with you, deaf or something?' He was grinning broadly. 'I was on my way here. Just now, for Christ's sake.'

Standish took the glass and held it with both hands. She was back, and he was still sitting here, drinking, listening to his own heart beating like a drum.

'Are you sure?'

'Sure I'm sure.' The Australian prodded his leg with a stick. 'Along that street by some crabby cinema. Hell, you take some convincing, you sure do!'

Standish was on his feet, his mind racing as he tried to think what he should do next. He felt dazed and sick, and cursed himself for drinking so much. It couldn't be true. It was impossible.

He heard himself ask, 'Did you ever meet another engineer called Winter?'

'What, the bloke who's got the big job up the coast here? Sure I have. Ours is a bloody small world, I can tell you. What about him?'

'What's he like?'

Something in his tone made the Australian stop grinning. 'He's young. Got a good head an' more degrees to his name than I've got teeth. He's the sort of joker you end up working for. Not one to really *know*.'

'You didn't like him then?'

'Hell, I only met him a few times when I was building a bridge a couple of years back.' He frowned, his eyes vanishing into red folds of flesh. 'Put it this way. He's a bloody perfectionist. Everything's got to be just right. Kind of bloke who'd wear silk pyjamas in the Sahara, get the idea?'

Standish looked round. 'I have to go ashore. If I'm not back

before you leave I hope everything pans out all right for you.'
He held out his hand. 'I'm glad we got to you in time.'

'Thanks. Me, too.' He looked at Standish gravely. 'I hope I
didn't put my foot in it just now.'

Standish smiled. 'No.' He beckoned to Wishart. 'I'm going
ashore, Sub. Tell the O.O.D.'

Wishart asked quietly, 'Shall I pipe for the motor boat?'

'No.' He cocked his head. 'I'll go in the Thai boat with the
libertymen. It sounds as if it's just leaving.'

As he left the wardroom Wishart said, 'It must be pretty
urgent.'

The Australian looked up from his chair and winked. 'I
would say that you have just made a fair judgment, young fella.
Now would you mind calling your steward to fill an old man's
glass before he dies of thirst?'

Caley lurched against the chair and said, 'Did I tell you
about my girl? She's gettin' spliced!' He swayed back on his
heels and tried to focus the Australian with his eyes. 'You know
what I think? I reckon that bloody bootneck's got 'er in the
family way!'

The engineer grinned. 'Sit down an' have another drink,
mate. It'll all be the same in a hundred years, so what the hell.'

Caley muttered, 'I'll kill that bastard when I get home. You
see if I don't.'

*   *   *

Standish hardly noticed the awkward silence in the launch
as it sped towards the jetty, its hull crammed with shoregoing
members of the ship's company. Some of the ratings who moved
up to make room for him had already been across his desk as
defaulters, and his unexpected presence caused a few uneasy
thoughts amongst them.

Nor did he see much of the town as he strode through the
lengthening shadows towards the Hotel Europa, the only place
he could think the girl would be. Where she had to be.

The same clerk was squatting behind his counter and stared
at Standish without recognition for several seconds. Unlike the
previous visit Standish was in uniform, but in his sudden

anxiety he put the man's blank stare down to another opening for a bribe.

As he tugged out his wallet he snapped, 'Miss Gail, is she here?'

'Oh it is you, sir!' His olive eyes dropped to the wallet. 'Yes, indeed. We were greatly busy when she came back, but I did all I could to make her stay a happy one. It is not often we get ...'

Standish asked harshly, 'The same room?'

He nodded, 'Yes, sir.'

'I'll go up.' He put a note on the counter and added, 'You'll be able to buy the hotel soon.'

The man watched him go and pursed his lips. Buy the hotel? Later maybe. But first a large American car, he thought dreamily.

At the end of the passage Standish paused, momentarily dazed by the speed of events since the Australian had unwittingly told him about the girl's return. Perhaps it was a temporary visit, until her new home was prepared? He looked up and down the deserted corridor with its flaking walls and long strip of threadbare carpet. No, that couldn't be possible. Nobody would send a woman here willingly.

He was outside the door, and was conscious of the silence pressing in around him. As if the whole building was holding its breath, waiting for him to act. Half the number was missing from the door, and beneath the paint he could see a deep scar, as if someone had once smashed a bottle against it.

He knocked, feeling the painful beat of his heart, the new dryness in his throat.

Her voice seemed to come from far away. 'Come in, please. The door is unlocked.'

Apart from a small lamp beside the bed the room was in darkness, and as he stepped inside the door Standish realized that like most of the accommodation this one opened on to a veranda above the street.

Then he saw her. She was standing just outside the window, her figure pale against the sky. Like that other night, when together they had looked at the ship.

She turned towards him saying, 'I am not really hungry, but

you can put it by the bed. If I want . . .' She broke off, one hand moving to her throat. 'Rex!'

'I heard you were back. I had to come.' He dropped his cap on the floor. 'Why didn't you tell me? I might never have known . . .'

She was still staring at him, her eyes shining in the small light as she watched from the shadows.

He moved towards her. 'What has happened, Suzane? Is there anything I can do?'

Before he could reach her she turned away and walked back to the veranda rail, seizing it with both hands as she stared straight out towards the sea.

In a low voice she said, 'I couldn't tell you. After all that's happened, how could I ask for help now? It would have been unfair to you.'

He stood just behind her left shoulder, his eyes on the sea where a pale sliver of moon had appeared above its reflection to make a small silver edge to the horizon. The ship was there as before, adding her own lights to the display. He wanted to touch her, to hold her, but knew it was not the moment. Even her voice seemed different, as if at last her resistance was crumbling and all the pent-up fears and despair were tearing her apart.

She said, 'He came in the night. It all happened so suddenly that I didn't really get a chance to say anything until we were on the road. Even then he didn't say much. He just kept driving, driving.' Standish felt her shudder. 'We got to the bungalow before dawn, but I don't remember much about it. He started to talk then, as if he could not stop himself. He was like a stranger, yet at the same time was just as I remembered.' She shook her head. 'I'm not making any sense, am I?'

'Don't stop. Get it out now. Put it behind you.' Very gently he slipped his arm around her shoulders. 'It's growing cold out here.'

She continued, 'He kept on asking about what happened. He wasn't angry or disgusted, or anything like that. He seemed to be fascinated.'

Standish squeezed her shoulder and tried to keep his voice level. 'I'm sorry.' It sounded so inadequate, so utterly opposite to the way he felt. He could see the bungalow as clearly as if

he had been there with her. The dawn light uncovering the
alien surroundings, and the man questioning and probing,
stripping her mind bare with his persistence.

'I tried to be calm about it, but nothing I said could move
him from this thing. So I told him I was tired, and then he
became almost attentive again. Even apologized for his not
being here to meet me.'

Standish knew there was more to come, but was totally
unprepared as she continued quietly, 'If I hadn't been so keyed
up and tired I might have realized.' Her voice shook. 'I was
undressing in a bedroom when he came in. It was his own
room of course. I should have seen.' She was speaking faster
now, as if she could not get the words out quickly enough.

'He took hold of me, and all the time kept saying how sorry
he was, over and over again. And that marriage wasn't important now, and things like that. I remember looking over his
shoulder while he was undressing me, and I think it was at that
moment I realized something.' She shivered. 'Before, I suppose
I had convinced myself that whatever happened I would
accept it. I would stifle my feelings, do as you said and put all
that other . . .' She cleared her throat. 'Put it behind me.'

She turned slowly and looked up at him, her face hidden in
shadow.

'But it wasn't like that at all. It was not that I could not let
him, I just didn't *want* him any more!'

Standish gripped her against his chest as she buried her face
and said, 'He started to shout at me, but I put my dress back
on, I made myself do it even though I wanted to run away and
hide, or be sick. When he saw I meant to go he called me names,
words . . .' It was then that the tears came, and as Standish
guided and half carried her into the room she sobbed, 'So I
came back here. The one place. The only place.'

'I know.' He lowered her into a chair and dropped on his
knees beside her. 'If only you'd told me earlier.'

The tears were pouring down her face, but her eyes were
wide open as she studied him as if seeing him for the first time.
Then she said huskily, 'I was going to stay here until the ship
sailed. I couldn't leave before then.'

He held her hand to his mouth. 'And I might never have
known.'

'I didn't want you to think I was running to you because of what happened. Not you, Rex, of all people.'

In the feeble light from the bedside lamp he saw she was wearing the same yellow dress, the one she had been saving for that special moment. It was crumpled now, and there was a smudge of oil on the hem.

He said, 'I'm the one who would come running. Ever since the first time we met, you've always been with me.' He felt her hair brushing his face as she bent over him. 'The ship leaves tomorrow morning. I have some money with me...' He reached up to touch her lips as she started to protest. 'Could you, would you wait for me? For three months?' She said nothing and he felt something like anguish as he added quickly, 'The ship will be returning to Singapore on or before that time. If you fly there, I know a place where you can stay. Where you could wait, make up your mind.'

She threw her arms around his neck, her words muffled in sobs although she seemed to be laughing at the same time.

'I don't have to wait three months to decide. I know *now*. I think that like you I have always known.'

He said, 'I must send a message to the ship. I will not be needed until morning.'

She slipped her arms from around his neck and watched as he got to his feet.

Then she said, 'Promise you won't be long. There is so much I want to hear about you.' She held his hand to her face and kissed it gently. 'Then I will feel as if I am already part of you.'

It took longer than Standish had anticipated to make the clerk understand what he wanted. Or perhaps he was to blame. His mind was still reeling from what had happened, and he had to force himself to concentrate as he wrote a message to be carried out to the ship.

When he returned to the room he found her standing by the window again, but instead of a dress she was wearing a white bath robe. The dress lay in one corner of the room and he looked at it as she said, 'I'm never going to wear it again.' Then she saw the bottle and glasses he was holding and asked, 'Is it wine?'

He nodded. 'The clerk downstairs has a sense of occasion, just as he understands the value of money.'

He poured two glasses of wine, conscious the whole time of her watching him, the sudden tension between them. He said, 'He gave me the same room as before. He handed her a glass and took her other hand in his. 'To us.' And thank God for that Australian.'

'Australian?'

'It doesn't matter. I'll tell you about it one day.' He squeezed her fingers. 'In Singapore.'

She asked, 'What time must you go?'

'Five in the morning.' He tried to smile. 'The Navy always does things at the crack of dawn. No one really knows why.'

She trembled and he said quickly, 'Come away from that window. It gets cold at nights here.' He bolted the shutters and then turned as she said in the same low voice, 'It's not that. I think I'm afraid.'

She did not resist as he took her in his arms. 'You don't have to go tonight. I want you to know that.'

He ran his fingers through her hair. It was like warm silk. 'I can wait, my darling. I just want you to stop worrying.'

When he tried to see her face she pressed it against his chest so that he could hardly hear her.

'I have to *know*, Rex. I don't want to fail you, or hurt you ever again.' She was shaking as if from cold, but when he lifted her chin her skin felt hot, even feverish.

He said quietly, 'You couldn't fail me, even if you wanted to.'

She shook her head, the hair tumbling around her neck as she said, 'I might. I couldn't wait three months with that on my mind. I love you too much.' She became very still and looked at him steadily. 'Do you understand?'

'Yes, I do understand.'

She stepped back from his arms and said, 'I love you. Remember that always.'

Then she reached for the bedside lamp but stopped as Standish said quietly, 'No. Not this time.'

Obediently she stood facing the bed, her hands hanging at her sides, then after another hesitation she undid the robe and let it fall to the floor.

Standish watched her in silence. The light played across her spine and over the gentle curve of her hip, so that in the glow her skin shone like pale satin. He waited, knowing she was holding down that same anguish. Willing her to overcome it.

Then she turned slowly and faced him. Her mouth was quivering and there were tears on her cheeks as she held out her arms and said, 'I do love you.'

She did not take her eyes from his face as he picked her up and laid her gently on top of the bed. Only when he started to undress did she speak again. 'Love me. Whatever I do or say, *love me!*'

For a while longer he tortured himself, standing beside the bed, looking down at her and the supple perfection of her body. Her eyes were closed, and her hands, which were pressed against her sides were bunched into tight fists. As if she was holding her breath, forcing her limbs to obey her.

As his shadow moved across her he saw her tense, and beneath one uplifted breast noticed the quick, nervous pulsating of her heart. He could hear roaring in his head, and was aware of the mixed and demanding emotions which flooded through him like fire. To love and protect her. Or to take her here and now no matter what protest or reluctance still hung to her memory of that torment aboard the *Cornwallis*. That and so many other things flashed through his mind; so that when his hand moved down to touch her shoulder it was like being a spectator. An onlooker to something over which he had no control.

Then he was beside her, feeling her flesh against his, her hair soft on his arm as he propped himself upon his elbow to look down at her face.

Along the corridor a door banged and someone shouted with sudden anger, but he did not hear any of it. He watched his hand as it moved down still further to encircle her breast, felt her shudder as she turned her face away, the hair hiding her face from him.

Her body was quite rigid and did not stir as he embraced and caressed it. Then as his fingers touched the soft curve of her stomach she gasped aloud, twisting her head from side to side, her forehead moist in the lamplight. He pressed his mouth on hers, murmuring unheard words, clasping her as if to defy and destroy the tension like a living thing.

As his hand continued to move he felt her arm trapped between them trying to force itself free, to push him away even

as she was endeavouring to turn her face from his. Then he held
her, the heat of his hand and her body, the desperate embrace
of their breath and lips joining together so that for several time-
less moments neither of them moved.

He drew his face away and saw that her eyes were open, and
he could taste the tears on his mouth as she said very quietly,
'Oh God, I love you . . .' Beneath his hand he felt her stirring,
knew that his own desire was matched by hers, but still could not
break the link held between their eyes.

Then as he raised himself above her, saw his shadow enfolding
her naked body like a cloak, she said, 'Now. Rex! *Now!*'

It was like falling, down and down, with her arms pale and
indistinct as they reached out on either side like parts of a white
crucifix. He felt her arch her back, closed his eyes as she rose to
take and enfold him, drawing him down still further until they
were one. Her hands were on his shoulders and his neck, the
nails biting into the flesh without pain, her breath hot against
his cheek until their combined passion spent itself in a climax
which neither wanted to stop.

Later, as she lay with her head on his chest, she said, 'Must
we sleep? Must we waste what time we have left?'

Standish reached out and poured two glasses of wine on the
bedside table. As he held a glass to her lips he said, 'You are
beautiful.'

She smiled, some of the wine spilling across his chest. 'So are
you.'

He saw her eyes move across his body and then she said
gravely, 'Your scars. I have not seen them before.' She touched
the discoloured flesh with her fingers and then bent down to
kiss it, her hair brushing across his skin like a warm breeze.

The glass rolled unheeded on to the floor, the sound like a
signal of their awakening desire.

When the first sliver of grey light filtered around the bolted
shutters Standish was still awake, holding her to him, listening
to her relaxed breath, to the steady beat of her breast against
his own body. He wanted to keep awake, to memorize every
part of it, so that nothing should be lost to him.

A car ground through the street below the window, and he
heard someone whistling, probably on his way to work.

Very gently he removed his arm from under her head and

swung his legs to the floor. He should have been exhausted, but as he groped for his uniform he was aware of an entirely different sensation. He felt alive, even light-headed, as if a great weight had been lifted from him.

When he looked again her eyes were open, watching him. He sat on the bed and touched her hair. 'It is time.'

She did not speak as he laid an envelope on the table and added, 'This is where I will meet you. I shall make the arrangements.'

He ran his hand around her neck and down across her breasts. This time there was no tension, and she watched for several seconds before saying huskily, 'If you touch me again I'll not allow you to go.'

Feet padded in the corridor and Standish imagined the perplexed servant calling at an empty room to rouse him.

He said, 'I shall be thinking of you all the time I'm away.'

She slid from the bed and pulled him against her. He knew from her voice she was trying not to cry. 'Have you any regrets? You must tell me.'

'Only that it took so long to find you.' He kissed her and then held her away, fixing her in his mind with the other memories. Her eyes were shining, both from happiness and with tears which she could no longer control.

'I will be watching from the window.'

Standish tried to hide his own growing awareness of loss. 'Not like that, my darling, or they'll raid the hotel!' He touched her bare shoulder and then picked up his cap.

'Until Singapore then.'

She nodded, her lip twitching as she said, 'Take care. Take good care of yourself.'

It had to be broken. He opened the door and then paused once more to look back.

She was standing beside the disordered bed, her naked body gleaming in the growing light from the window, her eyes on his face as he said, 'I love you.'

Then he found he was in the corridor and hurrying towards the same, shabby stairway. Strangely, it did not look so shabby now, he thought. He waved to a startled servant carrying a tray of coffee.

'Shan't be needing it now. But thanks all the same.'

The man was still gaping after him as he ran lightly down the steps and on to the road which led to the waterfront, and the sea.

*   *   *

The morning sunshine was hazy and the distant town already half hidden by a sea mist when the *Terrapin*'s anchor cable started to clank inboard through the hawsepipe.

Standish stood on the upper bridge, his cap tilted across his eyes as he watched Wishart leaning over the guardrail to study the cable's progress. Around the bridge the watchkeepers were at their stations, and on the fore gratings Dalziel was polishing his binoculars with a piece of tissue.

'Check that our new launch is properly secured.' Dalziel sounded irritable.

Standish heard the message being relayed across a telephone and marvelled that he still felt so remote from it all. He had received a few curious glances in the wardroom, and Dalziel had remarked, 'Just going to send a damned search party for you!' But he seemed content to leave it at that.

Overhead a steady plume of smoke billowed from the funnel, and Standish wondered if Quarrie was thinking about today. This might be the last voyage for the *Terrapin*. Except for the one to a breaker's yard.

Leading Seaman Neal climbed into the bridge and saluted. 'The outboard launch is secured on her chocks, sir.'

Dalziel swung round, his eyes hidden behind sun glasses. 'What? Oh yes, good.'

From forward came the cry, 'Up and down, sir!'

Neal had turned to go but Dalziel snapped, 'Wait!' Then he nodded towards Standish. 'Ring down slow ahead both engines.'

As the telegraphs clanged below the bridge Dalziel returned his attention to the expressionless leading seaman.

'When I pass an order of such value, I expect the buffer to come himself and report results, one way or the other, right?'

Neal eyed him flatly. 'Aye, aye, sir.'

'Both engines slow ahead, sir. Wheel's amidships.' Corbin's voice echoed tinnily up the pipe. But nobody was paying much attention to it. Every face was on Dalziel as he rapped, 'Well, tell Petty Officer Harris to get up here *on the double!*'

From forward again, 'Anchor's aweigh, sir!'

Neal said, 'P.O. Harris is dead sir. The executive officer has appointed me acting chief bosun's mate.'

Dalziel stared at him. 'Dead?' He looked around at the others. 'Yes, of course. Yes.' He did not seem to know what to do with his hands. Then he thrust them into his pockets and added shortly, 'Starboard ten.' He crossed to the gyro. 'Midships. Steady.'

Standish watched him, suddenly aware of the creeping sensation of apprehension returning. He saw the others nearby, their faces like masks. Hostility, anger or disgust, it was hard to tell what most of them were thinking.

Dalziel seemed to realize that Neal was still there and said, 'Well, you can carry on. Make a good job of it and I'll see . . .' He did not finish it.

Corbin again, detached and unaware of this tiny drama. 'Steady sir. Course zero-four-five.'

Dalziel lowered his head to the voicepipe. 'Steady as you go, Cox'n, until we clear the anchorage limits.'

Standish raised his glasses and tried to find the hotel. But it was just part of a shifting pattern beyond the mist. It was strange how difficult it was to find a small location on the shore. But she would be able to see the ship. Would be watching now as she settled on her course and moved slowly away from the land, her greasy smoke following her like a dirty banner on the sea's face.

Burch came on to the bridge, a big ensign rolled up under his arm. To one of his signal ratings he said gruffly, 'Not be needing this good one again for a while. Not till she 'ands in 'er notice.'

No one answered.

Standish stepped down from the gratings and a bosun's mate said, ' 'Ere, sir. You dropped something.'

'Thanks, Spinks.' Standish took it and held it in the palm of his hand. It was a small handkerchief. She must have dropped it when she had broken down on the veranda. He stared at it for a long moment, hearing her voice, feeling her touch.

It was something. He folded it carefully and put it inside his wallet.

Irvine was watching him from beside the chartroom door, his eyes opaque as Standish returned to the fore gratings.

Dalziel said, 'Not sorry to get out of that place. Can't abide inefficiency.' But he seemed to lack his usual bounce, as if his mind was elsewhere.

Standish raised his glasses again and looked at the town. But it was already gone, curtained off by the mist and shielded in the growing glare on the water.

Three months. But now, when the ship paid off it would not be the end for him after all. He touched the wallet in his pocket and smiled. Life had only just begun.

16 A Full Cargo

IT had been another hot day, and now that the sun had moved nearer to the western horizon the sea appeared to be steaming.

Standish stood loosely on the port gratings and trained his glasses abeam, watching the sharp wake left by the *Whizz-Kid*'s twin motors as she cruised amongst the scattered fishing boats.

Beneath him the ship heaved and rocked unsteadily, her engines stopped, her hull and upper works glowing tawny gold from the dying sunlight. The fishing boats were spread over a wide area, the nearest ones less than a cable away from the ship's bows, but because of the low, clinging haze they seemed to lack body and outline, their motionless ribbed sails giving them a kind of tattered dignity. They reminded Standish of an old water-colour which had hung in his mother's bedroom. Of brown autumn leaves drifting on a brook.

The yeoman said wearily, 'Nothin' there, sir.'

Standish did not bother to reply. It had been three weeks exactly since they had left the anchorage. In that time they had not set eyes on land, nor had they seen any vessel larger than fishing craft like these. Day after day, hour by hour, the *Terrapin* had pounded back and forth on her patrol. One hundred and twenty miles north to south and the same east to west. A giant, glittering box with little to break its monotonous sameness.

The area was not even on the main cargo routes, and smaller vessels were careful to stay close to the shore now that the likelihood of sudden storms and squalls was more evident. Only

the fishing communities of the countries which bordered the
Gulf had no choice. They followed their trade regardless of
weather or risk, relying on their carefully hoarded knowledge
rather than on the stability of their flimsy boats.

The log was full of such sightings as this one, and like all the
rest Dalziel had carried out his orders to the letter. At first there
had been some of the old excitement each time the *Whizz-Kid*
had skudded rakishly between the boats, and Standish had told
Wishart to change the boarding parties after each contact to
help break the lethargy.

He watched the *Whizz-Kid* shoving clear of a fishing boat and
steer towards another one. He could see Wishart, naked but for
a pair of khaki shorts and cap, sitting on the boat's gunwale,
a revolver at his hip, and could imagine his weariness with the
whole affair. It was a thankless task for him. Climbing between
stinking and overcrowded decks in search of something to
warrant his intrusion, which the fishermen resented almost as
much as the seamen detested being there.

There was not even any of the usual anticipation at paying
off. The ship seemed to be covered by a curtain of resentment.
Resentment at this fruitless patrol which they saw as some sort
of slur. At Dalziel, whom many now accepted as the main cause
of their discomfort. And at each other.

In the wardroom it was much the same, with a regular round
of routine and little more. For Standish it meant something else.
As he carried out his duties on the bridge or upper deck, or
consumed the unvaried meals with his companions, he kept his
mind busy with his new-found hope. He was even able to accept
Dalziel's brooding detachment as one day followed another with
nothing to show for it.

He heard a step on the gratings and heard Dalziel ask, 'How
is he getting on?'

Dalziel had been in the chartroom for most of the watch and
his reappearance was both noiseless and unexpected. Even he
seemed to have lost interest in the sighting reports after the first
signal from Wishart that all was well. He spent more of his time
with the charts than anything else. Making alterations to the
next course, or changing the search area at a moment's notice,
much to Irvine's obvious irritation, as he was never consulted.

Standish looked at him now and wondered if he had thought beyond the end of the ship's commission.

He said, 'Nothing, sir.'

Dalziel's lips came together in a tight line. 'Nothing *yet*, surely?'

Pigott appeared on the bridge with a sheaf of papers. He coughed and then said, 'The stores report that you asked for, sir.'

Dalziel took them and flipped over the neatly tabulated lists. Standish watched him narrowly. The food was certainly poor. Lack of fresh vegetables or meat had meant Pigott's department dipping further into the tinned stores, just as Quarrie's fuel tanks were already low even at the economical cruising speed of ten knots. It was just as if the ship was intended to be run down to the final pint of oil, the last pot of jam when she was handed to the dockyard.

Dalziel snapped, 'There's a mistake here!' He held out the bundle of papers. 'Quite wrong, Pigott. Even I can see you've made a bad miscalculation. Poor show, no wonder we're living like paupers!'

Pigott stepped forward, his face stubborn. 'But, sir, you've turned over *two* pages there, not one.'

Dalziel peered down and then ripped a paperclip from the corner of the top sheet before hurling it across the bridge.

'Don't you know you should never use paperclips?' He glared at Pigott angrily. 'I once knew a signals officer who used them just as you do. Two signals were clipped together and the lower one was overlooked. Result, a bloody cock-up of a shambles, which if it happened in wartime might have cost time and lives.' Pigott was looking at him blankly, his glasses slipping down his nose. He said, 'Yes, sir.'

Dalziel walked to the gratings and back again, his hands in his pockets as he added vehemently, 'Remember the horseshoe nail, eh? Well, a paperclip could be the same, so be more damned attentive to your responsibilities in future.'

Pigott swallowed hard. 'Is that all, sir?'

Dalziel nodded. 'Carry on.' To Standish he added irritably, 'If the Pigotts of this planet thought more of the *small* details we might be able to cope with the more important ones.' He stiffened and shot out his arm. 'What's Wishart doing?'

Standish raised his glasses and saw the blue painted launch tied alongside one of the fishermen. Wishart had probably intended it to be invisible from *Terrapin*'s bridge, but the fishing boat had swung slightly on the swell so that the little tableau was only too clear. Either out of the goodness of his heart, or in an effort to stifle the resentment of his men, Wishart had allowed them to take a break from their search operations. It did not need binoculars to see the naked seamen splashing in the water while Wishart and the boat's coxswain stood alone by the gunwale, obviously enjoying the spectacle.

Dalziel shouted, 'Of all the bloody idiots!' He swung on Burch. 'Recall the boat at once. I've had my fill of insubordination around here.' He glared at Standish. 'In future just try and keep my officers in order, eh?'

Standish nodded and turned to watch the startled reaction from Wishart and his men as the light began to flash towards them.

Quarrie had appeared on the bridge and said quietly, 'Hell, I could do with a paddle myself.'

Dalziel said from the opposite side, 'I will be in the chartroom. When Wishart gets the boat inboard let me know.' The door slammed.

Quarrie shrugged. 'You can feel sorry for him.'

Standish glanced at him with surprise. After Quarrie's fury during the storm, his obvious anxiety over the shaft, his remark was all the more unexpected.

Quarrie added, 'She's a good old ship. I'm finished with the Service after this. I'll miss her like hell.'

He said it so forcefully that Standish asked, 'You've known her a long while, Chief?'

Quarrie's face was suddenly tired and older than his years. 'I joined her as a rookie stoker when I was a lad of seventeen.' He grimaced. 'Can you imagine it? Seventeen and my first ship, and slap bang into the Western Approaches.' He shook his head. 'They call it the Battle of the Atlantic in the history books. But it weren't no battle, except to survive. It was sheer bloody murder.'

Quarrie smiled wryly as the *Whizz-Kid* started to turn towards the ship.

'These youngsters today don't know the half of it. Even now, when I'm down aft with my lads it keeps coming back. The storms, the explosions, and all the terrible dread of being scalded alive when that torpedo eventually found you. But it never did, and this ship taught me something. Not how to be without fear, but how to hide it, to control it before it shows on your face.' He looked along the screen. 'So in the end, I came back to her, just as I promised I would if I ever got the chance.' He grinned sadly. 'Never thought it'd be as Chief though.

Standish asked, 'Do you have a family?'

He shook his head. 'Wife was killed by a car.' He glanced at Standish. 'Like yours.' He paused. 'Except . . .'

'Except that she was knocked down, eh?'

He nodded. 'Yes. Still, I'll just have to think about it. Plan some little job where I can keep my hand in.' He sighed. 'I'd not want to be too far from the sea.'

'Boat's alongside, sir.'

'Very good.' Standish looked at his watch. 'Pipe the hands to the tackles and have it hoisted inboard.' He turned back to Quarrie. 'I imagine you'll soon get fixed up, Chief.'

Quarrie was watching the drifting boats, his eyes distant. 'Could do some fishing.' He chuckled. 'Like those poor bastards. What a helluva way to live.'

Standish heard Wishart calling his men by name.

Then Quarrie said, 'That's the only boat in the whole damn lot which has had a catch.'

Standish stared at him. 'Come again?'

'When I was a boy before I joined I used to live outside Grimsby. My dad took me to watch the trawlers coming home every so often. He was able to estimate the catch almost before they got to the pier.' He pointed at the fishing boat in question. 'Look at her. A full two planks lower than the rest of them.'

Wishart appeared at the top of the ladder, his face flushed and apprehensive. 'You sent for me, Number One?'

'The captain wants to see you, Sub.' Standish looked past him at Quarrie.

'The Chief just told me something.' He pointed to the boat's hazy outline. 'Did you search her?'

Wishart nodded. 'Yes. I was just going to do the last one when I got the recall. The lads had earned a dip. I'll take the responsibility.'

Quarrie grinned. 'You certainly will, my young hero!'

But Standish did not smile. 'What did you find in her?'

Wishart looked at him uncertainly. 'Nothing much. The usual stores, and two baskets of fish or thereabouts.'

'Get down to your lads and stop them hoisting the boat, Sub.' As Wishart hurried away he looked at Quarrie and said quietly, 'I may be sticking my neck out, Chief, but I think I'll risk it.'

At that moment Dalziel appeared in the chartroom door. Without his sun glasses his eyes looked tired and red-rimmed.

He asked, 'What's the delay now?'

Standish said, 'There's a fishing boat on the port bow, sir. It's been searched, but . . .'

Dalziel was already on the gratings, his glasses trained on the boats.

'But? But what?'

Standish pointed over the screen. 'She's lower in the water than all the others. It would take quite a weight to do that, but her catch of fish is negligible.'

He watched Dalziel's profile, the nervous tick in his throat as he muttered, 'That's strange.'

Quarrie said, 'During the war, after we lost Singapore and Hong Kong, some of the Chinese used to smuggle supplies and food to our people who were left behind.' He added slowly, 'They converted some of their junks and fishing craft for the purpose.'

Dalziel lowered the glasses and looked at Standish. His eyes were suddenly very clear, like a man coming out of a fever.

'False bottoms! God, I must be mad not to have thought of it!'

Standish asked, 'Shall I go across?'

Dalziel raised his glasses again. 'Yes. Watch out for traps and surprises. Once aboard I'll have the guns trained on you. Just to be sure, eh?' He showed his teeth, 'Jesus, Chief, you are a man of surprises!'

He made as if to control his sudden elation. 'Of course, it might be nothing.' But he failed. 'On the other hand . . .' He broke off as the *Whizz-Kid* landed in the water and the armed seamen began to clamber down the ship's side.

Then he ran to the chartroom and came out seconds later

carrying his sporting rifle. He saw Standish's expression and grinned broadly.

'If I see anyone molesting my executive officer I shall have no hesitation in making one large hole in his skull, right?' He gestured with the muzzle. 'Off you go then, and keep an eye on the light. It will be sunset in thirty minutes.'

As he ran for the ladder Standish saw Dalziel fitting a telescopic sight to his rifle, his face entirely engrossed in the task.

Quarrie was following him and added, 'Should have kept my damn fool mouth shut!' He slapped Standish's shoulder. 'But you see if I'm not right. My old dad knew a thing or two!'

Standish leapt down amongst the crouching seamen and shouted, 'Cast off! Start up the motors!'

Wishart was beside him, his face a picture of confusion. 'What are we doing?'

Standish stood up in the vibrating hull as the motors sent it hurtling across the placid water.

'About twenty knots, I should think!' He looked down and added, 'For God's sake, that was supposed to be funny!'

Wishart was still staring at him as if he had gone mad when they rounded the fishing boat's gaunt transom and glided noisily alongside.

There seemed to be about a dozen poorly clad fishermen in the crew, and as Standish hoisted himself over the bulwark they fell back towards a battered looking wheelhouse where another, dressed in a stained smock coat, was leaning negligently against the door.

Wishart said, 'He's the skipper. I've already spoken to him.' He stood aside as the armed seamen climbed up beside him. 'He's no English, but speaks French quite well.'

Standish glanced around the untidy deck space. It was a heavy boat for its size, with two masts and one large hatch in the centre of the hull. Judging from the oily stains around the transom he guessed she also contained a fairly powerful engine.

He said, 'Tell him we're going to search his boat again. His men will stay here on deck during the inspection.' He darted a glance at the seamen by the bulwark and added calmly, 'Unsling your weapons, but make it nice and easy.' He was smiling as he said it, and saw the sudden change in their expressions as his warning went home.

As Wishart strode to the wheelhouse Standish beckoned to a tall able seamen. 'You come with me, Maine. I may need a bit of weight.'

Below it was almost pitch dark in spite of one thick glass scuttle in the deckhead, and as they stumbled over crates and loose tackle Standish was very conscious of the appalling stink, and could forgive Wishart's haste with his earlier inspection. There was less than five feet between decks, and he heard the seaman Maine cursing softly as his head collided with a cross beam.

Standish called, 'Bring your torch over here.' For a moment he thought he was mistaken, a trick of the light, but as the bright beam cut through the gloom he saw a darker patch of dirt to one side of a great pile of old rope and fishing floats.

He said, 'We'll have to shift that lot.'

Maine spat on his hands and balanced the torch on an upturned bucket. Between his teeth he replied, 'If you say so, sir. But Christ Almighty, the stench is fair turnin' me up.'

Breathing as little as possible they worked in silence. Then as Maine hauled the last rotting bundle of cordage and fish fragments aside Standish knelt down and ran his fingers along the planking. There was a complete section, some ten feet by five, which was now recognizable as a well-disguised hatch covering. But even the carefully applied stains and trodden-in dirt could not hide the two parallel joins once the piles of rubbish had been removed.

He said quietly, 'Use your knife.'

The seamen opened the marlin spike on his knife and very carefully inserted it into the nearest crack. As he pressed down he muttered, 'We'll look bloody silly if this is goin' right through the bottom, sir!'

The crack widened very slightly and both men dug in their fingers and heaved with all their strength. Once it started moving it was surprisingly easy. Surprising too, there was a wire loop on the deckhead to hold the planked cover clear of the opening, which Standish had not noticed before.

He looked down at the black rectangle and beckoned for the torch. The air from the deep hiding place was very cool, even icy, and there was a different smell now which was very familiar.

Maine said, 'Hell, look at that lot!'

The torch beam moved slowly across the shining black shapes, and Standish had to lie flat in order to see where the cargo ended. There must be over fifty drums of oil, he thought grimly. Each drum containing fifty gallons of brand new diesel. The drums were very neatly stowed, and no amount of rocking would shake them, or betray their presence with a sudden grate of metal.

'We'll go and find out what the skipper has to say about this.'

As Maine went to return the knife to his belt it slipped through his fingers and bounced down into the opening with a sharp clang.

Maine said, 'I'll 'ave to wait till all that's shifted before I gets me pussers dirk back, sir.'

At that instant there was a chorus of shouts overhead and the sound of running feet across the deck.

Standish ran for the ladder and was almost knocked flat by a charging seaman as he emerged through the hatch.

During his search below the light had faded considerably, and as he paused to collect his bearings he noticed that the masts and patched sails were bathed in deep, fiery red from the setting sun. But his attention was riveted to the small, frozen group around the boat's stern. They appeared to have been caught in their various attitudes of surprise or anger and moulded there for all time. Then he saw the fishing boat's skipper beside the wheelhouse, his arm locked around a seaman's neck while with the other hand he held a heavy pistol to his temple.

Wishart was standing some six feet clear, his eyes fixed on the two motionless figures, his body quite still, as if by moving he might cause the gun to explode against the seaman's skull.

He seemed to sense that Standish was on deck again and said tightly, 'He heard you do something below. We were just talking when he grabbed Dolan, and . . .'

The seaman in question gasped hoarsely, 'Help me, sir! He's goin' to kill me!'

Wishart said in the same tight voice, 'He has said that unless our men put down their weapons he will shoot. I think he means it.'

Standish made himself speak very slowly. 'He hasn't got a chance. If you look at the ship you'll see that a Bofors is trained right on this boat. Tell him that if he has stolen those drums of oil he will have a chance to explain and get a fair hearing from the authority involved.'

As Wishart started speaking in slow, careful French he glanced swiftly at the surrounding sea. It was very much darker, and the mist was moving in like pink vapour against the dying sunlight. Unless they did something soon it would be hard to see anything at all.

Wishart said flatly, 'He refuses. Put down the weapons, or he will shoot.'

Able Seaman Dolan closed his eyes as the pistol nudged against his head with a sharp jerk.

Standish said, 'All right. Lay down your weapons. But stand by them in case the others try to rush us.' He heard the Stirlings clattering on the planking but kept his eyes on the two inter-locked figures as step by step they retreated towards the stern rail.

Maine whispered, ' 'E's goin' to jump over board, sir. Drown hisself, that's what 'e's up to.'

Standish shook his head. 'No. He'll swim for one of the other boats. In the darkness we'll never find him, and by dawn they'll be scattered to every point of the compass.'

The smock-coated skipper released his hold around the sea-man's throat but kept the pistol levelled at the nape of his neck as he edged closer to the rail, his eyes shining dully in the sunset.

As he threw one leg across the rail Standish heard a soft click and knew he was going to shoot Dolan even as he dived clear of the boat.

He yelled, 'Get down, Dolan! *Down!*'

His shout momentarily distracted the man on the rail, and in the brief, split-second silence which followed nobody moved. Dolan still stood where he was, either too terrified or too dazed to heed Standish's warning, and the pistol was as before, in line with his neck.

There was a sharp, abbreviated crack, and for a moment

Standish imagined the man had used a silencer. Dolan whimpered and clapped his hands to his face, but he did not fall. But the man on the stern rail had changed his position, was even now sagging forward in a tired bow, the pistol dropping at his feet as with one choking gasp he pitched down beside it.

Then everyone started talking at once. Men seized their guns while Wishart kept repeating, 'I felt the bullet pass me! Must have missed me by inches!'

Standish walked slowly aft and stood looking down at the corpse. The blood was starting to trickle through the thick coat, and he could see the man's teeth bared like the fangs of an animal caught in a trap.

He bent over and picked up the pistol. Dalziel must have fired his rifle at no less than half a cable. He felt the pistol shake in his grip. One hundred yards and into the eye of the sunset. The slightest error and he could have shot Dolan or Wishart. With such a high velocity weapon he could have killed both of them.

He said harshly, 'Try and get the engine started. We'll go alongside the ship and sort this lot out.' He heard the men moving around him, their actions jerky but determined, as if glad to be told what to do.

Wishart asked shakily, 'Is he dead?'

'Instantly, I should think.' Standish handed him the pistol. 'Souvenir for you. You'll be ready next time.' The deck gave several convulsions and then started to tremble. 'We'll be alongside *Terrapin* in a few minutes. I suggest you use the time to question some of the fishermen. It might save your bacon from the captain's wrath for letting Dolan get jumped like that.'

He left Wishart staring at the corpse and walked to the wheelhouse. Maine had taken the wheel and said, 'Sorry about the dirk, sir.'

Standish felt the cool air across his face and took a slow, deep breath. 'You probably saved us all a lot of time. But don't bank too much on getting the knife back just yet.'

When the boat finally bumped alongside the frigate's hull Standish saw Dalziel already at the guardrail peering down at him with obvious eagerness.

As he climbed up the ladder Dalziel asked sharply. 'What did you find out?'

'Hidden cargo of fresh diesel oil, sir.' Standish's limbs felt like lead. 'Very well concealed. Anyone could miss seeing it.'

'Really?' Dalziel eyed him searchingly, 'You didn't, did you?' He swung round as Wishart clambered on to the deck and gripped a wire stay as if to stop himself from falling. 'Well?'

Wishart said hoarsely, 'I questioned the others, sir. They seem to be genuine fishermen. The skipper was the one who told them what to do.' He swallowed hard. 'And he's dead.'

Dalziel peered at him. 'Any charts on board? Anything like that?'

Standish said, 'No, sir. That is why a determined man would use fishermen. They have little use for charts, as you know.'

'Makes sense.' Dalziel nodded quickly. 'Very clever idea. Drift in with a large collection of fishing craft, most of which are from a dozen or more different places, and there you have it.' He saw Rideout hovering in the gloom and barked, 'Fetch that corpse aboard and search it. I want a full report of every damn thing you can find.' He turned his back on him and added shortly, 'We'll have a conference in the chartroom in fifteen minutes, right?'

Standish replied, 'It will certainly prove our other report, sir. The diesel was destined for a submarine, unless I'm very much mistaken. I imagine the real objection to your theory was the difficulty in operating a submarine in the Gulf, with no available base for refuelling.' He glanced abeam and saw that the fishing vessels had melted away into the darkness. Maybe they knew of the captured boat's real function, or perhaps they did not care either way. They had known too much hardship, centuries of it, to have any interest beyond their own survival, he thought. He said, 'If you code up a signal right away, sir, we could organize an air search. Either way it might show the other side we're on to them.'

'Signal?' Dalziel sounded vague. 'Oh, that can wait for a bit longer.' He glanced up at the bridge. 'Don't forget. Conference.'

Quarrie joined Standish by the guardrail. He said quietly, 'He wasn't joking. That was a bloody dangerous shot with the rifle all the same.'

Standish watched Dolan being helped aboard, he was still suffering from shock and whimpering as he was led below.

Quarrie asked, 'Is that the end of it, do you think?'

Standish looked past him, recalling Dalziel's evasive answer. 'I'll tell you what I think *after* the conference.'

*　　　　*　　　　*

Dalziel came out of his sea cabin and glanced quickly around at the assembled officers. They were all present, except Caley, and it was possible to hear his restless pacing on the bridge gratings or the stamp of his feet as he tried to keep warm in the night air. Inside the crowded chartroom it was warm enough, and from the look of Hornby's shining face it seemed as if he had more than the heat to contend with. With her engines stopped, and drifting uneasily on a slow swell, the *Terrapin*'s motion was very uncomfortable, and high up on the bridge it felt at its worst.

Dalziel appeared to notice none of it. He nodded to Standish and then laid a chart on the table where they could all see it.

As they crowded closer Standish saw it was like no other chart he had ever confronted. Dalziel had shaded certain areas in colour, and there were little pins inserted around their various patrol areas, alongside pencilled notes and calculations.

Dalziel said briskly, 'Well now, gentlemen, what do we have?'

Nobody spoke, and Standish was conscious of the shipboard noises intruding all around them. The quiet purr of the automatic plot, the creak of metal from the bridge structure as the ship rolled on a beam swell, and the occasional stamp of feet as the watchkeepers eased their cramped limbs.

'Then let me sum up.' Dalziel leaned on the table. 'The diesel was obviously destined for that unidentified submarine. From the markings on the drums it would appear to be American, stolen from a military dump in Viet Nam.' He glanced at Irvine who appeared about to voice a question and added smoothly, 'Young Wishart has been to some pains to question the fishermen, and this is borne out by the fact that they come from the Mekong Delta, right?'

Quarrie said stubbornly, 'I still don't see why they should have let that chap take over their boat.'

Dalziel shrugged impatiently. 'The reasons are as varied as they are irrelevant. Fear of reprisals from guerillas, greed for easier reward than from fishing, who can say?' He looked at their faces individually. 'But it all points to the submarine. *Our* submarine.'

Irvine said, 'We have no power to interfere with foreign warships, sir. We can't even be sure the submarine was acting unlawfully.'

'Our job here is to *investigate*, Pilot.' Dalziel's tone was almost gentle. 'If that submarine was behaving lawfully, why all this bother? She could fuel at sea in broad daylight if that was the case. The powers-that-be have already stated several times that they have no information about her, some even doubted she existed. That hardly points to a run-of-the-mill patrol, or even a spying operation, now does it?'

Irvine persisted, 'Then someone else will have to sort it out, in my view, sir. There are no charts, and the doc has searched the dead man's body and found nothing.'

They all looked at Rideout. In the chart light his hands were very red, as if he had just finished scrubbing them.

He said, 'A few oddments, which I gave to the captain. The bullet entered his left upper . . .'

Dalziel held up his hand. 'We can manage without the post-mortem, thank you.' He smiled calmly. 'The man was most likely Chinese. He was carrying a copy of the Teachings of Mao, if you are interested.' He frowned. 'Also a scrap of paper with the name of a ship. The *Bombay Queen*.'

Standish watched him closely. Dalziel appeared very cool and relaxed, but he knew him well enough now to accept it as an act. He was enjoying it, playing with them, as he saved the most important piece to the last, while his officers were still mulling over his words.

Dalziel snapped, 'Don't bother, Sub!'

Wishart had been reaching for the manual of merchant shipping and dropped his hand to his side.

Quarrie said, 'Does that mean we've got to start searching for some ship again, sir?' He wrinkled his nose. 'Like a needle in a haystack, if you ask me.'

'Now, Chief, don't be so modest. You were the one to spot that the *Cornwallis* was behaving in a strange manner. It was you who noticed the fishing boat's unnatural draught, too.' He shot a hard glance at Wishart. 'When others were more concerned with taking a swim!'

He continued more evenly, 'The *Bombay Queen* is not on any list. She ceased to exist twenty-eight years ago when she foundered on a reef and was lost with all hands. As a point of interest, she was full of refugees and trying to escape from the Japs when she was hit by a typhoon and driven aground, that we *do* know of her.'

Standish glanced at the others. They were staring at Dalziel as if wondering what he would say next. He did not keep them waiting long.

He tapped the chart and said in an almost matter-of-fact tone, 'Here is our present position. Approximately one hundred miles to the north-east of us is that chain of reefs where the *Bombay Queen* foundered. There she still lies, although the wreck is unnamed on any chart. There are too many scattered along the reefs to bother making distinction.'

Irvine's eyes gleamed with professional interest. He said quietly, 'Sixty miles from the Cambodian mainland, sir.' He paused. 'And outside our patrol area.'

Dalziel ignored him. 'The reefs were said to be islands at one time, and there are many small islets along their entire length. Shipping avoids the area, and who can blame them? There are some reefs quite unmarked.' He looked up, his eyes very bright. 'But there are deep waters amongst them also. Deep and untroubled by unwanted observers, gentlemen. A most suitable location for a secret fuel dump, eh?'

Irvine said, 'We should make a signal with this information.'

'In due course, Pilot.' Dalziel smiled at him. 'But first we must investigate, and *verify*, do I make myself clear?'

'May *I* get something clear, sir?' Irvine was very erect, his features grim in the overhead lights. 'Do you intend to leave the allotted area without permission?'

'As my navigating officer I would have expected you to realize that earlier.' Dalziel watched him calmly. 'Anything else?'

'Then I must protest, sir. I . . .'

Dalziel interrupted harshly, 'Your protest will be noted. Now, if you have nothing more useful to add perhaps you would lay off a new course as I have shown on my own chart.' He tapped it with his fingers. 'One day this chart might be used as a blueprint for our entire Far East strategy, when no doubt even you, Pilot, will want to share in its construction!'

Dalziel looked at Standish. 'I will discuss details with you later. Right now I want four good volunteers to act as prize crew on the fishing boat. Give them a course for Kota Bharu and make sure they know what's expected of them. They'll run into a patrol in three or four days, I shouldn't wonder.' He smiled. 'By which time *we* will have something interesting to offer, eh?'

As the officers filed out on to the bridge Irvine caught Standish's arm and said urgently, 'You've got to stop him. He'll ruin everything if he's allowed to go on.'

Standish shook his hand away. 'This reef is about thirty miles outside our maximum patrol area. Is that so much to ask if it proves to be a secret base?'

'And if not, this ship'll be a laughing stock again.'

'Well, you won't have to worry, Pilot. Your written protest will exonerate you completely, and should look well when you go up for promotion.' He walked away adding quietly, 'Think about it, Pilot. And remember that mud has a habit of sticking, even to the one who throws it!'

Standish hurried down the ladder to the main deck, wondering why Irvine had made him so angry. He was probably right, and it would prove to be another fruitless search. But they were all in it together, whether they liked it or not. Quarrie, who had spotted the overloaded boat; Wishart, whose unlawful swimming party had delayed the search and had first drawn attention to it. And himself, perhaps most of all for giving Dalziel the one lead he had been seeking.

He paused and looked up at the dark silhouettes of funnel and foremast. In just a few more weeks it would be finished with anyway. It might be as well to have something worthwhile to remember when it was over.

17 The *Bombay Queen*

At daylight the following morning the *Terrapin* reached her destination, and using one of the known passages between the scattered necklace of reefs and islets began a slow and methodical search. As the sun rose higher in the sky the desolation and menace of the area became more apparent, and Standish could well imagine the ships which had perished being torn apart and thrown to the sea's bottom. Some of the islets were little more than craggy humps, and few were over two miles in length. While the frigate crept close by one of them, her echo sounder recording a constant warning, Standish studied it through his glasses, noting the steep sides with their swirling currents, and above all the total absence of vegetation. Bird life there was in plenty, and what had first appeared to be pale gorse along the cliffs proved to be an endless covering of droppings, and whenever the ship moved too close the air became filled with circling, screaming sea birds of every size and description.

Here the sea was very green, with deeper patches of dirty brown as the only visible evidence of the other menacing reefs below its surface.

A very dangerous place to be, and had the weather changed against them, Standish knew it would be madness to continue the search.

But the sky stayed clear and unmasked, and but for a steady swell the sea remained passive and indifferent to their presence.

At mid-day Dalziel ordered the anchor to be dropped, and

as the ship swung lazily at her cable the two power boats were lowered alongside.

Dalziel said, 'These two islands are the largest in the reef. The boats can take a look round. I want everything reported. I don't care how trivial it seems. We will keep at it until we find the evidence we want.'

The *Whizz-Kid* was away first, and after two minor breakdowns the motor boat chugged off in the opposite direction. Irvine had been sent in the latter, and when he returned an hour later he wasted no time in making his feelings known.

'Nothing, sir. There's not even a place to get ashore. It's like a damn great block of granite.'

When Wishart arrived on the bridge a few moments later his report was little better.

'I could have got ashore, sir, but it might have meant stoving the boat in. There's a pretty steep swell under the cliffs and a lot of caves. But nothing larger than a launch could get near the place.'

Dalziel had brought his special chart on to the bridge and was making pencilled notes against the two small islands. He said sharply, 'Well, we've made a start. It's going better than I expected.'

Irvine gave a brief smile. 'Really, sir?'

Dalziel did not seem to notice. He was still studying his chart and said, 'The reef extends in a rough north-westerly direction for another twenty miles. After lunch we'll weigh and continue the search.' He looked up. 'That will be all, gentlemen.'

But the afternoon's operations did not go quite so smoothly, for within an hour of anchoring again the motor boat's engine began to overheat and had to be stopped. While the ship's company watched helplessly from a mile away, the crew were fully occupied in warding off some wicked looking reefs with their boathooks and feet, and were in real danger until the *Whizz-Kid* arrived to tow them clear. By the time the fault had been put right the best part of the day had gone, and Dalziel said irritably, 'We will remain at anchor until dawn. We can finish the investigation tomorrow.'

Later that evening in the wardroom Irvine remarked on Dalziel's choice of words. '*Investigation* did you hear that? It's not a search any more. He knows damn well there's nothing to find, and never was!'

Wishart said, 'What about that paper with the ship's name on it?'

'Oh, for God's sake, it might have meant anything.' Irvine looked at him, his eyes scathing. 'It won't do much good when we make our report. You should have listened to me in the first place.'

Standish stood up. 'We don't seem to have much choice these days. I suppose you're gloating now? Waiting to make a big thing of it?'

Irvine looked away. 'I was merely pointing out the utter futility of it. The longer we frig around like this, the greater will be the wrath which lands on the captain's back. I should worry. He'll have to admit it himself soon enough.'

Standish walked from the wardroom and climbed to the quarterdeck. Beneath a ceiling of stars the nearest islet looked unreal and gaunt, like a section of the moon's surface, he thought. Across the unbroken water he could hear the dull boom of surf and the sound of the sea exploring the deep caves which seemed to be common to all the islets. One day the sea would eat them away and they would fall down to join the rest of the reef.

If only they could have found something. Even a tiny piece of evidence might have justified Dalziel's actions, and which added to the capture of the diesel oil would have distracted attention elsewhere. But Irvine was right. There was nothing here. It only needed a signal from Jerram, a demand for an exact position, to put Dalziel in line for an immediate court martial.

He put a match to his pipe and thought of the weeks ahead. Of the exact moment when he would step ashore and see Suzane again. It was strange to think of her having been aboard this ship. To have seen and shared the typhoon's fury with the rest of them. She would be on her way to Singapore now, and might even be thinking of him, and the *Terrapin*.

He turned as a muffled burst of cheering floated through the wardroom hatch. A figure scrambled across the darkened deck, and he heard Wishart say excitedly, 'Here you are, Number One! We've just got the news!'

Standish stared at him. 'News? What sort of news?'

Wishart waved his hands happily. 'A signal. It's the recall.' He leaned forward. 'It's all over. We've been ordered to cancel the patrol immediately and proceed to Singapore!'

'Is the captain in the wardroom?'

'No. He sent a messenger.' Wishart seemed lost in his thoughts. 'Now that it's happened I can't really take it in.' He dropped his voice and added more calmly, 'And I'm glad for you, Number One. It'll mean a new start for you. And after what you've done for me, I'd like to think we might meet again sometime.'

Standish thrust his pipe in his pocket. 'Thanks.' He tried to discover what was worrying him. 'I'll be back in a moment. I must see the captain.' He walked quickly towards the bridge, knowing that Wishart was still staring after him, his expression one of complete bewilderment.

He found Dalziel in his small sea cabin, the chart spread across his bunk below a reading light.

'I've just heard, sir.' He waited, seeing the look of set concentration on his face.

Dalziel did not lift his eyes from the chart. 'There is a good channel to the north of us here. And two more small islets. Maybe I was wrong to go for the larger ones first. But from the chart and the small amount of information available, it is hard to understand until you actually see them.' He looked up, his eyes blank. 'Heard what?'

'The recall, sir. We're returning to Singapore.'

'Quite right. Yes, it'll be quite a feather in our caps, eh? I told you when we left the place we'd make 'em sit up when we returned. And by God I was right!'

'Have you acknowledged the signal, sir?'

Dalziel smiled gently. 'Naturally. Don't want to arouse any unnecessary suspicions, now do we?'

Standish felt a cold hand on his heart. 'We are outside our patrol area. Any further delay here would certainly draw attention to the fact.' He hesitated. 'It would look bad for you, sir.'

Dalziel threw back his head and laughed. 'Bad? Why, they'd skin me alive if it was all to no good purpose. But you know, Number One, all through history it has been the same. If you are proved right after you have committed some trivial error the rest cannot harm you.'

'I take it that you intend to remain here until the search is finished, sir?'

'You may *take* it, yes. Why, do you have any objection?'

Standish eyed him steadily. 'I know I am as much to blame as anyone, sir. At first I agreed with you on this. But now that it looks so unlikely I think we should, no *must* return to Singapore as directed.'

Dalziel stared at him for several seconds. Then he said very quietly, 'I am surprised you should say that. I thought you were different. Perhaps I was wrong to place so much faith in that direction, but I needed your support, as I still do.' He stood up and paced restlessly to the open scuttle. 'But support or not, I have every intention in seeing this thing through to the end.' He swung round, his face suddenly angry. 'Do you hear me? I've had just about all I can take. And now, now that I'm on to something really important, I find you of all people are against me! What sort of bloody attitude is that?'

Two spots of colour glowed on his cheeks, and Standish could see the knuckles showing white as he bunched his hands into fists against the seams of his trousers.

'It's nothing like that, sir. I don't want to see you crucified, that's all.'

Dalziel looked away. 'Really?' He seemed momentarily confused. 'Oh, I see. Well, in that case.' He did not go on.

Standish put his hand on the door clip. 'But I will back you up.' He smiled gravely. 'Whatever happens.'

Dalziel's shoulders moved stiffly. 'Good. That's settled then.' In a faraway voice he continued, 'I had a young subordinate in the *Harrier*. Couldn't make decisions. Wouldn't take his proper responsibility, you know. But he would have made a fine officer if I'd had more time.' He faced Standish again, his face sad. 'He was killed in the collision. The one man who would have told those smug-faced idiots of the court martial what happened. But in this world you have to take chances. Life wouldn't be worth living if we just sat back like a lot of damn sheep, eh?'

'I understand that Captain Jerram was aboard your ship when it all happened, sir.'

'What?' Dalziel's head jutted forward. 'Where did you hear that?'

'I believe you mentioned it to me.'

'Did I?' Dalziel shifted his legs on the swaying deck. 'Bloody man saw it all. All it needed was one word, one small piece of evidence which would have cleared my name completely. But oh dear me no. He just stood there like a lump of wood. Didn't see anything. Didn't *want* to see anything, was more like it!' Dalziel was speaking fast and very loudly. 'Always was a crawler. Never trusted him right from the first. Even when my wife told me that . . .' He broke off sharply and then added, 'Long time ago. Finished.'

'I'd better leave now and do my rounds, sir.'

'Yes.' Dalziel watched Standish's hand on the door clip. 'Sorry I barked at you earlier. A bit strained, I suppose.' His whole face lit up with a grin and he said, 'But by God it will be worth it to see their faces when we make the headlines, eh? And you won't have to worry about your next appointment either. When I go up for mine I'll damn well tell them what you've done to make this last effort the success it *will* be. I remember when I first saw you. The day I stepped out of the helicopter. There you were waiting to meet me, wondering what sort of bastard you were getting, I'll be bound. And I thought to myself, now here's a young chap who's got the *makings*, that's what I thought. A bit scruffy, a bit weighed down with some old bother or hangover.' His grin widened. 'Like the ship, in a way. But you both had the makings. It just needed me to bring it out.' The grin faded. 'Goodnight, Number One. Tomorrow morning we'll get on with the job we came to do.'

Standish walked out on to the darkened bridge, his mind hanging on Dalziel's words, his eagerness, and the pathetic vulnerability.

In the wardroom he found the others cheerfully discussing the prospects thrown wide open by the recall.

He waited until they were all looking at him and then said, 'Tomorrow morning we will repeat the same routine as today. Boats' crews fall in at seven bells for instructions.'

Irvine was the first to break the stunned silence. As Standish knew he would be.

'So it's like that, is it? He's finally gone over the edge.' He glanced at the others, his voice very calm. 'I wondered if this might happen. In a way I suppose it will be interesting to watch.'

Pigott said thickly, 'Damn and blast it!'

Standish kept his gaze on Irvine. 'If you watch closely enough you should make a fine witness when required, eh?' Then he turned on his heel and left them in silence.

*   *   *

The last two islets lay about half a mile from the *Terrapin*'s anchorage, and in the harsh afternoon sunlight they looked like grotesque brown monsters. During the night the sky had been covered by a thin layer of cloud which had persisted throughout the day. While the ship had edged slowly amongst the outflung spurs of reef, her echo sounder and sonar hard at work, there was not a man aboard who had not looked at the occasional telltale feathers of spray across some protruding fang of rock, and held his breath.

The sonar had contacted several wrecks, some of which were shown on the chart as dangerously near the surface, as well as others which had been smashed and scattered into the deeper chasms and valleys beyond the reef. The *Bombay Queen* could have been any or none of them.

As the day dragged on Standish found himself thinking more and more of the wrecks. Remnants of past wars or victims of great storms, their ending made little difference. But to see the reefs gliding close abeam made him very aware of the ship's predicament. Beyond the deserted islets and spines of reef was another stretch of open sea. It was over sixty miles to the Cambodian mainland, but as he shaded his eyes against the million glittering reflections he realized that here distance made little difference. They were the only living thing, the last moving vessel these reefs had seen.

The *Terrapin* dropped her anchor as close as possible to the nearest islet, but even so it was necessary to keep constant watch on the cable and take regular bearings to ensure that she was not dragging. For here the sea's rocky bottom dropped more steeply, and it was possible to see a whole jumble of dark rocks protruding above the surface less than a cable from the ship's hull.

As the two power boats were dropped alongside Standish saw several groups of ratings looking up at the bridge as Dalziel called his instructions to Irvine and Wishart before they left on the final inspection. Most of the men were staring towards the bridge with expressions ranging from anger to critical impatience. It was probably all over the ship by now, Standish thought bitterly. That the captain was forcing all of them to remain here, when by rights, and in fact according to Dalziel's acknowledgement to the recall signal, they should have been steaming for Singapore.

It could not last much longer. If after the boats returned with another negative report Dalziel persisted with his search, anything might happen.

Wills appeared on the bridge with coffee and hard biscuits. There was no bread left, or any fresh food at all. Pigott had said there was not much coffee either.

Dalziel was peering through his glasses watching Wishart in the *Whizz-Kid* until they were out of sight around the nearest islet. At a more sedate pace, Irvine in the motor boat was chugging towards the nearer one.

He said, 'I have a feeling that this may be the day, Number One.'

Standish looked at him, suddenly moved by his trust. 'I hope so, sir.'

'It's all quite clear to me. No wonder our people and the Americans never had reports of a submarine passing through the area. Once in the Gulf she could stay as long as she pleases, knowing that her fuel supply was arriving at regular intervals. She could shadow and report on everything. I'll wager she tracked the *Cornwallis* until she was ready to home those junks on to her.'

Standish looked away and rubbed his eyes. The glare and the ship's uneasy motion was dulling his mind.

He said, 'Perhaps the submarine was making her last trip, sir. It's possible that the attack on the village could not be avoided. My guess is that her job was to ferry guerillas and supplies and then get the hell out of it. The coastal waters are too damn shallow for a submarine's liking.'

Dalziel nodded absently. 'Good point. Although you will have observed that around the length of this reef barrier the very opposite is the case. Beyond the twenty fathom line there are some quite considerable depths. That is why it would make such a good rendezvous point for . . .'

He broke off as Burch said heavily, 'Mr. Wishart's returnin', sir.' He lowered his big telescope. ''E's signalled a nil report, sir.'

'Thank you, Yeoman.' Dalziel picked up a cup of coffee and stared at it without recognition. 'Not to worry, eh?' But he was not smiling.

As the *Whizz-Kid* slewed round towards the port side Standish heard a brief chorus of derisive cheers from the main deck, and saw several seamen calling down to their mates in the boat's crew.

Dalziel said vaguely, 'Well, they sound cheerful enough. I think they understand the necessity for all this.'

Standish bit his lip. All at once he remembered Sarah Dalziel's words, as if she had just spoken to him. Anything he dislikes or mistrusts he shuts off from his mind. Completely. Was it really possible he had not noticed the cheers were just the men's way of showing what they thought of him and his delusion? And Petty Officer Harris. For just a few moments it had been as if Dalziel had put his death right out of his mind. Shut it off like a watertight door.

Wishart seemed genuinely disappointed when he reached the bridge.

Dalziel listened to him and then replied, 'Well, we shall just have to keep trying, eh?'

When the ancient motor boat returned thirty minutes later Irvine strode on to the bridge and faced Dalziel without even bothering to salute.

'I made a complete search, sir. There's an inlet, about two cables long and half a cable at the widest part. But the sides are as steep as a house.' He paused and added slowly, 'The *Bombay Queen* is just inside the mouth of the inlet, that's why we didn't sight it from seaward.'

Dalziel was staring at him, watching his lips as if he was afraid he might miss something. As Irvine fell silent he said urgently, 'Well? What else?'

'Nothing.' Irvine glanced round the watching faces to let his words sink in. 'No boats, no fuel lighters, and from what I could see of it, nobody has been there since that wreck went aground twenty-eight years ago.'

For a long time nobody spoke. Standish looked down at the main deck where an off-watch mechanic was unwrapping a fishing rod by the guardrail, oblivious and uncaring of the drama above his head. Further forward by the gun mounting Caley was leaning against a stanchion, arms folded as he stared at the anchor party in the bows. Probably still thinking of his daughter and what he would find when he eventually got home.

Dalziel said suddenly, 'You are quite sure it was the right ship?'

'Yes, sir.' It sounded like *of course*. 'Only the forrard half is still there, but the name is visible. The rest is so much rusty scrap.'

'All the same.' Dalziel crossed and then recrossed the bridge. 'There must be something. Any oil slick on the water? Some recent flotsam perhaps?'

'*Nothing*, sir.' Irvine was breathing heavily. 'Has it occurred to you that the fishing boat might have been *smuggling* stolen oil and nothing more sinister than that?' He glanced at Standish. 'This reef could be a rendezvous for almost anything.'

Dalziel looked at him and then around the bridge. All at once he seemed very tired, and the lines around his wide mouth more deeply etched.

Then he said in a low voice, 'I am going to look for myself.'

Wishart darted a glance at Standish, his youthful face suddenly troubled. 'My boat has to take on more fuel, sir.'

Dalziel walked past him. 'I'll go in the motor boat.'

Standish followed him down to the main deck and asked quietly, 'Why not let me go, sir?'

'No.' Dalziel faced him, his eyes empty of expression. 'I'd like to see. If the weather changes you can signal me on the siren.' Without another word he climbed down to the boat and sat in the cockpit staring straight in front of him.

Back on the bridge Standish found Irvine and Wishart watching the boat as it curved away from the ship and headed back towards the spine-humped islet.

Irvine looked at Standish and said, 'The doc would like a

word with you. He's in the chartroom.' For once he seemed less sure of himself. 'I'll keep an eye on things for you.'

Standish nodded and walked into the cool chartroom, trying not to think of Dalziel's face as he had left the ship. He would look like that when he left her again, for the last time, he thought.

Rideout was waiting beside the table, his scrubbed hands resting on a locker as he watched Standish for several seconds before saying, 'I suppose you know what I'm going to say?'

Standish sat down and looked at him. 'Say it anyway.'

Rideout raised one hand and studied it carefully. 'You may not know this, but I shall be leaving the Navy shortly. I have been offered an appointment in Manchester, which I have accepted.' He smiled briefly. 'Less exciting perhaps, but rather more rewarding. However, as this ship's medical officer I do have some responsibility, and in view of my early removal from the Service, I suppose I am doubly suitable for the task which I have at this moment.' He paused and glanced at Standish. 'I did not ask to become involved, let me make that clear. But certain suggestions and complaints which came my way, as well as the captain's recent behaviour, leave me no alternative.'

Standish tensed in his seat. 'Have some of the officers been complaining to you?'

Rideout did not answer directly. 'There were several things which first interested me. Later I discovered certain unusual behaviour patterns. Then there was a list which I compiled.'

'List?' Standish watched the doctor's immobile face as he glanced towards the open scuttle.

'The captain has done some things which might be construed as contrary to Service requirements. Misuse of stores, the matter of the sports fund which he controlled for his own purposes, things like that.'

Standish replied coldly, 'Some of the officers have been using you to do their complaining for them, it seems.'

Rideout shrugged. 'They are career officers. They probably realize that to make some sort of open protest would be as damaging to them as to the captain. But I am not interested in these symptoms from a disciplinary standpoint. There is a strong pattern here. The captain's single-mindedness, his utter absorbtion with his own personal interests. But I think you know more of this than you are willing to admit?'

Standish said quietly, 'Finish what you started.'

'At first I couldn't understand why Captain Jerram had me appointed to the ship at such short notice. That and other events made me curious. I suppose now Jerram wanted me here as a kind of watchdog, knowing of my earlier association with Duncan House.'

'Was that the letter you received?'

'It was. I wrote to a friend, but I think I knew anyway. It was Dalziel's mania for public speaking which triggered it off. I recalled there was a patient at Duncan House who took a course in it to help with his therapy, and was always addressing the other inmates about naval history, battles and so forth. I didn't see him, but I heard a good deal about him from others.'

'The captain was discharged as completely fit.'

'Quite. But one never really knows. Perhaps in a less demanding role he might have been adequate. Here, I am not so sure. Always he has to have a just reason for his actions. His refusal to recognize his own marriage for instance. It probably stems from the fact he cannot accept the truth. That his command was gained through his wife's favour and not because of his own ability. I gather that when you made your first serious contact with a junk and an innocent civilian was shot dead, Dalziel was absolutely convinced he was a terrorist. The fact there were actual terrorists hidden aboard is irrelevant, but lucky for Dalziel of course.'

Standish spoke very carefully, trying to hide his anger as well as his anxiety. 'Have you forgotten how he has pulled this ship together? Or the way he handled her in the typhoon?' Even as he spoke he saw a smile forming on Rideout's lips.

'With all respect, I think your behaviour was more valuable during the storm. As for the ship—well, it only *happens* to be the elderly *Terrapin*. Have you thought of a Dalziel in command of a carrier, or a Polaris submarine for instance?' He shook his head. 'I'm sorry, Number One, but it's too risky.'

'What do you intend to do?' Standish felt both helpless and sickened by what what was happening.

'I am afraid it rather rests on you.' Rideout watched him sadly. 'I can make out a report, giving my reasons for Dalziel's

immediate replacement, and you could put it in the form of a
signal. No blame will attach to you, whatever some might say
behind your back. But the longer we stay here, the worse it will
be for everyone aboard. Wherever they go, they will be marked
as people from a ship which strayed. A ship, which because of
apathy or incompetence, stood by while her captain slowly
drove himself insane.'

Standish stood up and walked to the scuttle. The islet with
its green backdrop of glittering water seemed to be mocking
him.

'I know you don't care about your own reputation.' Rideout's
voice was very gentle. 'You believe your loyalty to him is more
important. Sometimes perhaps that might be true. But now, at
this point in time, your loyalty and your responsibility is to
everyone aboard. You will be doing him a favour if you act at
once. It will soon blow over, and I am sure there are many
who would thank you.'

Standish turned and said harshly, 'And the captain. Will he
thank me?'

Rideout glanced at his hands. 'Yes. Later, I think he might.
He is basically an honest man. His main disadvantage was being
born two hundred years too late. The days of independent
action are finished. Now we have policy rather than individual
deeds of death or glory.'

'Suppose the captain agreed to leave here and now and take
the ship back to Singapore as ordered?' Standish listened to his
own voice, hating it, despising himself for failing to destroy
Rideout's case.

Rideout nodded. 'That of course would be the best thing for
everybody. Once at Singapore I could speak with the P.M.O.
who is not an unreasonable man . . .'

Standish held up his hand. 'You'll speak to no one! When we
get there I'll make my report and do what I can for the captain.
He's got enough to contend with as it is without another *expert*
stabbing him in the back!'

Rideout dropped his eyes. 'I'm sorry, really I am.'

Standish walked slowly to the door. 'When you get to your
new job in Manchester you'll be able to tell all your students
about this. It has been quite an interesting experiment for you,
hasn't it?' He opened the door and added bitterly, 'Just

remember when you do, that Dalziel, and men like him, were responsible for your being able to stay alive. While you were going through medical school he was probably at sea, keeping the Navy going when the country resented every damn penny being spent to protect them. Perhaps he has had his delusions,' he waved abruptly around the cramped chartroom, 'but by God he's not got much to show for all of it, has he? They're going to destroy him anyway, but at least you can leave him some dignity!'

He strode out into the filtered sunlight and saw Irvine by the compass.

Irvine said awkwardly, 'Sorry to drag you in like this. We all felt it was best.'

'Did you?' Standish faced him coldly. 'Then I hope you're satisfied.'

He ran down the bridge ladder to where Wishart was watching his boat below the rail.

'Take me after the captain, Sub.' He climbed into the small cockpit beside the three seamen and added, 'Fast as you can.'

Wishart glanced at him and said quietly, 'I had no part in it. They didn't even ask what I thought.'

'Well, that's something, I suppose.'

'I wish there was something we could . . .' The rest of his words were drowned by the roar of motors as the *Whizz-Kid* thrust from the ship's side and headed towards the reef.

Once through the arms of the narrow inlet the temperature fell away, so that it was like standing inside a giant ice box. The high craggy walls on either beam, the countless overhanging ledges kept the inlet in constant shadow, above which the clouded sky seemed suddenly remote and unreachable.

They saw the motor boat idling gently on a swirling current beneath one of the cliffs, and directly opposite, perched grotesquely on a ledge of jagged rocks lay the remains of the *Bombay Queen*.

She was just as Irvine had described. The bridge was still there, but everything aft had been carried away, and her rusting entrails were scattered across the rocks to mark the force of that final great wave which had hurled her into the narrow inlet and her last resting place.

Standish said, 'Go back to the ship, Sub. I'm going to speak with the captain.' He did not look at Wishart as the two hulls touched momentarily and with one jump he crossed to the other boat.

He waited for the *Whizz-Kid*'s noise to subside beyond the nearest cliff and then said, 'So you found her, sir.'

Dalziel stared up at the shattered hull with its flaking, rusty plates and gaunt holes along her bilge keel.

'I am glad you came to see her, too.' He sounded downcast. 'Not a pretty sight.'

The bowman, who was sitting with his feet dangling around the stem dropped his eyes as Standish looked at him. Like the boat's coxswain and an armed seaman, he was probably wondering just how long Dalziel would stay here staring at the wreck. Perhaps in her he saw the remains of his own life, Standish thought.

He said, 'It must have been one hell of a storm to carry her in here.'

Dalziel sighed. 'That's it then. No point in hanging about, I suppose.'

Standish watched him anxiously. He looked as he sounded. Beaten.

The bowman called, ' 'Er nameplate is still 'angin' there, sir! Shall I grab it with me boat'ook?'

Standish was still looking at Dalziel. He had already seen the forlorn plate dangling from one bolt below the broken stemhead. And why not? he thought. Maybe Dalziel had been saved in the past by some of his delusions, so what was wrong with one more? Perhaps in the years ahead he would be able to look at the old *Bombay Queen*'s name and find some small comfort there to sustain him.

He nodded. 'Right. Get it if you can.'

The engine coughed into life and the boat nudged slowly between two finely edged rocks as the seaman stood swaying in the bows ready to drag the plate down with his hook.

He heard the metal rasp across the rusting plates and then looked over the gunwale to make sure the boat was in no danger from the nearest rock. It was then that he saw it. A long black nozzle attached to two clean, bright shackles. Coupled to the nozzle was a thick hose, about eighteen inches in circumference.

He seized Dalziel's arm and pointed. 'Look! For God's sake,

it's a fuel pipe!' The boat swayed as Dalziel ran to the side and shouted, 'It goes up through the wreck, I can see it quite plainly!'

Standish swung round, seeing the coxswain's startled gaze as he called, 'Full astern! Let's get out of here!'

The bowman turned and looked at them, the boathook still above his shoulder. ''Ere, 'old on, I bloody nearly fell in that time!'

The sudden crack of automatic fire rebounded off the high cliffs so that it seemed to come from every direction.

Standish saw the bowman's expression change to stark terror, and then as the bullets tore into his back he gave one shrill scream and toppled headlong over the side.

Bullets were hammering into the hull, hurling splinters and ricocheting from the engine even as the boat started to go astern.

When he looked up Standish saw the telltale drift of smoke beside the wreck's eyeless bridge, heard the coxswain gasp with agony as he too was smashed down across the tiller.

The armed seaman jerked frantically at his Stirling and then fired blindly towards the ship's side, the bullets cutting away the rust and making a wavering line of holes between two empty scuttles.

And still the firing went on, joined now by another weapon higher in the bows from behind a heavy winch.

Feathers of spray lifted and danced all around the boat, and as he looked down Standish saw the water already seeping greedily through the bottom boards by his feet.

Dalziel groaned and threw one hand to his side, the blood shining in the hazy light like black paint.

Between his teeth he gasped, 'Take the helm! Back to the ship!'

Standish stumbled aft, realizing for the first time that the Stirling was silent and the seaman lay staring at the sky above the cliffs, a great hole in the centre of his forehead.

'It's no use!' Standish did not know he was shouting aloud. 'The bloody boat's sinking under us!'

Dalziel struggled across the cockpit and picked up the Stirling. He fired a short burst towards the wreck and then said, 'Empty!' He looked up at Standish and said hoarsely,

'They were there all the time!' He clapped his hand to his ribs and added, 'Keep going astern. If you try and turn they'll get you, too!'

Sweat poured beneath his cap, and he could feel his breath whistling in his throat as he struggled to hold the tiller against the engine's reversed thrust. It was hopeless. The boat was dragging badly, and when the water reached the engine . . . He looked up as something blue and white cut across his vision before turning end on towards him.

Dalziel muttered, 'God, it's that young fool coming back for us!'

The *Whizz-Kid* swung wildly, the spray bursting away on either beam as the coxswain headed straight for the sinking motor boat. Shots hammered against the wood, and Standish saw other bullets smashing into the *Whizz-Kid's* fibreglass hull while two seamen returned fire with the machine gun.

He saw Wishart right above him, felt his naked back under his hands as he dragged himself over the side while another man hauled Dalziel across the sagging bows.

He managed to grin and gasp, 'Back home now, Sub, and thanks for the ride!'

Wishart did not seem to see him, and as he ran aft to the stern Standish saw his face was like that of a hardened veteran.

With the hull bouncing and careering back across her own wash he had to crawl to Dalziel's side. As he opened his shirt and thrust his hand inside he heard Dalziel say, 'They thought we'd seen them, the bastards!' He bared his teeth as Standish's fingers probed at the wound. It was from pain, but as Standish glanced up at him it looked exactly like his old, mischievous grin.

Dalziel said through his teeth, 'Well, they made one bloody great mistake, didn't they?' Then he lay back and closed his eyes.

18 Sixty-five Days

As the boat came alongside the frigate's hull Standish saw the guardrails were crammed with watching men. It was then that he realized none of them had heard the shooting or knew anything of what had happened up to this moment. The walls of the narrow inlet had masked every sound, and now, as some jumped into the boat and others shouted questions from above, he felt his earlier reaction giving way to something like anger.

He saw Pigott leaning over the rail and calling, 'What happened?'

'The boat's sunk!' Standish stood aside as Dalziel was passed up and over the rail. 'There are three dead back there!' He noticed too that the swell was heavier and the boat was rising and falling steeply against the ship's plates.

He pushed between the seamen and saw the doctor running towards them, his face alive with questions.

Rideout reached Dalziel's side and said, 'Better get him to the sickbay.' Across the captain's shoulder he looked at Standish and added, 'I'll look after him.'

Dalziel seemed to come to life at that moment. He thrust Rideout aside and lurched against the rail, his voice harsh as he said, 'Take your hands off me! I don't need a refugee from the bloody National Health Service to tell me what to do. While I am in command I will give the orders, right?' He swung round, seeking out Standish. 'Help me to the bridge. There may not be much time.'

As they moved towards the first ladder Dalziel called over his shoulder, 'Tell the Chief to keep steam on the capstan. I will be shifting anchorage in a moment.'

Wishart asked breathlessly, 'The boat sir? Shall I get her inboard?'

Dalziel glared at him. 'I will tell you when I want it hoisted!' In a more level tone he added, 'You've done damn well, Sub. Don't spoil it now by being such a worrier, eh?'

It seemed to take an age to reach the upper bridge. Curious faces, peering figures were on every level, and by the time they lurched over the last coaming Dalziel was sweating badly.

As Rideout climbed after him he rasped, 'Just get a dressing on this gash, will you?' He tore off his shirt and threw it to the deck, seemingly unaware of the blood which ran unheeded down his side and leg to the gratings.

He saw Irvine and gestured fiercely, 'You were too damn hasty, Pilot! They were there right enough!' He looked round the bridge. 'But they're *prisoners* now. They can't get away, and I intend to keep them and their bloody secret oil dump until help arrives!'

He seemed to realize Irvine was still staring at him and asked coldly, 'What are you gaping at, man? Can't you admit you were wrong?' He held up his arms to allow Rideout and his medical assistant to wrap a large dressing around his ribs.

Irvine said haltingly, 'Just before we saw you returning we had a signal, sir.' He glanced at Standish before continuing, 'It seems some freighter is in difficulties. Shifting cargo. She's sent out an S.O.S. and we have been asked to verify our present position and state if we can reach her and give assistance.'

Dalziel dropped his arms and moved them cautiously. He winced, then replied, 'Show me.' He read the scribbled signal and said, 'Even if we had already left we couldn't get there before other ships in the area. She's on the main shipping lane. She'll be all right. Anyway, she's a Greek ship, so it's probably more panic than danger.'

Wills had appeared as if by magic and handed Dalziel a clean shirt.

'These bastards on the wreck could hold an army at bay.' His voice was muffled as he struggled into the shirt. 'This is what we'll do. There's probably a carrier somewhere in the Gulf. I shall request assistance and some helicopters. We can pin these characters down easily with a bit of air cover.' He groped for his cap and brushed some dust from it before saying, 'But remember, it's *our* pigeon!'

Irvine said, 'We have no choice, sir. We must leave at once.' He gestured towards the islet. 'They won't get far. We can call up additional support and let them handle it.' His tone hardened. 'You have no right to do this.'

Dalziel stared at him. 'No right? There are three men dead back in that inlet, mostly because you only saw what you wanted to see. Once more, your damn carelessness has cost lives, and now you've got the impudence to question my orders!'

Rideout interrupted quickly, 'I think it would be better if you went to my sickbay, sir. It is a nasty wound. No one could blame you for handing over command, *temporarily*.' He dropped his gaze. 'You have proved your point. Others can clear up the mess now.'

Dalziel walked unsteadily to the screen. 'You haven't understood a word, have you? Don't you realize that by the time we can get any sort of cover organized those murdering bastards will have been lifted off? Only our presence here is holding them and the evidence of their operations.'

Irvine looked at Rideout, but when he remained silent said bluntly, 'I do not think it is your decision any more, sir. If the doctor won't say it, then I will. I've got too much at stake to throw it all away on some fanatical gooks and a few gallons of oil.' Dalziel remained staring at the islet as Irvine continued, 'I suggest a signal is despatched immediately giving our *correct* position and relevant facts. If it is decided we should remain here to await support, then all well and good. But as the sea is getting up I think it unlikely.' He looked sharply at Rideout. 'It would be prudent if you would report sick at once. Number One can assume command until further orders are received and verified.'

Dalziel looked at Standish. 'Is that what *you* want?' His voice was very level, but in his deepset eyes Standish saw something more. He was pleading with him, throwing himself wide open as never before.

Irvine said, 'It doesn't matter what he thinks, sir. It is what is right which counts.'

Dalziel did not take his eyes from Standish. 'You know I'm right, don't you? If we waste time, and especially if the sea gets up, there'll be nothing here when help comes. In spite of what has happened and what we know, they'll turn their backs on it, because it is convenient for them.'

Standish replied quietly, 'Three men died just now. Without warning they were killed.' He looked at Irvine and saw that Pigott and Hornby had joined him by the compass. 'I don't think they should die in vain, sir. But you must make a signal. Tell the C. in C. and Admiral Curtis what has happened. Let them decide.' He kept his eyes on Irvine as he added firmly, 'But *you* will make the signal, sir. Nobody else will do it while you are in command.'

Quarrie swung himself into the bridge and said, 'I've still got steam on the capstan.' He glanced at the others questioningly. 'What's this, a conference?'

Dalziel walked to the telephones and picked one from the rack. 'W/T office? Captain. Stand by to despatch a signal. Immediate.' He covered the telephone with his hand and said, 'You should see yourselves. It's a sight I'll never forget, I know that!'

Marsh, the young signalman, crossed to the starboard gratings to keep clear of the assembled officers. He guessed what was happening, but could not quite understand it. Later he would ask the yeoman. Old Burch always had an answer. He gripped the glass screen as the ship heeled uneasily to her cable. When he spoke his voice was so quiet it was almost lost in the sounds of water sluicing against the hull. But the effect of his words was like an electric shock.

'Excuse me, but there's a submarine on the starboard quarter.' He swallowed noisily. 'Look, sir!'

Dalziel dropped the telephone and threw himself on to the gratings. Standish followed and stared hard at the low shape which was moving so very slowly past the other islet, about a mile and a half away. He seized some glasses and trained them over the screen, his mouth suddenly dry as he saw the submarine spring into focus. He could see the layers of sea-slime on her black hull, the air of menace which was so familiar to him, yet so alien when viewed from the *Terrapin*'s open bridge.

Dalziel said hoarsely, 'See? She's making for the inlet. Her captain has probably seen everything we've been doing. Now he's going in to take off his people, and will probably detonate the only evidence we have to show for all this.' His voice sounded near breaking as he added, 'Look at him. He thinks we're going to let him do it!'

Standish said softly, 'She's an ex-Russian boat. I heard they'd handed quite a few to the Chinese before relations got strained.' How could he be so calm when his whole being was screaming out to move and act?

Behind him he heard Irvine again. His voice like someone repeating a lesson. 'Make the signal, sir. There is nothing we can do. *Nothing.*'

Dalziel turned away as Standish said, 'If we could have got here *earlier*. Had we anchored across the inlet he'd have been helpless.' He made himself say it. 'As we are now.'

A voicepipe squeaked and the bosun's mate said, 'Call from the fo'c'sle, sir. Mr. Caley thinks the cable might be draggin'.'

Dalziel nodded dully. 'Hands to stations for getting under way. We will break out the anchor immediately.'

As the order was repeated and piped around the ship the watching figures along the guardrails seemed to melt away, while others appeared on the forecastle where Caley was staring down at the snubbing cable. Yet in spite of the noise and sudden activity it seemed quite remote on the bridge where officers and watchkeepers stood like statues, their eyes still watching the slow-moving submarine. On her conning tower it was now possible to see a few heads, and as the watery sunlight flashed momentarily below her periscope standards Standish knew her officers were studying the *Terrapin*.

He dragged his eyes away and looked at Dalziel, wondering how he felt at this moment. Frustration, despair? They were too empty to describe what he must be suffering. He had almost expected him to order an all-out attack, or at least make some show of defiance before this unnamed, unmarked enemy. It might have been better if he had. To be forcibly restrained and taken from his bridge would have shown all of them that the old spark was still there.

From forward came the steady clank of incoming cable, and on the side deck he heard Wishart yelling at his men to prepare the *Whizz-Kid* for hoisting.

Dalziel said tonelessly, 'You draft out a signal, Number One. Report the submarine's position and purpose here. You know what to do.'

Pigott muttered uneasily, 'At least they won't be able to use this place again.'

Dalziel did not turn his head. 'There will be other places. And there will be other people to ignore them until it is all too late.'

Irvine replaced a telephone, his features wooden. 'Engine room standing by, sir.'

A lookout called, 'Submarine has stopped, sir.'

Standish paused on his way to the chartroom and raised his glasses. There was still no sign of life on the submarine's casing, and apart from two heads on her conning tower she could have been abandoned. There was not even a gun as was usual in this sort of boat.

He blinked rapidly to clear his vision and then said quietly, 'Something's moving.' He steadied the glasses against the ship's uneven motion. 'Forrard of the tower, what the hell . . .' He sprang across the gratings and shouted, 'She's armed with rockets! She's training them on us!'

From the forecastle the regular clank of cable continued unhindered, and below the bridge Wishart's party had succeeded in raising their boat clear of the water like a gleaming blue pod.

Dalziel was already pressed against the screen, his voice carrying above the other sounds as he yelled, 'Break the cable! *Jump to it!*' He groped for the red button and jabbed it with his thumb. 'Action stations! Get those men off the upper deck!'

As the alarm shrilled and clamoured between decks Caley seemed to come to life again, pushing with his hands when words failed to move the men around him. They seemed stricken and unable to react until with an oath Caley dashed amongst them, his mouth moving soundlessly in the scream of the alarm.

Dalziel snapped, 'Signal. Immediate. We are . . .' He broke off as he saw Standish's face and turned his eyes back to the other vessel.

Standish stood quite motionless, watching the tiny blob of light as it left the submarine's casing and flashed low across the heaving water towards him. It was like a drip of molten lava, and had such a flat trajectory that he could see the surface of the water tearing apart as it ripped above it.

Pigott was yelling, 'He can't! He *couldn't* fire on us!'

Then came the explosion. It was like a thunderclap, and Standish felt the bridge shake as if it had been struck by the greatest wave in creation. As he reeled against some unyielding object he was partially blinded by a torrent of falling spray, his lungs burning as the air was squeezed out of them. All about him men were slipping and falling, yelling to each other, while the ship staggered and then rolled upright again. When he dragged himself to the screen he saw that the side deck was scorched black, the guardrails missing and the funnel buckled inwards like a crushed oil drum. In the streaming smoke, like two gaunt gibbets were the remains of the davits, and he guessed the rocket had exploded against the *Whizz-Kid* even as it was being hoisted up the ship's side. But for her, it would have burst right inside the hull.

He felt the ship swinging clumsily in a lazy roller and knew that the cable had parted, and when he peered forward he saw Caley and some men reeling aft towards the guns, while at his back three crumpled bodies lay spread-eagled around the empty hawsepipes, cut down by the blast which had somehow spared their companions.

Dalziel shouted, 'Make this signal. Plain language. Am under missile attack from unidentified submarine.' He ran to the voicepipe and snapped, '*Port fifteen!*' Then he looked across at Irvine. '*Did you get that?*' He watched the gyro again. 'Request immediate assistance.' His mouth hardened. 'Am engaging.'

Irvine prised his fingers from the screen and staggered towards the door of the chartroom.

'Midships. Full ahead both engines!' Dalziel's eyes gleamed like steel as he shouted, 'Here's another!'

This time the missile did not miss. As the frigate continued to turn in a wide circle it struck her below the starboard side of the bridge. The whole ship reeled wildly, and as Standish ducked to avoid flying glass from a shattered screen he saw smoke pouring through a voicepipe like steam under pressure, while on every side voices were shouting and cursing amidst the bedlam of creaking metal.

Through it all he heard Wishart over the intercom. ' "A" gun ready. Director out of action. Have switched to local control.'

Dalziel said thickly, 'Midships. Steady.' He was crouching over the gyro, watching fixedly as the submarine's low outline glided across the bows.

Irvine reappeared, a handkerchief balled in his mouth. 'W/T office is smashed!' He retched. 'Keeble and the others are . . .' This time he vomited helplessly against the side.

Dalziel looked at Standish. 'That's it then, eh? All alone.' He snapped, '*Open fire!*'

The right four-inch gun lurched back violently, and seconds later the shell made a tall waterspout rise slowly far beyond the submarine. As the other gun fired Standish found time to wonder how Wishart had survived the blast when the boat and most of his men must have been wiped out.

The bosun's mate said thickly, 'Damage control reports five killed in W/T and main fire point, sir.' He winced as the guns banged again. 'Fire under control now, sir. No damage to hull structure.'

Dalziel bared his teeth. 'Good.' He raised his glasses. 'Still shooting over. But I'll bet that gave 'em a nasty moment!'

The submarine was moving, and Standish could see from her rising bow wave that she was making real speed this time. 'A' gun crashed out again, and the waterspout which followed shot skyward less than half a cable from the submarine's bow. He heard Wishart call, 'Down one hundred.' He could picture the gunners peering over their sights, waiting for the sleek shape to emerge in the crosswires. One hit was all that was needed. The waters were too shallow for her to dive. She had to fight or run, and either way she had lost her first advantage of unprovoked attack.

Perhaps her commander had imagined the *Terrapin* intended to try and forestall her approach to the inlet. Maybe he even recognized the old frigate from some earlier encounter. As the one which had almost caught him at Kuala Papan, or had charged alongside the *Cornwallis* in total darkness.

He could feel the revolutions mounting with every second,

saw the bow wave surging abeam to break across some of those reefs which no longer seemed important or dangerous.

He saw too that the young signalman who had first noticed the submarine's stealthy approach was standing beside him, his hair blowing in the breeze while he stared wide-eyed at the target.

Standish groped for a helmet and held it out to him. Then he tapped the boy on the head and shouted, 'Put this on! You've got some valuable stuff in there!'

The signalman stared at him and then nodded dazedly. He was the same one who had accompanied Standish ashore to the burning village.

It was at that moment he felt himself falling. It was almost like being suspended in space, floating, while things and events all around took on an unreal and seemingly nightmare shape. There were jagged holes in the steel deck, and he saw Burch lolling against a flag locker with blood pouring from his mouth. The signalman was gripping his legs as if to hold him, to stop him from falling, but when he looked down Standish realized there was little left of him below the waist.

Only Irvine appeared to be alive, and as he staggered against the compass he was croaking aloud, yet no words came. Or maybe Standish could no longer hear. He might even be dead. With something like panic he clutched at the voicepipes, his shoes slithering on blood and pieces of torn flesh as he stared towards Dalziel.

The captain was crouching against the side, his cap gone, hair hanging loosely across his eyes and speckled with chipped paint. Then as his hearing returned Standish knew what Irvine was trying to tell him, and as he pulled himself towards Dalziel. he saw the great pall of smoke rising over the forepart of the bridge, heard the rip of tearing steel as something tore adrift and fell deep into the shattered hull.

'Wheelhouse doesn't answer!' Irvine's voice was suddenly very loud. 'Direct hit!'

Dalziel opened his eyes and licked his lips. 'Have to steer from aft. No good like this.' He lolled his head from side to side, and Standish saw blood soaking across his legs and the splintered remains of the gratings. 'Get down and see to it, Number One. I'm all right here. Just be a few moments, eh?'

Another great shockwave hurled the ship drunkenly from her set course, and as he ran for the ladder Standish realized that the rocket must have missed and exploded against one of the exposed fangs of reef. He threw himself down the ladder and then saw that the twin four-inch guns were pointing towards the sky, their muzzles still smoking as if they had just fired. Of the gunshield there was no sign at all, and he shut his mind against the thing which crawled sobbing from the charred remains, its clothing burning like a torch. It might have been Wishart, and he prayed that he was already dead.

As he passed the wheelhouse he heard a voice call, 'Able Seaman Macnair on the wheel, sir.' A pause and someone coughing. 'They're all dead in here for God's sake! But she's answering the helm again!'

A down eddy of wind cleared the funnelling smoke from the forecastle, and as he peered over his shoulder Standish saw that the submarine was no longer visible. Taking her time she had gone to complete what she had started. After that she would return and finish the crippled *Terrapin*. Her own radio operators would know Dalziel was sending no signals for help. That he could not.

He could tell from the vibrating deck that Quarrie had cut down the speed, and guessed the last explosion had punctured the old ship's skin and any increase would pare the plates away like flesh from a gutted fish.

He saw Rideout kneeling beside a seaman, his fingers no longer clean but bloodied like a butcher's as he worked busily with his dressings. He looked up and said hoarsely, 'They fired on us without any reason.'

'They had their reasons.' Standish looked aft at the clean paint and neat decks. It seemed incredible that the afterpart had survived with hardly a scratch. Not that it would make any difference now.

Rideout stood up and said, 'That's a bad gash on your arm. Here, let me . . .'

Standish pushed him away and wrapped a bandage around his arm. It was bleeding badly, yet he had felt nothing.

'Go and help the captain.' He met the doctor's glazed stare. 'I think he may be badly hurt.'

He found Hornby crouching by the depth-charge mortars, his face like a sheet.

'Gather your men together and check all circuits. You'll be in charge of damage control, right?' He shook his arm savagely, feeling the man quivering, unable to stand. Sickened, Standish turned and picked his way beneath the break in the forecastle.

He need not have bothered for he could see the sky quite clearly through the crater in the deckhead above.

Two stretcher bearers crunched over broken glass and splintered lockers, their burden lurching between them as if already dead. There was a bloody bandage completely covering his face with a tiny slit where the mouth should be. But as they hurried past one hand reached out and plucked feebly at Standish's leg. It was blackened and burned like a piece of wood, yet as the stretcher came to a halt he knew it was Wishart.

Mackie, the medical assistant, climbed through the tangle of torn steel and paused long enough to touch Standish's arm and give a brief shake of the head. Then he went on, calling out names as he ran.

Standish took the hand in his and held it gently, his heart aching as he watched the bandage moving around that one small slit. The two stretcher bearers stood like swaying statues while Standish lowered his ear to the bandage, one with a face like stone, the other sobbing helplessly as the tears cut bright passages down his smoke-stained cheeks.

'I'm here, Sub.' He felt the fingers move slightly. 'Take it easy. You'll be fine.'

The voice seemed to come from a great distance. Or like a man whispering in an empty room. 'Sorry—about—the—guns.' The hand twitched again. 'Had—no—proper—training—you —see.'

Standish heard more cries from above, the shrill of a whistle and Motts yelling his name. He had to go. Had to move.

He said quietly, 'You were bloody good.'

But there was no response, and when he released the hand it dropped against the stretcher and did not move again. Nor would it.

Mackie came back and stood watching him. Then he said, 'All right, you two. Put him down and go for another one.' As they tipped their burden on to the deck he said brokenly, 'My God, I think I've had it. I don't reckon I can take much more.'

Standish looked at him and replied, 'I think you can.' He took another glance at Wishart's body. 'Just a bit longer.'

Then he forced himself to walk back into the daylight, and when he looked up through the drifting smoke he saw that the cloud was breaking to allow a few rays of sunshine to reach them.

He had been away from the bridge for fifteen minutes, yet it seemed like an hour. When he reached it again he saw Dalziel was sitting on his chair, hunched forward to peer through the cracked screen, his cap once more in place and tilted across his eyes.

Standish said, 'The pumps are holding, sir. It's hard to tell how many holes we have in the hull, but we can still keep it under control.' He realized with surprise that Pigott was also on the bridge, some binoculars around his neck as he stood grim faced beside the wheelhouse voicepipe. Irvine was rubbing his eyes with a filthy handkerchief and seemed unable to time his movements to those of the ship, so that he swayed back and forth like a drunken man.

Dalziel nodded. 'I've been hearing the reports. We've lost nearly thirty dead and wounded.' He shifted painfully to look at Standish. 'And young Wishart. I'm sorry about him. You and he were friends, eh?'

Standish gripped the rail below the screen and tried to control his emotions.

'Yes.'

Dalziel grimaced. 'That bloody submarine has got to the inlet by now. Still, he'll be back here again very shortly. It won't be dark for another four hours.' He met Standish's eyes. 'You know what that means, don't you? The starboard shaft is overheating again, so we cannot even run away.' He smiled bitterly. 'Not that I would.'

Standish looked at the green, undulating water and the criss-cross of eddies around an isolated reef.

'And *he* can't reach the deep channel by any other route.' He ran his fingers through his hair. 'So that's it.'

Dalziel settled back in his chair. 'Ironic really. To think after all those years she's got to end her days fighting a submarine again.' He frowned and wiped his face with the back of his sleeve. 'Poor old girl.' He touched the stained steel with his fingers. 'Poor, misunderstood old girl.'

Caley appeared at the top of the ladder. 'My T.A.S. department is kaput, sir. All the circuits are done in.' He looked at the bodies which had been covered with coats and torn flags. 'I'm afraid I can't do nothing with Hornby. I think he's, well . . .'

Dalziel turned and looked at him. Then he grinned. 'Split his stack, eh?' He waited until the astonishment had given way to the shadow of a smile on Caley's rough features and added, 'Never mind. We have the Bofors, and we have a good company. Many have fought with less.'

As Caley clumped away he said sadly, 'Can't have him depressed. I expect he feels it badly, you know. His precious depth-charges out of action just when we might have been able to use them, although it was most unlikely.' The grin was coming back again. 'But perhaps he's still brooding over his bloody daughter, eh? That's almost worse in its way!'

Standish asked, 'How is the wound, sir?'

'If I said I felt fine you'd not believe it. So I'll tell you. I feel like screaming hell. Nevertheless, I think I can rise to the occasion.'

A lookout yelled, 'Submarine fine on the port bow, sir!'

It was more like an extension of the rocky outcrop which guarded the inlet, but as it lengthened and hardened Standish knew it was almost time. He thought of Suzane, and saw her very clearly, and wanted to take out his wallet just one more. As if by touching the handkerchief he would make some last contact.

He thought too of Wishart. As he recalled the hand in his he felt the slow return of the same madness which had almost overcome him before. It was unreal yet consuming, like Dalziel's grin, or the way this clapped-out ship kept going in spite of the destruction and punishment she had taken.

He looked at Pigott. 'Warn all guns to stand by.' He saw the bespectacled supply officer run to the handset, brushing against Irvine, who merely stared at him, his face quite empty of reaction or understanding.

Dalziel groped for the red telephone and then said, 'Chief? Captain speaking. Maximum revs when I ask for them, right?'

He paused and looked at the punctured deck by his feet. 'I know you will. It won't be long now, I'm afraid.'

Standish said, 'I put Motts on the wheel. You need a level head for this sort of thing.'

Dalziel seemed to be speaking to himself, or perhaps the *Terrapin*. 'Corbin dead, too. Lot of good men gone today. But by God, we gave 'em a run for it.'

The lookout reported, 'She's turning towards us, sir.'

Standish looked up at the sky and tried to think of a prayer. But nothing came. No thoughts and no more hopes.

He said vaguely, 'Christ, I'm thirsty.'

Then the submarine fired another rocket. At a range of nearly two miles it seemed to take an eternity to reach its target.

It struck *Terrapin* halfway along the port side, some four feet above her waterline, the explosion blasting inwards and then up through the steel deck like a fireball. The ship gave one great convulsion, and as Standish fell headlong he saw the lattice mast start to topple. With the billowing smoke all around it seemed to move very slowly, but as the ship gave another shudder it gathered speed to pitch over the side, dragging with it a clattering tangle of rigging and radar gear.

Standish struggled upright and ran to the bridge wing. For a moment longer he could see nothing beyond the smoke, and as he coughed helplessly and dashed his hand across his streaming eyes he imagined the ship had broken her back. When the smoked swirled clear the sight revealed was not much better. There was a great crater which stretched across the side deck and down almost to the waterline, and when he leaned over the rail he could see the full extent of the destruction below. Tangled frames and plates buckled and twisted like cardboard, dangling wires, and somewhere through the smoke the menacing gleam of water.

He heard Dalziel yelling behind him, 'Tell the Bofors to open fire!'

Standish dragged himself back across the tilting deck. 'No use! Knocked out!' His mind was still cringing from that last explosion, yet he was able to contemplate the bareness of his words. *Knocked out.* Did that really describe the horror he had just witnessed? One gun mounting wiped clean away, the other lying on its side, its muzzle twisted like a piece of piping.

Beside it, one of its crew lay gaping at the sky, his clothing gone, his naked body gleaming like flayed meat. Knocked out.

Dalziel stared at him, his eyes wild. The deck had stayed at the same angle. She was not coming back.

He shouted hoarsely, 'The pumps can't take it! God damn them, they won't hold it!'

Pigott was gripping a telephone, his face black with smoke while he pressed his sleeve against one eye. The blast had shattered his spectacles, and there was blood on his fingers.

He called, 'Engine room reports water gaining on remaining pumps, sir. It's already in the boiler room.'

Dalziel looked away, his shoulders hunched in the chair like an old man.

The bosun's mate ran to the broken gratings and yelled, 'Submarine's increased speed again! 'E's turning!'

Standish shook his head. That last rocket had swung the frigate off course, like someone kicking a toy boat. The submarine was still heading for the deep channel, her wash mounting as she gathered speed across the bows of her listing victim.

Dalziel said, 'She's getting away.'

Leading Seaman Neal had come to the bridge a few minutes earlier to help carry away the wounded. He was pointing up and away beyond the sea and the smoke, to a tiny sliver of silver which gleamed in the hazed sunlight like a star.

Standish nodded dully. An aircraft. Probably a Boeing en route for Saigon. It was unnerving to realize that over there, high up beyond sight and sound of their destruction, people were sitting comfortably, sipping drinks, maybe watching a movie. The submarine's commander must have seen it too, or had contacted it with his radar. He would take no chances now, but would make straight for deep water and dive. Like an assassin. A butcher.

Dalziel dragged his eyes from the submarine and said slowly, 'Better tell the Chief to get his people on deck.' He seemed hardly able to get the words out. 'She's taking it badly. Maybe you were right after all. Too old for this sort of thing.'

The submarine turned slightly, her arrowed bow wave streaming away across the reef, as if to dismiss them all, to show contempt for their puny challenge.

Dalziel said, 'Go yourself, Number One, and get our people ready. See what you can do for them.'

He tensed in his chair as something tore adrift deep in the hull and crashed heavily against a bulkhead.

Standish looked round. At Pigott with his one good eye fixed on the submarine. At Irvine, who was holding his hands locked together in front of him like a priest in prayer. At Neal and the others who still stood together on the shattered bridge, legs splayed to take the ship's deep list, their feet touching the sprawled corpses which had once been their friends.

He ran down the ladder, pausing to glance into the wheelhouse where Motts was leaning on the spokes smoking a cigarette while a seaman tied a bandage around his leg.

On down the main deck, past tangled steel and sightless bodies. Here and there a grimy figure stood up to watch him pass, and he saw Hornby sitting on a winch, his head in his hands, oblivious to a mechanic who was trying to fix a life-jacket around his fat shoulders.

He found Rideout in the wardroom tending to his wounded, his shirt and legs splattered with blood as he moved steadily amongst them. Sunlight dappled the bulkhead in a dozen bright stars, and Standish saw the holes where splinters had punctured the plating like embers through butter. His foot kicked something, and when he glanced down he saw it was Pigott's calendar, each date marked with a pencilled circle. He felt the deck tremble and heard some of the wounded sobbing quietly, lost in their own drugged world of fear and loneliness.

The calendar had been intended as a joke. It was nearly over now. The sixty-five days of Commander Dalziel. It made a good epitaph.

The phone buzzed on its hook and he stared at it for several seconds as more pictures probed his reeling mind.

Of Wishart answering it after speaking up for Dalziel against the others. Of Wills, the steward, who had dreamed of his pub. Standish had passed his body on his way here, sprawled across his broken cups. He had died as he had lived. Quietly.

He took the handset. 'Yes?'

It was Dalziel's voice, and for an instant Standish imagined something else had happened to the ship. That she was going down now, and fast.

'The submarine's turned again, Number One. She was going to dive, but . . .' In the background he heard Pigott's voice. Then Dalziel said, 'One of young Wishart's shells must have been a near miss. I don't think they can close their rocket mounting!'

Standish stared at the handset. 'I'll come up!' As he ran for the door he shouted, 'The Chief's sending some of his men to help you with the wounded, Doc. You may have to bale out in a hurry!'

He reached the bridge and seized Pigott's glasses.

There was more of a haze across the wider channel between the reef now, but in the powerful lenses he could see the small knot of figures on the submarine's casing, and several others climbing down from her conning tower.

He felt himself stagger, and when he looked round realized that the deck had come upright again.

Dalziel said, 'Another compartment flooded.' He smiled sadly. 'Strange all the same. Just as if she was bracing herself.'

Standish stared at him. He could feel his body shaking, his whole being quivering so badly that it was difficult to speak.

He said, 'Why don't we, sir?' He staggered across the broken glass, his feet slipping in blood. 'Why not have a go?'

Dalziel met his eyes, his mouth drawn back against the pain of his wound. Then, still watching Standish, he picked up the red handset.

'Are all your people out, Chief?' He nodded. 'Good. Send them to clear the wounded from the wardroom right away.' He swallowed hard. 'There is about a mile between us and that submarine, Chief. She can't dive yet, and we can't shoot.' He paused and closed his eyes as something broke clear of the hull and fell alongside with a heavy splash. 'The sea's getting a hold down there, is it?' His tone sharpened. '*Tell* me, Chief. I'll not have you fried alive for our benefit.' He smiled. 'Right then. Give me everything.' He looked across at Pigott. '*Everything!*'

Almost immediately the ship began to increase speed, the water surging dangerously close to the gaping crater in her side, spray lancing over the hull to make steam spurt from the smouldering wreckage left by the submarine's last missile.

Dalziel returned to his chair and looked at the blood on his legs without comment. To Standish he snapped, 'Take the con. I want to watch from here.'

The revolutions were still mounting, and astern across the creaming wake Standish saw the trail of greasy smoke mingling with that of the ship's wounds. How could she do it? What the hell was holding her afloat? He saw the wounded being laid right aft by Caley's impotent mortars, their bandages white against the smoke and glittering water. Other men stood around like spectators, some too shocked to realize what was happening.

But aboard the submarine someone had at last understood. He heard Neal bark a warning and turned to watch a lazy arc of tracer as it climbed from the rear of the conning tower before pitching down to rake the forecastle and lower bridge like a bandsaw.

Through the voicepipe he heard Motts yelling crazily, 'Shoot away, you bastards! Throw all you've bloody got!'

His wildness had an immediate effect, and below the bridge Standish heard more men yelling and cheering, their voices cracked but strangely defiant above the desperate roar of fans and the beat of Quarrie's racing engines.

He felt it for himself. So that he wanted to cheer and cry with the rest of them. As more tracer slashed at the bridge he heard himself mutter, 'You can't hurt us any more.' Who did he mean? The men or the ship? He thought of the blackened guns, of Wishart's crew blasted to fragments, and of the dead seamen who still lay by the empty hawsepipes. Nothing could reach them now.

Dalziel was leaning right forward, his face inches from the screen. Through his teeth he said, 'Get ready to clear the ship. All available rafts and anything which will float.' He turned and said sharply, 'Port a bit. She's turned slightly.'

Standish lowered his eye to the gyro. 'Port ten.' He held his breath, watching the submarine's black outline as it edged across the splintered jackstaff. 'Midships. Steady as you go.'

Up the voicepipe he heard Motts reply and then add, 'She's movin' now all right, sir!'

The whole bridge structure was jerking and vibrating as if to tear itself from the ship, and Standish saw the sea boiling back

from the stem in two great banks of white foam which looked
almost solid in the sunlight.

When he lifted his eyes again he saw the submarine was less
than four cables away, and that he could even see the slime and
scars on her hull without his glasses. The machine gun had fallen
silent, and several small figures were climbing back to the
conning tower which was swaying steeply on the current from
the reef.

Dalziel gripped the screen and pointed with his hand.
'Look! They're turning again!'

Standish did not speak. He watched the sudden frothing
commotion around the submarine's saddle tanks, the sluice of
water at her stern as slowly at first, then with gathering
momentum she began to turn.

He snatched the red telephone. 'Chief? The sub's altering
course again. I think she intends to use another rocket on us!'

It sounded like a sigh. 'I'll do what I can.' The phone went
dead.

Loose gear fell unheeded in the chartroom, and a corpse
beside the broken whaler vibrated on the deck as if returning to
life.

Faster, faster. Standish could almost feel the ship's desperate
efforts like his own heartbeats. Even when she had done her
first trials in that other living world she had never reached
nineteen knots. Now she was already doing seventeen, in spite
of her wounds, and he guessed that Quarrie's gauges had long
since passed the red warning mark.

A wire stay parted abaft the bridge and the buckled funnel
tilted to an even more grotesque angle. He saw the radar
mechanic, Vine, clinging to the bridge ladder, shading his eyes
against the glare as he watched the approaching enemy. He
was probably remembering how he had first seen it on his outdated set, Standish thought. How he had stayed alive when the
rear of the bridge had been savaged was anyone's guess.

Coldly he raised the glasses again and levelled them on the
submarine. For a long moment he stared at the hump below her
conning tower which housed the missile launcher. The weapon
which had killed and maimed so many, here today, and at the
village. As he watched, the steel doors started to close, and when

he looked at Dalziel he saw his realization stamped on his face, too.

'She's got 'em shut!' He looked round the bridge and said quietly, 'But she's *too damn late* this time.'

Frantically the submarine's commander tried to turn back on his original escape route, the slender hull rocking in the wash of power and rudders while he used everything to swing her away from those buckled, looming bows.

Men were clambering back into the conning tower, and as spray spouted above her tanks Standish knew they were going to dive. Above the din of fans and engines, of groaning metal and yelling men, he heard a klaxon, saw the submarine's bows begin to dip, the water creaming and sluicing back over the casing as she started to go under.

Standish watched her fixedly. 'Starboard ten.' *No, too much.* 'Midships! Steady now!' He blinked the sweat from his eyes to watch as the submarine swam across the bows like a giant whale.

The last fifty yards seemed to go in a flash. One second she was there lying diagonally across the *Terrapin*'s battered stem, her hull all but covered and the sea bursting around her tilting conning tower. The very next instant she was here, right here, the conning tower suddenly higher than the stemhead, the sea-slime bright green in the sunlight.

Standish wrapped his arms around the gyro repeater, his eyes fixed on the onrushing shape as Dalziel yelled, 'Stop both engines! *Prepare to ram!*'

Even so the shock was as sharp as it was agonizing. He felt the steel pressing into his chest even as the engines churned astern, the crashing, grinding embrace which seemed to go on and on until he could no longer record time or sounds. He watched, dulled and fascinated as the conning tower lifted until it was right above the port side of the forecastle, the casing beyond it twisting and reeling as the maddened frigate drove on across her hull, slicing it open, smashing it down so that even through the terrible noise Standish heard the triumphant inrush of water, the scream of tearing metal as victim and vanquisher changed roles for the last time.

Then it was over, with the *Terrapin* swaying drunkenly above her own shadow, the sea's sudden turbulence momentarily eased by a great widening spread of oil which seemed to reach out as far as the reefs and beyond that.

Dalziel slumped in his chair, his voice very tired as he said, 'Go and check the damage, Number One. We'd better get ready to leave her.'

Once more Standish left the bridge, past those same faces and familiar figures. When he returned shortly afterwards he could feel the unreality gripping him like some intoxicating drug.

When he saw a seaman adjusting his orange lifejacket he stopped and said thickly, 'You can forget that. There'll be no swimming just yet!'

It was incredible. With her stem smashed in and her hull battered almost beyond recognition, the *Terrapin* was refusing to die. The forward bulkhead was not even weeping, in spite of the fact it was the only solid thing between the sea and the rest of the forecastle. Perhaps the loss of both anchors had made just that much difference? But as one of the pumps started up again and Quarrie peered from his engine room hatch to give him a dazed thumbs-up, he began to think otherwise.

When he reached the bridge he saw Rideout standing beside the captain's chair, his face pale as he looked blankly at the others. Standish reached him in three strides. Dalziel was watching him, his expression one of curiosity and tired satisfaction.

Standish asked quietly, 'How do you feel, sir?' He did not have to see the great dressing which Rideout had placed above Dalziel's thigh to know the answer. It was already sodden with blood.

And when he glanced at Rideout the doctor dropped his eyes, his lips ashen as he whispered, 'All this time. Just sitting there. It's not possible!'

Dalziel reached out and gripped Standish's sleeve. 'You were just going to tell me, eh? That she's all right?'

He peered at Standish's mouth as he replied, 'She is, sir. God knows how or why, but we'll get her home. Just as you always wanted.'

Dalziel nodded. 'You understood, eh?' He grimaced and then said, 'Make 'em all sit up.' He shifted his head stiffly as

Quarrie clattered on to the bridge. 'Sorry about the mess, Chief.'

Quarrie's eyes widened slightly, then he replied, 'I can raise about five knots for you sir. The pumps have got control now.' He looked away, unable to watch Dalziel's face. 'Always said she's a good 'un!'

Standish put his arm round Dalziel's shoulder, seeing the life going from his deepset eyes even as he said, 'It's getting damn dark. You know, Number One, I can't abide . . .' His head dropped forward and the oak-leaved cap rolled against Quarrie's feet.

Quarrie picked it up and said fiercely, 'Say what you like.' He handed it to Standish. 'By God, he was a *man!*'

Standish placed it below the shattered screen. There was so much to do, and a long way to go.

He looked at Quarrie and the others. 'We will take it in easy stages. See how she answers.' He half turned, almost expecting Dalziel to interrupt him. For a long moment he stood looking at him, his head moving gently to the ship's motion, one hand still on the glasses around his neck as if he was about to use them.

What was it Rideout had said? He tried to clear his mind from the ache and the sense of loss.

'*His trouble is that he was born two hundred years too late.*'

He looked sadly at the splinter holes and dark stains, at the men around him, and the small, battered ship around them.

Maybe he was. But for him none of this might have happened. But for him also, none of them would have survived.

He said quietly, 'Carry on, gentlemen. We will get under way in ten minutes.'

But they still stood there, their faces strained and suddenly aged as they accepted that they had survived.

Standish added, 'Well, let's get on with it. We haven't got all bloody night!'

Behind him he could almost imagine Dalziel laughing.

Epilogue

ONE week to a day after Dalziel's death, in a long, austere room above Singapore's great naval anchorage, a court of enquiry was convened to hear the circumstances and to pass judgment on the loss of Her Majesty's frigate *Terrapin*.

While Standish had stood before the baize-covered table with its grave-faced senior officers in their white drill and glittering decorations he had listened to his own level voice with something like disbelief, as if still unable to accept that in spite of all their efforts the *Terrapin* had actually gone down. As if by turning his head slightly he would be able to see her lying at her buoy, battered and pitted with splinter holes, with all that jaunty defiance he had come to love.

If he had chosen the exact time and position for the final moment he could have done no better. Twenty-four hours after they had smashed through the submarine's hull they had sighted an American destroyer, and for the *Terrapin* it seemed that the slow, lonely journey was ended. The destroyer had swept towards them, her signal light flashing, then Quarrie had reported that the engine room was flooding. The pumps, unable or unwilling to stem the sudden inrush of water, stopped altogether, and while the other ship edged carefully alongside, the *Terrapin* started to settle down.

As he spoke Standish had been aware of the complete silence in the long room, like the tension he had sensed when the commander of that same American destroyer had given his own account of what he had witnessed during the old frigate's last moments. How she had looked, and the damage which he had seen perhaps better than anyone.

On the face of it there had been no reason, no one true cause for the *Terrapin*'s behaviour. The sea had been flat calm, without even a breeze to ruffle its surface. There had been sufficient time to take off every man, and only when Standish had followed the rest aboard the destroyer did *Terrapin* decide to make the final gesture.

With something like tired dignity she had started to lean on to her side, exposing for just a while longer the great gaping holes left by the rockets, the weed and dents on her bilge keel. Then, almost eagerly, she had gone, taking with her her own dead to the untroubled depths. She was in good company.

All the way to Singapore Standish had thought of those last minutes, and as he had described them to the silent court he had been reminded again and again of so many small events, once familiar faces and voices, as if he was speaking for them, and not of them.

The enquiry lasted all day, with evidence from technical advisers as well as witnesses from amongst the *Terrapin*'s survivors.

As he completed his summary of events Standish glanced slowly at the others who had gone before him, wondering how they were feeling behind their various masks, how they would suffer or benefit after today.

Captain Jerram had spoken of Dalziel at some length, his tone grave and unhurried as he had outlined his past record before assuming command. It was hard to know what Jerram was really thinking. Perhaps in his own way he was glad that both ship and captain were beyond human reach. Relieved to be spared the embarrassment of Dalziel here facing him in the courtroom.

The American admiral, Curtis, had described loosely the function of his unified command and the part played in it by the *Terrapin*. His evidence was short to a point of brevity. Maybe he thought it pointless to elaborate when the rest of the world had already formed its own opinions. They had been as varied as they were predictable. The British and the Americans had condemned the attack on the *Terrapin* as wanton aggression, and had praised the courage and determination of her company.

The Russians had said very little, grateful perhaps at seeing China involved in the undeclared struggle between East and West while the world's eyes were momentarily diverted from their own affairs in Europe.

The Chinese had denied even losing a submarine, but in Peking the British Embassy had been attacked by Red Guards and two English journalists were arrested for espionage. They would, it seemed, wait for the next round.

Lieutenant Rhodes had been present throughout the hearing but had said nothing. Standish had watched him while Curtis had been speaking, and had tried to see beyond the American's outward calm. He more than anyone might have been able to give the full truth of that last savage encounter. With or without Admiral Curtis's consent, he could have been the one to fix the final obsession in Dalziel's mind, knowing that he above all would act at the least chance of success. If Curtis did know or suspect, he gave no hint to the court.

He had looked around the watching officers and had said quietly, 'This was no ordinary sea fight, gentlemen. There were no flags, no emblems of country, and maybe in what we have heard today we will recognize our path for the future. Nor was this another *Pueblo* incident, but one where a small, outdated ship fought with honour and total bravery, values which still rate high in a free society.'

Occasionally a member of the court had put a question or requested that a point be made more clear. When Irvine had been giving his description of the battle a senior captain had asked, 'Did you at any time expect, or perhaps hope that your ship would surrender to what was obviously a much superior enemy?'

Irvine had been relaxed and quite assured up to that moment, but then as he had glanced quickly at Standish his voice had faltered for the first time. Like Standish he was probably seeing himself in those last moments before the *Terrapin* had righted herself and had dashed madly to destroy her attacker.

Without effort Standish had recalled Irvine's stricken features, his complete helplessness as Pigott had brushed him aside to take over his duties from him.

In a small voice he had answered, 'No, sir. I knew the captain would think of something.'

Surprisingly, it had been Quarrie who had brought some of the tension and bitterness to the surface.

Possibly more than any of them he had felt the ship's loss as something very personal. Something which in his simple mind he could not replace with detached evidence and vague sentiment. Or maybe he no longer cared. He was leaving the Service, and had lost the one thing he had left to care about.

When asked his opinion of Dalziel's actions he had said slowly, 'I never really knew him, sir. I disagreed with some of the things he did, but not with his reasons or his motives.' He had let his eyes rest on Irvine. 'But before you try to decide where the strength or weakness lay in that ship, you must ask yourself who stood for country, duty and personal pride.' He had brushed his face angrily with his hand. 'Also, whose standards would you commend to a young officer today? Commander Dalziel had those standards, while some others . . .' He had been unable to continue.

In the stillness which had followed the president of the court had looked at the littered papers on the table, his face obviously moved by the engineer's sincerity.

There had been a short interval while the court considered its findings. Standish had walked alone below the building, his eyes unseeing as he watched the anchored ships and the first lights appearing across the water.

What was Dalziel to those who debated his actions? An enigma, or an embarrassment? Hero or scapegoat? He thought too of Sarah Dalziel. She had got her freedom and had retained her honour. But in the years ahead, when she faced her new husband, what would she really find to sustain her?

The findings were announced fifteen minutes later. No blame was attached to Commander Dalziel, and his efforts were recorded as being beyond the highest praise and in accordance with the finest traditions of the Service.

As Standish walked from the room he had repeated the statement in his mind. Dalziel would have liked it, he decided. Down the stone steps beyond the entrance doors he saw the girl waiting in an open car. Watching his face as he hurried towards her.

Terrapin was gone, but not before she had given him another chance. A chance, like her memory, which he would never waste or forget.